MW01538987

CITY

OF

STEEL

AND

SHADOW

THE LAST ETERNAL
Book Five

by

JACOB PEPPERS

This book is a work of fiction. Names, characters, places and incidents are either the product of the author's imagination or are used fictitiously. Any resemblance to actual persons, living or dead, or to actual events or locales is entirely coincidental.

City of Steel and Shadow: The Last Eternal Book 5
This book is licensed for your personal enjoyment only. This book may not be re-sold or given away to other people. If you would like to share this book with another person, please purchase an additional copy for each person you share it with. If you're reading this book and did not purchase it, or it was not purchased for your use only, then you should return to the retailer and purchase your own copy. Thank you for respecting the hard work of the author.

Copyright © 2023 Jacob Nathaniel Peppers. All rights reserved, including the right to reproduce this book, or portions thereof, in any form. No part of this text may be reproduced, transmitted, downloaded, decompiled, reverse engineered, or stored in or introduced into any information storage and retrieval system, in any form or by any means, whether electronic or mechanical without the express written permission of the author. The scanning, uploading, and distribution of this book via the Internet or via any other means without the permission of the publisher is illegal and punishable by law. Please purchase only authorized electronic editions, and do not participate in or encourage electronic piracy of copyrighted materials.

The publisher does not have any control over and does not assume any responsibility for author or third-party websites or their content.

Visit the author's website:
www.JacobPeppersAuthor.com

For the best dog a man could ever have.

Sleep well, Pepper.

And when you dream,

Let it be of green fields and doggy treats unending.

That's a good dog.

Sign up for the author's mailing list and, for a limited time, receive a *free* copy of *The Silent Blade: A Seven Virtues Novella.* **Head to JacobPeppersAuthor.com to get your free book now!**

CHAPTER ONE

THE AIR WAS filled with silent screams.

The wanderer walked the lonely mountain trail as those screams echoed in his mind.

He had been here before, when he and Dekker and the others had fled the Accursed in search of sanctuary.

This time, though, was different.

Before, the trail had led them to a village, to a bright spot of life and civilization in the hostile wilds of the Untamed Lands.

Now it led only to death.

He felt that death, recognized it even before he reached the village and how not? After all, he and death were well acquainted— he knew the signs of death's comings and goings as well as anyone might.

He knew the taste in the air, like ash on his tongue. He knew the smell—meat left to rot in the sun. And then there was the feel of it, the feeling of an inevitability realized, a charge to the air as if the world itself had drawn in its breath. Only the wanderer had seen enough of the world to know that if it had drawn in its breath, it had done so not in shock but in pleasure.

For the world, he had come to believe over the years, loved nothing so much as it loved death.

Yet it was not the taste or the smell, not even the feel which affected him the most, which made each lonely step he took up the mountainside a trial, a challenge all its own.

It was the silence.

A silence that was as complete as it could ever be. A silence a man felt more than heard, that seemed to seep into his flesh, his bones, his *mind,* bringing with it a creeping despair, one that filled his limbs and made continuing farther up the trail a test of will.

No birds chirped. No squirrels skittered. No people breathed. Not in this silence.

For this was not a natural silence but one that had been forced upon the world, one that only ever meant one thing—death had come this way. He could see it as clearly as he might see the footprints of some thirsty beast which had crept upon some forest pool to drink its fill. And if one thing could be said about death, about that beast, it was this—death was always thirsty. And it always drank its fill.

He saw the first body a short while later. A middle-aged man, lying on his stomach, his face hidden. Yet even still, the wanderer recognized him. After all, when he and the others had left the village, some had remained, and each of those had been etched into his memory, burned into his mind. He did not know the man's name, but he knew him, remembered that he had seemed doubtful about staying, remembered thinking that he might be swayed during the wanderer's speech.

But he had not been swayed. He had remained...and he had died.

There was a bow lying beside the body and a quiver hung from the dead man's back. Several arrows lay strewn about the rocky ground. A scout then, or a sentry, one whose job had been to warn the others of danger come upon them, yet he had fallen to the very danger he had been meant to guard against.

He wondered idly if the sentry had gotten off a shot before his death had come upon him, but he did not think so. There was a long, deep gash across the man's back or, more precisely, four long, deep gashes. It was a wound with which the wanderer was familiar, having seen it on others and, on some few unfortunate occasions, having experienced it himself. It was the kind of wound left by the claws of the Unseen.

No, he doubted the man had managed a shot, had likely not even managed a scream before his death had come upon him.

He had perhaps suspected something, seen a shimmer in the air, heard a footstep, and he had turned, likely meaning to flee. And so he had not seen his death come—not that he likely would have any way. He had died running from that death, as all men did, in the end. And that death had come because of the wanderer, because he had brought it.

"I'm sorry," the wanderer told the dead man.

He rose from where he'd knelt beside the body, glancing around at the silent, scree-covered mountain trail, feeling as if something regarded him. It was as if the world itself watched him, perhaps holding a cruel smile the way a malicious child might as it struck a mongrel dog with a stone and watched it whimper away. Enjoying the product of his labors.

The wanderer walked on.

He came upon the next body a short while later at the village's edge. An old woman, bent with age. She lay in a small garden. She had been tending her crops, it seemed, when the death which had found the sentry came for her. She'd only managed a few steps before it had taken her, and now she lay on her side, her upper body in the street, her lower still in the garden.

Her cold, dead gaze seemed to study the wanderer with accusation. He pulled eyes away, feeling like a coward, and choosing instead to regard the garden she'd tended. Already, the grass had begun to grow up. Soon, one passing by would not even be able to tell that it had been a garden at all. The world would take it back, make it what it would, erasing the woman's efforts and wishes as it did all the works of men in time.

Another might have shed tears at the thought, but the wanderer had shed such tears already, many times, and there were none left any longer. What he found instead was that the emptiness inside him, an emptiness where once, as a child, had existed a belief that the world was a good, magical place had been, grew a little. As if someone, or perhaps it was nearer the truth to say some *thing*, were inside of him, scouring him out a bit at a time.

He wondered what would be left when that scouring was complete.

He wondered if anything would.

But he was aware of the others, Dekker and his family, Clint and the Perishables, waiting for him at the base of the mountainside, and so he did not wonder for long.

He continued deeper into the village, to see if anyone survived, if there was any way he might help. He knew that he would find no one, find only death, knew it as surely as he had ever known anything, and yet, as was so often the case with men, he had to look, to *see* for himself. Otherwise, he knew that in the days and nights to come he would be haunted by what-ifs and could-have-beens. If he did not look, then a certainty would grow in the weeks and months and years to come, a certainty that someone *had* survived, and that in his selfish desire to avoid witnessing anymore death, he had left them on their own, had abandoned them.

The wanderer was haunted by a dozen ghosts already—he did not think he could handle anymore.

He walked farther into the village.

He saw three more bodies in the street as he moved through the village. Each had fled, hoping to reach safety. And each had failed.

The village of Alhs had not been large, and so it did not take him long to discover where it was they had fled *to*. The door to the sheriff's station lay ajar in its frame, and by the holes gouged into it and the splintered wood, it was clear that it had been broken down.

The room's desk—which normally sat against the wall—lay only feet inside the door, broken and shattered along with several cabinets. The villagers had barricaded the doors then, hoping to keep the creatures which had come for them at bay. But death, as always, had proven persistent.

He stood in the doorway, regarding the corpses. There were nearly twenty in all, scattered in a semi-circle in front of the door. Weapons of various sorts—some few rusted swords, a crossbow, and several shovels and hoes—lay around them. And so, with nowhere else to go, no other shelter left to seek, they had stood, and they had fought.

It had ended the only way it could, of course, the corpses evidence of that, yet still the wanderer was glad for them, for they had faced the inevitable and met it with courage, had met it standing. In a world where all men fell eventually, it was the most that any man could hope to do.

Among the bodies were two corpses of Revenants, and this also made him glad for the villagers. Glad and impressed. It took much to bring down one of the creatures, and clearly they had fought hard and well.

He saw two women's forms beyond the semi-circle of combatants. Drawing closer, he was surprised to realize that their backs were to the rest of the room. They were facing toward one of the room's cells, the same cell in which the wanderer had been imprisoned what felt like a lifetime ago.

They'd both suffered wounds in the back, had never even seen the blows coming. He frowned as he moved farther in, stepping carefully over the bodies, wondering what it was that had captivated their attention so much in their last moments.

Peering through the bars, the wanderer saw that the cell's small cot had been tipped over. He tried the cell door and found it locked. His frown deepened, and he stepped to the side of the cell, so that he might see around the upset cot.

What he saw behind it, or more precisely, *who* he saw made his upper lip peel back from his teeth in a silent snarl. Deputy Ward's corpse lay on the cell floor, and it was clear that he'd locked himself in the cell, taking shelter behind the cot. The two women had sought to be let in, and judging by his position behind the cot—and by the cell keys lying on the floor beside him—the deputy had obviously had no intention of sharing his sanctuary.

As he stared around the room, the wanderer recreated the scene in his mind, his thoughts getting grimmer by the moment. How long had those women screamed and begged to be let in, only for their pleas to fall on deaf ears? How long had they sought aid by the very man whose duty it was to protect them, only to find that the man who was supposed to keep them safe had, instead, abandoned them to their fate?

The wanderer regarded the deputy's corpse and noticed something that made him angrier still. The man bore no wound. No claw mark, no cut where a sword had struck him. Not an arrow or a bruise, so far as the wanderer could see. He had not died in battle at all, it seemed, and by his withered, emaciated look, the wanderer suspected that he had died of thirst.

It seemed that, when Ranger had come through the village, he had left one of his Revenants, perhaps more than one, to watch over the deputy, to kill him, should he dare leave his cell. And the man had been too afraid even to do that. Instead he had crouched behind the cot, *cowered* behind it. He must have huddled there for days, suffering, his throat growing dryer and dryer, his stomach growling and cramping with hunger pains, yet as bad as his suffering must have been, how *prolonged,* still it had not been enough to bring him out of the cell. And so he had died as he had lived—a coward.

Staring at the bodies of those two women in front of the cell, the wanderer decided that however much the deputy had suffered, it had not been enough. And the man *had* suffered, that he did not doubt. The wanderer had traveled long and far, had gone days without clean water or food as he'd fled from the enemy's attempts at finding him, and so he was acquainted with hunger pangs, knew well the grittiness of a throat gone too long without water.

The deputy had suffered, that was not in doubt. He had suffered for days after the other villagers were long dead, for however terrible their fates had been, at least they had been quick. The deputy had not been so fortunate. And here, at least, was one visage that would not haunt his dreams, that his guilt and shame and regret would not call up in his mind's eye during the late hours when darkness has overtaken the world and light was no more than a memory.

No, the deputy's death would not bother him. If the wanderer had any regret on the man's demise it was only that he had not been here to see it, that he had not had the privilege of watching the man squirm and writhe as death slowly consumed him, bit by bit.

He blinked.

That had been a strange thought, had felt cruel and angry and not his own. In that moment, the wanderer was very aware of the cursed blade at his back. He found himself thinking of Oracle's words of warning, that the cursed blade was an insidious threat, one that might disguise its influence as his own thoughts, his own feelings.

He pulled his gaze away from the deputy and looked once more around at the dead. He could not save them, for the time for saving was long past, but he could to this, at least—he could remember. And, in remembering, he hoped he might honor them. "I am sorry," he told them.

They did not answer.

He took a slow breath then turned and stepped out of the sheriff's station, back into the dusty street. He might have left then, might have reunited himself with Dekker and the others, for he knew they were waiting. But he was not quite finished—not yet. He would be a witness to the dead, for he could be nothing else, and there was one that remained, one who he had not yet seen. The wanderer started down the street once more.

***

He found him where he'd thought he might. Not inside his large, opulent home but in the graveyard, among the other dead.

The mayor of Alhs knelt before his wife's grave, and from the way he had fallen, still half kneeling, half leaning against his wife's tombstone, a sword wound in his back, it was clear that the man had not even bothered to turn when his death came upon him. He had only thought of her, in that moment, and the wanderer thought that there was some solace to be found in that.

Or so he hoped, and since there was no way to know one way or the other, he chose hope. He chose love.

"I hope you find each other quickly," he told the dead man.

And that was all of them then, all the dead, all those who had been left behind.

The wanderer stood there for a moment, then another, giving the dead their due, wishing things might have been different. But then, things were only ever as they were. A man could waste his life away wishing they were not, or he could get on with the business of living, the business of doing what needed to be done.

The wanderer gave the dead their moment but no more than that. For their fate, their destiny had been met already.

He turned and started down the street.

The dead were dead and beyond help.

Now it was time to worry for the living.

CHAPTER TWO

HALF AN HOUR later, the wanderer walked down the mountainside to find Dekker and the others waiting for him. The big man gave him a questioning look as he approached, and the wanderer gave him a slight shake of his head.

Dekker heaved a heavy sigh. "I'd have gone with you. You didn't need to go alone."

"I know," the wanderer said. But the truth was he was glad the big man hadn't gone, nor Clint. Both had volunteered, but they had already suffered much because of him, had been through much tragedy. He had not been able to protect them and the others from it as he would have liked, but this, at least, he could protect them from, and so he had. After all, it was one thing to know that those who had remained in Alhs had died. It was another to *see* it, to witness their broken bodies, their slack, empty stares that seemed to hold everything and nothing all at once. It was not much, perhaps, saving them from that, but it was something.

But while none of them might have seen the devastation of the village, they still *felt* it, and it was a grim, silent company that started back through the forest, in the direction of the border of the Untamed Lands.

***

The wanderer rode through a land of monsters.

Perhaps he should have been afraid, but he was not.

Perhaps he should have been eager to leave that place, to escape the tall trees with their enormous trunks that might have hidden anything or anyone. And yet...he was not.

As he, Dekker and his family, as well as Clint and the Perishables, approached the border of the Untamed Lands, it was not fear nor eagerness that he felt. Instead, it was sadness.

And with that realization came another—he did not want to leave.

It was ridiculous, of course, for the Untamed Lands was a place of dangerous creatures and beings most would not think existed anywhere save in dreams. Or, more likely, nightmares.

Ridiculous, yet the fact remained...he did not want to leave.

And a glance over to his left, where Dekker and his wife, Ella, walked, glancing behind them from time to time, showed him that he was not alone in this. Even their daughter, Sarah, who rode atop Veikr's back beside them, looked near tears.

Clint and the Perishables all shared grim expressions as they neared the tree line. They, too, it seemed, were reluctant to leave the Untamed Lands behind. Or perhaps, he thought, they were worried of being pursued. But he dismissed that idea in another moment. After all, a creature of the Untamed Lands *did* track their progress, stalking their footsteps, but it did so not to hunt them, but instead to protect them.

The giant cat was out there, somewhere, in the trees. The wanderer did not need to see her to know that which was just as well, as despite its enormous size, the creature was incredibly skilled at blending into its surroundings. The wanderer caught no more than a passing sign here and there—a snapping tree limb to one side, a flash of fur to the other—that it still followed their progress.

The creature had chosen to help them leave the Untamed Lands as a way of saying thank you to the wanderer for rescuing its cub back on the mountainside, and he was glad of that. After all, while he had come to appreciate the uncivilized beauty and purity of the Untamed Lands, he did not doubt that, without their lethal escort, some of that beauty would have long since tried to take a bite out of them and made their trip considerably shorter.

As it was, the trip had been what the wanderer, at least, would consider blissfully uneventful. Even the Whisperers posed no danger, for before they left the wizard had cast what he'd called a concealment spell upon a stone, one that the wanderer could activate when they neared the Whisperers territory and one that, the wizard had assured them, would last until they were past it.

The wanderer, though, while he thought that he and the wizard had come to like or at least respect each other, had entertained some doubt, particularly because the wizard had given him a small smile when he gave him the stone and told him that it should last, so long as they didn't tarry.

They had not tarried. They had moved quickly and had found themselves on the other side without incident. The great cat had not been within the spell's bubble, but apparently the Whisperers had been unable—or, more likely, unwilling—to attempt to turn the giant creature into their prey.

And so they were close now, no more than half an hour from the border of the Untamed Lands, a border that he had only crossed in the first place because he'd had no choice yet one that he now found himself anticipating with regret. The only one among them, in truth, who seemed not to share that regret was Veikr. The great horse walked stoically, uncomplaining, as always, yet the wanderer had spent enough time with him to know that he was tense. Neither did he miss the way the horse's gaze traveled around them as they moved, tracking the giant cat's movements in the trees far better than the wanderer might have. Here then, at least, was one who'd had his fill of the Untamed Lands.

He smiled, giving his horse a pat on the muzzle. "It's okay," he said softly. "That's alright."

Veikr's eye rolled up to regard him with a look that seemed to say he might want to reconsider his criteria for what was okay, then the horse gave his head a toss as if to wash his hands of the whole affair.

They rode on.

Night was no more than fifteen minutes away, the border of the Untamed Lands little more than that when the wanderer called for a halt, and they set up camp. They might have waited until they were across the border, but he found himself averse to the idea. After all, beyond the forest of the Untamed Lands lay cultivated fields, wide, open spaces where any person—or thing—hunting them might easily find them.

The Untamed Lands had its own dangers, it was true, but with the giant cat lurking in the shadows around them, he thought they had little enough to worry about.

While the trip out of the Untamed Lands might have proven nowhere near as perilous as the trip into it had been, it had still been long, and they were all excited to rest.

All of them, at least, save the wanderer. While the Untamed Lands had held its dangers—dangers that he did not doubt would haunt his dreams and nightmares in the days and weeks to come—it had, in some ways, been an escape. An escape from civilization, yes, but mostly an escape from himself. After all, he had spent so much of the last days and weeks reacting that he'd had very little time to think about things.

Things like the cursed blade and its influence on him, an influence that seemed to be bleeding over into his dreams, coloring them, changing them into visions of blood and violence and death, ones from which he woke gasping and bathed in sweat, unable to remember any specifics of the dreams except blood and screams. So much blood that it seemed like a river of it in his mind. So many screams that they were deafening.

And while the cursed blade was a concern, it was far from his only one, or his greatest. The greatest was those who had chosen to follow him. Dekker and his family, Clint and the eleven Perishables who accompanied him. The wanderer was well aware of the fact that they had given up a life of almost guaranteed safety—or as guaranteed as anyone ever got—to follow him. They had done so because they believed in him, and he could only wish that he shared their belief.

The truth was, he had doubts.

The bald truth was that he had little else.

So, as the others lay down to get some sleep, the wanderer moved a short distance away from the camp, found a likely tree with a trunk large enough to hide him—not hard to do in the Untamed Lands—then sat with his back against it, his arms draped over his knees.

He sat and watched the camp, watched over those who had placed their trust in him. And his greatest fear, perhaps the greatest fear of his life, was that he would fail in that trust, that their faith in him would turn out to be misplaced. People spoke of leaps of faith as if they were positive things and perhaps sometimes they even were. But sometimes, most of the time, he thought, that leap was just what it appeared to be—suicide.

So while the others got comfortable, a few of the Perishables sharing berries they'd picked along the way, the wanderer sat in the fading light and thought dark thoughts.

He thought of the cursed blade, seeming to thrum on his back with something akin to eagerness. He thought of Dekker and his family, of Clint and the Perishables. He thought, also, of the wizard, of Sheriff Fred and the others, of Deputy Ward and those dead in the village of Alhs. But mostly...he thought of failure of leaps from cliffs that were that and that only.

He was still thinking half an hour later when a shadowed figure separated itself from the others, rising and starting toward him.

"Ungr," the Perishable's leader said quietly, giving him a nod as he came up.

"Clint," the wanderer said, nodding back as the man sat beside him, grunting as he propped his own back against a tree. "Couldn't sleep?"

"I rarely can," the Perishable leader admitted. "Guess I just never had the knack. Or, at least, if I did, I lost it some years ago." He considered that, scratching his chin. "Just about the time I formed the Perishables, I reckon."

"The responsibility?"

The man considered again, then grunted. "Somethin' like that. Though it ain't the lookin' after folks or their well bein' that always got to me."

"It's the thought of failure."

"That's right," Clint said. "That's it exactly."

"I understand that."

The man watched him for a moment, slowly nodding. "I think maybe you do."

"It's hard," the wanderer said. "To know the right thing."

"That's pretty much been my thought on the matter," the other man agreed. "Speakin' of thoughts, you don't mind my sayin', it don't take a mind reader to have some idea as to your own. Is it the folks back at the valley that got your mind workin'? 'Cause if so, I think you can lay that worry to rest. That wizard fella, he might have been a bit of an asshole, but he was at least a capable one. I expect with him watchin' over them they ain't got all that much to worry about."

"It's not them I fear for," the wanderer said, his gaze traveling, of its own accord, to where Dekker and his family lay and then to the Perishables who had finished their meager meal, such as it had been, and were now all lying down.

Clint followed his gaze then let out a soft grunt. "I don't mean to tell you your business, Ungr, but you've got nothin' to worry about as far as they go. Dekker and his family are as solid as they come. As for my people, they know well all that you've done, all that you've sacrificed. For the world, sure, but for them, too. They'd all die for you."

"That's what I'm afraid of," the wanderer said quietly.

Clint hissed. "Damnit, sorry. Listen, Ungr, that's not what I meant. All I was saying is—"

"I know, Clint," the wanderer said, giving the man the best smile of which he was capable—not particularly good just then. "It's alright."

The two of them sat in silence for several minutes, each of them thinking his own thoughts. They remained so until a figure separated itself from those sleeping around the dying fire, rising. The wanderer could not make out specifics of the figure, not with the darkness having settled in in full, but then he didn't need to, for there were few people walking the face of the world who matched Dekker in sheer size.

The big man picked his way gingerly around his family and the other sleeping figures, moving to where the wanderer and Clint sat.

"Done sleepin' already?" Clint asked as Dekker drew close.

The big man grunted. "Done pretendin' to, anyway. What of you?" he asked, glancing at Clint. "Not plannin' on takin' a trip to dreamland?"

"I find that the older I get, the less welcome I am," Clint admitted. He shrugged. "Anyway, I like the night here. Quieter than I'm accustomed to. Besides, I don't guess I'm all that tired."

Dekker nodded, sitting down beside them. "Yeah, me neither."

The wanderer glanced at the two men, neither of them looking in his direction, both staring off into the night instead. They were trying for casual but not quite making it. It was touching, though, to see that they would put on the show for his benefit when the fact was they were both tired—a blind man could have seen that at a glance—and both in need of sleep.

No, it wasn't lack of weariness nor enjoying the night that kept them from their bedrolls, the wanderer knew the truth of that just as he knew that it was worry that kept them from sleep. He knew that as much as he knew another truth—they were right to worry.

By coming with him instead of staying with the wizard and the others, they had started on a dangerous path, one that would likely end in their deaths and that, likelier than not, sooner rather than later. After all, the wanderer was done with running—he'd told the creature posing as Ranger as much before he'd killed him, and he'd meant it. Now he would stand. He would pit himself against creatures who had defeated the most capable, most gifted, most powerful men and women he had ever met, and likely he would die.

Certainly he saw no other option. He thought that, were it just him, he might have been able to reconcile himself to the idea of that, might have even been able to have found something noble, something *worthy* in standing against evil, even if he knew that doing so only meant that he could fail. But there wasn't just him to think of—there were the others. Dekker and Clint, yes, but also those they meant to protect.

"So," Dekker said after a few seconds, glancing at the wanderer. "We'll be out of here soon enough, won't we?"

"Yes."

The big man nodded. "If you'd have asked me a week or two ago if I'd ever feel sad at the idea of leavin' the Untamed Lands behind me, I'd have thought you were crazy."

"And now?" the wanderer asked.

The big man shrugged. "Now, I'd still think you were crazy, only, I reckon so am I."

"There's something...beautiful about it," Clint said. "About how...how unspoiled it all is. How wild."

"Yeah, I reckon I like the wilderness," Dekker agreed. "Just so long as that wilderness doesn't try to take a bite out of me, that is."

Wild. Unspoiled. Listening to the two men, the wanderer found himself thinking of the Wizard of the South, of Earl. He couldn't keep the small grin from coming to his face and he didn't try to. Not a name of any wizard he'd ever heard of before, but then Earl hadn't been like any wizard he'd ever heard of before either. The man had loved the creatures of the Untamed Lands, that much was clear. Had respected them, including the Free, those that the Eternals had always taught him were called the Accursed. And while the wanderer had always been taught that they were evil, he'd begun to rethink that during the time he'd spent with them—hard not to when one of them had saved his life.

Thinking of the Free and of the wizard made him remember what the man had said, that he'd claimed someone had tried to make them into weapons before, had tried to turn them into an army. He thought, too, of how the wizard had felt about the Eternals, how he'd claimed they'd only ever cared about themselves, about how he held them responsible for his son dying. The wanderer would have dismissed it all as ridiculous except that, over the time they'd traveled together, he'd come to know the wizard pretty well, and the man had never struck him as foolish or cruel. After all, he'd spent much of his time and energy creating safe places within the Untamed Lands for the relatively weak mortals such as those of the village of Alhs.

"Ungr?"

The wanderer blinked, turning to glance beside him and saw that Dekker and Clint were both staring at him with poorly disguised worry. "Yes?" he asked.

"Everything alright?"

No. "I'm fine," he said. "Why do you ask?"

The big man shrugged. "Only on account of I said your name three times, and you didn't answer."

The wanderer winced. "Sorry. I was thinking."

"That's what I smelled," Dekker said, giving him a smile.

The wanderer tried to return it, but the expression felt odd, unnatural on his face, and he let it slip.

Dekker sighed. "Alright, out with it, you bastard."

"Out with what?"

"You know damn well what I'm talking about—whatever's botherin' you. Shit, Ungr, I've seen fellas that've just got done drinking a glass of poison that looked less sour'n you."

The wanderer said nothing, only raised an eyebrow, and the big man grunted. "Well. Maybe that ain't completely true, but you still look like miserable in a shirt and trousers. So what gives?"

He sighed. "I do not know what to do," he told them honestly. "I don't have a plan." The words felt like the pronouncement of some great doom coming out of his mouth, and he found himself tensing in preparation of the recrimination, of the great anger and wrath that must follow.

After all, the two men had trusted him, had risked not just themselves but those they cared for the most to follow him. It would not be a comfort to learn that the man they had chosen to follow, that they had put their faith in, had no idea where he was going or what he was going to do.

The two men slowly turned and looked at each other, their expressions unreadable, and the wanderer waited, doing his best to school his features, for the inevitable but deserved scorn they would heap upon him.

But when the men finally showed a reaction, it was the last one he might have expected. They began to laugh. To howl with laughter, in fact, both of them tipping their heads back and roaring it out as if the wanderer had just told the world's funniest joke.

The wanderer was left speechless, could only stare in confusion as the two men glanced at him and then, seeing his befuddlement, began to laugh all the harder.

"*Dekker,*" a hiss came, and the three of them turned to see that Ella had risen to a seated position and was staring at them from her place nearby the glowing coals of the fire.

That did the trick, cutting Dekker's laughter off as abruptly as a brick to the head might have done. "Sorry, dear," he called back in a voice that might have been meant to be quiet but in truth was like the rumble of thunder.

The wanderer, with his keen eyes, could see the woman shake her head before lying back down.

"Shit," Dekker said quietly. "I'll be hearin' about that in the mornin' and with no one but you to blame, Ungr."

"I...don't understand," the wanderer said.

Dekker glanced again at Clint who grinned before looking back. "No. No, I don't expect you do. Did you think we were goin' to be pissed off that you didn't have a plan, is that it?"

The wanderer blinked. "Well...yes."

Dekker barked a laugh then tensed, glancing back at the sleeping figures. "Shit, Ungr, if we were the type of fellas that would be thrown by you not havin' a plan, don't you think we might have cut ties with your ass a long time ago? After all, in my experience, the types of folks that find themselves facing giant cats or climbing the sides of mountains—or with even a fraction as many scars as you carry—ain't exactly the plannin' type. If you catch my meaning."

"I think I do," the wanderer said slowly, not sure whether to be offended or relieved and landing somewhere in between the two.

Dekker must have seen something of it on his face, for he gave another quiet laugh. "Oh, don't go getting sour again. You might not be much of a planner, Ungr, but in my experience you're a damned fine figure-it-out-on-the-flyer. You also ain't a bad stab-it-if-it-gets-out-of-liner, and that's come in handy quite a few times since I've met you."

"I'm...not sure if that's the compliment you think it is," the wanderer said.

"I think what Dekker here is tryin' to say," Clint interjected, "is that if you need help, we're here to help. We might not spend our free time climbing cliff faces or fighting invisible creatures that move as fast as a thought, but it might be we could help you to come up with a plan."

"That's what I said, ain't it?" Dekker asked in seemingly genuine confusion.

The wanderer gave a soft laugh. "Something like that. You're right, though. I value both of your opinions, likely more than my own."

"Can I get that in writing?" Dekker asked.

"So I could certainly use your help," the wanderer went on as if the big man—who was currently grinning like a child given a treat—hadn't spoken.

"Well, I guess, as far as that goes, what we need to answer first is what you aim to do," Clint said.

"What I aim to do?"

"It's a pretty common saying," Dekker said. "Surprised you ain't heard it. Means what's your goal—what are you tryin' to accomplish?"

"I know what it mea—" The wanderer cut off as he saw the big man's eyes dancing with mirth.

Clint laughed, shaking his head. "This is what happens when the big bastard doesn't take his nap," the Perishable's leader explained.

"Anyway, what I mean is, what's your goal? You still tryin' to stay ahead of those things or not? Are you wantin' to run...or to fight?"

"I meant what I told Ranger's impostor," the wanderer said. "I'm done running."

Clint and Dekker shared a look then nodded, both of them clearly satisfied. "Was hopin' you'd say that," Clint said. "It don't sit real well with me, the thought of our leaders being some sort of monsters that killed the Eternals and are takin' their place."

Dekker grunted. "Like findin' out vegetables really are good for you."

The wanderer shared a look with Clint, and the Perishables' leader gave his head a slight shake as if to say they had too much on their plate and couldn't get into that just now. "So then," Clint said, "if we want to fight back, how's the best way to do that? How do we go about it?"

"That is the problem, I think. It will be difficult for us to make any move without them being ready for it."

Dekker frowned. "How's that? I mean, last they saw us, we were in the Untamed Lands. Unless there's some of those Unseen bastards lurkin' around, I don't know how they'd reckon we were leavin'. Why, for all they know, we're goin' farther south or stayin' with the wizard and all the others from Alhs."

The wanderer shook his head slowly. "I was foolish before, when fighting Ranger. I told him that I was done running, and it will not be so great a leap from that to know that I will not remain in the Untamed Lands."

"Even if you did say that, and even if that bastard did somehow realize that you meant to leave the Untamed Lands to come and fight them, what difference does that make? It seems to me that what he knows and doesn't know ain't all that important considerin' that you showed him the business end of that sword of yours."

The wanderer winced. "I wish that were true. The problem is that while we know very little of the enemy, we do know that they are able to communicate with each other—as well as those abominations they create and which carry out their bidding—over great distances. No," he said, shaking his head again, "if Ranger knew of it, the others do as well. I do not doubt that they were watching everything transpire through his eyes."

"Huh," Dekker said.

Clint frowned. "That's damned inconvenient."

"Yes."

"Still," Dekker said, "even if they can talk to each other through their minds or whatever it is, its not like they can read your mind and figure out your plans. Particularly since, you know, you don't have any."

The wanderer nodded. "That is true enough but of little comfort. We may have destroyed two of the enemy, but there are plenty more of them. And among those is one who is posing as Tactician, the greatest military mind not just of this age but of any age."

"Yeah, but the key word there is 'posing' isn't it?" Clint asked. "I mean, it isn't as if the creature *is* Tactician."

"Perhaps not," the wanderer admitted, "but in practice I do not know if that will make as much difference as you might think. After all, judging by the creatures who took Ranger and Soldier's places he will possess much, if not all, of Tactician's military genius. At least, I think it is enough to say that if there is a significant difference in the impostors and those they impersonate then it is small enough as to make little difference."

The two men nodded slowly, taking in their situation. "What about that amulet of yours?" Dekker asked.

The wanderer blinked. "Sorry, what?"

Dekker grunted, shaking his head, and he and Clint shared a knowing look before the two men turned back to regard him. "Shit, Ungr, we're not fools, are we? Or, leastways, if we *are* fools, then we're not as big as you make out. There's somethin' to that amulet of yours—anyone with eyes to see would know that much. Whenever you're worried or trying to figure out what to do you toy with it—the way you're doing now."

The wanderer frowned, glancing down in surprise to see that, indeed, the amulet was in his hand. He'd been running his thumb over its worn surface without even realizing he was doing it, a nervous tic he hadn't even been aware he had.

"You talk to yourself sometimes too," Clint said, sounding almost guilty. "Or...well, it seems like you're talking to yourself only..."

"Only you're not. Are you?" Dekker asked.

The wanderer stared at the two men, once again impressed by how much they picked up and annoyed with himself for not considering it. "No."

The big man nodded as if he'd just confirmed a suspicion. "We reckoned you were a bit crazy at first," Dekker said. "Not that we could blame you. After all, a fella spends a hundred years on the run, the only significant company his horse—damned fine horse though he is—well. Stands to reason he'll be a bit rough around the edges, don't it? But as time went on, we realized that amulet of yours, it ain't just an old heirloom or somethin' you bought at some random shop."

"No," the wanderer said. "It is not."

"Magic, ain't it?"

"Yes."

"So," Dekker said. "My question remains. Any magic in there that can help us?"

"I...don't think so," the wanderer said slowly. "At least not at the moment. The amulet, you see...it isn't magic in the way you might think. It...it carries the essences of the Eternals in it. The real Eternals. Their minds, their memories."

Clint's eyes went wide. "You mean...Soldier. Healer. Leader. They're all in there?"

"Yes."

Dekker grunted. "Seems a bit small. Poor bastards got to be cramped."

"But...if that's true," Clint said, choosing, likely wisely, to ignore Dekker's jibe, "then...I mean, we should be fine, shouldn't we? I mean, it isn't as if we're alone—why, we've got the Eternals themselves to consult and help us."

"Shit, he's right," Dekker said. "I mean, the Eternals, they're damned legendary. I ain't sure of what use Clint and I can be for givin' advice when you've got the Eternals to talk to, the most powerful men and women ever to live."

"The same Eternals who have already been defeated by the enemy once," the wanderer reminded them.

"Ah, right," Dekker said, frowning. "Forgot about that for a minute there."

"Besides," the wanderer said, "while the spell Oracle cast imbued their essences in the amulet, that is a far cry from having them present, here, to help us. Anyway, if the two of you have any thoughts on what we might do, I'm listening."

"Makes it harder," Clint said, "knowin' that, so far as it goes, we're going to be against a mind as good as Tactician's. A bit daunting, truth to tell."

"I have had a similar thought," the wanderer said.

"Well," Dekker said. "My father once told me that if a fella sees a thorn bush on his land and don't cut it down, then when he finds himself wanderin' into it one drunken night, he's got no one to blame but himself."

Clint frowned, glancing at the wanderer who gave shake of his head to show he wasn't sure where Dekker was going.

"What I mean," the big man said, "is that if this Tactician fella— or, well, his impostor at any rate—is our biggest problem, then that's what we deal with first. The same way that a fella, if he's got a lot of chores to do for the day, starts with his hardest. That way, once it's done, it's all downhill from there."

"I always preferred putting my chores off as long as I could," Clint said with a small smile, then he turned to the wanderer. "But I think he's right. It makes sense to take out the biggest threat first."

Dekker nodded. "If you want to make a snake not dangerous, you don't take away its tail first—a snake ain't nothin' much but tail, come to it. You cut off the head. And, failing that, you pull the bastard's fangs. The rest might wriggle about for a bit, but a snake without fangs ain't nothin' but a worm."

The wanderer found himself nodding along as the big man spoke. It would be dangerous, of course. However clever they might think themselves, however many possible plans they might come up with, Tactician would have thought of dozens more, would have seen the eventualities, the possibilities, and would have planned accordingly. But then, when a man sets himself against such powers and such forces, it could not help but be dangerous, and even a very small chance of success was better than none.

"Tactician's territory is far to the north, in the frozen mountains. It will be a long trip."

Dekker shrugged. "Been meanin' to get a vacation in."

"It will be cold."

Clint shrugged. "Been tired of all this heat anyway. A man can only sweat so much."

The wanderer glanced between the two men, shaking his head in wonder. He had often thought that he had no luck or, if he did, only bad. It was a thought that had accompanied him for the last hundred years since he'd been left alone, the last living Eternal. Now, though, he decided that it simply wasn't true. After all, it was the best of fortune, the best luck that anyone could possibly hope for, that would see him run into two such men.

Still, he knew that it was one thing to speak of the distance, of the cold. It was quite another to experience it. Few people living had traveled as far as the wanderer—in truth, he doubted if anyone had—and so he knew that better than most. "We will have to find a carriage or a wagon, and even then it will take weeks," he warned.

"You got some pressin' appointment you haven't told me about?" Dekker asked. "That it?"

"No," the wanderer said. "I am only trying to make sure that you understand what's before us. As for the weather...it will be very cold. Have either of you been to the north before?"

"No," Clint said, "but I've seen cold before."

"Not like this," the wanderer said. "Tactician did not choose the location of his kingdom by happenstance. He told me, once, that it is precisely for the weather and the natural obstructions that he settled there. And the weather is more than just the cold—blizzards are commonplace, as are avalanches, ice storms with hail the size of fists falling from the sky, chunks of ice hard enough to kill a man, if he finds himself out in the open. And as for cold...the temperature sometimes drops by twenty or thirty degrees or more in minutes, so quickly that a man might set out thinking the weather was fine and die before he ever made it home. I spent three months in Ildwald during my training, and they were the longest three months of my life."

"Who in the name of the Eternals would want to live in such a place?" Dekker asked, and the wanderer saw by the stricken looks on the two men's faces that they were not taking his words lightly.

"No one," the wanderer said. "And, for Tactician at least, that was the whole point. He told me once that he chose the spot of his kingdom precisely because no one else would want it. He said that, that way, even if he and the other Eternals were to somehow find themselves at odds, no one would ever envy or be jealous of his holdings. That, of course, is before you even consider the many dangers any invading army might face."

"Must be some miserable people that live there," Clint observed.

"They are some of the hardiest, toughest people I have ever met," the wanderer said honestly. "They have learned to endure hardships that most of us can only imagine, the price of the remoteness that they enjoy. The trade off, of course, is that they don't have to deal with bandits or bands of outlaws, for such men do not dare brave the frozen wastes. And it must be said that it is beautiful there. Cold and barren...and beautiful."

"Doesn't seem like much of a trade, you ask me," Dekker said.

"Maybe not," the wanderer agreed, "but then the people of Ildwald and its outlying areas are not like you and me. Besides, there are other reasons for them to travel to such a place or, in the case of those born there, to remain. You see, out there, in the ice, men and women are able to find extremely rare minerals and rocks, items which scholars and users of the Art will pay a fortune for."

"You ask me, there are better ways to make a coin than freezing your balls off."

"I tend to agree," the wanderer said, "but if we are to face Tactician it is to the frozen mountains that we must go."

Dekker grunted. "Well. Say we worry about avalanches and hail the size of my fist later. For now first thing's first. We need to find a wagon."

"We could easily hire one out back in Celes," Clint said, but the man was frowning doubtfully even as he said it.

It was a frown the wanderer understood, for whatever else the creature who had taken Tactician's spot might think they would do, it and its companions would certainly be watching Celes, what had served as Soldier's capital.

"I think it'd probably be best if we avoided Celes for a while," Dekker said, no doubt remembering, as the wanderer was, how they had been chased from the city what felt like years ago by a band of Revenants and several Unseen, only just escaping with their lives and *that* only because they had fled into the Untamed Lands.

Clint nodded, frowning. "You're probably right. Still, it's too damned bad. I've got some connections in Celes, connections that might have proven useful to us, and the carriage only the least of them."

Both men turned and looked at the wanderer, a question clear in their gazes, leaving it up to him to make the decision. He scratched at his chin, thinking it over. Clint was right, of course. The Perishables' leader knew plenty of people back in Celes, and even aside from that, it was a big city. A city that would have everything they would need to be getting on with their journey. Food and provisions yes, a carriage certainly, but more than that, they would have also been able to procure horses and furs for the journey. There were plenty of benefits to stopping at the city...but then, Tactician—or at least his impostor—would know that.

"No," the wanderer said finally, shaking his head. "We can't risk it. They would have to be fools not to prepare in case we decided to come back to Celes, and the real Tactician once told me that any strategy that relies on a man's enemies to make a mistake isn't a strategy at all but a fool's hope and one that often leads to a fool's death."

"Sounds like a real pleasant fella to be around," Dekker observed.

The wanderer smiled. "We all have our strengths—there is a reason he has the role he has instead of Charmer's."

"But if not Celes then where?" Dekker asked.

The wanderer considered that, shaking his head slowly. "I'm not sure."

"Might be I have an idea," Clint said. Both men turned to him and the Perishables' leader went on. "There's a settlement by the name of Ingleton about an hour south of Celes."

"Huh," Dekker said. "Thought I knew all the towns of any count around here."

"May be that's true," Clint said, "but apparently you don't know the ones that aren't any count." He shrugged. "To call Ingleton a town would be like selling a fella a mule and calling it a horse. Unfair to the fella buyin' it but unfair to the mule, too. Truth is, Ingleton barely even qualifies as a village, I reckon. Less than fifty souls living there altogether, most from just half a dozen families or so. Folks that got tired of livin' in Celes and moved farther south, close enough to the city that they can buy what they can't produce themselves or can take shelter in time of war. That sounds ridiculous now, but then they don't know that Celes's ruler is the true enemy, or at least was, until thanks to Ungr here, he came down with a case of the dead."

"And this village, this Ingleton," the wanderer said, "you think we should go there?"

Clint shrugged. "I know some of the folks there—one of 'em's a friend of mine. Murphy's a good man—hard but good as they come. Not a tougher son of a bitch walkin' the face of the world." He paused, glancing at the wanderer, then at Dekker. "Well. Not many anyhow. They might not have a pony-drawn carriage with gold and silver trappings, but I imagine they have a wagon or two we could trade for, not to mention provisions for the journey."

The wanderer and Dekker shared a look and, after a moment, the big man shrugged as if to say that is was up to the wanderer. "It sounds good to me," the wanderer said.

Clint nodded, smiling. "It'll be good to see Murphy again—and if we're lucky, his wife'll fix us a meal. If there's a better cook on this side of the grave than Gerta, I ain't ever met them."

"Poor Ella ain't even in contention, I can tell you that," Dekker said.

"Sounds more like poor you," Clint said, grinning.

Dekker barked a laugh, and the wanderer found a smile coming to his own face. He felt better than he had since they'd first left the wizard and the sheriff and all the others back at their new home. True, the threat they faced was still very real—and very threatening—but at least, now, they had a plan. "Thanks, both of you," he told the men. "For your help figuring out what to do."

Dekker shrugged. "If everybody's stranded on the same life raft, Ungr, it don't make sense for only one fella to do all the paddlin'."

"True," Clint said, "and maybe next time you'll ask us for help instead of making us lose sleep to give it," he finished, grinning to show that he meant no offense.

The wanderer laughed. "It's a promise."

"Well," Dekker said, grunting as he rose, "on that note, I'm for bed." He glanced at the wanderer. "You make sure you wake me when it's my time—don't go tryin' any stupid heroics. You and I both know some beauty sleep would do you good, though I reckon it's likely a lost cause."

The wanderer and Clint laughed at that, and the big man gave them a smile of his own, then nodded before turning and walking toward where his wife and child lay.

"I think I might get some sleep too," Clint said. "Just so long as you'll promise to wake us."

"That I can do," the wanderer said.

The Perishables' leader nodded, rising to his feet. He started away then glanced back at the wanderer. "You're not alone, Ungr. Not anymore." He shrugged. "Just thought I ought to remind you of that, remind you that that burden of yours ain't only on your shoulders. There's plenty of us that'll help you carry it for just as long as you have to."

"Thank you, Clint," the wanderer said. "That means a lot."

The man gave him a wink then turned and moved to his own bed roll.

The wanderer sat in the darkness of the night, looking over the sleeping figures, feeling good, liking their chances better now than he had since he could remember, perhaps for a hundred years.

He was not alone.

In time, the moon traced its slow way across the sky and finally the wanderer rose, moving to wake Dekker to take the next watch. The man did so without complaint—at least not any complaint loud enough to hear as he grumbled what might have been some choice curses—as he rose and rubbed wearily at his eyes. When he was settled, the wanderer moved to his bedroll, lying down.

And then, one of the most shocking things imaginable happened.

The wanderer slept.

CHAPTER THREE

THEY WOKE EARLY the next morning and resumed their journey. Instead of moving farther north, where they would break out of the Untamed Lands the quickest, they instead chose to move east, skirting the boundary between the Untamed Lands and what was considered the civilized world.

Still, they stayed close to the boundary, no more than a few hundred feet away, in case they needed to flee toward it for any reason, but the wanderer did not expect to see any of the forest's creatures, not this close to the edge of the Untamed Lands. No, they would remain deeper in their own territory, where they felt safer.

They walked on until the wanderer judged them directly south of Celes—or near enough as to make little difference. Then they began making their way north.

It did not take them long to reach the boundary of the Untamed Lands. The wanderer stared at the fields beyond the thick snarls of trees, hesitating, as the others did, before he finally stepped out. Standing in the field the world seemed to stretch on forever, and he suddenly felt very small, very vulnerable, and very exposed.

The others came to stand beside him, and Dekker sighed. "Well," he said. "We're back."

"Yes."

There was a mewling sound, and the wanderer turned to see that it had come from the giant cat's cub. The mother stood at the edge of the boundary, presenting a clearer view of itself than he had seen since leaving the valley the wizard had escorted them to.

It stood staring at him, its amber eyes shining as its cub pushed its face at its leg, purring. Then the giant cat flicked its head at him, a purposeful gesture, before turning and walking back into the Untamed Lands, vanishing out of sight in seconds.

"What do you reckon it was sayin' there?" Dekker asked. "Tellin' you that if you ever come back to stop by for dinner?"

"Or maybe to stop by to be dinner," Clint offered.

"I don't know," the wanderer said honestly, silently wishing the great cat and its cub well. "Ready?" he asked, glancing at Clint and Dekker.

"Reckon we gotta be," Dekker said.

Clint nodded. "Ready. I know we're all a bit sad now about the idea of leavin' this place, but I can tell you that as soon as we get to Ingleton and you try some of Gert's cookin' you won't give it another thought," the man said grinning, and there was something childlike about the expression, about Clint's excitement, that made him appear far younger than he was.

The wanderer shared a glance with Dekker and the big man grinned. "Excited, are you?" he asked Clint.

The other man colored. "Well...yes," he admitted. "Murph's a good friend—Gert, too. We used to see each other I guess about every day when we were younger. But then a blind man could look at me and see that it's been a long time since I was young."

"When was the last time you saw them?" the wanderer asked.

Clint considered that, scratching at his chin. "Let's see...I came south to visit 'em half a year or so ago, durin' the drought, remember?" he asked Dekker, and the big man frowned, nodding. "Yeah, guess that woulda been six...no, seven, yeah, that's it seven months ago now." Clint shook his head. "Damn but where does the time go?"

"I don't know, but if you find out you let me know, eh?" Dekker said. "I wouldn't mind havin' a few years back myself. I took a nap here while back—just a nap, understand. Stood up and my knee hurt for three days. Not for nothin' but standin' up. And here I thought that standin' up and walkin' were what the damned thing was *for.*"

Clint laughed. "I had a nose hair I found the other day, fella was stretched from one nostril and curlin' into the other. Like maybe they were gettin' ready to have a meetin'."

Dekker howled with laughter at that. "What about you, Ungr?" Dekker said. "Got any marks of old age on you?"

"More than I can count," the wanderer said honestly.

That made him think of the way he'd gotten those aches and pains, those scars, and he found the smile fading from his face at the memories. For while he had walked away from the many dangers and tragedies which had left their mark upon him, there were plenty of others who had not. Clint and Dekker got far-off looks in their own eyes, no doubt thinking similar thoughts as their own smiles faded.

Dekker hocked and spat. "Well, shit."

"Yeah," Clint agreed.

"Let's get to it then," Dekker said.

And then they were moving.

***

Morning gave way to afternoon as the wanderer traveled through the open fields, followed closely by Dekker, his wife and daughter, and then, at the rear, Clint and the Perishables who'd chosen to accompany them. No houses or villages stood as far as they could see, for no one would dare think to build so close to the Untamed Lands. Instead, there were only flat plains interrupted intermittently by rolling hills of green.

It was beautiful, in its way, that landscape unmarred by people, and yet after having spent so long beneath the great boughs of the giant trees of the Untamed Lands, the wanderer couldn't shake the feeling of being exposed, of being vulnerable. And judging by the way the others walked, with their shoulders hunched as if expecting a blow, their gazes moving around them as if they were mice scurrying through a field and expecting to see a giant bird of prey swoop down upon them at any moment, he wasn't alone.

But despite their worry, they continued unmolested and the sun was midway through the sky when they came to the top of a small rise in the land. In the distance, woods spread out before them.

"Never thought I'd be so happy to see some damned trees," Clint said.

Dekker grunted, nodding in agreement. "It ain't the Untamed Lands, but damnit they ain't bad, either."

29

"Language, Dekker," Ella said.

"Sorry, dear," Dekker said, winking at the wanderer. "I meant 'damnit, they *aren't* bad.'"

He smiled, like a kid who'd just pulled a trick and was particularly pleased with himself, and the wanderer couldn't help but laugh as Ella rolled her eyes.

"Never get a husband, Ungr," she told him. "They're far more trouble than they're worth."

"I'll try to keep that in mind," he said.

"She says that," Dekker said, "but if a bear comes barreling through the door who do you think's going to handle it if I'm not around?"

"So the best reason you can come up with for getting a husband," Ella said, raising an eyebrow, "is so that he can be a chew toy in the event that a mad bear decides to break into our home? I think I'd be okay risking that one."

Dekker shrugged. "Just sayin'. Bears are nuisances."

"As are men resembling bears," Ella said.

Dekker opened his mouth, clearly meaning to retort, but apparently he was out of ideas, for he closed it again, sighing. "Best keep moving, huh?" he said, glancing at the wanderer.

"Oh, I don't know," the wanderer said, grinning. "I don't suppose we need to be in all that much of a hurry."

"Bastard," Dekker said quietly, though not so quietly that anybody within twenty feet couldn't have heard it.

"Go on then, Clint, you smilin' son of a bitch," Dekker said. "Lead the way."

"If you insist, Majesty," Clint said, sketching a mock bow before stopping halfway and turning to Ella. "Or perhaps, I should say, Your Highness," he said, sketching a far deeper—and shockingly good—bow to her.

Ella blushed, laughing. "Go on then, you."

"With your blessing, Your Grace," Clint said, and several of the nearby Perishables snickered and laughed as he turned and started away again.

Everyone fell in behind them save Dekker, and the wanderer patted the big man on the shoulder. "Oh, I wouldn't worry about it, Dekker. You win some, you lose some."

"In my experience with being married, Ungr," he said, "you mostly just lose." He shrugged then, grinning. "Still, if I got to lose to somebody, I'm damned grateful it's her."

And with that, the man started forward, and the wanderer was left to follow, a smile on his face.

As they walked, he reflected on the fact that, not so long ago, every day had just felt like another struggle, another day where he could never win, could only not fail. That might seem like the same thing to most people, but for a man who had spent a hundred years traveling the world, doing his best to keep the enemy's cursed blade out of their hands, when any slip meant his death and the death of the entire world, the wanderer knew that was simply not true.

Just as he knew that now, as impossible as it seemed, he had allies, people he cared about and who cared about him and with their help he might have a chance not just of surviving, not just of *not* failing, but of actually succeeding.

He felt good.

They all did.

They felt hopeful.

But it was a goodness, a hope, that could not last.

CHAPTER FOUR

CLINT LED THEM into the woods, and the wanderer found himself glancing around at the trees. Many of them were fifty feet tall or more, yet they all seemed like little more than saplings to him after spending so long beneath the giant boughs of the ancient trees of the Untamed Lands.

They reached an intersection in the wood, and Clint glanced back at them, smiling widely. "We're close now. An hour away—no more."

They'd followed Clint down the trail for another fifteen minutes when Veikr began to shift, giving his head a nervous shake. The wanderer frowned, patting the horse softly on his muzzle as he gazed around him looking for what might have bothered the horse, for Veikr was not easily upset. He saw nothing though, and they continued on.

Five minutes later, he realized what had bothered the horse, for he picked up a scent. The others had not smelled it yet, likely would not for some time, but his heightened senses, a product of the trials he'd undergone to become an Eternal, recognized the smell instantly.

Smoke.

But not fresh smoke. No, this was old, not the smell of something burning, but the smell of something burnt.

As they continued, the smell grew stronger, and a knot of worry began to form in the wanderer's stomach.

It was another fifteen minutes later, when Dekker gave a sniff, frowning. "You smell something?" he asked, glancing at the wanderer.

"Yes," the wanderer said, watching Clint's back, watching the way the man moved eagerly down the trail, looking as if he might break into skipping at any moment. He was excited to see his friend again, and why not? From what he'd said it had been some time since he'd seen him and from the way Clint had spoken of this Murphy it was clear he had nothing but respect and love for the man.

The wanderer wished that he could be excited too but something felt...wrong. He couldn't quite put his finger on what it was that was bothering him, but there *was* something, something that niggled at him, a feeling of dark foreboding that he couldn't seem to shake no matter how much he tried.

He told himself that it was the smell—that smell of something burnt. That he was worrying more than he ought, his mind, accustomed to assuming the worst-case scenario without any real proof. As for the burned smell, well that could be anything. He had traveled the world for a very long time, and he knew that a forest fire could be started by something as simple as a campfire getting out of hand or a candle being tossed away carelessly.

Several times over the course of the years he'd been traveling through the woods only to find evidence of vast fires miles from the nearest living soul, fires caused by lightning striking a tree in a dry season where there was no humidity in the air or ground to stop it and the flames were left to rampage until, eventually, they burned themselves out.

No, it was not the burnt smell that bothered him. Or, at least, it was not only that, and despite how he might want to dismiss the worry he felt as nothing more than nerves, he could not. After all, much of his training with Oracle had been learning to accept his feelings, his instincts, even if he did not always know from where those feelings originated.

"Hey, what's this?"

They all turned at Dekker's voice to see the big man move to the side of the trail, lifting something from where it had been all but hidden from view underneath a bush.

The wanderer walked up, along with Clint, to see what the big man was holding only to find that, gripped in his thick-fingered, calloused hand was a small doll in a pink dress, the kind that every little girl in the world seemed to own.

At another time it might have been comical seeing the big man holding the girl's toy in his massive hands, but at the sight of the small child's toy the wanderer's worry increased, and he found that he couldn't have been further from smiling.

Clint, on the other hand, seemed unaffected by whatever was troubling the wanderer, grinning as he stared at Dekker. "Well, Dekker, I got to say I had no idea you were into dolls. If I'd have known I might have got you one for a present, though I must say that her dress really does bring out your eyes."

"Oh yeah, laugh it up you bastard," Dekker said, then frowned. "Still, seems a bit strange, don't it? The doll bein' here?"

Clint raised an eyebrow. "A child losing a toy—you're right, that never happens. Probably whatever little girl—or big man—" he paused, grinning—"owns it was out here playing in the woods and forgot about it when they went home."

Dekker grunted. "Yeah, probably you're right."

Clint nodded. "Anyway, if you're done playing, we aren't far now—a few minutes, no more. That is, if you're okay with it—the Eternals know I wouldn't want to interrupt teatime."

Dekker grunted. "Go on then, you bastard. We're behind you."

Clint winked at the wanderer, grinning widely, then turned and started away again, whistling.

Dekker continued to stare at the doll, not following along.

"Everything alright?" the wanderer asked.

"Maybe...maybe not," the big man said.

"What do you mean?"

Dekker shook his head slowly. "I've got a daughter, Ungr. She's got a doll a lot like this one. Sarah loves that doll—I reckon she loves it more than anything in this world, save maybe that horse of yours. Marsha, she calls it."

"So?" the wanderer asked, thinking he knew well enough where the man was going.

"So she wouldn't leave that doll anywhere. Shit, she wakes up and can't find her for five minutes the water works start. When I was a boy, sure, I'd leave my toys all scattered about, but then that's what boys do—they mess shit up. Girls, though, they're different. They wouldn't anymore abandon one of their dolls than a man'd walk to town and leave his feet behind him."

"So what are you saying?"

Dekker considered that for several seconds then, finally, let out a frustrated sigh, shaking his head. "I don't know," he said. "But I've got a bad feeling."

You and me both, the wanderer thought, but he only nodded. "Come on," he said. "Clint's waiting on us."

"Aye," the big man said. "Reckon it's probably just my imagination anyway."

"I hope so," the wanderer said, then they turned and followed after the Perishables' leader.

CHAPTER FIVE

THEY ARRIVED at Ingleton half an hour later.

Or, at least, what was left of it.

A dozen burned-out husks in a clearing, no more than that. Piles of gray ash and collapsed, scorched wood. Detritus that had once been homes and was now only a grim testament that something had happened here. Something bad.

"I...I don't..." Clint said, stopping in the path and staring at the devastation, his face pale, his eyes wide and disbelieving.

"Dekker, what...what happened?"

The wanderer and Dekker turned to see that Ella had walked up with Sarah, the young girl's face pressed against her.

Dekker glanced at the wanderer, his expression grim, and the wanderer nodded. The big man turned back to his wife. "Best keep everybody back for a bit, El, while we figure out what's going on."

"O-of course," she said, glancing at Clint's back, where he stood staring at the burned-out homes for a moment before she finally turned and made her way toward where the other Perishables waited, motioning them back.

That done, the big man turned back to the wanderer, meeting his gaze again, and the wanderer gave him a nod before the two of them started forward, moving up to stand beside Clint.

"Do...do you think there was an accident?" Clint asked, glancing at the wanderer, his expression afraid and fragile.

The wanderer took a minute to turn and regard what was left of the settlement. The burned-out buildings were all small, simple, what had no doubt served the citizens of Ingleton as homes. "Give me a minute," he said. Then he moved forward, letting his gaze slowly move over the buildings, over the surrounding trees, and the partially scorched ground.

Whatever had happened, it had happened some time ago, likely weeks, but not much more than that. Proof of that could be seen in the state of the homes. Any less time and the smell would have been considerably stronger than it was, any more and the area would have been grown up with weeds and creepers. The wanderer had seen it before in his travels, many times. Villages ransacked by bandits or destroyed by plague or lost for a dozen other reasons. And no sooner had the last villagers died or fled than nature began to creep back in.

It was what nature did, after all. It grew. It lived. It proliferated. But it had not yet reclaimed this part of the land where men had once lived. It would, soon enough, but that time had not yet come. Now there was no life here, only what the fire had left, and the fire, as always, had left little enough. Only ash and more of it.

The wanderer moved about the clearing the way Ranger had taught him, not looking for any specific thing, but instead only letting his mind take in all that he saw, ash and destruction and churned-up dirt at his feet. All that he smelled—smoke, and something else. Decay. All that he heard, too—muted sounds of the forest, as if even the animals that called it home were not prepared to venture here, not yet, at least.

The wanderer looked, he saw, and as he did a picture began to emerge. Or rather, a series of pictures. There had been animals here. Livestock. Goats and chickens mostly, perhaps a cow or two. There had been gardens, also, and the two together had no doubt provided the vast majority of the village's food, if so small a settlement could even be called a village.

The people had been close—in such a small community, they'd have to be in order to survive. No doubt they had each had their own reasons for coming here. Reasons that likely ranged from a simple desire to live and live simply, to a disillusionment with society or with large cities, either of which the wanderer understood for such sentiments were very close to his own desires.

And like his own desires, it seemed that the wishes of the villagers were destined to be disappointed. They had lived and lived simply—at least for a time. He paused, glancing down at the ground surrounding him, at the churned-up mud, the footprints and hoofprints marring its surface. The villagers had been setting about another day when men had come. And as was so often the case when men came, they had brought steel and fire and death with them.

Weeks had passed since the attack, yet blood was not so easily forgotten—that was a truth the wanderer knew well. Among the mud he could see a darker crimson shade, here and there, proof that who or whatever had come upon the settlement of Ingleton had not come in kindness.

A metallic glint in the mud a dozen feet away caught his eye, and he was just turning to move toward it when Clint and Dekker walked up. "Ungr?" Dekker asked.

"It...they're okay, right?" Clint asked. "I mean...that is, there must have been just an accident or something and..." He trailed off, meeting the wanderer's eyes with a desperate expression. "Right?"

The wanderer stared at the man, seeing what he wanted to believe, what he *desperately* wanted to believe. But he would not lie to anyone, particularly a friend. It was a line he had not crossed—perhaps the only one—and he would not cross it now. On the other hand, he did not want to believe what his senses, what his mind was telling him anymore than Clint did, so instead of answering immediately, he walked toward where he'd seen the metallic glint.

It was almost completely hidden, and he was forced to brush aside mud and ash to uncover the object he'd seen. He wiped it off on his trousers before turning back to Clint and Dekker, a grim expression on his face. "I don't think this was an accident," he said.

The two men shared a look and then they moved forward, staring at the object the wanderer held.

"But...is that..." Clint began, trailing off.

"An arrow," Dekker growled, looking around the clearing with an angry expression as if searching for someone to blame.

"But...what does it mean?" Clint asked.

"Nothing good," the wanderer said, rising and examining the arrow, its broken shaft. He glanced around them, taking in the scene again. "They came at night," he said, narrating it even as he thought it through. "Two dozen riders armed with swords and bows."

"How do you know that?" Clint demanded. "You can't know that."

The wanderer knew well that it was the man's anger at what had happened, his worry for his friends, that made him defensive. "Listen, Clint—"

"No," the Perishables' leader said, giving his head a shake and backing away from the wanderer as if somehow by doing so he might take back what had happened, as if his denial might in some way protect those for whom he cared. It wasn't logical, of course, but in a very real sense, when faced with the prospect of losing someone or something he loved, denial was the most logical thing any living creature could do. "No," Clint said again. "I just saw Murphy and Gert, what? No more than six months ago. They can't be...that is, this can't...*they* can't...you're not going to tell me that they're dead."

"Hey, hey," Dekker said, moving forward and putting a hand on the other man's shoulder, "nobody here is sayin' that, alright? Ungr's just trying to help."

The Perishables' leader winced, glancing at the wanderer. "I'm...sorry, Ungr. I didn't...that is..."

"Think nothing of it," the wanderer said immediately.

The other man nodded, running an arm across his eyes where tears had begun to gather. "You're sure? About the riders, I mean?"

"Yes. They tried to cover their tracks, but it is no easy thing to hide so many."

Clint nodded slowly. "And...and the people who lived here?"

The wanderer glanced around at the burned-out buildings then at Dekker.

"Listen, Clint," the big man said, turning to the Perishables' leader, "I wonder if you couldn't check on Sarah for me, make sure she's okay?"

Clint left off wiping at his eyes to give the man a weak, trembling smile. "You're trying to get rid of me—I've seen the look enough to know it, though it's usually from women."

"As if any woman would let you spend time around her in the first place," Dekker said, giving the man a small smile of his own.

Clint grunted. "Bastard," he said.

"You and Ella ought to talk," Dekker said. "Seems you've got a lot in common as she thinks the same."

Clint gave a soft snort, then finally nodded. "Alright. Okay. I'll go check on your girl for you. But..." He paused, glancing around at what was left of Ingleton. "These were good people here," he said, turning to the wanderer. "If..."

"We'll do everything we can—you have my word."

Clint nodded again, then turned and walked back down the path where Sarah had led the others.

The two of them watched the man walk away and Dekker waited until he was out of ear shot before turning to glance at the wanderer. "Bandits, do you think?"

"Maybe," the wanderer said, looking around him. He glanced back to see that Clint and the others had moved around a bend in the path, beyond their sight. "We'd best do a search, see what we can find."

And so they did, Dekker starting on one side of the houses, the wanderer the other. It was a grim business, sorting through ash and collapsed homes, seeing small bits of evidence that people had lived here, that they had called this place home, little pieces that the fire hadn't managed to eradicate completely.

In one small house the wanderer found a small scrap of silk that seemed as if it belonged to a fine dress, probably what had been a prized possession of the woman who'd lived there—certainly such items wouldn't have been readily available in so small a village.

There were other things, too, hiding like precious gems in the dirt. A child's shoe, a pipe, another kid's toy, this one not a doll but a small wooden horse, scorched and broken beyond repair. It was a macabre search, one that left the wanderer feeling greater and greater despair with each moment that passed. Yet, it was not as bad as it could have been, as it *might* have been, for among all the things which he found, there was one thing that was conspicuously absent—bodies.

Yet even that was little comfort, for whoever had come to the village had clearly not cared for its inhabitants and so if they had chosen to leave them alive there was a reason for it. And no matter how he looked at it he could not imagine a reason that would mean anything but pain and loss for the villagers of Ingleton.

The wanderer finished searching another house, finding nothing to indicate who had attacked the village or why they might have come here, then sighing heavily, he stepped out of the crooked, charred doorway and moved to the final house, the one that sat at what would have once been the village's center.

He noted Dekker walking up as well. "Find anything?"

"Nothin' of any consequence, I don't think. Well, except this." The big man reached into his pocket, producing a small torn piece of black cloth. It was no greater than half the size of the wanderer's hand, singed and torn, but upon that strip of black cloth was a stylized, crimson-embroidered patch. Or, at least, part of one.

Less than half the patch, not enough to know what it was by the looking, but the wanderer felt a shiver of cold dread run up his spine at the sight of it. A normal person, looking at it, might not have known what it was, but the wanderer knew well enough, for he had seen its like before, long ago.

"Probably just trash," Dekker said, shrugging, clearly not noticing the inner turmoil going on within the wanderer. He started to toss it on the ground.

"*Don't.*"

The word came out of the wanderer's throat in a harsh hiss, so abrupt that the big man started. "Everything okay, Ungr?" he asked.

"I don't think so," the wanderer said, looking at that scrap of black, soot-stained cloth, staring at the partial patch on it. He reached out, taking the cloth, examining it, hoping that he was wrong, trying to convince himself that he was. The problem, of course, was that he knew he wasn't.

"What is it?" Dekker asked. "What's wrong?"

The wandered swallowed hard, shaking his head. "Later—for now, let's finish the search. The others are waiting."

Dekker frowned but nodded. "Alright."

The house, like the others, was small, consisting of two rooms, a bedroom and the main entry which must have served as the primary living quarters as well as the dining room.

The wanderer left Dekker to check the main room, moving to the single bedroom. There was nothing left of the mattress save a burned and collapsed frame. There was a small bureau in the corner that had been broken into and tipped over, as if whoever had attacked had been searching for loot. What caught the wanderer's eye, however, were two simple hooks on the wall, of the kind that would be used to hold a weapon.

Frowning, he moved to the bed, pushing some of the burned timber aside with his foot to reveal something metallic. He knelt, clearing more of the rubble away, until finally he revealed a sword. There was no scabbard or, if there had been, it had been burned away in the fire, but even a glance could tell the wanderer that the blade had been well cared for. He lifted it, seeing that most of the leather-grip handle had also been burned away, but the blade was well-balanced.

"Murphy's sword," a voice said, and the wanderer turned to see Clint walking through the shell of the burned-out doorway, followed closely by Dekker.

"Clint," the big man said, "are you sure you want to—"

"I'm alright, Dek," Clint said. "Or...at least, I will be." He nodded his head at the blade the wanderer held. "Murphy used to be a soldier—did I tell you that?"

"You did not," the wanderer said quietly.

"Well, he did. That's his sword there, from his time as a soldier. Murph never would have gone anywhere without it. He told me once that he loved that weapon. Told me that he hated it, too."

The wanderer nodded slowly. He had carried the cursed blade—and his own, more mundane sword—for many years, had been forced to use both on more occasions than he liked to contemplate and so he understood well enough what Clint's friend had meant.

"Come on," he told the two men. "Let us go back outside."

Dekker nodded, leading the way, but Clint hesitated, staring at the sword lying in the ash.

The wanderer watched him for a second. "You should take it."

Clint spun to look at him with an expression that would have been more suited for if the wanderer had told him he should kick a puppy. "That's Murph's sword."

"Yes," the wanderer said, "and you should take it. That way, you might return it to him."

Clint watched the wanderer for a minute, then finally he nodded, kneeling and gingerly picking up the sword. He gave the wanderer another look then turned and walked outside.

The wanderer followed him out to where Dekker stood. He glanced down the path and saw to his relief that the others were still out of sight somewhere beyond the curve in the path.

"Wish I could get my hands on the bastards that did this," Dekker said.

"Good luck," Clint said. "After all, we don't know where they are. Shit, we don't even know *who* they are."

"Bandits, surely," Dekker said, glancing at the wanderer. "I mean, all the homes looked looted."

"Bandits don't normally burn down the homes of those they rob though, do they?" Clint asked, frowning.

"Don't know," Dekker said. "I don't know a lot of bandits or criminals. Not anymore, anyway, since I met Ella and gave up the bloody life. You?"

Clint grunted. "No, I s'pose not. Still, what reason would they have for burning the village down? And where are all the people?"

Dekker shrugged. "Who knows? But what reason would anyone else besides bandits have for attacking a settlement out here in the middle of nowhere? Anyway, we know that they went through and looted everything—you ask me, that's the sort of thing bandits would do."

"Or the sort of thing someone trying to make it appear as if bandits were responsible might do," the wanderer said.

The two men turned on him, frowning. "Something on your mind, Ungr?" Dekker asked.

"Yes," the wanderer said. "First, as I mentioned before, there were around two dozen riders, perhaps more than that. In my experience, bandits rarely travel in so large of numbers."

"Rarely, sure, but it still happens," Dekker said. "Why, what about the Bandit King? That bastard caused all that havoc a hundred years ago? It was said he had over a thousand men at his command."

The wanderer knew well who the big man meant, for history and military tactics had made up a substantial amount of the education the Eternals had given him when he'd been training to become one of their number. And whatever else he had been, the Bandit King—eventually defeated by the Eternals—had proven to possess a great military mind, one that had been said to rival even Tactician himself.

"He was called the Bandit King," the wanderer acknowledged, "but he was not, really. He was a revolutionary. Either way, Clint makes another good point—bandits don't tend to burn down the villages they rob, nor do they tend to kidnap people. Sure, they might hold a person for ransom," he went on before Dekker could pose the obvious counterpoint, "but who would attempt to ransom an entire village? And even if they *did* intend to do such a thing, who would they ransom them *to?*"

"I don't know," Dekker said. "But I don't know what keeps the sun up in the heavens, shinin' down on us, either. Doesn't mean it isn't so."

As always, the wanderer found himself being impressed with the big man's mind. "True," he admitted, "but whatever other reasons we have for thinking it, I know that this time, at least, it was not bandits, only someone wanting people to think it was."

Dekker frowned, thinking that over. Then, finally, he shook his head. "I'll admit that's a scary thought, Ungr, but if, you ask me, bandits are the sort of thing that, if you impersonate closely enough, you ain't impersonating at all, if you see what I'm saying. Anyhow, why are you so sure it wasn't bandits?"

The wanderer glanced at Clint, saw the man frowning, his fear for his friends writ plain on his face. "Because," the wanderer said, reaching into his pocket and withdrawing the scrap of cloth he'd put there when they'd entered the last house, "bandits don't wear insignia like these."

Dekker took the piece of cloth, eyeing it doubtfully, then handed it to Clint.

"And this..." the Perishable's leader said, examining it, "this somehow let's you know it isn't bandits?"

"It does," the wanderer said.

Dekker grunted. "I ain't tryin' to be contrary, Ungr, but it don't look like much of anything to me—certainly it don't look like any insignia I've ever seen, and I've seen more than a few."

"Nor would it," the wanderer said. "Few indeed are those who know the significance of this insignia," he went on grimly, meeting the two men's gazes, "for it stands as proof that the bearer is part of the Shadows."

"Shadows? Only shadow I know is the one follows me around everywhere I go," Dekker said.

"The Shadows are an elite group of warriors," the wanderer said. "Men and women who have been trained since childhood. They are perhaps the deadliest warriors the world has ever seen."

Dekker grunted. "Never heard of 'em."

"Nor should you have," the wanderer said. "No one knows of the Shadows existence save the Eternals themselves."

Dekker raised an eyebrow. "Seems to me, Ungr, that a group of warriors ain't all that useful if they got to remain hidden—that's the thing about war. Whatever else it is, it's loud."

"You misunderstand me," the wanderer said. "The Shadows are not meant for open battle—not any more than a blacksmith's hammer is meant for war. No, they are a tool of an altogether...different nature."

"What kind of nature?" Clint asked.

"The Eternals were considered, by many, to be gods. They were looked on as paragons of virtue, unparalleled in wisdom and compassion, in mercy and love. But..." The wanderer trailed off, finding himself thinking of the Wizard of the South, of his own distrust and dislike of the Eternals. He gave his head a shake. "They are considered a guiding light for the people of the world. But for some tasks it is not the light that is needed but the darkness. For in some places the light does not, *cannot* reach. And for those times, the Shadows were made."

"I'm not following you, Ungr," Dekker said.

"Sorry," he said. "That is how it was explained to me, long ago. The Shadows were created to solve problems that would prove...*difficult* for the Eternals."

"Difficult?" Dekker asked. "What sort of problems could prove difficult for men and women who had the powers of the gods?"

"Not difficult in that way," the wanderer said. "Not difficult to overcome but difficult to...to be associated with."

"Go on," Dekker said, frowning.

"There were some instances in which certain things—or people—needed to be dealt with," the wanderer said. "Situations in which certain individuals posed a very credible, very real threat to the peace of the world, but hid it well so that, should open action be taken against them, the people might disagree. And so, in such cases, the Shadows were sent to deal with it."

"Deal with it," Dekker repeated slowly.

"Assassins," Clint said. "You're talking about assassins."

"Yes."

Dekker scratched his chin. "No offense, Ungr, but the more I hear about the Eternals—the real ones, I mean—the less I like 'em."

The wanderer winced, remembering that when he'd first heard of the Shadows his reaction had been much the same. After all, the Eternals were held up as the embodiment of the positive virtues. True, they all had their individual strengths, but as a whole they were taken to be the very best that the world had to offer. The kindest, gentlest, most loving, selfless individuals. It was not easy then to consider that those same individuals, those same examples of perfect moral virtue, might make use of such a secret army as the Shadows.

"Maybe you don't like it," Clint offered, filling the silence, "but you have to admit it makes sense. I at least can see where such a force would be necessary."

"Takin' a shit's necessary too," Dekker countered. "That don't make it pretty. Anyway, you don't mind my sayin' so, Clint, I'm surprised to hear you defendin' 'em. Considerin' that if what Ungr thinks is true then it was the Shadows that came here to Ingleton, that attacked your friends."

Clint turned to the wanderer. "But...why would they do that, attack an innocent village?"

The wanderer shook his head slowly. "I don't know," he told the man. "But I mean to find out."

"Find out?" Dekker asked. "I know you're a damned good tracker, Ungr, but you'd have to be a magician to be able to track those bastards after weeks of wind and rain and who knows what else."

"I don't have to track them," the wanderer said, looking back down the trail.

"No?" Dekker asked. "How do you figure that?"

"Because I know where they're going," the wanderer said, meeting the big man's gaze. "The Shadows serve the Eternals. Each of them. They are sort of a personal force employed to their aid. Men and women who have been trained since birth not to think on their own initiative but to follow orders, whatever those orders might be. If the Shadows are here, there is only one place they can be—Celes."

"Celes?" Dekker asked surprised. "But...why would you think they'd be there?"

"It is by far the closest capital city of the Eternals," the wanderer said, "one ruled by an Eternal himself."

"Was ruled, you mean," Dekker said. "As I recall you dealt with that bastard pretty definitively back in Alhs."

"So I did," the wanderer agreed, "but the enemy will have sent someone else. They would not have allowed Celes to go on without being overseen."

"And you're sure about that?" Clint asked. "That they went to Celes I mean?"

"The puppet does not stray far from the hand of the puppet master," the wanderer answered.

"So...the others, the villagers, Murph and Gert and all the rest...you think they took them to Celes?"

"There is no way to know for sure," the wanderer said, "but I believe so, yes. If they'd wanted to kill them they would have done so already."

Clint's regarded the woods to the north, beyond which lay Celes, and the wanderer could practically see his thoughts written across his face. "Listen, Ungr..." he said after a moment, "I know I said I'd go with you to the north and all, but...but I was thinking, maybe I ought to go to Celes. You know, see if I could find out about Murph and Gert. I'll get a horse there and catch up with you somewhere along the path. It doesn't, that is—"

"No."

The Perishables' leader cut off, his eyes going wide, and he glanced at Dekker then back at the wanderer. "I...I guess I'm not sure what you mean."

"I mean no, Clint," the wanderer said. "You're not going to Celes." He paused, glancing over at Dekker who gave him a nod. "Not alone, at least."

Clint blinked. "Do...do you mean—"

"We're coming with you," the wanderer said. He turned back to Dekker. "If, that is, you agree."

"Any son of a bitch that would do this deserves what's comin' to him," the big man said.

"Twenty-four," the wanderer offered.

"What's that?"

"There are twenty-four sons of bitches. Maybe more."

"Fine," Dekker said. "Any sons of bitches that would do something like this, burn down a whole village, they deserve what's comin' to 'em, and I mean to bring it to them. Anyway, if there's even a chance we could save the villagers, we have to take it, right?"

"Right," the wanderer said.

"But...but you can't risk your family," Clint said.

"It's a risk just wakin' up in the mornin', Clint," Dekker said. "Seems to me, if all paths lead to risk, we might as well take the one that takes us to somethin' worth doin'."

"That...but you don't even know them," Clint said.

"We know you, Clint," Dekker said. "And if you say they're good people, that's all I need. Ain't that right, Ungr?"

The wanderer smiled at the big man, giving a nod. "That's right."

"But what about your...your mission?" Clint asked. "To defeat the...the enemy?"

"I told you," the wanderer said, "the Shadows work for the Eternals, and the Eternals—or, at least, those posing as them—*are* the enemy."

"Besides," Dekker said, "the bastard hasn't managed to finish his mission in a hundred years. I reckon a few days won't matter all that much either way."

Clint studied the two men, a mixture of respect and relief on his face as he grinned. In moments, though, the grin faded, and he shook his head. "No. No, it wouldn't be right. What if somethin' happened to your family?" he asked Dekker. Then he turned to the wanderer. "And what if something happened to that weapon you carry on account of your tryin' to help me? It wouldn't be right, riskin' the whole world for me and my friends."

"Once I would have agreed with you," the wanderer said, "but not anymore. You, your friends, you *are* the world, Clint. And last I checked, the best way to save a thing isn't to stand by and watch while it's destroyed."

"And if we get caught in Celes, and the enemy gets that artifact you carry?"

"Or what if he's got an army waiting just up ahead on the path?" the wanderer countered.

"Or what if a storm comes and a tornado blows us all away, cursed sword and all?" Dekker added.

Clint sighed. "Alright, alright, I get it. Truth is, I'll be damned glad to have you two along—even if you are both bastards."

"Yeah, sure, flatter us," Dekker said, "my question is, who's the *bastardiest?*"

Clint grunted a laugh, shaking his head.

"Ready?" the wanderer asked, letting his gaze travel between the two men.

Dekker shrugged. "Sure, why not? Been what, a few days since we've risked our lives? Reckon I'm gettin' a bit antsy."

CHAPTER SIX

THE OTHERS WERE waiting beyond the bend in the path. Ella glanced at her husband who gave her a grim shake of his head, and that was all. No one asked after the villagers, for they could see the answer clearly on the three men's faces.

The wanderer hesitated at the bend in the path, turning to look back at Ingleton. Only it wasn't really Ingleton, not anymore. It was nowhere. Just a few ransacked buildings that had once been homes, a place where people *used* to live. Soon, nature would begin to reclaim the land. In months, people might pass here and wonder what had happened to this place, might wonder who had lived here and what had become of them. In years they might pass and never know that anyone had ever lived here at all.

As he stared at those ruins, the wanderer found himself thinking of a conversation he'd once had long ago with Assassin. The woman had not spoken much, but she had been troubled that day. She had drunk much wine, something she never did, for she always said that to lose oneself in drink or herb was to invite disorder and chaos and death.

She had spoken then, while he'd been in the room, but even now he was not sure if the words had been meant for him or for herself. It had been cold that day, and they had been sitting before a fire.

"We think ourselves eternal," she'd said. "We tell ourselves that we will live forever, that the works of our hands will persevere. The truth, though, is that the moment a work is finished, however great, it begins to fall into disrepair. The truth is that at the moment in which we are born, we begin to die."

Assassin had often been quiet, speaking little or, usually, none at all, but she was sharp, clever. Soldier had always said so—as sharp as the knives she carried, he'd said. As clever as a fox. And certainly his time spent training with her had reinforced this to the wanderer. But while he had known her as many things, clever and sharp and more than a little frightening, capable of seemingly disappearing and reappearing out of nowhere, as if she could travel through the very shadows, could step into and out of them the way a man might a door, what the wanderer had never known her as being was maudlin.

And so he had dared, in that moment, to ask her what was wrong, what troubled her. She had gone several seconds without speaking, so long that he had thought she would not speak at all. And then, she had said simply, *It is the anniversary.*

He had asked her about that, about what it was the anniversary for, but she had lapsed into a grim silence, refusing to comment further and, after a few more futile attempts, he had let it go.

Often, because she was so quiet, so unobtrusive, the wanderer and the ghosts seemed to forget that she existed at all, and he thought that, too, was intentional, for the woman had never done anything without a clear intent. She had a way of disappearing from people's minds the same way she disappeared from their sight, so that he rarely thought of her.

Yet he thought of her now, as he stared at those ruins, thought of her words on that cold night, with the fire burning bright and doing nothing to touch the cold and the darkness her comments raised in him. He thought of her as one of his hands drifted into his pocket, touching the patch there, the patch that would mark a man or a woman as one of the Shadows, troops who she had personally trained while she was still alive and that, so far as he knew, her impostor still trained.

Assassin who, according to Soldier and Leader, both legendary warriors in their own right, had been the deadliest person to ever walk the face of the world. A woman who the entire world walked in fear of, who had reached the very pinnacle of deadliness of which mortals were capable and so could be more confident than anyone else in the world that she might be safe.

Assassin who the wanderer had never seen smile.

He wondered about that, as he and the others made their way down the forest trail in the direction of Celes, leaving the dead village behind them.

He wondered about many things.

He considered, as they walked, opening the amulet and asking the ghosts for their thoughts on what he should do, on what path he might take, moving forward. But in the end, he decided against it—and not for the usual reason that he decided to forego opening the amulet. Indeed, he was confident that should he open the amulet they would go to great lengths to explain to him just how much of a fool he was, but while that had been what dissuaded him in the past, it was not what dissuaded him from seeking their advice now. Instead, it was because of one very simple thought, a thought that he had not even considered a year ago. And that thought was this—whatever advice they gave him...they might be wrong.

There had been a time, not so very long ago, when he had never questioned the Eternals. Certainly before he'd become one himself he had thought of them as gods. Even after having been accepted into their ranks, he had never truly considered himself one of them, had always thought them better, smarter, cleverer than himself. In many ways, he still did. It was odd to him, then, that only now, when they were all long dead, the only thing left of them the ghosts which inhabited his amulet, that the wanderer realized the truth...they were not gods at all. They were—or, at least, they *had been*—people.

And while gods might be infallible, the wanderer had seen enough of people to know that even the best had flaws and that the greatest among them were those who recognized those flaws within themselves. And he was not sure that the ghosts did that—was not sure that they *could* do that.

So, he left the amulet unopened, only walking onward with the others. The fate of the small village weighed heavily on him, as it did on his companions, and they spoke little as they made their way toward Celes.

They were silent, and in that silence a feeling began to creep over the wanderer. An instinct, nothing more, but then he had learned long ago to trust such feelings. Had been *taught* to trust them. So as they walked, he pushed aside his anger and grief and worry for the people of the small village of Ingleton.

And then, in the silence, in the stillness that was not just without but within too...

He listened.

He watched.

At first, there was nothing.

Then, he began to make out tracks along the road. No strange thing, that—after all, that was what the road was for. Although it had to be said that the road out of the southern part of the city was rarely traveled as it led only to a few small hamlets beyond which loomed the Untamed Lands.

Still, the road was traveled from time to time, mostly by villagers seeking to sell their wares or goods in Celes's market. There was nothing strange about their presence in and of itself. What *was* strange, however, was that the wanderer had been trained by the best tracker in the world, and so he recognized the signs that someone had tried to hide their passage. They'd used a branch and its leaves to try to brush away their footprints, but they had not managed it, at least not completely. Not exactly someone rushing at him brandishing an axe, but try as he might, the wanderer could think of no benign reason for someone trying to hide their passage on a main road.

And the poorly hidden tracks weren't the only thing that bothered him.

The woods around them were quiet, no birds chirping, no squirrels scampering about the trees, not even so much as a single call from a loon or whippoorwill.

As he noticed this, the wanderer remembered a lesson Ranger and Assassin had both taught him, in their own ways, long ago. Sometimes, the sign a man looked for wasn't to be found in the presence of something. Sometimes—oftentimes, in fact—it wasn't about what was there but what wasn't.

The woods were quiet, yes—too quiet. A silence, a stillness had descended on them that was nothing short of unnatural. Or, perhaps, it was more accurate to say that it was the most natural thing in the world. After all, such a silence, such a stillness, was common enough when a predator roamed nearby. And no lion, however sharp its teeth, no wolf however keen its claws, could ever compare to the world's greatest predator.

Man.

Perhaps another might have thought that the silence was due to their passage, but the wanderer was confident that it was not. After all, at the coming of a predator the creatures of the wood and air often flew and scampered away, but they did not fly at his and the others' approach. No, they had flown already.

"Stop," the wanderer said.

The others did as he asked, turning to regard him with questioning expressions.

"Everything alright, Ungr?" Clint asked.

Instead of answering, the wanderer turned and stared back down the path. Empty as far as he could see. Silent. Still. And while there was nothing that he could put his finger on to say why, he thought that it would not remain so for long. Someone or something was coming.

"Ungr?"

The wanderer turned from studying their back trail to regard Dekker and Clint who stood beside him. "Someone's following us."

Dekker frowned, looking behind them at the empty trail with no sign of life or movement, then turned back to the wanderer. "You sure?"

He considered that for a moment then, finally, shook his head. "No."

Dekker grunted. "Good enough for me. So what do you want to do? Try to outrun them?"

The wanderer considered that for a moment, regarding the tracks he could make out on the road. "No. There'll be more up ahead, waiting."

"What makes you say that?" Clint asked.

"I have seen it before," the wanderer said, thinking of the bandits he'd encountered shortly before meeting Dekker and his family what felt like a lifetime ago.

"Wait for them, then?" Dekker asked thoughtfully. "Lay a trap of our own, show the bastards they ain't the only ones that can ambush someone?"

The wanderer considered that. It wasn't a bad idea on the surface—after all, rarely indeed did the predator expect the prey to turn and attack. The problem, of course, was that there was a reason for that—no matter his level of aggression, his courage, when the rabbit faced down the lion there was only one real outcome. They had no way of knowing just how many they would be up against, and that wasn't his only fear.

He suspected that those stalking them were bandits, but then he might well be wrong. After all, they were close to the enemy's place of power, close to Celes. He didn't know how the enemy possibly could have learned of their coming, but then they had surprised him before. It was conceivable that those who hunted them weren't just bandits but that they worked for the enemy.

"No," he said after a moment, shaking his head as he turned and glanced in the direction of where Sarah and Ella, along with the Perishables, waited. "It's too dangerous."

"Well," Dekker said slowly, "if we can't move forward—on account of we'll die—and we can't wait on account of we'll die, then I'm not sure where that leaves us to go."

The wanderer turned back behind them, regarding the trail they'd so recently traveled. "Back."

Clint raised an eyebrow. "Back? I don't mean to quibble, Ungr, but it seems to me that going back presents the same danger as moving forward...don't it? I mean if what you're sayin' is true—and I don't doubt that it is—" he added hurriedly, "then there's a group ahead of us as well as behind, makin' one direction pretty much as good as another, right?"

"Wrong," the wanderer said.

"Mind educatin' us fools on why that is?" Clint asked.

"Because they're countin' on us goin' forward," Dekker said, answering for the wanderer who nodded.

"That's right," he agreed. "Anyway, I don't mean for all of us to go back."

Dekker frowned. "You got that look in your eye."

"What look is that?"

"The one you get before you set about doin' some fool heroics that'll get you killed, like as not," the big man said.

"I do not see another way," he told the big man. "We cannot face both groups at once, surrounded."

"And you mean to go on your own," Clint said. It wasn't really a question but he decided to answer it anyway.

"Yes."

"Not a chance," Dekker said immediately. "We're goin' with you and that's it. This time you'll just have to share the glory, that's all, but at least you'll be alive to do it."

"I don't care about the glory," the wanderer said, turning and regarding Dekker's family and the other Perishables, all of whom were watching the three men with troubled expressions. "I care about them."

Dekker frowned at that, his mouth working, but it was Clint who spoke. "All the more reason for you to have backup," the Perishables' leader said.

"For what I mean to do, I will need to be quiet," the wanderer said, "and quick. It is better that I go alone."

"Until it ain't," Dekker said. "Look, Ungr, do you have any idea of how many of the bastards are coming up behind us?"

"No."

"And any clue as to how many might wait ahead?"

"No."

"So your plan—such as it is—is to take on an unknown amount of armed men by yourself. Any fool can see why they didn't call you Planner or Wisest. And just what do you expect the rest of us to do while you're takin' on what, for all you know, could be an army? Twiddle our thumbs? Hide under the blankets, maybe?"

"I will be faster alone," the wanderer said. "Make no mistake," he went on, meeting the two men's gazes in turn, "we have stepped into a trap. One that is closing around us even as we sit here and debate what to do about it. It is too far gone now for us to simply remove ourselves from it the way a man might lift his ankle before the trap's teeth bite. The only option, now, is to force it open and to do so quickly before it takes hold of us. I have a better chance of doing that alone."

Dekker shook his head, hocking and spitting. "Leavin' again, the same way you tried to slink off in the middle of the night while everyone slept back when the wizard was workin' that spell on us."

"I'd like to think there was more strut than slink," the wanderer countered.

He was hoping for a smile at that, but he was bound to be disappointed, for Dekker only frowned, and it was the Perishables' leader who spoke.

"And what are we supposed to do in the meantime?" Clint asked.

The wanderer considered the question. "You should go into the woods," he said. "Far enough not to be seen or heard from the road but not so far as to get lost."

"Okay," Clint said. "You can meet us after you're done. We'll tell you where we're headed and—"

"Better if you didn't," the wanderer said. "Just in case."

There was silence for several seconds then until Dekker spoke. "Bullshit," the big man said. "If we're not goin' with you then we're at least going to wait here for you. I know you're a tough son of a bitch, Ungr, but unless you've got a crystal ball tucked in your pack somewhere you can't know that you'll be able to find us."

In fact, the wanderer thought it was safe to say that he did. No matter how good the men were at covering their tracks, there was simply too many of them to conceal their passage completely. But time was of the essence, and he thought there was a quicker way to make Dekker understand the necessity of it. "And if those waiting ahead grow impatient?" he asked. "If they choose to come back and check? Likely those behind have alerted them to our presence somehow already—some sort of signal. Even if they have not, the two groups certainly will have some way of checking in with each other. If you wait here, in the road, it might be that they will backtrack to check, reaching you before I do."

It was also true that, should those behind kill him, Dekker and the rest would have to worry about that group as well but judging by the grim expressions on the men's faces it was clear that there was no need to say as much.

"How long will it take, do you think?"

The wanderer glanced behind them again. "They will want to be close but not too close. Likely they are an hour, perhaps two behind us."

"It's gettin' late already," Dekker observed, turning his gaze to the sky. "It'll be dark before you reach 'em."

"I'm counting on it," the wanderer said.

"Still sounds like suicide to me," Dekker said, sighing. He turned to Clint. "Go on, Clint. You got somethin' to say on it?"

The Perishable's leader considered that. "Good luck," he told the wanderer.

Dekker hissed. "That's not what I meant, damnit."

"This is the best way," the wanderer told the big man.

Dekker grunted. "Fine, damnit. I'll go and get your horse."

"Not for this."

The big man turned, raising an eyebrow. "You don't mean to take him? Seems to me you'll need every advantage you can get."

"Veikr is an amazing horse," the wanderer said, "the greatest of his kind, the noblest and bravest beast to ever live, so far as I'm concerned. But while he has many talents, I'm afraid subtlety cannot be counted among them. And for what I plan, subtlety is required."

"Subtlety," Dekker said. "For what you have planned."

"That's right."

"You mean assassination, don't you?" Dekker asked.

"If necessary."

The big man considered that for a moment then finally gave a single nod. "Good luck. I hope you're right about this."

"So do I," the wanderer said, then he gave the two men a nod, turned, and started away.

CHAPTER SEVEN

HE TOOK the path for a time, leaving the others behind him as the sun sank lower and lower, and the shadows spread out to claim the world of the living once more.

The wanderer did not worry that he might stumble upon those who followed, for he was confident he still had some time yet, was confident that his heightened senses would detect anyone sharing the woods with him before they might detect him.

He thought, as he walked, of what he and the others planned. Not that there *was* much of a plan—just a bunch of hope cobbled together. They would go to Celes and hope that they weren't identified as soon as they entered the city, where they hoped to find Clint's friends in a city with tens of thousands of people. And the wanderer's greatest hope was that he was not leading them into a trap, a trap like the one they even now found themselves in.

He had told Dekker that it would be better for him to investigate those following them on his own, and that was true. After all, he had been trained by the greatest woodsman and the greatest assassin ever to walk the face of the world. But the *complete* truth was that was not the reason he had come alone. He had come alone because it was his fault they were here in the first place, and so he would not risk the others, not if he could help it.

That led to dark thoughts about what awaited them even should they somehow find their way out of this latest debacle, and he found a knot of despair, of hopelessness growing inside of him as he made his way farther down the trail.

He glanced at the sky and saw that there was little moon tonight, no more than a sliver, one so thin it was easy to think he imagined it, and he thought of something Assassin had told him long ago. *Dark thoughts and dark deeds are most often done on dark nights.*

He had not thought much of it at the time, had even thought it a little silly—almost like a child's rhyme. It had seemed a strange thing for the normally reticent Assassin—who never said anything more than was absolutely necessary—to waste breath on. Now, though, he understood, for knowing what he planned, the darkness of the night seemed to seep into him, becoming part of him, tainting his thoughts. For it *was* dark, dark enough that a man might find himself unable to remember the light of day, might find himself thinking that the light did not exist at all, that his memory of it was no more than a construct of his imagination.

But that darkness only grew within him as he walked, and after a time he did not fight it. After all, dark deeds were done on dark nights, and he thought there were some dark deeds ahead of him, for as he moved down the path he began to doubt that those who hunted them were just bandits. After all, bandits had never dared operate so close to Celes, for Soldier had been aggressive in hunting down such men, who he considered no better than vultures.

It seemed all the more likely, then, that those who hunted them did so at the behest of the enemy. He did not know what incentive might cause men to side with the creatures, had no idea how much they might have been told, how much they might know, and the truth was that he did not care—he could not.

All he cared about was keeping Dekker and his family and the Perishables who followed him safe. He could do no more than that.

He continued down the trail until he saw what might have been the flicker of a torch in the distance. Then he left the forest path, stepping into the shadowed woods. He moved in a slow, methodical circle around where he'd first seen the orange flicker, catching a glimpse of it from time to time. Mostly, though, he paid it little attention, instead allowing his gaze to roam over the silhouettes of tree trunks and bushes, looking for any shape or unnatural angle that might give away the presence of someone lurking in the woods.

Despite the fact that he was anxious to get back to the others where they waited somewhere in the woods, the wanderer forced himself to remain patient, to move slowly, for he knew that in such matters haste often spelled a man's doom.

That was another thing Assassin had taught him—patience. Many talented contractors, men and women who had mastered all other aspects of their trade, still found themselves on the wrong end of a sword or rotting in a dungeon cell due to a lack of patience.

And patience wasn't the only important thing—so, too, was focus. He pushed aside thoughts of the others, opening a box in his mind the way he had been shown, and shoving all of his worries and fears and doubts inside. There was a place for fear, a purpose for it, but that purpose would not serve him now—instead it would serve only as a distraction, one he could not afford.

A calm descended on him as he continued his wide, meandering circle around the distant flame. He would not have called it peace, not that, for he was not anymore peaceful than the sharpened blade, free of its sheath. Not in a state of peace but in a state of waiting for its time to come so that it might fulfill its purpose.

So that it might cut.

In another few minutes' walking he was able to hear voices. Distant, muffled and unclear, for even with his heightened senses, given him by the Trials, still he could not make out the words.

He stalked closer.

There were a dozen of them, at least, shadows gathered around the dancing flames of two campfires, silhouetted in the darkness.

He stalked closer.

As he moved, he glanced at the men gathered around the fire from time to time, but the majority of his attention was focused on the woods around him and in front of him as he moved. It was for this reason that he saw the silhouette of a man seated twenty-five feet ahead of him, his back propped against the trunk of a large tree.

In the deepening gloom, the man was nearly indistinguishable from the woods around him. But as Soldier had so often told him when the wanderer had nearly—but not quite—managed to parry a strike during training, life and death existed on either side of almost.

The bow he'd fashioned in the Untamed Lands when preparing for Ranger's arrival hung at the wanderer's back, but he did not reach for it. Neither did he reach for the cursed blade or his own sword. An arrow fired from the bow might leave the man wounded, and wounded men could still scream. As for the swords, amid the thick undergrowth and reaching branches it would be far too easy for one of the blades to get snagged on something.

Instead, he drew the knife he always kept sheathed at his belt. A short blade but sharp for he kept it so. The wanderer had been trained by the greatest woodsman in the world, had been taught how to move through the trees and underbrush, leaving no more sign of his passage than necessary. He had been educated on the finer points of skulking and sneaking by the world's greatest assassin, taught how to blend in with his surroundings, how to become little more than a shadow among shadows.

He took care with each step, each movement, focusing on economy of motion, moving no more than he had to so that even should some slight sound cause the guard to turn, still he might go unnoticed, covered by the shadows of the falling night.

But the guard did not turn, did not even so much as look up as the wanderer drew in front of him. And as he gazed down at the sentry, the wanderer realized that he had worried over his approach in vain, for the man seated before him, whatever else he might be, was a terrible sentry, for he was asleep.

The wanderer stared at the sleeping man, knowing that he should kill him, that he should let the blade he held do its work and in that way ensure that the sleeping sentry would not give him away. Certainly it was the wise thing, yet he found himself hesitating. The man and those with him had not done anything to the wanderer, at least not yet. Perhaps they meant to—why else would they be following them?—but as of yet the man was guilty of nothing. Or, at least, nothing save being a terrible sentry who fell asleep at his post.

You're hesitating, he told himself, *not doing what you know you should, and you know well that hesitation always has a price.*

A truth he had been taught by Assassin herself, and, as if the universe meant to remind him of its veracity, there was suddenly a shout from the campfire.

The wanderer spun, expecting to see men rushing toward him.

But after a moment he realized that the man who'd screamed— and who was currently on his feet, jabbing his finger into the woods, still yelling—wasn't pointing in the wanderer's direction at all.

The wanderer was peering into the darkness of the woods where the man was wildly gesticulating—still trying to figure out what he might be attempting to indicate—when he heard a voice.

"What the fuck?"

This voice, though, was not one of those around the campfire—it was far closer than that. The wanderer turned and saw that the sleeping sentry was staring at him, no doubt woken by his fellow's shout.

"Hey," the man said, "who is that? Clive, is that—"

The wanderer knelt in an instant, clapping one hand around the man's mouth and bringing his knife to his throat. "Do not cry out, or you will die," he said, and the man gave a shaky, terrified nod, his eyes wide and wild in the darkness.

Not that the wanderer was all that worried—whatever was causing the commotion among the others gathered around the fire didn't seem in any danger of stopping soon as there was shouting back and forth.

The wanderer set them and whatever was causing the shouting aside, at least for the moment, for a man could only solve the problems in front of him and the problem in front of *him* could ruin his night simply by voicing a cry. "I am going to ask you some questions, you either nod or shake your head in response. Do not speak. Am I clear?"

The man gave a shaky nod, his eyes trained on the blade poised at his throat.

"You and those with you—you were following me and my companions. Correct?"

The man met his gaze for a second, and in his wide eyes the wanderer could see him considering it, trying to decide whether or not to lie. In the end, his shoulders slumped, and he gave a trembling nod.

"And there are others of your men waiting farther down the road?"

Another consideration, another shaky nod.

The wanderer was preparing to ask another question when there was another shout from the fire, this one loud enough that he could make out the words clearly. *"I'm tellin' you, I fuckin' saw something, Merle!"*

The wanderer forced his attention back to the man in front of him. "How many?" he hissed, deciding he had little time left—whatever was causing the scene with the man's fellows didn't seem to be getting better but worse.

The man didn't answer, giving his head a slight shake, and the wanderer leaned forward. "*How many?*" he growled again.

The man's eyes went wider still as a tiny droplet of blood formed around the knife's blade, then he stared down at the wanderer's hand, mumbling something he couldn't understand, and that was when the wanderer realized that his hand was still clamped around the man's mouth.

He pulled the hand away. "Speak."

"Wh-what's happening over there?" the sentry asked, his voice breathy with panic. "Wha—"

"Don't worry about them," the wanderer said. "Worry about me. How many are waiting farther on?"

"H-half a dozen men," the sentry said. "N-no more than that. Now, please, listen, we didn't mean you any harm, it's just—" There was another loud cry from the campfire only this time, the wanderer didn't think it was a shout of alarm—instead, it sounded like a scream of terror.

He decided that he'd learned as much from the sentry as he had time to learn.

Kill him.

It was a voice in his head, not his own but a strange, alien voice. The words struck him like some magical command and, for a moment, it was all the wanderer could do to keep from dragging the blade he held across the man's exposed throat.

Kill him, the voice said again.

"P-please," the man said, "I-I have a wife, a boy."

"Then you should find a new profession," the wanderer said. He pulled the knife back and before the man could move, before he could so much as speak, the wanderer reversed his grip on the blade and brought the handle into the man's temple. The sentry's eyes rolled up in his head, and he slumped to the ground unconscious.

The wanderer rose, looking back to the campfire in time to hear another scream, and he saw the dozen men gathered around the fire had all rose and were staring in the direction of the dark woods.

"I tell you, Merle, there's somethin' out there!"

"And I'm tellin' you there ain't!" another man, presumably Merle, shouted. "Nothin' leastways save the imagination of some damned fool gettin' ready to piss his pants over a squirrel or a loon passin' by."

"Ain't ever seen a squirrel or a loon that big," the other man said doubtfully. "Nor have I ever known one to sit and watch folks with beady amber eyes, like maybe it's thinkin' of doin' 'em harm."

"Know a lot of squirrels, do you?" the other man, Merle, demanded. "And if a squirrel is out here that bastard is a lot more worried about us than we ought be about him. Now stop your bitchin'. It's gettin' late, past time to sleep. We'll catch up to those bastards tomorrow mornin'. If we're lucky, they got some food on 'em. Ain't no problem you got that a full belly won't cure. Understand me?"

"We hear you, Merle," another man said, standing near the first. "And we ain't tryin' to argue—honest, we ain't. But Clive ain't the only one as saw somethin'. Why, I thought I did too. Somethin' that was...well, it was like...like darkness."

"Damn me if whatever you got ain't catchin'," the man named Merle said to the first speaker. He turned to the second then. "Of course you're seein' darkness! It's dark, ain't it? What did you expect to see?"

"It ain't that sorta dark, Merle," the first man protested. "It's...well, shit. It was darker'n that."

"Darker than what?" Merle demanded. "Darker'n dark?"

"That ain't—" the second man began. There was a shout from someone else, interrupting him, and they all turned, along with the wanderer, to the man who'd shouted.

The shouter stood closer to the forest than the others, as if he'd heard something and had gone to check it out, so that he was on the very edge of the circle of orange, ruddy light the fire gave off before that light faded and gave way to the shadow.

It was the man's shout that had drawn them, but he was not shouting now. Instead he only stood silently with his back to them, staring out into the night as if contemplating some deep question, unmoving.

"Well, what the shit are you yellin' about now, Brandon?" the man, Merle, asked.

Brandon did not answer, and as the wanderer gazed closer at the man he realized that he was moving after all. Or, at least, trembling. Trembling, shaking the way a dog in pain might shake.

"*Brandon?*" Merle barked, and the man tensed, turning to regard Merle.

"Th-the darkness, Merle," the man said, his voice a dry, croaking whisper. "It...it looked at me."

"You've got to be kidding me, you too?" Merle asked. "What in the—" But before he could finish something happened which stole the words right out of the man's mouth, which caused the breath to freeze in the wanderer's lungs.

The shadows reached out, gliding along the man, Brandon's, throat. Only for a moment, and then they retracted again, but what was left was a bloody ruin as something had torn the man's throat open. This time, Brandon did not scream, was no longer capable of screaming. Instead, his eyes bulged in their sockets as blood sluiced from the ruin of his throat. He let out a wheezing, wet, gurgling croak and collapsed.

"Ooh, no," someone sobbed, "oh Eternals be good, it killed him. Roscoe was right."

"That ain't...that ain't possible," Merle said, staring at the man lying face down on the ground. "It—it can't be."

The wanderer found himself tensing, wondering what manner of creature had just taken the man's life, for he had seen nothing but a shadow himself. He was still wondering when, a moment later, he noticed something strange.

One of the other men stood near the edge of the firelight, had backed away from it when he'd witnessed what had happened to his fellow, but it was not the man who captured the wanderer's attention. Instead, it was the shadows behind him, shadows that pooled at his feet like water so dark a man could not see into it.

Even as the wanderer watched, that pool of shadow seemed to tremble and move, to *bulge,* and in another instant those shadows shot up in a form that vaguely resembled the silhouette of a man. The shadows surged forward, and as they touched the man he threw his head back to utter a scream he never got out, for he suffered the same fate as his companion. The shadows clawed at his throat, tearing away the flesh as if it were paper, wet and soggy from rain.

The unfortunate man's body had not even hti the ground before the shadows were already moving again, seeming to lose all physical substance and melting into a pool of darkness. The pool bubbled and spat as if boiling, and as the wanderer watched that boiling substance slithered along the ground like a thing alive while he and those others gathered around the fire stood frozen in shock and horror and confusion.

At first, he thought that it moved along the forest floor but as he watched it, he realized that such was not the case after all. In fact, the thing—whatever it was—seemed to move from shadow to shadow like spilled ink. But if it was spilled ink then it was spilled with a purpose, for its path along the shadow did not seem chosen at random, but was instead the shortest path to the next closest man who screamed as he watched it come on. Screamed but did not move, for in his horror he had lost control of his feet, and so he only stood, watching his death come.

Whatever else the man Merle might have been, he was no coward. While the other men around the fire shrieked and fled, abandoning the light in favor of the darkness, leaving their whimpering companion to his own devices, Merle rushed forward.

"Move your ass, Gilbert!" he shouted.

Gilbert did not move, though, and Merle had only closed half the distance between them when the shadows seemed to rise up, like a snake preparing to strike. Only it was not fangs that the shadows bared at the poor man but amber eyes that shone like death in the darkness.

The creature—if creature it might be called—glided forward, as quiet as a dying breath. The man, Gilbert, finally seemed to regain control of his body, and he screeched in terror as he raised his arms in front of him as if to shield a blow, as if to stop an attack. The shadows struck the man's arms, but they did not slow, and they did not stop.

The man's entire body tensed the moment the inky darkness touched him, and his cries of fear turned into shrieking screams of agony, though the wanderer could not imagine how he might have been hurt.

The man was still screaming when the sprinting Merle finally reached him. Merle did not try to attack whatever the creature was, and to his credit neither did he hesitate. He charged into his fellow, his shoulder leading.

Gilbert was sent flying by the impact, and the shadows peeled away from his flesh like sticky tar as he was sent careening away until he fell, hitting the ground hard. Yet despite the fact that the shadows no longer touched him, the man's screams continued, sounding as bad, perhaps even worse than they had before.

For his part, Merle managed to keep his feet, stumbling and drawing a crude, rusted sword from a sheath at his waist. A simple movement, but it was enough for the wanderer, who had been trained by the best fighters in the world, to see that the man knew nothing of the use of the weapon he wielded, yet that did not stop him from facing off against the bubbling shadows in front of him which had now risen to over six feet high.

Merle didn't wait for an invitation. Wielding the rusty blade in two hands, he stepped forward, roaring a battle cry and swinging it at the figure, hoping no doubt to make up for his lack of skill with ferocity and the power he put behind the blow.

But that power, that strength, was destined to be of no use, for when the blade struck the creature it did not sever any part of it but instead seemed to pass harmlessly through it, as if Merle did not strike a living thing at all but the night itself.

The swing had been powerful, but that power had come at the cost of Merle losing his balance, a problem exacerbated by the fact that his sword passed through the creature as if it were made of air. The man stumbled away, nearly falling, but it was this stumble that saved his life, for part of the creature's wavy, insubstantial form suddenly solidified, shooting forward like an ebony spike, one which was no doubt meant to impale the man and would have done so had he kept his feet.

Instead, it struck him a glancing blow in the side, along the sleeve of his shirt. It was no more than a brushing impact, yet Merle roared in apparent pain as he lost his grip on the sword, his stumble turning into an uncontrolled, spinning fall that ended with him lying on his back.

When he'd first came upon these men, the wanderer had thought it likely that he would be forced to kill them. For any men that the enemy had sent after him—and he'd grown more and more sure that these men *had* been sent—would not have been stopped any other way. If anything, it was likely that the creature—whatever it was—was doing him a favor by killing some and sending the others fleeing into the woods.

But despite this, despite the fact that the men would have almost certainly killed him if given the chance, the wanderer found that he could not stand by and watch the man, Merle, be murdered. Perhaps he was a good man, perhaps he was a bad one. The wanderer did not know for sure—all that he did know was that the world was full of evil, full of strangeness, and in such a place of darkness and dangers, it was enough that he was a man.

The wanderer charged into the firelight, drawing his sword free of its sheath as he did, the familiar metallic *snick* of the blade leaving its place like the call of a trumpet to announce that battle was to be joined.

The shadow figure collapsed back into a pool. As he ran the wanderer tracked its progress as it seemed to bubble across the shadows of the ground toward Merle.

It was clear to the wanderer that the man was not going to get up in time to defend himself, just as it was also clear that he would not reach him before the creature. Seeing this, the wanderer did the only thing he could do. Snatching his knife out of its sheath where he'd put it back at his waist and, slowing only long enough to pivot, he hurled it through the air even as the shadows began to coalesce in front of the fallen man.

He was disappointed—though not surprised—when the blade behaved much as Merle's had, flying through the creature as if it weren't there at all. The creature did not seem to even take notice of the wanderer's approach. Instead, part of the shadow began to bubble and shift tumultuously, as it had before that tendril of solid darkness had shot out before.

"*Hey!*" the wanderer shouted, and the creature spun, its amber eyes alighting on him in what might have been surprise. It glanced back at the man, Merle, where he was still lying on the ground, and the wanderer almost felt that he could read its thoughts.

"*Move!*" he yelled at the fallen man who hissed a curse, rolling to the side. But even as he moved the wanderer saw that he would not be quick enough. Still, his shout had distracted the creature, making it hesitate, and just as a shadowy tendril coalesced, shooting toward the man lying on the ground, the wanderer arrived, swiping his sword at the darting appendage.

It was a desperate move, and he expected the blade to prove no more effective in that moment than his knife or the fallen man's sword had. He was surprised, then, when the sharpened steel did not pass through the shadowy tendril as it had the previous times. Instead, it struck the protruding limb as if it were something solid, knocking it away.

It was so unexpected, that impact, that the wanderer hesitated for a moment in surprise. It was a moment that very nearly cost him his life, for the creature did not seem at all discomfited by the sharp steel, and no sooner was the shadowy tendril batted aside than it retracted, vanishing altogether into the creature's shifting, shadowy form. A moment later, another tendril shot out from a different location on that inky mass, and the wanderer was forced to give a hasty step to the side, only just managing to get his blade up in time to deflect this latest blow.

And then it began in earnest, tendril after tendril shooting toward him. Had it not been for years of tutelage under the best swordsman in the world he would have died in the first seconds of the fight. Even with Soldier's training, it was all he could do to parry the incoming blows, let alone even conceive of mounting an offense. Not that he had any idea of how to do such a thing anyway considering that each strike made against the creature had, so far, passed harmlessly through it or seemed to have had no lasting effect at all.

He was forced to back pedal under the constant barrage, relying more on instincts honed over years than any conscious thought as his sword moved in a blur, weaving a web of steel in front of him. By chance, his constant retreating brought him back toward the blaze the men had been gathered around.

The wanderer barely noticed this, though, for it took all of his concentration, all of his considerable skill to keep those flashing tendrils at bay. Yet despite his best efforts, he was unable to parry or dodge all the attacks, and one made it through the steel net he'd woven in front of him.

The wanderer pivoted away from the blow so that it only barely brushed against him, but he hissed in shocked pain as a line of agony traced its way across his forearm where the shadow had touched him. He turned, growling in anger and lashed out with his sword, a vicious blow to the tendril that had touched him. And while it did not seem to faze the creature any more than those which had come before, it was powerful enough that it forced the shifting shadows back, giving the wanderer an opportunity to gather himself and catch his breath.

As he did, he glanced at his arm where the creature's extending shadow had touched him and saw instantly why its touch had caused such agony. It had only grazed him, no more than that, and he was thankful for where the creature had touched him his shirt was frozen over as if left in frigid temperatures, and there was a rime of frost along it.

He frowned, looking back at the shifting mass of inky darkness where amber eyes stared back at him. He had never encountered such a creature before, but he did not have to think long about where it might have come from. The world produced terrifying things, it was true, creatures and beasts that might be considered monsters by many. But if they took the time—most didn't—to learn more about those creatures, a person would discover that however scary, however unusual, the creatures were only creatures, not so different from themselves. For every creature, big or small, terrifying or not, wanted the same thing—not to kill, but to live. True, sometimes killing was a part of that, but such killing was not done for sport but for sustenance, so that the creature might continue its line, might live and reproduce. Scholar had taught him that it was that simple act—of beast and of man striving to survive—that shaped the world.

Therefore, however unfortunate it might feel to be the one on the wrong end of the she-lion's jaws when she meant to feed her family, it was, in every way, completely natural for the lion to do what she does, what she *must* do.

But the creature before him was not part of that world, was no member of the intricate dance which kept it all glued together. It would not reproduce, did not care about survival, not anymore than the Revenants or the Unseen did. It cared about one thing and one thing only—death. And its makers—those same creatures, he was confident who were the authors behind the twisted existence of the Unseen and Revenants—had given it the tools to accomplish its task, a fact evident in the two dead men lying sprawled around the campfire.

But he could not spare any concern for them, not at the moment, for the creature was re-orienting itself, the shadows which comprised its form beginning to shift and bubble angrily once more in preparation for an attack.

Indeed, a moment later it glided forward and renewed its assault, black tendrils launching themselves at the wanderer, one after the other. He parried with his blade as quickly as he was able, but he was forced onto his back foot once more, retreating under the barrage.

The creature's attack was constant, coming from multiple angles at once. The wanderer managed a few counterattacks, but they did not seem to affect the creature anymore than those before, not even so much as slowing its assault.

And so the wanderer continued to retreat, growing more and more desperate with each passing moment as he was forced to parry and dodge at a pace that he knew he could not keep up for long. Already his arms were sore from the repeated impacts, his breath heaving in and out of his lungs.

Yet another inky tendril shot out at him, and the wanderer brought his blade up to block. The blow was hard, and he took a step back. As he did, his foot struck a loose stone, turning his ankle. Not badly, and he was able to right himself in another moment. But because of this, his next parry was a half a second too slow, no more than that.

In a duel against a normal opponent the slight hesitation would have almost certainly gone unnoticed and unpunished. The problem, of course, was that what the wanderer faced was no normal opponent, but a creature designed and created to kill with powers and skills far beyond that of any normal man. So it was, then, that the wanderer's parry, a fraction slower than normal, meant that the creature's attack slipped past his guard.

Even as he saw it happening the wanderer pivoted desperately to the side in an effort to avoid the darting tentacle—a feat which he managed...mostly.

While he was not impaled, the side of the tendril struck his sword arm. He cried out in shocked pain as a bitter cold deeper than any he'd ever known shot into his arm as if he'd been touched by winter itself. His fingers and hand where they gripped his sword immediately went numb, and the blade toppled from his lifeless grip. He might have tried to retrieve it but the creature's blow also had the added effect of knocking him to the side.

He lost his balance again, but this time was unable to right himself. He fell, rolling as he did, which was all that saved him. For the shadow creature, whatever it was, did not sit idle as he fell. Instead, it seethed forward across the ground, appendages lashing out from it and shooting toward the wanderer, impaling the ground where he'd been only an instant before.

The wanderer continued to roll as the creature came on, unable to spare the second it would cost to get to his feet. The creature pursued him relentlessly, its darting tendrils tearing into the grass and soil.

The wanderer caught sight of the flames of the dying fire and realized that his rolling was bringing him closer to it. Seconds later, he struck something solid and biting cold lanced through his already numb sword arm. He jerked back by instinct, trying to roll to the other side, but once more he struck what felt like ice, and he turned away, lying on his back.

He realized in a moment that what he'd fetched up against had been the creature's form, for a protrusion of darkness penned him in on either side. There was nowhere to go, nothing to do but to stare up at that inky, shifting blackness, at the amber eyes that studied him from inside of it.

Staring at the creature, the wanderer felt revolted, disgusted in a way any living man might have, for the creature's very existence felt profane, an insult to the natural world. He felt revolted, and his arm felt cold—freezing, in fact—with a cold that seemed to have reached all the way to the bone where the thing had touched him, as if someone had filled his veins with ice water.

But cold and revolted were not the only things he felt. He felt one more—heat. Heat on his face from the fire where it still burned only feet away. His sword was far out of reach, and it had proven of little use even when he'd had it, so as the shadows looming above him began to boil and bubble the wanderer did not try to make a break for his blade. Instead, he reached out in desperation for the flames, the fingers of his left hand scrabbling and clawing across the burning embers of the campfire. There was pain, but in some ways it was a welcome pain, heat to battle the cold filling him, a distraction to take his mind away from the bitter numbness in his right arm.

As the creature surged forward toward him, meaning to finish it, the wanderer scooped up a handful of burning embers and flung them at the amber eyes. The shadow had shrugged off blows from the keen edge of his sword easily enough, just as it had shrugged off the sharpened steel of his knife, but it did not shrug off the burning embers.

It let out a scream, one that started as a piercing, shrieking wail that sounded like what a person might expect to hear in some underworld of the damned but one that, in another moment, sounded very much like the agonized cry of a man.

The creature recoiled, the shadows that comprised its form flitting and tearing away like dozens, hundreds of pieces of fabric blown about in a high wind, and the wanderer caught sight of something beneath that darkness. Something that he could not quite make out before the shadows began to reform, the way water might settle after a stone had been thrown into it, disturbing the surface.

The wanderer used the creature's momentary distraction to roll his way to his feet, swiping his singed hand at his trouser legs to knock free the remaining, burning embers that still clung to his palm and fingers. He stared at the creature as it slowly seemed to come back together, the tattered shadows reforming and once more beginning to cover whatever he had glimpsed beneath them, and as he did, an idea struck him.

He had tried his sword and knife and found them both ineffectual, but he had been a fool to think they would be otherwise. After all, the creature before him was no natural beast, one of flesh and blood and bone that might be harmed by the keen edge of sharpened steel. It was something else, something *unnatural,* not a creature or beast at all, really, but some abomination formed by the dark magics of the enemy, crafted by their malicious intent. It was darkness personified, shadows given form and function, the night set loose upon the world.

And the night, the dark, could not be slain by swords or maces, axes or arrows. The night could only be slain by one thing—the first human weapon ever to exist. The first which mortals discovered how to fashion and wield to their purpose and, in that discovering, paved the way for the civilized world. It was the weapon that acted both as a blade to carve out their own desires upon the flesh of the land but also as a shield to protect them from what the shadows hid.

It was fire.

"You are shadow," the wanderer panted, trying to flex the fingers of his numb arm. "And shadows flee before the light, before the flame, for they cannot abide it. I wonder...can you?"

The creature seemed to read his intent, and it surged forward, a bubbling, boiling, seething mass of darkness.

The wanderer rolled to the side, allowing his movement to carry him along the edges of the still-burning fire. A fire into which he reached, ignoring the heat searing him and pulling out a burning brand of one of the branches the men had stacked on the fire.

The creature was still pursuing him, and so it was an easy enough thing to turn and bury the makeshift torch in its shadowy form. There was another inhuman screech, this one far worse than that which had come before it. This time, the shadows didn't just flit away—they seemed to rip and tear, bursting apart. And as they did, they began to reveal something beneath. It was unclear at first, but as more and more shadows fell away like fluttering pieces of ash, disintegrating even as they fell, the wanderer realized, with horror, that what they had concealed was not some*thing* but, instead, some*one.*

For staring at him in agony, a look of pale, stricken terror on his face, was a man who appeared to be in his fifties. The man was thin, that much the wanderer could see, his cheeks shrunken, his eye sockets looking hollowed out. There was a wasted, dying look to him as he screamed in pain, finally collapsing to the ground on his back.

The wanderer moved forward, raising the burning torch above his head, prepared to renew the attack, but he needn't have bothered. Whatever the thing lying on the ground had been, whatever sort of abomination it had been turned into, it was that no longer. Instead, it was only a man. A man who mewled and whimpered in apparent agony as he twisted and contorted on the ground, seemingly unaware of the wanderer's presence at all.

Examining the man closer, the wanderer saw something that sent a shock of horror and anger through him. The tattered shadows which still writhed and flaked and burned around the fallen man, were not thrown about him like a cloak or mantle, as the wanderer had first thought. Instead, they were *part* of him, seeping into the skin of his face and naked chest, his arms and legs. It was as if the darkness itself had somehow become fused with the man's flesh.

"*Damnation,*" a voice said, and the wanderer turned away from the pitiable sight to see the man, Merle, standing beside him, the wanderer's sword hanging loosely in one hand. "They're men," the man said breathless, his voice revealing his own horror at what they gazed upon. "The damned things are men. I can't damned believe it—that bastard Roscoe was right."

"*Please...please,*" a voice said, and the wanderer and the man named Merle turned back to regard the man lying on the ground, writhing in pain. "*Help me.*"

The creature had nearly killed him moments ago—and his arm still felt frozen where it had touched him—but the wanderer found that he was not angry at the man lying there, looking so wretched. Instead, he felt only pity.

He moved forward, kneeling before the man. As bad as the man's state had appeared, as he drew closer it revealed itself to be worse. The shadows penetrated his body in dozens, hundreds of places, like inky fingers of darkness stabbing into him.

"*I beg you,*" the man croaked, his voice rasping and hoarse and barely recognizable as human at all. "*Help.*"

The wanderer glanced back at the man, Merle, who was watching with a grim expression that was a mixture of horror and sadness. The man gave the smallest shake of his head and the wanderer turned back to the man lying on the ground. "I...I don't know how," he said honestly as the man continued to whimper and writhe, the shadows that were part of him slowly burning away.

"*You...do,*" the man said. "*Kill...me. Please.*"

The wanderer recoiled at that as if he'd been struck.

"*Hurts,*" the man said. "*Always...hurts.*"

The wanderer stared at the man writhing there, dying, he thought, but he also thought that he might be long in the doing of it. How much pain, how much suffering before it ended, before the flames consumed enough of the shadows that made part of him up that he finally succumbed?

The wanderer found himself thinking of the Eternals. He was confident that none of them had ever seen anything like what lay before him, for if they had he felt sure that they would have told him of it during his training. But while they might not have seen such a creature before, he also thought that if anyone knew how to help the man, how to save him, it would have been them.

He opened the locket.

We know what you are going to ask us, Youngest, Leader said, his voice full of compassion. Compassion and sadness but something else, too—regret. A regret that made it so that the wanderer knew what the ghost's next words would be even before he spoke them. *But we do not know a way. Perhaps, given time enough, Healer or Oracle might find some way to undo what has been done but...*

The ghost did not finish the thought, but then he did not need to. Perhaps, given time enough, one of the Eternals might find some way to fix it, to heal what had been contaminated in the man, but not quickly enough to save him.

You know what to do, Youngest, Assassin said, her voice quiet, subdued as it always was. *It is a kindness.*

The wanderer took a slow, trembling breath, and closed the locket. He was on his own, and there was no help for him, just as there was no help for the man lying writhing before him. He rose to his feet, turning to regard the man Merle then glanced down at the sword in the man's hand, his sword.

Merle winced, giving a shaky nod and passing him the sword. The wanderer stared at it for a moment, at the steel. It was sharp, for he kept it so. Sharp enough to do what must be done. He just wasn't sure that he was.

He turned back to the man. "I'm...I'm sorry," he said.

"*Please,*" the man begged, his voice breaking. "*It hurts so mu—*" He did not get a chance to finish, for the blade pierced his heart, that part of him which was still a man, which had remained largely uncorrupted by the enemy's power. His words turned into a gasp and the gasp into silence. A silence of which the dead were the only ones capable.

"What...what is it?" the man named Merle asked from beside him, his voice little more than a whisper.

77

The wanderer considered that, staring at the unfortunate soul before him. "Something new," he said.

They continued to stand there in silence for several seconds. Dark thoughts filled the wanderer's mind, his heart. Thoughts of hate and violence and revenge.

Kill them, a voice said in his mind. *Kill them all.*

It was the voice of the cursed blade again, for the wanderer had come to recognize it since it had first begun to speak to him. That was not what bothered him—or, at least, not what bothered him the most.

Instead it was that the voice had begun to sound familiar to him in a different way, like a voice he had heard for a very, very long time. Like a voice he had heard all his life.

His voice.

And while he had thus far been able to resist the pull of the sword's will, he found that this time, at least, he did not want to.

He would go to Celes. He had told Clint that he would go to help him find his friends, and so he would, but just then, as he stared at the dead man, a man who had suffered unimaginable horrors before he'd finally found the peace of death, the wanderer had another, greater reason for going to the city.

He would go to Celes. And when he got there, he would find those responsible for the dead man's suffering. He would find them and, as the sword demanded, he would kill them. Not because the magical artifact wanted it but because *he* wanted it. It was not violence for violence's sake that he was after. It was not murder and death.

It was a reckoning. And if that reckoning meant blood then so be it.

"You're...you're him, ain't you? The fella?"

The man's voice pulled the wanderer from his thoughts, and he turned away from the dead man lying before him to regard Merle. "Tracking so far," he said.

The man gave a nervous laugh. "Right. The one we was followin', I mean. Me and the boys."

"The one you meant to kill," the wanderer said, watching him. "Me along with those I've come to care about. Tell me, Merle—it's your name, isn't it?"

Fear was in the man's eyes, shining bright in the firelight, but he squared his shoulders and nodded. "That's right," he said.

The wanderer nodded back. "Tell me, Merle," he said, his fingers tightening around the grip of his sword, the blade still slick with the dead man's blood, "what would you do to someone who meant to kill those you loved?"

Merle considered that, watching him, watching him the way a man might watch a beast, refusing to look away for knowing that the moment he did, it would pounce. He was not far wrong.

"Guess I'd kill 'em," he said. "I got a boy, a wife, too. Anyone messed with them...well. A man ain't much of a man, he ain't willin' to protect what's his."

"You'd kill them," the wanderer repeated.

Kill him, the sword told him. *Kill him now. His life mocks you, each breath is like spit in the face of your friends, of those you love.*

The wanderer frowned at that. It was strange, hearing the sword talk of love, even if it only did so as a reason to kill, for to that point it had spoken of death and that only, eschewing any need for a reason, as if death, murder, was something that existed beyond any necessary reason or catalyst but was a means and an end all its own. He wondered what it meant that the sword was beginning to communicate more.

Likely nothing good.

"Look," the man, Merle, said, "I see well enough what you're thinkin', the way you're standin' there. I've had such thoughts myself. Shit, such thoughts are the reason me and the boys were out here in the first place. Thoughts of killin', thoughts that some folks have gone so sour they ain't good for nothin' but worm food. I know what you're thinkin'."

"You know what I'm thinking," the wanderer repeated.

"Sure, ain't no thought easier to read than murder," Merle said. "And at this point, I figure anythin' I say is goin' to sound like an excuse, a go at savin' my own hide. But it's the truth, whether you believe it or not, so I'm gonna say it anyway. Me and the boys, we didn't mean no harm to you and yours. Leastways not to your health, just your coin purse. And your supplies—we'd have taken those, 'course. Bread and victuals and such, if you'd had any."

"You want me to believe that you followed us only intending to rob us?"

"You believe what you want to believe—you strike me as a man that can't be made to do anythin' against what he's set himself to. You can cut me down now, if you'd like—I saw the way you fought that...that thing. The way you moved. I reckon if you decide you want me dead there ain't a whole lot I can say on the matter. But know that if you kill me, you're killin'...well, I won't say an innocent man, but an honest one anyhow."

"A lie," the wanderer said. "Those you work for would not be satisfied with robbing me and the others. They would want our deaths, would demand them."

"Work for? What are you on about?"

The wanderer frowned. "The Eternals, of course." He glanced back at the dead man, found his upper lip peeling back from his teeth in a silent snarl as sudden, blooming rage threatened to overcome him. "The ones responsible for creating and sending this...thing."

"Look, fella," Merle said, "I try to make it a habit not to argue with men of a mind to kill me and enough talent to see it through, but I reckon I'm gonna have to break my rule, here. The only folks I work for is a wife that thinks I'm mostly a pain in the ass—and is mostly right, I'm afraid—and a boy who I'd swear is part tornado." He paused, frowning and the wanderer saw what could only be fear—fear greater even than the threat of imminent death had elicited in the man—flash across his gaze. "Or was, anyway." He gave his head an angry shake. "As for those Eternals—I don't give a damn about them, wouldn't piss on 'em if they was on fire to put 'em out. Shit I'd tend the blaze, best I was able."

The wanderer frowned, watching the man, looking for any sign of deceit.

He did not find it though, only a sort of offended incredulity, as if even the implication that he might be working for the Eternals was enough to provoke him almost to attack. "I mean shit, give it a think, why don't you?" the man said. "You reckon those bastards as created that damned thing there are in the habit of sending it after those as work for 'em? Must make recruitin' a bitch."

The man had a point, one that resounded clearly enough that the wanderer felt his hand, which to that point had gripped the pommel of his sword so tightly it hurt, began to loosen its grip a little. "If you don't work for them then why were you following us?"

"I told you," the man said, looking ashamed. "We meant to rob you."

"You're bandits, then?"

Merle's eyes narrowed at that, and when he spoke the wanderer could hear the anger in his voice. "A man'll become a lot of things, *do* a lot of things he might never have thought himself capable of if he's made to watch his wife and boy starve."

The wanderer needed a moment to think on that, for the man sounded sincere, but then he had been tricked before. So, instead of addressing it directly, he asked another question. "Your man— Gilbert, I think I heard you call him. Is he..."

"Dead," Merle said, and it was not fear that flashed in his eyes then but anger. "That fuckin' thing did for him right enough. Gil was a good man. Young, a bit stupid as only the young can be, but a good one. He's got..." He paused, his frown growing deeper still. "He *had* a wife. Mary." He sighed heavily. "I wish there's somethin' I coulda done, but I failed him. He deserved better. They all do."

"All? Including those that ran and left you and your man?"

Merle shrugged. "Those others, Clem and Sheb," he said, nodding toward the two dead lying on the outer edge of the firelight, "they got families too, both of 'em. They all do. I don't blame the bastards for bein' smart enough to run when runnin's required. Leastways they'll make it home to their families tonight. I wouldn't have, if not for you." He paused, glancing at the wanderer's blade. "Reckon I still might not. All I ask is if you're goin' to do it, make it quick. I like to think I'm brave, but after seein' what the fuckers done to this poor bastard here, well...seems to me that when it comes to dyin', quicker is better. I reckon that won't be a problem for you though, after watchin' you fight. I don't know much about swords." He paused, givin' a nod to his own blade that was lying on the ground a short distance away. "That'n there was my granda's and reckon it looks just about as bad as he does, though he's been in the grave goin' on thirty years. But while I may not know much—I don't tend to get invited to the fancy balls with their duels, if you can believe it—I don't s'pose there's a lot of folks walkin' around breathin' air that can wield a sword like you. True?"

"True."

The man nodded. "So, as I said, if you could make it fast, I'd appreciate it. And...I've got one more thing to say, if you've a mind to listen."

The wanderer didn't say anything, only watched the man and after a moment Merle grunted. "Well, thing is, I reckon I mentioned before about my wife and boy. He's sick, my boy..." He paused, clearing his throat, and the wanderer saw something of the man's fear, not for himself but for his boy, in his grim, tear-filled gaze when he looked at him. "Not doin' well. Not at all. Has a fever he just can't seem to get quit of. There's medicine the healers have, but I can't afford it. Can't even afford to feed him proper. It's why we're out here, all of us. If...if you could see your way to checkin' in on 'em, maybe...maybe give them a little somethin' to keep 'em over until Charlotte—that's my wife—figures out what to do...I'd sure appreciate it."

"You meant to rob me and now you're asking me to look after your family?" the wanderer said.

The man grunted. "Stupid, maybe, but I'll be stupid if it means a chance at helpin' my family. Fact is, I'd be a lot worse than that—the stupid bit I reckon I've pretty much been for free my whole life. I guess you're right, though. Not a lot of fellas in the world that'd try to rob a man and then ask him to look after their family. Problem is all the other folks I'd ask are dead or fled. Either way, they're both beyond me right now."

"Not a lot of fellas in the world that would throw themselves at a creature like the one you faced to try to save a friend, either."

The man shifted uncomfortably. "As I said, the stupid part's been a particular talent of mine my whole life."

"Some would call it courage."

"Suppose so, and I reckon most of those that'd say as much are dead. You know, on account of they were too stupid to live."

"Being dead doesn't make them wrong."

"No, but it makes it damn hard for 'em to argue their point, don't it?"

The wanderer stared at the man, Merle, and as he did he realized something. He liked him. A hard man, it was true, but then he had been taught that a man—a real one, not the posturing bully or the coward that blew whichever way the wind took him—sometimes had to be. Real men, he had been taught, were soft and hard, were kind and sometimes, yes, even cruel. They were sober and humorous, men of thought and action. In short, they were whatever they needed to be to protect those they cared about.

And that, he realized, was what Merle was. Not a bandit, but a man. A real one.

The wanderer sheathed his sword.

Merle looked at him, then at the sheath, then back at him. "You ain't gonna kill me then?"

"Not yet," the wanderer said, giving the man a small smile.

"Well. I appreciate that."

"Don't mention it."

"Any way...I suppose I ought to ask if there's a way I can repay you?"

The wanderer considered that. "You live in Celes? You and those other men that were with you?"

"We die in Celes anyway," Merle said grimly. "Ain't been much livin' goin' on for weeks now, truth to tell."

The wanderer nodded slowly. "What do you do, if you don't mind my asking?"

"Well, I reckon that, considerin' you're sparin' my life, you might be entitled to gettin' a bit personal, though..." He paused, wincing sheepishly. "Well. I'll tell you the truth, but I'll warn you that it might be just as hard to swallow as the fact that we didn't mean to kill you."

"Try me."

He sighed. "Alright. Here it goes—I work for the church."

The wanderer wasn't sure what he'd expected to hear but this certainly wasn't it. He blinked. "The church?" he asked, thinking that maybe he'd heard the man wrong.

Merle grunted, holding his arms out to either side. "What, don't I look churchly?" The wanderer looked at the man, his hair in tangles, his skin stained with dirt and his clothes looking one good washing or shake from falling apart. He was trying to come up with an answer to the man's question—at least one that wouldn't give offense—when Merle dropped his hands and gave him a small smile.

"Relax, fella, I know what I look like. Ain't no offense to call a spade a spade, nor an ugly bastard an ugly bastard."

"It's just...well, the way you speak—"

"Don't know a lot of priests that talk this way, eh?"

"Not many."

Merle nodded. "Good thing I ain't a priest, then. Just a fella that helps out, when he can."

"And the others?"

"Sure, they work for the church, too."

The wanderer considered the men he'd seen around the campfire. Rough looking men, all of them, filthy from time spent out doors and hungry. Men who, it had been clear, had no idea how to hunt and find food for themselves.

"I know what you're thinkin'," Merle said. "You're thinkin' we don't look like much, and you're right—we don't. That's on account of we ain't. Just a bunch of orphans, is all."

"Orphans," the wanderer said.

"That's right. You wonder why a fella like me might work for the church? Well, it ain't on account of the Eternals, I can tell you that; they don't seem to give two shits about us, so I don't give two shits about them. But there's good folks at the church, folks as helped me out of a dark spot when I thought there wasn't no way out. The way I see it, least I can do is try to help someone else the same way. I guess the other boys feel pretty much the same."

"I see," the wanderer said. "But if you work for the church, then why are you out here? Don't they pay you?"

"Pay us with what?" Merle countered. "Coin? A bit of shiny metal? And how's a man supposed to feed his family with that?"

The wanderer raised an eyebrow. "It's my understanding that most people use it to buy things, food and water." He let his gaze travel up and down the man's stained, ragged form, his frayed trousers and threadbare shirt. "Clothes too."

Merle snorted. "Maybe once they did. Maybe they still do in other places—but not in Celes. In Celes, coin don't mean shit. Turns out when things go sideways, it ain't gold that men look to but food and with all that's happened of late there's scarce enough of that to go around."

"I don't understand," the wanderer said. "You're saying that Celes is out of food?"

"I hear there's folks in the palace eatin' damn fine, Soldier and all the rest," Merle said, "but as for us lowly folks, yeah, I'd say we're just about out. Things are bad and gettin' worse, and that's a fact, and it ain't even just the hunger pains you've got to worry about neither. It's come to a place where a fella don't dare let his family go out at night nor go out himself. There's whispers, you see, of folks disappearin' in the night." He turned and regarded the dead man. "Of shadows comin' to life and takin' 'em."

"You mean...creatures like this?"

Merle shrugged. "I don't know. Maybe. Be honest I didn't think they were real right up until one tried to rip my throat out—that has a way of changin' a man's mind. Even now I find it hard to believe. But while these damned things, whatever they are, might be roamin' the streets of Celes, they ain't the only dangers lurkin' in the dark. Rumor is there's folks that decided starvin' weren't for them, decided that just about anythin' would be better. Anythin' includin' eating others. It's gotten so that the undertakers started hirin' guards to watch over 'em while they were buryin' the deceased. Not that they're doin' it now—the undertakers up and stopped comin' to work. Ain't much good to risk your life against folks tryin' to eat a corpse if you're gettin' paid in coin that ain't worth no more'n a rock."

"Eating the dead," the wanderer said slowly.

"Sure," Merle said grimly, a haunted look coming over his eyes. "But not just them. See, Celes is a big city, ain't it? Lot of folks in it, lot of those not keen on starvin'. Just ain't enough dead to go around. So if a fella ain't dead sometimes he's made to be, understand? Shit, it's worth a man's life to go down some streets, and that even in the broad light of day. After all, the day's got it's own shadows, don't it?"

"But don't the guards do anything?"

"Oh they do something alright, the sons of bitches," Merle snapped. "You ask me, they're some of the worst of the lot. Nothin' but bullies and thieves. Not that I think that Soldier is any better— if he were then he'd have done somethin' by now."

The wanderer frowned at that. Clearly word hadn't gotten out about the death of the creature impersonating Soldier, which made sense. The Eternals were supposed to be *eternal,* after all. It wouldn't do for people to discover that a man who was thought to live forever, to be nothing short of a god was dead. It would make people begin to ask questions, questions that the enemy would no doubt rather not have them ask. But while it made sense that the enemy might want to conceal the death of Soldier's impostor, he didn't understand what motive they might have to be so cruel to the people of Celes.

"But...why?" the wanderer asked.

Merle gave him a humorless smile. "If it's some grand plan you're lookin' for, there ain't one. Or, leastways, if there is, I don't know it. I don't know why the farms outside the city were burned just as I don't know why those...those *things* are takin' people. All I know is that sometimes folks that go out at night don't come back in the mornin'. All I know is that folks are starvin'. Desperate. And there ain't much a desperate man won't do."

"Desperate," the wanderer repeated thoughtfully.

"That's right," the other man said. "Desperate enough to follow a group of twenty, give or take, meanin' to rob 'em in the woods."

The wanderer nodded as he considered all the information the man had told him. "And Celes...I'm guessing the guards aren't letting anyone in?"

"Oh, gettin' in's easy enough," the other man said. "It's gettin' out that's the problem. Anyway, I wouldn't recommend visitin' the city if you're out for a lark. There's better ways to die and better places to do it in, after all."

"You managed it. Getting out, I mean."

"Not all of us," Merle said. "Anyway, we only made it out on account of I know one of the guards—we used to live on the streets together, back when we was kids. Or well...suppose it'd be proper to say I knew him. He's dead now, him and half a dozen others that meant to come out with us."

"He was your friend," the wanderer observed.

Merle considered that then shrugged. "Maybe. You don't really have friends when you live on the streets, stranger. You just have folks that you know won't stick a blade in you while you're sleepin' to get what you have. Not sure that makes 'em a friend, but...he wasn't an enemy, anyway." Merle sighed, seeming to deflate. "He was a good man. Suppose that I can take some solace in the fact that whatever sort of afterlife he's headin' toward, he won't be alone. There's been a lot of folks that died lately and a lot of them that were good. Why, I reckon if there's a gate they're all passin' through, the folks as run it are havin' to pay some overtime hours. Now, if it's all the same to you and if you're still sure you ain't plannin' on killin' me, I need to be goin'. Those fools as ran into the woods don't know the first thing about survivin'. They'll be dead by tomorrow night without help, and that ain't to mention what'll happen if they should run into somethin' like this poor bastard here," he said, glancing at the dead man lying beside them.

Merle gave him a nod then started away.

"No."

The word stopped the man in his tracks, and he turned, regarding the wanderer. "No? Changed your mind after all, then?"

"Not quite," the wanderer said. "I want you to lead me and my friends into Celes."

Merle frowned. "Ain't you been listenin' to a word I said?"

"I've listened."

"I'm not sure you have," the man said. "If your plan is takin' your friends to Celes, you might as well slit their throats now—at least then you'll save 'em a walk, and maybe they'll even get to go out on a full stomach. A blade's bad, sure, but it beats starvin' any day. Celes is a city of the damned, stranger."

"Nevertheless."

The man considered that, glancing at the dead men lying around them, then turned back to the wanderer. "What's your deal, fella? You lookin' for damnation, that it?"

The wanderer's gaze traveled to the poor soul lying dead on the ground, a man who had clearly been used as a weapon against his will, his existence bent and twisted to the enemy's purpose. "Not my own."

Merle shook his head slowly. "Look, I know you're good with that blade you carry—maybe even great, who am I to tell? I've only seen one man wield a sword that way, and that's been a long time ago now. But as good as you are, even you can't take on a whole city of guardsmen, not to mention the Eternals alone know how many of those...those *things*. And as bad as they are, they ain't the only thing lurkin' in Celes. There's rumors of other things, too. Things that look like men but don't feel pain, ones as can take a knife to the belly and not even so much as pause to wince."

"Revenants," the wanderer said.

The man frowned. "And others. Invisible bastards with claws like knives."

"Unseen."

Merle's frown deepened further. "Know somethin' of 'em, do you?"

"More than I'd like."

"Aye, well that's sayin' a lot without really sayin' anythin' at all, ain't it?"

"Maybe."

"So all that's happenin' in Celes...you mean to do somethin' about it, that it?"

"Yes."

The man made a show of glancing around the wanderer, over his shoulder, under his feet.

"Looking for something?" the wanderer asked.

"Damn right—I'm lookin' for that army you must have hidden somewhere. You know, the one you'll need if you're to do anythin' besides die and die badly."

The wanderer gave the man a grim smile. "They're waiting a little farther on."

"Pikes and swords, horses and trumpets, the whole deal?" the man asked.

"Something like that."

The man paused to consider that, and the wanderer could almost see the thoughts going through his mind. There was fear, there, it was true, but there were other emotions too. Anger. Doubt. And something else, almost buried beneath all the rest but just barely visible—hope. The wanderer waited for what the man might say, what he might do. He believed that he knew, believed that he had taken the man's measure already, but then he had been wrong before, so he only waited, saying nothing.

"And this army of yours, that's the folks you were traveling with?"

"That's right."

"No offense, but that ain't much of an army."

"None taken," the wanderer said. "Even small blades can cut deep."

The other man considered that then nodded slowly. "And after I meet this...army?"

"We'll find your friends."

"And then?"

The wanderer gave the man a small smile. "And then we march to battle."

Merle watched him for a minute. He glanced around at the dead men, then back at the wanderer. "I've had enough of shadows," he said, offering his hand. The wanderer took it, and Merle gave it a firm shake. "Let's shine some light on the bastards."

The wanderer nodded, and they set out.

They stopped to check on the sentry he'd knocked out, but apparently being unconscious hadn't been enough to keep the man from fleeing into the darkness.

"We can search for him and the others—" the wanderer began, but Merle shook his head.

"Don't much love the idea of searchin' through the darkness after seein' that...that thing. Anyway, we had a plan, in case we became separated, a meetin' place on up ahead. If they're...well, if they made it, they'll be waitin' for us there."

"As you say," the wanderer agreed, and then they were moving.

CHAPTER EIGHT

THE WANDERER LED Merle back to where Dekker, Clint, and the others waited, relieved to find that the only thing they had suffered while he was gone were a few uneventful hours. They made a fire—he normally wouldn't have wanted to draw attention but considering the shadow creature he'd so recently faced he decided there were worse things than being noticed—and he, Merle, Dekker, and Clint gathered around it. Then the wanderer began to recount to them all that had occurred, watching their expressions slowly growing grimmer and grimmer, their faces paler and paler as he did.

When he was finished, Dekker sat back, glancing warily out at the night. "Damn," the big man said. "As far as scary campfire stories go, Ungr, I'd say you pretty much win the prize."

"Do...do you suppose there are any more of them out there?" Clint asked, licking his lips nervously as he glanced around them.

It was only the four of them. Ella, Sarah, and the Perishables were gathered around a separate campfire, and so the wanderer was able to speak honestly.

"No," he said.

"Why are you so sure?" Dekker said.

"Because if there were, we'd be dead by now," the wanderer said.

The big man watched him for a moment then grunted what might have been a laugh. "With jokes like that, Ungr, you ought to be in some king's court, wearin' motley and turnin' flips."

"I'll keep it in mind in case things don't pan out with my chosen profession," the wanderer said dryly.

"You're assumin' that if things don't pan out you'll be around to choose another," Dekker said. "You ask me, that sounds pretty unlikely."

"I won't argue with that."

"But...have things really gotten so bad in Celes as all that?" Clint asked, glancing around at the other men. "I mean...it seems like we were just here little more than a month ago."

"A lot can happen in a month," Dekker said, his voice kind.

"Yeah but...but *why?*" Clint asked, a note of desperation in his voice. "Why make everyone in the city suffer so much? Why burn the farms? For that matter, why would they take Murphy and Gert?"

They all turned to regard the wanderer then, and he shook his head. "I don't know," he said. "But I mean to find out."

"So we're still going to Celes then?" Clint asked, and in his voice the wanderer could hear a note of hope. "I thought maybe, considering how bad it's gotten, you might change your mind."

"Yes, we're still going," the wanderer said. "We cannot let things stand as they are. The point of it all is to save the world—a healer does not save his patient by killing him nor by letting him die."

"Save the world?" the man, Merle, asked. He grunted. "I'll leave the savin' to you boys. I'll settle for some bread, maybe a bit of jam to spread on it, if I'm bein' real greedy." Even as he said it the man glanced at the plate Dekker had set aside after they'd eaten, upon which was some meat from a deer the wanderer had slain and a half-eaten chunk of bread.

Dekker shook his head, glancing at the thin man. "Go on then and eat it," he told the man," though I can't figure where you're puttin' it all."

Merle didn't wait for a second invitation, leaning forward with indecent haste and snatching the plate, immediately beginning to eat.

"Anyway," the wanderer went on, "our reasons for going to Celes are stronger than ever. Though, of course, we must speak to everyone else and let them know that, should they choose not to go, there will be no hard feelings. We will give them as much supplies as we can spare, and they can go on their way."

Dekker grunted. "Oh, come on, Ungr. You know damn well we ain't leavin' you. Why, El'd kill me, and if she didn't get to see that horse of yours again I'm pretty sure Sarah'd help her."

"You ain't got to worry about the Perishables," Clint said. "They'll stick."

"Tell them anyway," the wanderer said, meeting the gazes of both men. "This is not to be taken lightly. If what Merle says is true then it will be very dangerous."

"*If*," Dekker repeated.

That made the man, Merle, pause in his eating, and he glanced at Dekker. Clint looked between the big man and the thin one, a sheepish expression on his face.

Dekker shrugged. "No offense, fella. Probably you're a nice man—the sort that'd lend me a cup of sugar, if I needed it, maybe help me with a lame horse. But I don't know you from any damn body, do I?"

"I get it," Merle said. "I do. And fact is, I don't blame you. Considerin' all I'm tellin' you, well, I ain't for sure I'd believe me neither. Probably I wouldn't. That don't make it not true though, does it?"

"Doesn't make it true either," Dekker countered.

"Fair enough," Merle said. "I tell ya what, big fella. How about this? How about the first time you catch me in a lie you can go to work on me with those big fists of yourn, the ones you're flexin' just now, with fingers look like damn rolled sausages stickin' out of a dinner plate."

Dekker blinked at that, and the wanderer tensed, noted Clint doing the same. Dekker was a kind man, just as he was a clever one, but he was also possessed of what was sometimes an unpredictable temper, and the wanderer was far from sure how he would react to Merle's nonchalance.

The moment seemed to stretch on forever, the wanderer tensing in preparation of having to launch himself forward should the big man attack. Then, suddenly, Dekker tilted his head back and roared with laughter, slapping his knee. "Fingers like sausages," he said through tears of laughter, shaking his head as if he'd never heard anything so funny.

Clint started to laugh too and then, after giving a surprised expression that showed he'd been expected a beating as well, Merle began to laugh along. Then they were all laughing, but it was laughter that died quickly as each of them considered the path laid out before them.

"Maybe I was wrong," the big man said, his smile slowly fading. "Maybe you're an alright fella after all."

"I'd like to say my wife'd agree with you," Merle said, "but then that wouldn't be true."

Dekker grinned at that. "Wives," he said.

"Wives," the other man agreed.

The wanderer glanced at Clint who gave him a small smile.

"Still," Merle went on, "I won't lie to you—I'll be damned glad to see mine again. It's been three days since me and the others left Celes, hopin' we'd find some food to bring back. I miss her. Miss my boy, too."

"You've a boy?" Dekker asked.

"Aye," Merle said. "Elmer. He's seven."

"I've got a daughter, Sarah. She's six."

"Sarah," the thin man repeated. "It's a good name."

And just like that, the wanderer thought a bond had grown between the two men. It was not so surprising, the wanderer thought, not really. The one positive thing that might be said of living in a world full of devils is that when a man came upon another man, more often than not he recognized him.

"It's a crazy thing, havin' a child," Merle said.

"Aye," Dekker said, glancing back at where Sarah sat with her mother. "A crazy thing."

"Elmer's a good boy," Merle said, partly to himself and partly to Dekker for the wanderer thought that, for the moment, at least, he and Clint might as well not have been there at all. "Stubborn, sometimes, when he sets his mind on somethin'—accordin' to his ma he's me to thank for that, and I wouldn't argue. Stubborn but good. Good through and through. That he don't get from me, I'm sad to say, but his mother. I miss him. I miss him terribly." He frowned then, his eyes flashing with anger. "And I promise you, if I can help you do what needs doin' with Soldier then I'll do it. Damn but if I had my way I'd see every last one of those damned Eternals dead."

"Well," Dekker said slowly. "Not every one." He glanced at the wanderer who gave him a small nod.

"What? What am I missin'?" Merle asked.

"Anythin' else we need to go over?" Dekker asked the wanderer.

"I'd say that just about covers it."

The big man grunted. "Good." He slapped Merle on the shoulder, and the wanderer saw the thin man wince as he accepted the blow. "Come on then—there's some things that need sayin' and now's just as good a time as any to say 'em."

Merle glanced back at the wanderer once, a curious expression on his face, then, slowly, he nodded. "Alright," he said.

The two men walked away, leaving Clint and the wanderer alone at the fire. The wanderer was exhausted—it had been a long few days and his fight with the shadow creature had taken it out of him. More than that, he yearned for some solitude so that he might open the amulet and speak with the ghosts, might ask them about the creature. He also wanted to ask them about Celes, their thoughts on why the enemy might have given up even the pretense of civility and kindness in Celes and chosen instead to make its inhabitants suffer so terribly.

Yet he could tell by the man's expression that Clint had something on his mind, something he wanted to say. So he waited, doing his best to not yawn or blink his weary eyes.

"That...that thing you told us about," Clint said finally. "The shadow?"

The wanderer thought he knew, then, what Clint would ask, but he thought, too, that the man needed to ask it, to confront it, so he nodded. "Yes?"

"It...you said it was a man, right?"

"Once."

Clint nodded slowly, his mouth working. "Thing is...I've been thinking about it." He finally raised his gaze from his fidgeting hands and looked up at the wanderer. "About Murph and Gert, I mean. About those...Shadows, isn't that what you called them?"

"That's right," the wanderer said.

Clint rubbed at his chin, a pained look on his face. "Anyway, I was thinkin' about it. About why they wouldn't just kill them. Why they'd take them instead. And...I was thinking...that is, I was wondering, you don't...you don't think they mean to do to Murph and Gert what they did to that poor bastard, do you?"

The wanderer leaned forward, putting a hand on the other man's shoulder, trying to communicate through that simple gesture what he thought he could only fail to communicate through his words. "I think...I think we will do everything in our power to make sure that Murph and Gert and all the others of Ingleton, all the others of Celes, are safe."

"Of course. Right," Clint said, running his hands along his eyes to wipe away the tears gathered there.

The wanderer sat there awkwardly, wishing that there was something he might say, some words of comfort he might offer the man. Not comfort about the safety of his friends because that was knowledge far beyond him, and false comfort, false hope, he'd learned long ago, was worse than no hope at all.

He wished, as he stared at the Perishables' leader, the man's shoulders slumped, his head hung low with grief, that Healer were here. Healer who had been a master of curing whatever ailed not just a person's body, but their mind as well. Necessary, she had told the wanderer, for a person was not their body, and they were not their mind, but both of those things and one could not call them "healthy" or "healed" unless both were in order.

Healer had always known what to say, what to do. She had known what salves and medicines to apply to heal a person's body, had known what words, what sentiments to use to heal their heart, their soul. The wanderer was no Healer, for death had always come far more naturally to him. Yet, as he stared at the man before him— not broken, not yet, but certainly bending—he found himself thinking of something she had told him once, long ago.

It had been after he had helped her see to a regular patient of hers. This patient—a man in his forties—had been savaged by a bear. He had survived, but only just, yet the bear's attentions had not left him unscarred. Had not, in fact, left much of him behind at all. Under the care of any other healer, the man would have succumbed to his wounds and died. But, as it happened, Healer had been nearby, visiting Scholar's domain. The family had come to the Eternals, begging for assistance, and Healer, as was her nature, had immediately gone to see what might be done.

In the end, she had saved the man's life, but the bear's attack had cost him both of his legs and one arm. That had been years before the wanderer had met him, a story he only knew because he'd been told by others—not Healer, for she never spoke of such things, unwilling to approach anything that might be considered boasting of her own talents.

The wanderer had looked on that man and felt pity. And, like most men and women of the world, he had felt something else, too, something that floated in the deep currents of that pity. Revulsion. Revulsion not really because of the man's state but because of what that state did to the wanderer when he saw it. Because anyone gazing upon such a thing could not help but consider that it might be them, and so pity for another, as was also so often the case, gave way to self-pity.

He had felt compelled, when the man left, to speak to Healer about it, to wonder aloud what point there was in such a man living, why he kept going on at all. After all, what sort of life could a man have when he was only able to experience the world through one hand, five fingers?

He had not often seen Healer angry—had sometimes thought that, like a fish expected to walk ashore, she was simply incapable of it. As if whatever part of a person, in a madman, was so overgrown that it caused them to lash out in furious anger at anything or anyone had simply been left out of her in the forming.

But he had been wrong. Healer *had* been angry then. She had scolded him for being in the wrong as, of course, he had been. And so now he did not seek his own wisdom—little enough of that to be found, he'd discovered long ago—but instead relied on hers. He did not have to search for the words, for he remembered them well enough. A man always remembered words that wounded him just as he always remembered the blade that did the same.

"I do not know what will happen tomorrow, Clint," he told the man. "But I can say this with confidence. Tomorrow, like every other day, there will be sunlight and there will be shadow. And I will seek the sunlight. Even if that means that I travel through the shadow to do it."

Clint stared at him for a minute. "Shadows and sunlight," he repeated.

"That's right," the wanderer said, giving the man a small smile.

"And if a man can't find the sunlight?"

The wanderer gave a small shrug. He had asked the same question, and so he gave the same answer he had been given. "Then he hasn't looked hard enough."

Clint considered that for several seconds, scratching at his beard. "Huh. I like that."

"So did I, when I was first told it."

The Perishables' leader gave a sigh and a small smile appeared on his face. "Well. I s'pose I'm for bed—looks like we have a long day ahead of us tomorrow."

"It looks like."

Clint turned away then paused, glancing back. "Oh, and Ungr?"

"Yeah?"

"Thanks."

The wanderer smiled in answer to that, a smile that faded as the Perishable's leader turned away and headed toward where the others slept.

After all, the truth was he did not feel much like smiling. He believed the words he had told Clint—believed them now as much as he had when he'd first heard them. When he'd heard, in them, the ring of truth, of a wisdom undeniable, a wisdom which had been around before the first man had breathed his first breath and would be there long after the last man had breathed his last. A wisdom not of men at all but of the world, of nature itself.

Each day brought with it sunlight and shadow, that was true, and it was a wise man who chose the sunlight, even when it was not easy to do. That was also true. The problem, though, the truth which had stolen the smile from the wanderer's face, was that while he wished more than anything to lead those with him to the sunlight, he did not know that they would all make the journey.

He did not know that any of them would.

After all, to reach the sunlight, first they had to travel through the shadow.

CHAPTER NINE

THE WANDERER, troubled by his own concerns, his own fears, did not sleep well.

The morning came quickly.

The wanderer suggested searching for Merle's companions, but the thin man once more assured him that there was no need, claimed that they'd all agreed that, should they become separated for any reason, they'd meet up ahead, nearer Celes where their second group had lain in wait for the wanderer and his companions. He said this with a pale expression, watching the wanderer nervously as if he thought he might strike him down in a fit of rage at any moment.

The wanderer had noted, upon waking, that since Dekker had shared his true identity with the thin man, Merle had treated him differently, had seemed awkward and unsure in his presence, like a country peasant suddenly finding himself in a king's court. As they prepared to leave, the wanderer tried to put the man at ease but with little success. Dekker, meanwhile, watched the thin man's strange behavior—and the wanderer's awkward attempts to reassure him—with a wide grin on his face, one that made the wanderer forget about what they faced, made him, at least for a moment, forget his own exhaustion, and want nothing more than to give the big man a good kick in the shin.

In the end, though, he only did his best to ignore both Merle's anxiousness and Dekker's mirth as they planned their route to where the thin man assured him his companions waited. And soon—though nowhere near soon enough, as far as the wanderer was concerned—they were on their way.

They packed up their increasingly meager belongings and supplies—reduced to little more than empty packs from their journey out of the Untamed Lands—and started out. They spoke little, and judging by the quiet and their grim expressions, not to mention the bleary-eyes and yawns, the wanderer did not think that he was the only one who had allowed his fears to rob him of sleep.

They walked on.

It took them nearly two hours to reach the spot where Merle claimed his companions would be waiting, at a bend in the trail where it skirted around a tree that was significantly larger than those around it.

They all came to a stop, Merle—who'd walked at the lead along with the wanderer, Clint, and Dekker—glancing around, his hands on his hips. "*Well, what are you waiting for, an invitation? Come on out, you bastards,*" he called, "*and Shep you make sure to keep that damned itchy finger of yours off that crossbow's release, for the Eterna—*" He cut off, glancing wide-eyed at the wanderer, before turning back. "*I, that is, just don't damned shoot is all, it's me, Merle.*" He winced, casting a furtive look at the wanderer. "Sorry about that uh...sir. Just...well. A manner of speech, isn't it?"

"It's fine," the wanderer said, only just managing to hold back the sigh that threatened to come. There was a sort of strangled snort, and he glanced over to see Dekker grinning widely. The sigh did come then.

Merle, though, didn't notice. Instead he was staring around, a frown on his face. "*Well? Come on, damn you! I've got some folks here you all ought to meet!*"

Still there was no answer, and Clint cleared his throat, studying the woods around them. "Are...that is, are you sure this is the right place?"

"You see a lot of trees with a figure like that?" Merle countered, jerking a thumb at the giant tree on the roadside.

The wanderer followed the gesture. At first, he didn't see what he meant. Then, a moment later, he did. One part of the trunk of the tree had formed strangely so that, if one looked closely enough, he could almost see the figure of a woman. One that, it had to be said, would have no doubt contended with back problems.

Dekker snorted another laugh, reminding the wanderer of nothing so much as a child drawing what he thought was a naughty picture in the dirt with a stick, and Clint colored. "Oh. I see," he said.

"His lady, Gil calls it," Merle said then frowned. "Or...well. Called it, I guess. He and his brother used to hike around here back when they were kids. He was fond of sayin' she was the only woman hadn't ever led him astray."

"With a body like that, even if she meant to lead him astray I reckon a lot of men'd be happy to follow," Dekker said.

"Careful, husband mine," a new voice said, and they all turned to see that Ella had walked up. "It would be a shame," she said, her voice low and calm, "to die over a tree."

"But *what* a tree," Dekker said, grinning. His wife did not grin back. Not, at least, until he scooped her up into his arms, spinning her in a circle. Then she did grin, laughing as she slapped him.

"You put me down right now, Dekker!" she half-laughed, half-squealed.

"Don't you worry, love," Dekker said. "You're the only woman for me, tree or no."

She smiled at that, rolling her eyes, and the wanderer found himself grinning as she shook her head at him as if to ask if he could believe Dekker's behavior. Clint was grinning too. But as he glanced at Merle, the wanderer saw that the thin man, at least, was not smiling at the big man's antics. In fact, he didn't seem to be aware of what had transpired at all. Instead, he was still staring around at the woods, a grim expression on his face.

"Maybe they just...stepped out for a bit?" Clint offered, his expression sobering.

"Stepped out to where?" Merle asked, waving a hand at the forest around them. "You see any taverns nearby?"

Clint winced, nodding to acknowledge the man's point. "Any thoughts, Ungr?"

The wanderer was barely listening, though. He had caught sight of something in the grass near the large tree, and he moved toward it, kneeling.

"Ungr?" Dekker asked. "You good?"

The wanderer looked at the object lying in the grass, then back at the three men. "Your man—Shep—you said he was an archer?" he asked Merle.

"That's right," the thin man said. "A good one, too. Leastways, he is when he isn't in his cups. Though, truth to tell, he's just about always in his cups."

The wanderer nodded slowly, turning back and picking the object out of the grass, holding it up for the others to see.

"What is that?" Dekker asked.

"Piece of trousers, maybe?" Clint asked.

"No," the wanderer said, glancing at Merle who was staring at the small piece of leather as if it were a bloody knife. "It's a finger tab. Archers use it to protect their fingers from the bowstring."

"I've seen him with that thing," Merle confirmed grimly. "Used to give him shit about it."

"So that means they were here," Dekker said. "The real question is—where did they go?"

The wanderer glanced around them at the ground, studying it closer. He could make out the indentations of feet where the man and those with him had waited. Likely, had he checked the other side of the road he would have found more. They had been here then, that was certain. The question, as Dekker had said, was where they had gone.

"Dropped it, do you think?"

The wanderer turned to regard Dekker who had crouched down beside him, then looked back at the piece of leather. "Maybe," he said. He glanced around at the ground, reading it the way another man might read a map. There had been three here—if there were six, total, as Merle had said, then that likely meant the other three had waited on the other side of the road.

They had remained there for some time—the depth of the indentations in the ground showed as much. They had waited, as they had been tasked to do...until they hadn't.

Until something had changed.

The wanderer raised his gaze to the forest beyond the road. A person who hadn't been trained in woodcraft by the best in the world likely wouldn't have noticed anything of import. Bushes and trees a man might see anywhere.

But the wanderer *had* been trained by the best woodsman in the world, and so to him they were more than that. A small branch, freshly broken—evidenced by the not-quite dried out exposed end of where it had been snapped—showed that someone had gone through there recently. And, judging by the spacing of the slight footprints, only just visible on the ground as it had not rained the day before, they had been running.

He rose, his gaze studying the forest in front of him, then he turned back to the men, meeting Merle's gaze. "I'll go look. Perhaps...maybe it would be best if you stayed here."

"You think you'll find 'em," the man said grimly. It wasn't really a question, but the wanderer decided to answer it anyway.

"Yes."

"And you don't think you're goin' to find 'em alive."

"Perhaps you ought to wait here," the wanderer said again.

"No," the man said instantly. "I've lived my whole life without bein' a coward—a fool, sure, an asshole, no doubt, but never a coward. I don't mean to start now. If you think the boys are out there some place," he went on, nodding his head at the woods, "then I mean to find 'em. With or without you."

The wanderer watched the man for a minute, gave him a second to change his mind. When he didn't, he nodded, glancing at Dekker and Clint. "I wonder if..."

"We'll look after the others while you're gone," Clint said immediately. "Just yell if you need us."

Dekker was frowning as if he didn't like the thought of the two men going off alone, but he nodded. "Be careful."

The wanderer nodded back, then turned to Merle. They did not have to travel far before the wanderer became aware of two things. First was the buzzing of flies somewhere up ahead. Second was the smell. It was one he knew well, one that any living thing did, for who better to recognize the dead than their opposite?

He glanced at Merle. "Are you sure you want to see this?"

"I'm sure I don't," the man said. "Now let's go."

The wanderer nodded, finding that he respected the thin man even more. After all, some things weren't pleasant—most things weren't. That did not mean they weren't worth doing or that a man, being a man, did not have an obligation to do them. That one had come from Leader during one of their "talks" as the man had been fond of calling them. In truth, the wanderer had done very little talking. When you are listening to the wisest person ever to walk the face of the world, you don't speak—you *listen*, and feel privileged to do it.

"Okay," he said.

They pressed on through the woods. It did not take them long to reach the source of the smell, and what had drawn the flies. The wanderer stood with Merle at the edge of a small clearing. Six bodies lay sprawled in a rough circle. It was obvious that the men had chosen this spot to take their stand against that which had pursued them.

They had fought back-to-back, forming a circle of defense, one which, against most normal foes would have been difficult to penetrate. A wise tactic, but it had not helped them.

Proof of that could be seen in the simple fact that all the dead scattered about the clearing were Merle's men. There was no sign of whoever—or whatever—had killed them. But then the wanderer needed none. For one, four of the six had had their throats torn out in a grisly but familiar fashion that matched the fate of those two others the wanderer had seen fall to the shadow creature. The other two did not possess such wounds, but their bodies were stiff in death—too stiff—and as the wanderer approached, kneeling before them and examining them, he saw why.

The two men were frozen, their clothes and exposed skin iced over as if they had spent days unprotected in the frigid wilderness of the north where the snow fell in a perpetual white curtain and it was worth a man's life to spend an hour without a flame.

Such cold never reached this far south, and so it took no great leap of logic to figure out what had happened. The touch of the shadow was a cold one, bereft of life and warmth. The wanderer knew this, for he had felt that touch himself. Even now there was still an aching tingle in his arm where the creature's substance had brushed against him, a tingle akin to the pins and needles a man felt when one of his limbs had gone to sleep and was just beginning to wake up again.

He had suffered only a slight brush of that touch, had avoided the worst of it. The men lying before him, their faces pale white and tinged with blue, had not been so fortunate.

"Dead. All of 'em are dead."

Merle's voice was ragged and hoarse with grief and anger. The wanderer rose, turning to him and seeing that grief, that anger, writ plain on his face.

"It was that damned thing, wasn't it?" Merle asked, glancing at him. "The thing that got Gil and the others?"

"Yes. Or another like it."

"Another like it," Merle said quietly, his voice shocked and horrified at once, as if he hadn't even considered, until that moment, that there might be more than one of the creatures. The wanderer, though, had spent the last hundred years of his life being hunted and pursued by uncountable numbers of creatures out of nightmare, and so he had thought of it, for he was aware that whatever else the enemy were, they were not the sort who took half measures.

Merle shook his head, hocking and spitting. "The boys never stood a chance."

There was nothing the wanderer might say to that to offer the man comfort, so he said nothing at all.

"I've known most of these fellas for years. Good men. Or at least as close to good as men come. They didn't deserve to die like this. Shit, nobody deserves to die like this."

They continued to stand in silence for several moments then. The wanderer knew the others were waiting, but he knew, also, that Merle needed those moments. Not to make peace with what had happened—for some things, there was no making peace with them. But instead to say goodbye in the only way a man could say goodbye to the dead. By remembering.

"That's Thurman there," Merle said, nodding to one of the men who had felt the shadow creature's touch and been frozen. "Can't tell it now what with…" He cleared his throat. "Well. He used to be a good lookin' fella. He loved women, did Thurman, and they loved him back." He smiled, a tear running down his face, one of which, it seemed, he was unaware. "Didn't much matter to him whether they were spoken for or not, just as, when it came to it, it didn't seem to much matter to the women, at least not so far as Thurman was concerned. Another fella step toward 'em, they'd give his face a good slap, but with Thurman it weren't ever like that, not so far as I saw. No, Thurman didn't even have to do much steppin'—far as I could tell, it was most always the women steppin' to him. I always told him all that womanizin' would get him killed sooner or later, that some time or another he'd be a bit too slow climbin' out of a wife's window as her husband come in, and that'd be all for him." He sighed. "Guess I was wrong after all."

"A woman's man, then?" the wanderer asked because sometimes a man needed to talk and sometimes he needed someone to listen. Besides, he knew that it wasn't the words that were important, not really—it was the memories. It was saying goodbye.

"Oh, sure," Merle said, giving a soft laugh. "Bastard never met a woman he couldn't bed, and most without effort. Or, well..." He paused, smiling. "I suppose there was one."

"Your wife?"

"That's right. Charlotte, she chose me. The Eternals alone know why." The man winced as if he'd just eaten something sour, his smile of remembrance fading to be replaced by a grim expression. "Dekker...what he told me back at the camp—it's true? You're...an Eternal?"

"Yes."

The man shook his head. "Hard to believe."

"Not much easier on this end," the wanderer said honestly.

"So...what am I s'pose to call you then? Sir? Highness? Milord?"

The wanderer winced. "I'd rather you didn't."

"Ungr, then?"

"I've been called worse."

The other man nodded slowly at that. "Truth to tell, I've never been much a fan of the Eternals. Always seemed to me that they got a whole lot of credit for a whole lot of nothin'."

The wanderer smiled. "Some more than others."

"So it's all true?" Merle asked. "What Dekker told me? I mean, the Eternals, the ones folks are always prayin' to, the ones they call *eternal.* You're tellin' me they've been dead since before I was ever even born—before my *father* was even born?"

"Yes."

Merle shook his head in wonder. Then he glanced back at the dead men lying sprawled on the ground, and a cold, hard expression came into his face, into his eyes. He turned and looked at the wanderer. "It ain't right. Not a fight, this, but a slaughter. Not a battle for land or money or women but killin' for killin's sake. I ain't never had much time for the Eternals, half-men half-gods. Don't put much faith in 'em, and it seems I was right not to, considerin' they're monsters that have taken their place. But I'll tell you this, Ungr, if your aim is to find those responsible for this and all the rest of what's happening in Celes, what I reckon is probably happenin' all over, well, I'm your man. Whatever you need from me, you got it. The bastards behind this need to be put down, the same way a fella'd put down a dog what's taken to bitin'."

"Thank you, Merle, for the offer," the wanderer said earnestly. "But...you don't know what you're saying. You have a wife, a son. The ones behind this...they do not take kindly to people or things who attempt to stand in their way, and I have done so for a hundred years. They don't just want me dead, they want to make me suffer. Me and whoever is with me."

"Like that fella Dekker? And his wife and girl?"

The wanderer winced at that. "Yes."

"You been around a long time. So I don't mean to argue with you. But these folks—my friends. Or, at least, as near to friends as a grumpy bastard like me can have...they weren't tryin' to bring down any corrupt official. Weren't tryin' to get in anybody's way. They were just tryin' to find food for their families. Not in the right way, maybe, waitin' for innocent folk to come by on the road the way we done but...well. After a while, a man gets hungry enough, he sees his wife and his kiddies get hungry enough, listens to 'em cryin' while they try to go to sleep with the hunger gnawin' at their bellies like a rat inside 'em...well. After a while that fella stops carin' about gettin' food for his family the right way. After a while, he just wants to get it for 'em *any* way."

The wanderer had experienced hunger a few times himself over the years—times when risking stopping to hunt or forage would have risked the entire world—and so he knew what the man spoke about. Civilized man, he'd been told—and had come to learn on his own—was always one step away from a savage. One terrible tragedy or one week spent without food away from becoming little more than a beast, yet capable of far more atrocities, far more destruction than any beast might imagine. "I understand," he said quietly.

Merle watched him for a moment. "I think maybe you do," he said. "But I say all that to say this—in a world gone mad, it don't much matter what a man does or don't do. That madness'll find 'em just the same. Ain't no way to get on in such a world, not and keep safe those things a man treasures. Can't avoid that sorta madness—you gotta kill it. Put it down. Because if you don't, like a weepin' sore, it'll grow and fester and sooner or later it'll be too big to put down at all. I aim to help you, if I can, to make the world a better place, if I can, just so long as me and mine are livin' in it. And Eternal or not, I don't think you got any business tellin' a man he can't try to improve on the world."

He squared his jaw, staring at the wanderer, clearly prepared to argue, to fight. The thing was, he was right, the wanderer knew that, too. "Okay," he said. "But," he warned, "it will be dangerous."

Merle nodded. "I once knew a fella—I won't say friend, but an acquaintance, anyway, who decided on a whim to take a different walk to work over at the clerk's. Ended up gettin' mugged, killed. Death finds a man, whether he goes lookin' for it or not. Now, do you want to keep standin' around here jawin' or find the bastards responsible for this and maybe use that sword of yours to poke some daylight into 'em?"

The wanderer gave a small smile, thinking of his conversation with Clint. "I choose daylight," he said.

CHAPTER TEN

THE OTHERS DID NOT ask what had become of Merle's men when they returned, no doubt able to determine what the answer might be by the expressions on his and Merle's faces.

They set out for Celes, slowly following the road that led up at an incline, over a hill. At the top, the wanderer surveyed the area before them. Beyond the hill, the forest ended, giving way to farmland where hundreds of farmers worked their plots, planting and harvesting, shepherding and raising cattle to provide food to the great city of Celes that was visible in the distance.

Or, at least, it was where the farms *had* existed. The stables and barns and houses that had been used by the farmers and their livestock had all been burned down, leaving charred ruins similar to those they'd discovered in Ingleton.

Here and there, the wanderer's enhanced sight picked out lumps lying in the fields. At first, he couldn't identify what they might be but in another moment he did. Dead animals. Cows and horses, sheep and chickens and oxen that would have been used to pull plows.

There were no vultures, not now, for the dead animals had been picked at already, their flesh given way to decay so that they were little more than bones. And the wanderer felt confident that, should he look closely enough, some of those skeletons would be human.

"Why?" Clint asked from beside him. "Why would anyone do such a thing? These folks didn't harm anybody."

Kill them. Kill them all. It was the sword's voice in his head again. Or, perhaps, it was his own. It was growing increasingly difficult to tell the difference.

"I don't know," the wanderer said quietly. He glanced at Celes, the great city with its white marble walls standing beyond the fields, looking as it always had. Like a bastion of hope shining in the morning sun. Like the promise of better days.

It looked perfect. Or, at least, as close to perfect as the works of men could get. But then the wanderer had lived long enough to know that looks were often deceiving. Celes was like a corpse, similar to those others lying in the hot sun. This corpse was dressed up, the way undertakers will dress the dead in face paint and fine clothes, but what lay beneath that expertly-crafted illusion was decayed and spoiled. Rotten.

The southern gates of Celes yawned open, like the mouth of some sneaking creature lying in wait for its prey to come. And that prey, such as it was, lined up at the city's front. Dozens, hundreds of men and women. The wanderer could not make out much of them, not from so great a distance, but it appeared as if they were seeking admittance into the city. He wondered if they knew how bad it was in the city and went anyway, or if they were unaware. He thought it likely they knew, but when a man has lost everything, when he has had it all taken from him, where might he go for safety but to the capital city of his leaders? True, those leaders were evil, but then they did not know that.

The wanderer frowned. "I don't know why they would do this," he said again, glancing around at the green fields beyond them, at the churned brown earth where the farmers had worked the land, at the white bones peeking up here and there. "But I mean to find out."

Veikr gave his head an agitated toss beside him, and the wanderer absently patted the horse's muzzle. His equine companion was not immune to the anger and frustration he and those with him felt. "Easy boy," the wanderer said quietly, hoping to calm the horse. Hoping to calm himself.

They started down the hill.

As they drew closer to the devastation, the wanderer examined the bodies they passed, the burned-out buildings, and determined that the devastation that had come upon the farmers and their livestock had happened weeks ago.

That bothered him, for it had been little more than weeks ago when he and the others had escaped Celes, and he wondered—feared—that the enemy had wrought the devastation they walked through as a form of revenge against him and the Perishables, against the men and women of the city of Celes who had aided him.

He wanted to believe that no creature, however evil, could be capable of making an entire city suffer for the crimes—or, at least, perceived crimes—of a few dozen, but then he knew that such was not the case, however he might wish it. Animals, beasts, might not be capable of such hatred, such vileness, but then he thought the enemy likely would be. They impersonated men and women, after all, and men were certainly capable of such evil—the wanderer knew for he had seen it firsthand and that more than once.

Several weeks since the tragedy had occurred, long enough that the crows had already eaten their fill and even the flies had no interest in what little dried, desiccated flesh still clung to the bones bleached white in the sun.

Neither did any people move or run around the burned-out shells that had once been homes where families had lived their lives. Everything was still, silent, a land of the dead where the living had no place. The others might have felt despair as they moved about the remnants of lives ended prematurely, but the wanderer did not. No, it was not despair that filled him—it was rage.

Not the fiery hot rage that often burned the man from which it came as much as anyone else. No, this was a cold rage, one that did not feel like fire in his belly but instead like a shadow in his heart. A shadow that was spreading slowly through him, bringing with it what the shadows always brought...darkness.

Kill them, the voice in his head hissed.

I will, the wanderer promised. He did not know whether that voice was his own in truth, or if it was the sword's—which he suspected. And at that moment, at least, he did not care. His words were true ones. He would find those responsible for this atrocity, and he would kill them, or he would die in the attempt.

It felt as if they walked forever through those fields of soot and ash and corpses, and no matter how many steps they took it seemed as if they never drew any closer to the white marble walls of Celes that stretched toward the heavens.

They walked in grim silence, all of them doing their best to keep their eyes on the path in front of them instead of letting their gazes drift to the wreck and ruin on either side of the path and each of them failing in the attempt. Everyone, that was, save for Sarah. Dekker and his wife, Ella, had left nothing to chance when it came to their daughter, the big man having retrieved his spare shirt from his pack and used it as a blindfold to tie around his daughter's eyes, blocking them from view. Even with this precaution, he carried her against him, one hand on the back of her blonde hair, pushing her face into his broad chest.

The wanderer was glad to see that much, at least. The girl was innocent. Such sights as those which lay on either side of the road would not spoil that innocence completely, but it would dirty it, would steal a piece of it away. And the wanderer knew from brutal experience that once that innocence was gone there was no getting it back again.

Sometimes, he thought that was all aging really was, in the end. A loss of that innocence. Men and women started like great masterpieces created by the gods themselves, but over the course of their lives things—people, sometimes, tragedies, themselves—chipped away at those masterpieces. A chunk here, a sliver there, taking those wonderful works and making of them increasingly disturbing oddities.

The world would do its work on Sarah in time—there was no preventing it, not so far as the wanderer could see—but that did not mean that it needed to be today. He thought that childhood—the innocence, the simple joy, the exuberance only the young felt at even the smallest of things, the hope and belief that everything would be okay—was something worth fighting for. Something worth dying for, if it came to it.

And so he was glad, as they walked, to see Dekker holding his daughter against him, speaking quietly to her, words too low for the wanderer to hear, but he did not think that the words themselves mattered, not really. Not anymore than the words mattered when he spoke to Veikr to calm the horse down. It was just the familiar voice that mattered, that was all, a voice whose very presence assured the horse—and the girl—that everything would, of course, be okay.

In time, they left the worst of the devastation behind, their path carrying them over a hill and then down it so that they could no longer see the destruction. At least not with their eyes. The wanderer thought that they would be witnessing the scene in their minds for many nights—and many nightmares—to come.

As they drew closer to Celes they caught sight of the line of refugees they had spotted from the hilltop, and however bad, however desperate the people had looked from a distance, they looked far more so as the wanderer and the others drew near.

"Poor bastards," Dekker muttered. "But shit, what in the world has got them comin' here? I mean, if what we just walked through ain't the clearest damn 'stay out' sign I ever saw, then I don't know what it is."

"And where would you have them go?" Merle asked.

"Shit if I was in their shoes, I don't suppose I'd be all that picky," Dekker countered. "Rather stay in a cave than here."

"With all that's going on," Clint said, "the darker and deeper the better."

"Tried that," Merle said, "or close enough to it. Thing is, there ain't usually a whole lot to eat in caves. Worms, that's about it, and not enough to keep a man alive even if eating worm for breakfast lunch and dinner is anyone's idea of livin'."

"What are you saying?" Dekker asked.

"I'm sayin' that you ain't the first to have the idea—the idea of diggin' a hole and climbin' in. The problem is that the world don't stop movin' just cause we do. These folks here, they're hungry and desperate. I guess they figure they can be hungry and desperate by themselves or hungry and desperate with others. After all, I ain't never met a man in my life wanted to die alone. You?"

Dekker frowned. "I ain't never met a man that wanted to die at all, truth to tell."

"No?" Merle asked. "Then you've been lucky—but you ask me," he went on, glancing back at the line of refugees, "I think that's just about to change."

"They're letting refugees in?" Clint asked.

"Sure, why not?" Merle said, the disdain clear in his voice. "More bodies to disappear in the night."

"Letting *them* in, sure," Dekker said, "but will they let *us* in? I gotta figure we look a bit different than the folks they're used to seein' come in."

"Think so?" Merle asked, raising an eyebrow and glancing at each of them.

The wanderer frowned, following his gaze to the others then to himself, realization slowly dawning. He hadn't considered, until that moment, just how rough their journey through the Untamed Lands had left them, had been too concerned with moving forward—with surviving—to take much notice of their appearance.

Their clothes were worn and threadbare, stained with dirt and grass and blood. Their hair was tangled and knotted with dirt and burrs from the trees and bushes they'd walked through. There was also a noticeable smell—one that he must have gotten used to without even realizing it. After all, it wasn't as if a man running for his life thought to stop and take a bath. Each of them seemed filthier than the last, save Ella and Sarah, the two looking a bit worn and a bit unkempt, but by some magic exclusive to women, looking far more put together than any of the men.

"I think we'll be okay," the wanderer told Dekker. In fact, if they stood out from the refugees currently making their way into Celes it wouldn't be because they were too clean but because they were too dirty.

"You sure, Ungr? I mean these poor bastards look like—"

"You've got a little somethin', Dek," Clint said, giving a small smile of his own. "Right..." He paused, waving his hand to indicate everything starting from Dekker's cracking, stained boots to his matted, tangled hair and his unshaven, unkempt growth of beard. "There."

Dekker frowned, glancing down at himself and grunted. "Fine, so maybe I could do with a bath, but you don't look so damned presentable yourself, you bastard. And you smell like you rolled around in pig shit."

"Some pastimes are just hard to give up," Clint said dryly.

There was a laugh, and all of them, including a frowning Dekker, turned to see that it had come from Sarah. Dekker had passed her to her mother once they'd made it past the burned-out farms and slaughtered livestock, and the girl was smiling now.

"That's funny," she said.

They had seen some terrible things that day, some sights that the wanderer knew would be long in leaving, but the sight of the little girl's smile, the sound of her laughter stood as an answer to all the badness, and he found himself smiling. The others smiled as well, even Dekker.

"Still though," Sarah said, "you said a bad word. That's not good, Daddy."

More laughter from the men at that, and Dekker scowled at them, his mouth working but no words coming out—likely because any that he allowed to escape just then would only get him into more trouble. "Sorry, love," he told his daughter. "I'll try to do better."

"Now that we've got all that out of the way," Merle said, glancing at the wanderer, "there is a problem needs seein' to afore we go into Celes."

The wanderer was about to ask what he meant, but then the thin man's gaze traveled to Veikr, standing beside him, and he knew. "You think Veikr is a problem?"

"I think Celes don't see a whole lot of horses these days—nor any animal. And certainly not one so big. I think that there's folks in the city—more'n a few—who'd risk their lives to take a bite out of him."

"It'd be the last thing they ever did," Dekker said. "Horse has got a kick on 'em that'd bring down castles."

"I don't doubt you're right," Merle said, still looking at the wanderer. "He's a magnificent beast—anyone spares so much as a glance in his direction can see as much. But then..."

"But then that's the problem," the wanderer finished.

"That's the problem."

Dekker frowned. "We could...maybe smudge 'em up a bit? Rub some dirt on 'em. Make him walk with his head hung down a bit? Give 'em a bit of a slouch?"

"A giant slouchin's still a giant," Merle said, "and a giant's gonna get remarked on. That's for damn sure." He glanced at the wanderer. "And I'm thinkin' maybe you don't want that."

The wanderer considered that, turning to regard his horse. His oldest friend. Veikr stared back with a gaze that told the wanderer that if he didn't know precisely what they were talking about he knew enough.

He didn't worry as much about people trying to make a meal out of Veikr—as Dekker had intimated, the person who tried ought to be pitied more than anything else. But Veikr *would* draw attention—he couldn't help that, for all the finest things of the world drew attention. And considering that the wanderer was the most hunted man in all the world, and that the others were looking to him for protection, attention was the very last thing they wanted. Right up there with an axe to the throat which, if the enemy figured out they were in Celes, was more than likely what they were in for. Eventually. The enemy would not rush such a thing as the revenge they sought—they would make sure to make the wanderer pay for all of his perceived crimes and would make the others pay for helping him.

"But...but I don't want Veikr to leave," Sarah said, her voice desperate and pleading, sounding panicked at the thought of being without Veikr, a sentiment that the wanderer understood all too well.

"We ain't leavin' him, darlin'," Dekker said, glancing at the wanderer with very much like a child's fear in his own gaze. "Are we?"

"We can't bring him with us," the wanderer said quietly, turning to regard the horse.

"Can't leave 'em behind, either," Clint said. "Where would he go?"

"Can't take him and can't leave him behind," Dekker repeated slowly. "Now there's a riddle for ya. Suppose we could cover him in burlap, carry him on our backs."

"Maybe you could, you big bastard," Clint said. "I just caught a cramp for listenin' to you say it."

"There might be I have an answer for what to do with that horse of yours," Merle said slowly.

"Oh?" the wanderer asked.

Merle scratched his chin. "I know a fella owns a stable in the city."

Dekker grunted. "I thought we just decided that—"

"At the *edge* of the city," Merle interrupted. "Just through the gate, yonder."

"Well, shit, why didn't you say so in the first place?" Dekker asked. "Why have us all guess at what's for dinner while you're holdin' the platter behind your back? I mean if you're friends with a guy that runs a damned stable, then—"

"Never said we were friends," Merle interrupted. "I just said I knew him, is all. And yeah, he owns a stable, just as his daddy owned it before him. He took it over when his old man died. Ran that stable alright. Ran it right into the damned ground."

"I...don't understand," Clint said. "Is there a stable or not?"

Merle shrugged. "It was still standin', last I checked. The buildin' anyway." He glanced at Veikr, "Though, I'm afraid the furnishin's might not be up to the standards that this magnificent beast here is accustomed to."

The wanderer shared a look with Clint and Dekker, the men no doubt remembering their trek through the Untamed Lands where they had been confronted by all manner of creature and dangers. "He'll adapt," he said. "Veikr is not so picky as that. Though, this man...the one you speak of—your not-friend. Is he reliable?"

"The only thing I'd rely on Jessup for is to start the day drunk and end it the same way."

"Has a drinking problem, this Jessup?"

Merle turned to regard Dekker. "Sayin' Jessup's got a drinkin' problem is like sayin' a dead man has a breathin' problem but yeah."

"You're not exactly convincing us this is a good idea," Clint offered.

Merle shrugged. "Never said it was a good idea. Fact is, I wouldn't trust Jessup to put his own boots on without fallin' and crackin' his head open. But the fact is you need a place to put your horse, and he has one—if'n he hasn't sold the lumber off to pay for drink, that is."

"Don't much care for the sound of this, Ungr," Dekker said.

"Me neither," the wanderer said, "but I don't see that we have much choice."

And so, with that grim truth hanging over them, the wanderer and the others stepped back into the line. The line moved faster than he would have expected, and despite the fact that there had to be at least a hundred people seeking admittance into the city it took them no more than ten minutes to reach the gate.

As they walked through the entrance, the wanderer saw the reason the line had moved so quickly. At a typical city gate, guards would be stationed, guards who questioned those entering about their reasons for coming to the city, examining their belongings to make sure they did not bring in anything that might pose a danger to the city or its inhabitants.

Here, there were guards—eight in total, four times the number that had once been assigned to guard the city gate the last time the wanderer had visited Celes. Which was strange. Stranger still, none of the eight were facing the gate. Instead, they were all positioned so that they faced into the city, gazing down the street or at the people entering the city with a disgust and revulsion they made no attempt to hide.

The guards did not say anything to the refugees, nor direct them on what they might do, where they might find shelter or food. In fact, aside from the slight sneers they shot at the steady stream of ragged people entering the city the guards paid them no attention at all. At least, that was, until a hunched old woman, only managing a shaky, uncertain walk into the gate with the use of a walking stick, fell, upending the burlap sack she'd held over one shoulder onto the ground.

The woman's possessions, such as they were, spilled out onto the ground. What appeared to be a flint and tinder, a single dress that looked as worn and faded as the one the woman currently wore, a small rusty tin pan and a chunk of dried, crusty bread. Not much. Certainly meager enough belongings to represent what the wanderer suspected was at least sixty five years of the woman's life.

The wanderer waited for whoever the woman was traveling with to step forward and help, but he realized in another moment, as she struggled down to her knees with grunts and whimpers of pain, that she was alone. She had no one. Perhaps she had once, perhaps she was coming to the city to find them. Or, perhaps, she was alone.

He did not know. All he knew for sure was that the woman was struggling to try to gather up her belongings with shaking hands while the line of refugees stalled at the city gate behind her.

This finally roused the guards, one of which slapped the shoulder of one of his fellows. The two of them rose, walking forward and looming over the woman. At first the wanderer thought they meant to help her, but as the one in front flashed a cruel smile he realized that they had no intention of doing that.

"Bastards," Merle muttered from beside him.

"Move your shit, you old bag," one said.

"O-o-of course," the woman said, out of breath from the small exertion, her frantic struggles to gather her meager belongings increasing. But try as she might, she couldn't hold the burlap bag and stuff her things inside, not while also keeping herself upright with her walking stick, a task which, judging by her increasing trembling, was growing more and more difficult by the moment.

The two guards shared a laugh, as if there was nothing funnier than watching an old lady struggle. "Come on already," the second said, "you're blockin' the way. Don't you see all these folks wantin' to come into our fine city?"

"Forgive me," the woman said, "i-if you could just, give me a little help, I—"

"Of course, of course," the first guard interrupted, kneeling beside her. "Got to get all your stuff, right?" he said, then he abruptly snatched away the woman's walking stick, and she fell. She cried out in surprised pain, and the guard rose, his smile vanishing. "You've got three seconds to get your ass up, get your shit, and get out of the way."

The wanderer became aware of someone snarling, like an angry hound preparing to bite.

Kill them. Kill them both.

So far he'd held the sword's urgings at bay, but this time, he could think of no reason not to listen. In fact, he didn't want to. His swords were wrapped in a threadbare blanket at his back in an effort to conceal them lest they arouse questions, a precaution that the others had taken with their own weapons, but the wanderer knew he could draw them in a moment.

He stared at the old woman, at the guards, and saw that there was a line of blood trickling down the woman's forehead where she'd struck it on the cobbles of the street. That was what did it, overcoming whatever meager defense the rational, logical part of his brain had been trying to summon.

He reached for his sword.

His hand was only halfway there, though, when another hand clamped around his wrist like an immovable vice, and he glanced over to see Dekker watching him, his expression grim. The big man gave him a shake of his head. "Why don't you let me take this one?" he asked softly.

Dekker didn't wait for a response before moving toward the woman and the two guards. The wanderer watched him go, blinking and feeling as if he'd just woken from a dream.

"Just what in the fuck do you think you're doing, you big bastard?" one of the guards demanded, and although he tried for threatening the wanderer could hear the fear in his voice at Dekker's approach.

The big man stopped a couple of feet away from the old woman. "I just mean to help her, sir, that's all."

The two guards glanced at each other, then the first licked his lips, a slow grin spreading on his face as he realized that Dekker didn't mean to attack after all. "That right? What is she, your mum, that it? Dear old mommy?"

"Say that she is," Dekker said.

The guard smiled. "Well go on then, you big oaf," he said, stepping to the side away from the old woman and gesturing toward her. "Help mommy dearest before she falls again."

Dekker nodded, starting forward. The guard waited until he was past then gave him a kick in the back.

The big man grunted, stumbling and falling to one knee on the cobbles, and the wanderer tensed, expecting Dekker to react. After all, the wanderer had seen him fight, and he would have given Dekker easy odds against the two men, if he decided to attack them.

He didn't, though. Instead he only glanced back at the guardsman. No more than that, yet the guardsman in question took an involuntary half-step back, as if he was afraid Dekker might charge him. As far as the wanderer was concerned, they were right to be afraid. Sure, Dekker might be gentle at the moment, but then so too might a tamed bear raised from birth to perform in some traveling circus troupe. But however well-trained the bear, any caretaker that wasn't a complete fool had to keep one thing in mind—beneath that gentleness, the creature was still a bear, capable of terrible violence.

But Dekker did not leap toward the nearest man, roaring a battle cry as the wanderer half-expected him to do. Instead he turned back to the old lady and helped her to a sitting position. "You alright, Mum?"

"I-I'm f-fine, thank you," the old lady said.

Dekker nodded, glancing at the cut on her forehead with a frown. A shallow cut, but it was still bleeding. The big man tore off a piece of his shirt, glancing back at the old woman with an apologetic expression. "Not as clean as I'd like, I'm afraid," he said as he folded it over, "but it ought to stop the bleeding, if you hold it pressed against the cut."

The old woman took it, giving him a grateful smile and pressing the ragged square of cloth against her forehead.

"We're not a healer's shop," the second guard said. "Get your shit and get out of the street. Now."

The old woman started to lean forward, but Dekker stopped her with a gentle hand on her shoulder. "Relax, Mum," he said. "I'll take care of it."

Then he set about the task of grabbing the woman's belongings and putting them back into the burlap sack. He folded the dress, quickly but gently, and replaced it, then he retrieved the tin cooking pan. He was reaching for the crust of dried bread, when one of the guardsmen stepped forward, stomping his foot onto the big man's wrist.

But if he was looking for a hiss of pain or for Dekker to cry out then the guard was destined to be disappointed. Instead, the big man only turned a questioning look up to the guardsman, and the wanderer was impressed to see that Dekker still seemed in no danger of losing his temper.

"Oh, I'm sure she doesn't want *that*," the guardsman said. "I mean, just look at the state of it. Falling on the cobbles like it did." He sighed, shaking his head. "Tell you what," he went on, grinning, making a game of it, "leave the bread—I'll take care of it."

"P-please, mister," the old lady began, "it's all I—"

"Easy, Mum," Dekker said, turning and putting a hand on the old woman's shoulder. "That's alright." He turned back to the guard. "After all, this friendly fellow is right—a person'd have to be pretty desperate to eat bread like that. Why, I reckon most dogs wouldn't touch it, and they're taken to sniffin' each other's rear ends."

The guard's malicious smile soured at that. "Something you want to say, you big son of a bitch?" he asked, bristling.

"Not at all," Dekker said, responding lightly, even going so far as to give the man a smile. "We thank you for your help—you know, with the bread."

He rose then turned and offered a hand to the old woman. Her eyes flickered nervously to the guards then back to his hand before she finally took it and Dekker pulled her effortlessly to her feet.

"But...my bread..." the woman said, a desperate, mewling sound to her voice.

"That's alright," Dekker assured her, reaching into his own pack and withdrawing a large banana leaf in which he'd wrapped what was left of his portion of berries they'd foraged while on their way. "Here, maybe this'll help."

She stared at the small, not-quite-ripe blueberries inside the leaf the way most would have gaped at a sack of gold coins. "A-are you sure?" she asked, staring at him with wide, disbelieving eyes.

"Sure I'm sure," Dekker said, smiling.

"But...what will you eat?"

"I ain't all that hungry just now. Now go on, please—take them."

"Berries?" one of the guards asked, for the moment forgetting to be cruel and instead sounding only surprised.

"Blueberries," the second guard confirmed, staring at the leaf, not quite salivating but not all that far from it either. "Seems forever since I've had one."

The other guard started forward, but Dekker stopped him with a hand on his chest. "If you've waited forever, I don't suppose a bit longer'll hurt," the big man said, his voice not unkind.

The guard stared at Dekker's hand on his chest as if he couldn't believe the man would have the audacity to touch him. "You dare?" the guard asked.

Dekker considered that for a moment then nodded. "I dare," he said.

He spoke calmly, casually, but he might as well have uttered a death threat the way the guard reacted, beginning to tremble, the expression on his face shifting like a storm as he vacillated between anger and fear. "If I want those damned berries, I'll take those damned berries," the guard said.

"You can certainly try," Dekker responded, giving the man a small, honest smile.

The second guard let out a hiss. "*Fuck this,*" he snarled, starting forward toward the old woman. "Get the fuck out of my way, you big ba—" The man's words cut off as Dekker buried a fist in his stomach.

The air exploded out of the guard's lungs in a great *whoosh,* and he bent over the fist planted in his gut like he was trying to touch his toes—and making a pretty damned good effort at it, so far as the wanderer could see.

Gasping, the man went for his blade, and Dekker struck him again, this time in the temple. The guard practically did a flip at that, unconscious even before his limp body collapsed to the cobbles in a heap. Dekker turned back to the second guard, looking as calm and relaxed as he had moments ago.

It had all happened so fast, so abruptly, that the remaining guard hadn't even thought to draw his sword, only stood staring at his fallen companion in complete shock.

Finally, though, the man seemed to overcome the worst of his surprise, hissing and fumbling at the sheath at his waist in a panicked effort to draw his sword.

"I wouldn't," Dekker said calmly. "Somebody might get hurt."

He didn't make the words into a threat, delivering them without any particular inflection, but then he didn't need to, for the threat spoke for itself—that could be seen in the way the guardsman's hand froze.

He glanced back at the old woman, deciding she was an easier target than the big man looming over him. "Give me those berries," he said. "I'm confiscating them."

The woman started forward, pausing as Dekker raised a big hand. "That's not going to happen," he said apologetically.

The man looked back at him, then at the other refugees waiting in line, sneering as he noted the audience of so many watching him be put in his place. "You have to obey me," he said, a discernible squeak in his voice. "I'm a city guardsman!"

"So is he," Dekker said, nodding his head at the unconscious man. "But, more's the pity, even the best of us—like a noble city guardsman, say—can get hurt, if we aren't careful."

The guardsman licked his lips nervously at that, looking around as if for help, but the only help he had was busy hanging out in the land of dreams—to which Dekker had sent him so forcefully only moments ago.

He sneered. "They're not even ripe yet anyway—probably sour and taste of piss. Who'd want 'em?"

"Exactly," Dekker said, nodding. "Who'd want them?"

The man's eyes narrowed. "It's a crime, strikin' a city guardsman. One punishable by death."

"It's a good thing he tripped and fell then," Dekker said. And now he did take a step forward so that the guard was forced to look up at him. "Isn't it?"

The man swallowed, his face paling. "Yeah, he fell. Fitz...he always has been a clumsy bastard."

Dekker nodded, glancing at the man lying on the ground. "Had a cousin like that, once. Are we good to go on through?"

"S-sure go on then, damnit," the guard said.

Dekker inclined his head, going back to where the wanderer and the others waited, staring at him as he approached.

"That's my husband," Ella said with obvious pride and love.

The wanderer glanced at the unconscious man then back at Dekker. "Who knew you had such a way with words?"

"Oh sure could talk himself out of just about anything, that one," Clint said, "just so long as those wagon wheels he calls hands weren't bound, of course."

Dekker winced, clearly uncomfortable. "Listen, Ungr, I was wondering if Veikr—"

"He'd be happy to," the wanderer said, and without being told or urged the horse stepped forward to where the old woman stood and lay down to the ground to get as low as possible.

Dekker moved toward her, helping her into the saddle and speaking with her quietly. In another moment, he came back to the wanderer. "Names Ada. She doesn't have any family—used to live a bit to the north in a village, but men—" He paused, frowning. "*Bandits* she claims, came and took everyone, burned their homes down. Only she escaped—on account of she hid."

"Bandits," the wanderer repeated.

The big man nodded. "Reckon it's more of those Shadows?"

"Yes," the wanderer said. "Yes I do."

"Anyway, I was wondering if she could come with us, maybe we could help her find a place to stay?"

"Of course," the wanderer said.

Dekker smiled gratefully, nodding. "Thanks."

"Thank you," the wanderer said. "For stopping me."

Dekker grunted, trying for a smile, but the wanderer thought he could see the worry beneath it. "You lost your temper a bit, that's all—happens to me all the time."

Not like this, I think. The wanderer did not speak the words aloud, for the big man had enough to worry about. Besides, he was already moving back to the old woman where she sat awkwardly atop Veikr's back and soon they were all traveling down the road, Merle at the front, Clint walking beside the wanderer, and Dekker and his family, along with the old woman on the horse, behind them.

"Reckon trouble's gonna find us on account of that business at the gate?" Clint asked quietly, not so loud that there was any chance of Dekker or his family overhearing. "Don't get me wrong," he went on quickly, "Dekker kept his calm a damn sight better'n I would have. I ain't sayin'—"

"I know you're not," the wanderer said. "As for your first question...I think, considering what we're doing here, trouble is going to find us either way. I also think that a good man doesn't do things because they're convenient or because they serve him the best—he does them because they're the right thing to do."

"Dekker is a good man," Clint said, "ain't no doubt of that."

It was a true sentiment and that was what worried the wanderer the most. After all, the Eternals had been good men and women—the best in the world, or so he had always been taught. Now they were all dead.

In a bad world, a man's goodness was not a shield on his arm—it was a target on his back. For that which was sour hated that which was sweet, for in its sweetness it served to underscore the other's sourness.

"Damn guardsmen," Merle said, coming up beside him.

"All of them are like that?" Clint asked.

"More or less," Merle said. "All the good ones have either vanished, left, or are staying at home with their families. The ones as are left are the cruel ones, bastards who don't care a whit about protecting people, only care about taking advantage of 'em. Come on," he went on, frowning. "Jessup's this way. It ain't far now."

***

As soon as they were out of sight of the gate, the old woman who Dekker had helped excused herself from their company. She thanked the blushing big man profusely before departing, but the wanderer couldn't help but notice the nervous glances she cast about her before fleeing down an alleyway. She didn't want to be seen or associated with them, that was obvious, but then the wanderer couldn't blame her. In fact, he didn't suppose there was another person walking the world who it was as dangerous to associate with as himself. Which just went to prove that the old became old for a reason.

True to Merle's word, they traveled for no more than fifteen minutes from the southern gate of Celes before the thin man left the main road behind, leading them down an empty side street. The wanderer trusted Merle, felt that he had taken the man's measure and taken it truly. But that did not stop him from looking at the doors and windows of the buildings as they passed to ensure himself that no one waited in ambush. Silly, perhaps, considering he'd already trusted the man this far, but it occurred to him that his meeting Merle at the campfire, saving him from the shadow creature, might well have all been a sort of play, orchestrated by Tactician or one of the others. Such a thing might have seemed far-fetched to another, to imagine that the enemy might know he would catch on to the "bandits" following him, and might furthermore conclude that he would help Merle, that the man's easy-going manner, that the courage he'd shown, would put the wanderer off-guard.

True, that was complicated, involved, but then the enemy was also complicated, and the wanderer had seen Tactician himself have such convoluted plans, ones where he accurately predicted the actions and reactions of a bandit group or a political figure to a tee, seemingly controlling them like a puppet master controlled his puppets, or like a man might move pieces on a game board.

But despite the wanderer's caution, despite his worry, no shadowy figures appeared out of the alleyways to accost them. Neither did any guardsmen charge after them. After less than fifteen minutes of walking down sidestreets and back alleys, Merle stopped in front of a rundown building that had clearly once served as a stable and which had also clearly not done so for some time.

At the front of the building stood two double doors, built large enough to accommodate horses or wagons. They both hung askew in their frames. There were windows at the front, likely built so that, when opened, they might allow more air into the stables, but at least two were shattered.

"The stables you spoke of?" the wanderer asked, glancing at the thin man.

"What's left of them anyway," Merle muttered.

The wanderer nodded. There was a small house attached to the stables. He had seen such a thing before, where the stablemaster had built his home adjoining the stables so that he might more easily be on hand to see to the needs of horses and customers alike—not that it was likely that the stables had seen much of either recently judging by the state of it.

The wanderer started toward the house then paused, turning to raise an eyebrow at Merle. The thin man sighed then gave a nod, moving toward the door. He had to knock three times before someone answered. After the third, the door opened a crack, but unless the wanderer was very confused, the person peering out at them from the other side was not Jessup.

"What do you want?" a sour-faced woman who appeared to be in her fifties asked. The wanderer could tell by her drooping jowls and sagging cheeks that the woman had been overweight once but had recently lost a lot of weight very quickly. Her eyes widened a bit as she took in the twenty or so people standing in front of her home, more than would have fit inside.

"*Help,*" she shrieked. "*Help, thie—*"

"We're not thieves," Merle interrupted. "Honest, ma'am, we're not."

The woman did not seem convinced, scowling out at them with narrowed, suspicious eyes, but the wanderer was glad, at least, that she had stopped screaming. Not that there was anyone in the street to either side and, if the city really was as bad as Merle had said, he doubted that anyone would have come to her aid. Certainly the city guards didn't seem interested at all in helping anyone...except for helping themselves to an old lady's bread perhaps.

"If you ain't thieves or vagabonds out to steal my virtue—" the woman began, then paused at a snort from Dekker. They all turned to regard the big man who cleared his throat.

"Sorry about that," he said. "Swallowed a fly

"As I was sayin'," the woman went on, turning back to Merle, "if you ain't bandits, then just who are you and why are you bangin' on my door in the early morning?"

In truth it was closer to noon, but the wanderer didn't think there was any point in saying so, and judging by his response neither did Merle. "Sorry, ma'am, but I used to know the man that lived here. Jessup. I was wondering—"

"Jessup, is it?" the woman said. "I'd ask if you were a friend of his, but then I know damned well that ain't the case. Jessup don't have friends, leastways not for long for any friend he meets, it's only a matter of time 'fore he screws 'em over one way or another."

"Got you too, did he?" Merle asked.

The woman raised an eyebrow. "You're sayin' Jessup owes you?"

"There anybody in the city he don't owe?" Merle countered.

The woman watched him for a minute then gave a smile, the same sort of smile a crocodile might give when it crept along the water toward its prey. "And these fellas here, those as are behind you—they come to throw a party for Jessup, that it?"

"Look you've got it all wr—" Clint began, but Merle spoke over him.

"Something like that," the thin man agreed.

The woman watched him for another moment then gave a nod. "Good. That bastard's been deservin' that sorta party for a long time now. Anyway, he ain't here—don't live here no more. Poor bastard sold me this house at a steal on account of he was out of money...and thirsty, of course. You know how Jessup gets thirsty, don't you?"

"I do."

She gave a grunt. "Anyway, you'll find the no-good bastard over there, sleepin' it off no doubt" she said, jerking her thumb at the stables. "That is if he ain't out tryin' to bum or steal money for another bottle."

Merle inclined his head. "Thank you, ma'am, for the—" The woman slammed the door shut, then, and he didn't bother continuing, instead turning and moving back to the wanderer.

"I didn't know this Jessup owed you," the wanderer observed.

"I wasn't exaggerating—the bastard owes nearly everyone in the city. It's a miracle he ain't dead yet, but then, my experience, the good suffer and the bad linger. You ready?"

"Lead the way," the wanderer said.

They followed Merle to the stable doors. He knocked, and no answer came. He knocked again and still no one came to the door, though the wanderer heard a faint, muffled curse.

Merle sighed, glancing back at him with an apologetic expression before banging on the door loud enough that it rattled and shook, looking in danger of collapsing. "Jessup, it's me, Merle, not the damned city guard—get off your ass and open the door!"

"*Merle?*" a slurred, befuddled voice called from somewhere inside. "*That you?*"

"Said it was, didn't I?" Merle called. "What, you got so many visitors you don't recognize me, that it? Or is it just that you've finally drunk yourself into a permanent stupor?"

More cursing from inside, then a loud *thump* followed by yet more hissed curses and, in another minute, the stable door creaked as it swung open. Or, at least, it started to. It got stuck, the downward angle at which it hung making it dig into the ground, and the man on the other side—presumably Jessup—hissed and spat as he lifted it up and pulled it back.

The man standing in the open doorway looked far worse even than the refugees the wanderer and the others had seen at the gate. His trousers were unbuttoned, and his shirt—stained with a mixture of what looked like dirt and, the wanderer thought, alcohol—hung awkwardly from his lank frame, so thin it made Merle look like Dekker by comparison. It didn't take the wanderer long to find the reason for the shirt's strange fit as the man had apparently only managed to get one arm inside the sleeve of his shirt. The man had long hair, lank with sweat and smelling thickly of spilled liquor. He sported a dirty, unkempt beard with pieces of straw stuck in it. The wanderer thought he was in his early forties, though given his current state he looked closer to sixty.

"Mornin', Merle," Jessup said, wincing, one hand raised as if to block out the sun. "I didn't know you was back in town—tale was you up and absconded."

"Spell it," Merle said.

"What?"

"Never mind," Merle said. "I'd ask what you've been up to, Jessup, but it seems obvious enough that you've been in the drink again."

"What, me?" Jessup asked, blinking dumbly. "Naw, Merle, you got me all wrong—I gave up drinkin'."

"When, just now?"

"Haha, Merle. Funny as always."

"Well we all have our talents, don't we?" Merle asked, letting his gaze travel up and down the disheveled, half-clothed man's form.

"I was just taking a nap is all," Jessup said defensively. "You woke me."

"Sleeping it off, no doubt," Merle said, sighing. "Listen, Jessup, I need your help."

The man blinked. "Sorry?"

Merle sighed. "Your help, damnit. I need your help."

The man grinned. "Well, now, ain't that a thing? What can I do for you, Merle?"

"My friend here," Merle said, gesturing back at the wanderer, "he's got a horse that need's tendin', and a place to stay."

"And...you want him to stay here?" Jessup asked.

"Well, it's a damned stable, ain't it?"

"O-of course, of course it is," Jessup said. "But look, Mer, thing is...well, it's gonna cost you."

Merle sighed. "How much?"

Jessup considered that, biting his lip and avoiding Merle's eyes. "A gold coin ought to do it."

"*A gold?*" Merle demanded in shocked annoyance, and that was no great surprise, for normally such a service would cost a silver or two, and that would include oats or hay.

"I know it's a bit high, but, times being what they are—"

"It's not a *bit* high, Jess," Merle said, "but maybe you are. You're drunker than I thought if you think I'm going to pay you a gold coin for stabling a horse."

Jessup winced, clearing his throat. "Look, Mer, it ain't like that, me tryin' to rip you off or nothin'."

"No? Then why don't you tell me what it is like, Jess, because I'll tell ya, from this end it sure does look like you're tryin' to bend us over and without even takin' us out to dinner first."

The drunk man scratched at his beard, shaking his head. "Thing is...I messed up, Mer. Borrowed money I probably shouldn't have borrowed, truth to tell, and—"

"How much?"

"Well, you got to understand, I heard about an underground duel, a sure thing, they said. I was hurtin', you know, since my da's business went under—"

"You mean since you ran it under the ground."

"Anyway...it just, things being what they were, it didn't seem as though I had much choice except to—"

"How much, damn you?" Merle asked.

Jessup hung his head, giving it a shake. "Five gold."

"*Five gold?*" Merle demanded. "Are you out of your damned mind?" He pinched the bridge of his nose between his thumb and forefinger. "Forget it, never mind. How much is left?"

Jessup cleared his throat, shifting his feet, and Merle's eyes went wider still. "You lost all of it?"

"It was supposed to be a sure thing, Mer," Jessup said again. "And...look, I needed the money for—"

"I know damned well what you needed the money for, Jess. Just...damnit, who do you owe?"

The man glanced up at him from underneath his eyebrows, and Merle hissed. "Don't you dare fuckin' tell me. You didn't go to Haggarty. Tell me you're not that damned stupid, Jess."

"Go ahead and sit back and judge me, if you want, Merle," Jessup hissed. "Sure, maybe I made a mistake, but it was my mistake to make, and I'll pay for it like a man does."

Merle snorted. "Like a man does. Seems to me you're tryin' to make me be the one as does the payin'."

The man, Jessup, gave a sour expression at that. "I'm just tryin' to make it by, best I can, Merle. I know you think I'm a fool—maybe I even am one. I've fucked up—what, you don't think I know that? Well, I do. But all I can do is to try to be better. I was goin' to use the winnings to get my da's stables going again. Buy oats and hay and repair the damages, replace all the stall doors."

"I won't ask what happened to the stall doors," Merle said, "as I think I know already. But damnit, Jess, why didn't you just come to me? Why go to that criminal Haggarty? You know damned well what he does to folks that don't pay him."

"It was a *sure thing*, Merle!"

"If it was a damned sure thing you wouldn't be sittin' here hiding in the damned stables scared to answer the door, would you!?"

Jessup sighed. "You're right, Merle. It ain't your problem—two silver'll do fine."

"Oh?" Merle asked. "And if I pay you two silver, just how much are you going to have to pay Haggarty back when his goons coming looking for you? And they *will* come looking for you, Jess. Haggarty ain't the sort to let his ledger go untended."

"You think I don't know that?" Jessup snapped. "Anyway...with your two silver added in...I reckon...well. I'll have two silver."

"Fuck me running," Merle said, shaking his head. "Some of the dumbest folks in the world, Jess, got to touch the fire to see that it's hot, but it seems like your ass just keeps on reachin' back in, never mind how much you get burned." He fished into the pocket of his trousers, coming out with his coin purse and offering it to the man. "Take it—it's all I got. There's about three gold in there, though I don't know what good coin is to anyone these days—if you can't eat it or drink it it seems to me that it ain't worth nothin'."

"I said as much to Haggarty, but he has a different way of thinking," Jessup said, wincing. "Says that right now things might be tough but that they'll go back to normal again. Says that, when they do, the folks who have looked to the future are goin' to find themselves sittin' prettier than ever."

"Yeah, that's Haggarty alright," Merle said, "always lookin' to the future, figurin' out where the pitfalls are so he can make sure it's someone else falls in 'em, then maybe he can rob 'em blind while they're layin' there dyin'. That's all I got for now, but you hold on to it. I'm goin' to go check on Charlotte and Mack here directly. I think she's got some coin squirreled away—don't know how much, but I'll do what I can."

Jessup nodded, looking on the verge of tears. "Thanks, Mer. For everything. You're my best friend."

Merle snorted. "I'm your only friend, you bastard. Now, how about we get onto business?"

"Of course," the man, Jessup said. "So, where is he, this horse of yours? Let's see what we're working with."

Veikr moved forward, and the wanderer noted the drunk's eyes go wide as he began to tremble. "By the gods, it's...it's..."

"A horse," Merle said. "Damn, Jess, just how hard have you been hitting the drink?"

"No, Mer, you don't understand," Jessup said. "That ain't just any horse, not any more than a shark is just a fish or an eagle a bird. That there, Merle, is one of the Gyllir, the greatest breed of horses to ever walk the face of the world."

The wanderer felt a shock of surprise go through him at that, for it was the first time that Veikr had been recognized as what he was in over fifty years.

"What nonsense are you on about, Jessup?" Merle said. "It's a horse is all, and—"

"You're right," the wanderer said, stepping forward, aware of Merle giving him a confused look. "But tell me, how do you know of the Gyllir? It is a name that has been long forgotten by the world."

"Maybe by most, stranger," Jessup agreed, "but not by my pops. He had a love for horses unmatched by any man that ever breathed, I'd guess. Made it his business to know everything there was to know about them, to learn everything that could be learned—that included studyin' on the Gyllir, and it also included him makin' sure his son knew it all too, so that, when he died, I'd be able to run his stables and treat the horses the way they ought to be treated."

"I see," the wanderer said, making sure to keep his expression neutral for he saw the way the man was studying him, a vulnerableness in his gaze that was unmistakable. No doubt he waited for the wanderer to make the obvious, derisive joke about how poor of a job he had done looking after his father's stables.

When it was clear the wanderer wasn't going to, the man took a slow breath. "Anyhow, back then, I guess I was just about as crazy about horses as my father," Jessup said. "I'd have gladly spent an eternity listenin' to his stories and reckon I wasn't all that far from it. Not many of those stories were about the Gyllir—fact is there ain't much known about them and what is known is thought by most to be no more than myth, the inane ramblings of some ancient drunkard or a few hundred-year-old practical joke. Certainly I never really believed them. My father, though...he always did."

The man shook his head, moving forward to stare at Veikr in wonder, seemingly completely oblivious of his state of near undress or of the twenty or so people looking at him. He paused in front of Veikr, glancing at the wanderer. "They say the Gyllir are not just the strongest and biggest of all horses, but also the smartest, able to think as well, maybe even better than most men."

"I'm sure he'd agree with you," the wanderer said, and Veikr snorted, giving a shake of his head.

Jessup reached out a trembling hand toward Veikr's muzzle and then froze, glancing at the wanderer, "M-may I?"

"It's fine by me if it's fine by him."

The man turned back to Veikr. "May I?" he asked.

The horse watched him for a moment then bent so that he offered his muzzle to the man's attentions. Jessup grinned, looking in that moment not like a drunkard woken from an alcohol-induced slumber but like a young child encountering some mythical creature out of a storybook. He laid his hand on the horse's muzzle with a touch so gentle the wanderer wasn't entirely certain he touched him at all.

The man went on stroking Veikr's muzzle carefully, reverently, as if he thought the horse were made of glass or, perhaps—and the more the wanderer watched the closer he thought this was to the truth—as if he considered Veikr something almost holy, almost sacrosanct.

"I never would have thought..." Jessup said, his voice little more than a whisper. "I never would have thought to see one of the Gyllir myself. Why...all the stories say that they went extinct over a hundred years ago. Guess they were wrong."

"Not by much," the wanderer said sadly, looking at Veikr. "He is the last."

"The...the last?" Jessup asked.

"Yes."

"Ah, damn," the disheveled man said, looking even closer to tears than he had when speaking with Merle about his situation. "That's a tough thing to hear. Damn tough. Just wish my pa was here—he'd have lost his shit to see this fine horse of yours." He shook his head. "You're magnificent," he told Veikr, and the horse gave a noble shake of his head, glancing at the wanderer with what could only be smugness.

"So anyway, Jessup," Merle said, "what about it? Will you watch the horse or not?"

"O-of course I'll watch him," Jessup said as if Merle were insane. "I'll make sure he's got everything he could need or want, sir," he went on, turning to the wanderer, "you've got my word on it."

Merle snorted. "Like havin' a thief promise that he's just borrowin' your coin."

Jessup shot the man a scowl then turned back to the wanderer. "It's true my word don't mean much to most, not anymore. But there was a time when it did, and I swear to you, I won't let anythin' bad happen to this fine beast of yours 'less it happens to me first."

The wanderer glanced at Merle, and the other man shrugged. "It's up to you," the thin man said.

The wanderer shared a look with Veikr, the horse meeting his eyes, then giving a nod of his head at the man, Jessup. Jessup let out a mewling sound of surprise and shocked excitement.

"It sounds like Veikr's made his decision."

"Veikr," Jessup said in an amazed whisper as if the name was some magic spell. "Of the old tongue."

"He is an old horse," the wanderer said.

"It means...it means 'weakest,' doesn't it?"

The wanderer blinked, deciding that there was more to this drunk than he'd first thought. "So it does. And you said two silver, correct? To care for him?"

Jessup looked at him as if he were insane. "Forgive me, sir, but I won't take a copper penny of payment to watch this fine horse. If anythin', I ought to be payin' you. Any stablemaster worth his salt would count it a privilege to house him in his stables."

"Nevertheless," the wanderer said, "I think I must insist. After all, as you have observed he is no normal horse, and as such he requires more than normal attention. I can personally assure you from experience that he eats far more than a normal horse might."

The other man winced. "Very well, if you insist."

"I do."

The man took the proffered coins, putting them into the pocket of his limply hanging trousers. "I'll look after him as if he were my own," he assured the wanderer.

"I've seen how you take care of your own shit, Jess," Merle said, giving the man a smile to take some of the sting out of the words. "Better if you looked after him as if he were someone else's. And listen, just as long as that horse is under your roof—"

"No drinkin'," Jessup said. "I know, I know. I've screwed up plenty in the past, Merle, and likely I'll screw up plenty more in the future, but I can tell you now that, so far as this horse is concerned, I'll do what needs doin'."

Merle seemed impressed by that, and he nodded. "Soundin' a bit like the old Jessup. I wondered if he was still in there somewhere."

"So did I," the other man said, giving him a small, fragile smile.

The wanderer walked up to Veikr then, removing his pack from the horse's saddlebags and standing in front of him, the drunk man reluctantly giving way. "I'll be back soon," the wanderer told the horse. He found himself running a hand along the horse's muzzle much the same way the drunk had, careful and reverent all at once.

People were funny. Give them something fine, something beyond measure, of incalculable value, and they would cherish it, at least for a time. But in a week or a month, in a year or, in his case, a century, they would, sooner or later, become accustomed to that thing. It would just become a part of their lives and, in doing so, they would forget about its value, would begin to forget the privilege it was to possess it.

He didn't possess Veikr, for no man could possess a beast in truth, certainly not one so fine as the horse, but he'd enjoyed the privilege of his company for many years, was only alive because of it. And while he and the horse had been separated a few times recently, he found that this time, it was more difficult than those others for the man, Jessup, had reminded him of the true value of his friend.

"I'll be back to check on you as much as I can," he assured the horse, but the words were more for himself than Veikr.

Veikr gave a snort and a shake of his head, and the wanderer sighed, giving the horse's muzzle a pat. "Alright," he said. "Alright. I'll go. But I'll be back soon."

He turned to the man, Jessup, who nodded, approaching again with a timid, half bowed walk the way a man might approach a king. "If you will," he told the horse, "it's this way." The wanderer watched as the man led Veikr away, struggling with the sudden feeling that he would never see his friend again.

Don't be ridiculous, he told himself. *You have faced long odds before, the two of you, and you have always made it through.*

And that was true, but then it was also true that they had largely survived for the last hundred years by running, by Veikr's speed and

Veikr's wits and by the wanderer's ability to...well, to walk into a supply house and buy feed, mostly.

Now, though, they weren't running. They had chosen to stay, to fight, and so the risks they now faced were greater than any they had known before.

"Please, keep him safe," he said quietly, though he wasn't sure to whom he spoke, only that the words needed to be said, that, more than that, he needed to say them.

He was still staring at the stables when someone spoke from beside him. "Never knew Jessup to pass up coin. Must be some horse."

The wanderer turned to regard Merle. "He is."

"A Giller, that what he called it?"

"A Gyllir."

"Right. Anyway, I don't know much about horses, but even I can see he's a fine one. Just as anyone could see that he means a lot to you, don't he?"

"He means everything," the wanderer said simply.

Merle nodded. "Had a dog like that once, a mongrel, truth to tell, but I loved that son of a bitch as much as anything. Couldn't ride 'em though. Anyway, I wanted to thank you."

"For what?"

"Bein' kind. To Jessup, I mean. He's had a tough life, that one. Just about as tough as anyone, I reckon. I won't say he came out of it unscathed, for anyone with eyes to see knows better'n that. But then, I can't say that I'd have come out any better. Matter of fact, I think it likely I'd be a damn sight worse off, I was in his shoes."

"What happened to him?"

This from the wanderer's other side, and he and Merle turned to see Dekker and Clint standing there. The thin man grunted. "You wouldn't believe it, seein' 'em now, but Jessup used to be a damned fine duelist. Best I ever saw, and that's the truth."

"That fella?" Dekker asked in disbelief.

"Oh yes," Merle said. "Though that was, what? Fifteen years ago, I'd guess. Jessup was doin' quite well for himself, fightin' in the tournaments around Celes, travelin' to other cities, too. Got him a wife. A fine woman. Mattie was a beauty, inside and out. Jessup loved her just about as much as a man can love anything. And, stranger still—she loved him back. They had them a nice house, too, and if it weren't a mansion then it was a mansion's close cousin, that's sure."

"Sounds like they were livin' the dream," Dekker said.

"Aye, they were," Merle said quietly, staring at the stables. "At least, that was, until Jessup fought one particular up and coming duelist."

"He was beaten?" Clint asked.

"No," Merle said. "No, far from it. It was clear soon as the match started that this young man—this young *noble*man who had been puffed up by all of his fellows as being the next, greatest duelist—was terribly outmatched. Don't get me wrong—he was good. Damn good. Only, Jessup wasn't good—he was amazing. He was as different from the fella he was matched against as that horse of yours is from a normal breed," he told the wanderer.

"So...he won, then?" Dekker asked, confused.

"Aye, and that handily," Merle said. "Why, I'd say he could have taken on six copies of the fella and still come out the victor. Anyway, the whole thing was over in less than five minutes, and we— Jessup's friends and family—back when he *had* friends and family, that is, celebrated. You see, it was a big bout, all blown up by the nobles and all, lot of money riding on it. Enough that Jessup might have had to sell that almost-mansion of his, if'n he lost. Enough that he wasn't goin' to bet on it at all 'til Mattie made him."

"But he didn't lose," Clint said.

"No," Merle said slowly, shaking his head, a grim expression of sadness on his face, "no, he did not. Better if he had, though. You see, that fella, the young, puffed-up nobleman, convinced of his own greatness? Well, he got it in mind that it was a fluke or that Jessup had cheated him somehow. A foolish notion, of course, for anyone who'd been there knew he'd been beaten fairly and nearly the whole city'd been there. But then there are few things more difficult in the world than separating a fool from his foolishness or a prideful man from his pride, and this fella was both."

Merle seemed overcome with emotion then, going silent for a time, and though the wanderer thought he knew well enough where this was headed—or at least had a general idea of it—he nodded. "Go on, if you want," he told the thin man, "but know that you don't have to."

Merle gave him a grateful nod. "Anyway," he said, clearing his throat, "this fella, he wanted to beat Jessup—wanted to beat him just as bad as anything, I reckon. Figured, I s'pose, that it'd be a salve for his bruised pride. Only, as much as he went around claimin' that Jess had cheated and that he could beat him in a fair fight, that didn't stop him from bringing four of his boys with him when he came upon Jessup, meanin' to find himself a rematch. Jessup was out with Mattie that day, walking the streets of the city, shopping at the shops. Didn't even have his sword on 'em, but it didn't matter. Jessup borrowed a broom from one of the nearby shops."

"A broom," Dekker repeated, glancing back at the stables with something like wonder.

"That's right," Merle said. "I wasn't there for that one, but everyone I spoke to agreed that they ain't never seen a broom used that way before or since, ain't ever thought it *could* be used that way. Said he did with that broom what anyone does with a broom— swept out the trash, cleaned up the street. Sent that nobleman fella and his cronies runnin'. I reckon his pride weren't just wounded then but dyin' a painful death. Figured, when I heard of it, that he must have learned his lesson, for there ain't no teacher quite as good as pain. Only..."

"Only he didn't learn his lesson," the wanderer said.

Merle glanced at him. "He did not. We all laughed about it at the time, all save Jessup. He didn't laugh. Maybe even then he knew that the nobleman wouldn't let it go...I don't know. But for us, his friends and all, it felt mostly just like a game. Weren't no game to the nobleman, though. He wasn't done. Done with Jessup, maybe, but one day, while Jessup was out at another match and his wife home alone, that nobleman and some of his cronies showed up at his house."

"No," Dekker said, his voice a hoarse growl.

"Yeah," Merle said, his own voice little more than a dry croak. "Showed up and...well. Did to Mattie what they couldn't do to Jessup. Left her there so he'd find her and find her he did. She'd put up a fight—Mattie was kind, but she had a fire in her. One of the fellas who'd broke into their house didn't leave with the others, wouldn't ever be leavin' anywhere again. But then...neither would Mattie. Jessup found her, dead, and I guess he just about went crazy. He tracked down that nobleman and his cronies—knew it was him on account of he recognized the dead man lyin' in his entry way. Found 'em at a tavern, if you can believe it. Drinkin' and celebratin' I s'pose, though what such as they might celebrate, I've no idea."

He shook his head grimly, his eyes taking on a distant, far away look as he traveled back through the grim memories. "Jessup was always a kind man, patient to a fault, I used to think. Soft spoken and soft actin', like his father. I always thought it funny, that, considerin' what he did for a livin', that he was the best duelist I ever saw, and competed—and won—in plenty of jousts, too. Anyway…he wasn't kind that day. Not to the nobleman and not to the fellas he had with him—five in all. Six it'd been when they set out, but then Mattie had accounted for that last with a firepoker in the eye—not the sort of thing a fella shrugs off. Jessup *did* have his sword on 'em then, and like a skilled artist wielding a brush like no one else can, he went to work. The men fought, of course, at least at first—didn't make no difference, though. To a man of Jessup's skill—not that there are many—they were like children wavin' toy swords about."

"After a bit, they musta realized the truth of that. You see, Jessup could have beaten 'em fast, could have killed 'em fast, but he took his time about it. Cut 'em apart piece by piece, bit by bit. Way I hear it, the fight leaked out of those fellas pretty quick, right along with their blood. For them, the whole affair changed from a fight to them tryin' to flee any which way they could, to get away from the demon with the bloody blade. Only…Jessup was fast. Real fast. Too fast for those poor bastards. He cut them down and cut them up, left ribbons of 'em on the floor. By the time he was finished, it would have been damn near impossible for anybody to know which part went where. I don't reckon an undertaker coulda put 'em back together again 'less he had a map."

"Damn," Dekker breathed. Then, after a moment. "Damn."

"Surprised he's not wasting away in some cell," Clint said.

"Or whetting a hangman's axe," Dekker agreed.

"Likely he would have—after all, that nobleman's family was rich indeed, powerful, too. I don't doubt the guards would have hauled Jessup off to rot in the dungeons or killed him then and there. Only, by the time someone went and fetched 'em, Jessup was long gone, as was any sign he'd been there."

"Any sign?" Dekker said, his voice thick with disbelief. "But...you said it happened in a tavern common room, didn't you? Folks had to have seen."

"Oh, there were plenty of witnesses," Merle said. "Only, you see, that nobleman and those sons of bitches who'd helped him at his bloody work, they might have chosen any tavern in the city to do their celebrating. Instead they chose the closest one. Thing is, the folks at the Hangman knew Jessup. After all, he'd been coming in there for years. Not to drink, mind, at least not then—he said it dulled his wits and his sword, too. No, just to socialize, mostly at my urging. Anyway, those folks at the Hangman, they knew Jessup. Knew Mattie too. So, you see, it weren't no problem findin' witnesses—the Hangman was always packed back then. The problem was finding any witness who would tell the guards what they saw."

He shook his head, something like wonder on his face. "Thirty, forty people in the tavern that night when Jessup...well. When he done what he done. Some of 'em his friends, some of 'em not, some folks he'd even got into it with a time or two—folks from when he and I were kids who knew us, grew up poor like we did and were sour that he weren't livin' hand to mouth no more. Yet for all those people, there wasn't a single one who seemed to have got a clear look at the fella that came in and did for those men. Not a single soul."

"But...but surely, later," Declan said, "I mean...when they found out about his wife—surely they would have put two and two together."

"Maybe you're right—maybe they did." Merle shook his head. "Shit, I figured back then they must've. I mean, that nobleman, he hadn't made any effort to hide what he thought of Jessup. I reckon he'd told it to just about anybody who'd listen. S'pose it'd be a bit of a hard pill to swallow to think that Jessup's wife gets murdered and, on the same night, that nobleman and several of his cronies find themselves cut to ribbons. Certainly there were quite a few people—me among them—who urged Jessup to go into hiding, to leave his house and things behind. He wouldn't, though. You see, it wasn't just his house in his mind—it was Mattie's house. And they weren't his things but the things of his departed wife, all he had left of her. No, I don't reckon a team of horses could have dragged him away from that place. So he was sitting right there, ready for the guards to scoop him up, if they meant to. Only...it seemed they didn't."

"But...why?" Clint asked.

Merle shook his head slowly. "I don't know. I thought about that a lot, then and since then. Maybe they were aware of all that had happened, figured that the nobleman got what was comin' to him. I'd like to believe that—it'd go a long ways toward restorin' my faith in this shit show of humanity. But I'm afraid I just don't. Knowing people like I do—knowing city guardsmen like I do, I figure there musta been another reason. I mean, sure, there are a few good ones, but they're as rare as a virgin whore, if you ask me. Most folks become guardsmen, they do it for a reason. After all, ain't nobody better placed to impinge on another man's liberties, his freedoms, than the very man meant to protect them."

"I think you're bein' a little hard there, fella," Dekker said. "I've known some good men who chose to be guardsmen and soldiers because they looked around at the world and saw plenty worth protectin', figured they'd help do it."

"Maybe," Merle said, but he didn't sound convinced. "Myself, I don't see a whole lot worth getting out of bed for, not anymore. At least not beyond the walls of my own home."

"But if you don't think it was the guards' sense of justice that kept them from imprisoning or executing him...then what?" the wanderer asked.

"Honest?" Merle said, considering. "I think they were scared."

"Scared?" Dekker said. "Look," he went on, glancing at the stables, "I don't care how good that bastard was with a blade—and I don't doubt your word on it—no one could take on an entire city's worth of city guardsmen, if they came at him." He raised an eyebrow at the wanderer. "Well. No one that hasn't lived more than a hundred years and all of that as a bit of an asshole anyway."

"Probably you're right," Merle said, "though I don't doubt quite a few of those bastards would end the day with more holes in 'em then they started it. It would have been a damn show, that's for sure. Anyway, it's one that we never got a chance to see. See, it weren't just Jessup the guardsmen had to fear—it was just about every man, woman, and child in the poor district. Shit, I expect that if it had come to it, the damned dogs and cats woulda shown up, showin' their support with their teeth and claws. You see, Jessup's family might have had more than most in the poor quarter—certainly his pa's stables made enough that they could have moved to another part of the city, put on airs. After all, his da ran the best stable in the city, took such good care of the horses he tended that even noblemen found themselves venturin', many for the first time in their lives, into the poor quarter to make use of his services."

"Don't see what that has to do with anything else," Dekker said, not rudely but simply honestly.

"Well, I say all that to say that Jessup and his da, they were well-liked around these parts. Made plenty of coin, they did, but they used a lot of that to help others, and they never forgot who they were, where they came from. Shit, I don't suppose I could even guess at how many times his da and, after he was gone, Jessup himself, helped folks in need. If he had another passion besides duelin', that was it, and it was one Mattie, his wife, shared. They helped the people of the poor district, and so, when it came to it, the people of the poor district helped Jessup, coverin' for him. And the guards, while they might be assholes—or not—" he said with an aside glance to Dekker, "what they certainly ain't is fools. Why, a fella didn't have to look too close to see the way the land lay, and I reckon they decided that if they tried to take Jessup in or execute him they'd have a riot on their hands. Figured, in the end, it was better to let it lie, to leave him alone. Though," he went on, grimly, glancing back at the stables with an unmistakable expression of sadness, "if you ask me, they didn't do him no favors. A man loses everything he loves, particularly when he loves it as hard as Jessie loved Mattie...well. What he does after that ain't livin'—it's lingerin'. That was years gone now, and I don't reckon Jess has shown a spark of life since, at least not until he seen that horse of yours. But then I don't doubt he'll drown that spark just as soon as he can find a place to buy some drink." He shook his head grimly. "Anyway, enough about old pains, old tragedies—we're facin' plenty enough now, we don't need to go borrowin' from the past."

The wanderer nodded, his eyes trained on the stables. He wished there was something he could do for the man Jessup, something he could say, but even had he known the words there was simply no time. The longer they stayed in one place, the better the chances that the enemy would discover their presence in Celes.

If they were lucky, their entrance into the city wouldn't have been remarked upon, and their presence was still unknown to the enemy. But then, Tactician had taught him long ago that only a fool relied on the world givin' him luck—a wise man made his own.

"So...what now?" Dekker asked, turning to the wanderer.

The wanderer glanced around at their group of nearly twenty people, his eyes settling on Ella and her daughter, Sarah, as he considered the question. He wanted to start investigating what was happening in Celes and its outward areas—he could practically see Clint hopping with eagerness to find out what had happened to his friends—but there was something to see to first. "We need somewhere to stay," he said.

Dekker followed his gaze to his family and nodded slowly. "Right," he said, scratching at his chin. "Well, let's see..." He looked to Clint. "What about the Tankard?" the big man asked, clearly referring to the tavern where the wanderer had first met Clint, searching for the leader of the Perishables so that he might dissuade him from his mission of going against the Eternals. In the end, he had been the one whose mind had been changed.

Clint considered Dekker's question then, after a moment, gave a single nod. "It'll be cramped—the Tankard ain't exactly big, but then I suppose there's worse things than being cramped."

"Sure, like gettin' our heads lopped off," Dekker agreed.

"Wait a minute," Merle said, his gaze traveling between the two men, "you don't mean the Spilled Tankard, do you?"

"Aye, that's the one," Dekker said. "You know it?"

"Sure I know it," Merle said. "Not that there's much to know—not anymore, at least."

Clint frowned. "What do you mean by that?"

"I mean it's gone, that's what," Merle said. "Leastways everything but bits and pieces of the foundation—what the flames didn't take."

"You mean...the Tankard caught fire?" Clint asked, stunned.

"Aye," Merle said. "Went up in a damn blaze, it did."

"Shit," Dekker said. "Do they know what the cause was?"

"I don't reckon. If they ever found who was responsible they never said."

Clint turned to regard the wanderer. "Do you think..."

"Yes," the wanderer said, nodding slowly. "I do." To him, it was clear enough what had happened. When they had left Celes months ago, they had been being pursued by a band of Revenants, as well as two Unseen. Not all of those Perishables who had tried to escape the city with them had made it out, and it seemed clear that some of those who had failed to escape had not been killed. At least not at first. The enemy would have left a few alive long enough to ask them questions and ask them hard. Hard enough that anyone would answer.

Clint nodded grimly, a dark expression on his face that said he had reached a similar conclusion.

"What about Sammy's?" Dekker asked.

"Sammy's Inn, you mean?" Merle asked.

"Aye, that's right," the big man said, sounding a little defensive. "Sure, Sammy might be a bit of a handful, but the place is plenty big enough to accommodate us. Sammy might overcharge us, but he'll be happy enough to let us stay and that without asking any questions. As good a choice as any."

"Sure, it would be as good of a choice as any," Merle said. "If it was still open."

"Wait a minute," Dekker said. "You mean to tell me Sammy closed up shop? Bullshit," he went on. "Sammy might have been an ass but he loved that place. Nothing short of murder'd make him close it."

"Murder," Merle said, "or disappearing."

The big man's eyebrows drew down into a frown. "What do you mean, 'disappearing'?"

"Sammy vanished a few weeks ago. The neighborhood kids noticed first."

"Sure, they would," Dekker said quietly. "Probably wonder why he wasn't sittin' out front, throwin' rocks at 'em."

"That's right," Merle agreed.

"But...he disappeared?" the big man asked. "I have a hard time believing that. Whatever else he was, Sammy wasn't a pushover. Nor was he quiet. Not the type of man to be led away meekly into the night."

"Maybe not, but he's disappeared just the same, and he ain't the only one. Like I told you before, disappearin's been goin' around."

He glanced between the two men. "How long you say you been gone again?"

"Just a couple months," Dekker said. "No more than that."

Merle grunted. "Damn. Is that all it's been since things went to shit? Seems like a lifetime." He shook his head. "Damn sure didn't take long for things to fall apart."

"It never does," the wanderer said quietly.

"Well, I'm running out of ideas," Dekker said.

"Look," Merle said, "I've got to go...my wife and child—"

"You don't need to explain yourself to us," the wanderer said. "We really appreciate all that you've done, getting us in the city."

"I wouldn't thank me just yet," Merle said. "After all, you just got here—you don't have any idea of the shit show Celes has become in recent days." He gave a slight bow then hesitated, turning back. "Look," he went on, meeting the wanderer's eyes, a hard cast to his own. "I meant what I said. I want the sons of bitches responsible for all this just as much as anybody else. You tell me where you're goin' to be, I'll meet you there—just as soon as I know my wife and son are alright."

Dekker, Clint, and the wanderer all shared a look, each of them trying to think of somewhere that might accommodate the number of people with them while also not revealing their whereabouts to the enemy.

For his part, the wanderer could think of nothing, despite his best efforts. After all, he was not accustomed to traveling with so many people, was far more used to traveling alone. A man alone might find a place to hide easily enough, but the twenty people with them would be far more difficult. He was still thinking, still coming up empty, when Clint spoke.

"Well..." the Perishables' leader said in a voice that sounded reluctant, "that...it might be that I know a place that could work."

"If it ain't burned or closed up," Dekker grumbled.

"Right..." Clint said slowly.

"Well, out with it, man. Unless you mean to hang around out here until some of those damned shadow-things Ungr told us about show up."

The Perishable's leader turned to Merle. "You know Pearl's?"

The name didn't sound familiar to the wanderer, but the thin man clearly recognized it, blinking. "You mean to take them to Pearl's?" he asked in apparent surprise.

"Better than the street," the Perishables' leader answered. "Anyway, do you know where it is?"

The thin man gave a small grin. "Been a while since I been, but aye, I think I can find my way back easily enough."

He nodded to three men. "I'll be by tonight, tomorrow at the latest." He gave a wink. "Tell 'em to leave a light on for me, will ya?"

And with that, Merle turned and walked away.

"Just what are the two of you on about?" Dekker asked.

"I…I'm not sure what you're asking," Clint asked, avoiding the wanderer and the big man's gazes.

"What I'm asking is, why did he just strut away with a smirk like you just told a joke?"

Clint winced, giving his head a shake, and if it was a joke it was one that he didn't find funny, not at all. "Come on," he said in a grim tone of voice like a man heading toward the executioner's block. "Pearl's is this way."

CHAPTER ELEVEN

THE PERISHABLES' LEADER might have been reticent to answer Dekker's inquiries, but they didn't have to wait long to figure out what had struck Merle as so funny.

As they made their way through the city the wanderer and those with him moved in small groups so as to arouse less suspicion by anyone that noted them. A precaution that was likely unnecessary, as what few people traveled the city streets seemed far more concerned with not being noticed themselves than anything else, skittering away into alleys and side streets like rats fleeing from a storm when they saw the wanderer and the others.

The wanderer had spent a significant amount of time in Celes when training with Soldier, and having been born and rasied in a backwater village, he had always been shocked and excited by the vibrant, constantly moving life of the capital city. It had always seemed to him that no matter what time of the day or night, the streets were teeming with men and women and children. Hundreds, thousands of families going about their lives.

Now, though, those streets were desolate, or at least nearly so. He remembered a time, long ago, when he and Soldier had been staring out one of the high windows of his castle at the city below, full of people. The lifeblood of the city, the man had called them. He had been teaching the wanderer a lesson about leadership—or at least trying to. Explaining that it was not a city's castle or leader, nor its soldiers and guards, nobles or merchants, which made it thrive, which kept it alive. Instead, it was its regular citizens. The people who worked and lived within it.

If that were true—and the wanderer believed that it was—then indeed the city of Celes was sick. And maybe not just sick...maybe dying. And those men and women he saw giving them furtive glances as Clint led them toward the poor district were no more than the vultures and flies gathering at the signs of that death, waiting to feast upon the remains of what had once been one of the finest cities in the world.

The walk depressed him, seeing a city he had once loved fallen to disrepair, most of its shops and buildings boarded up, windows and doors both. Trash and filth littered the street. As Clint led them down one side street they saw the corpse of a mongrel dog that looked as if something—or some*one*—had taken bites out of it. Anything living was always in a state of dying, of course, but a city—unlike a person—might be renewed, its life, as it was, extended pretty much indefinitely. Such renewing was done by the guards and the street cleaners, by the shopkeepers and the people who visited their shops, but now those renewers, it seemed, had, like a healer deciding their patient's affliction was beyond their ability to cure, given up.

Each boarded window, each looted building or piece of detritus that littered the street felt like a stab in the wanderer's gut, and he was glad when they finally turned a corner and Clint stopped, nodding at a building across the street. "There it is," he said reluctantly. "That's Pearl's."

The wanderer glanced over at Dekker and the two shared a look, the big man giving a small grin. Meanwhile, Ella let out a small, surprised gasp and snatched up her daughter, hugging her to her chest and putting one hand on the back of her head, burying it in her shoulder.

"Mommy," Sarah said, her voice muffled, "why didn't that lady have a shirt on? Isn't she cold?"

"I'd say, based on all the evidence," Dekker said, grinning wider as he looked up at the second story window where the woman in question lounged, "that she's feeling at least a bit...nippy."

"*Dekker!*" Ella said, sounding scandalized as she slapped her husband on the shoulder.

Dekker, meanwhile, grunted a laugh. "Oh, come on, love. That's a good one, and you know it. Besides, don't you worry none. She ain't got nothing on y—"

"Finish that sentence, husband mine," Ella said, her voice low and menacing, "and you'll regret it. Just as you'll regret it if your eyes don't find something else to look at and quickly."

Dekker cleared his throat at that, pulling his gaze away from the woman in the window. "Sorry, El," he said. "It...it's hard, not to look, you know, what with it being on display like that. Seems almost...rude to ignore it, don't it?"

"If you think that's rude then you'd love what's going through my mind right about now."

Dekker cleared his throat again, glancing at Clint with a scowl as if to say this was all the Perishables' leader fault. "See what you done, Clint? You got me in trouble—hope you're happy. A brothel, man? You bring us to a damned brothel?"

"It's big enough for all of us," Clint said defensively, though the wanderer didn't miss the way he avoided the big man's gaze.

"Yeah, so's a mass grave," Dekker countered, shooting an uneasy glance at his wife. "That don't mean we ought to go jumpin' in, does it? Anyway, I don't know if you're aware or not, but brothels ain't into renting rooms—at least not for anything but an hour or so, that is."

"Know a lot about brothels, do you?" This from Ella, her voice low and dangerous, and Dekker's eyes went wide like a man who has just stepped, unwittingly, into a trap. Which, of course, he had.

"That's not...that is...I mean—"

"I think what Dekker is trying to say," the wanderer said, deciding to end the big man's suffering and never mind how much he enjoyed watching it, "is that brothels are not in the habit of accommodating men and women who intend to stay for any significant length of time."

"Yeah, that's it," Dekker said, still avoiding his wife's gaze. "All I meant was, brothel owners—I've *heard*—" he added quickly, "focus on turnaround time. You know, the more swinging d—"

"*Dekker,*" his wife warned.

"Doors," the big man spurted, "I was going to say doors. The more swinging doors, the more coin is made."

The wanderer grinned as Dekker fidgeted under his wife's scowl, then turned to Clint. "He's right," he said. "How do you know that he—the brothel owner, that is—will let us stay?"

"She," Clint corrected. "Pearl's the owner."

"Ah," Dekker said, "and here I thought the name meant..." He glanced at his wife, saw her watching him, then cleared his throat. "Never mind."

"And you know this Pearl?" the wanderer asked.

"I did," Clint agreed. "Once. But...that was a long time ago."

"And the two of you, you're close?"

Clint winced. "We were, once. It...it's a bit complicated."

"My experience, when it comes to women, it always is," Dekker said, obviously avoiding looking at his wife. "Anyway, do you think she'd even let us stay?"

"I think so, yes," Clint said.

The three men lapsed into thoughtful silence then as they considered it. "Look," Clint said, "if I thought there was a better option, I wouldn't have brought us here. But Pearl...she's a good woman, and I trust her. She won't give us up or anything of that sort."

The wanderer nodded, glancing at Dekker, waiting to hear the big man's thoughts.

"Thing is," Dekker said, "I ain't even sure we could afford it. I mean...how much coin do we have? Brothels are expensive—" He paused, clearing his throat. "Or so I've heard. And that's when a fella is payin' for an hour, maybe two if he's feelin' particularly...ambitious. I ain't all that sure I want to calculate what it'd run to stay at one for any length of time."

"Probably best if you leave the calculating of brothel times to others, dear," Ella said, and though the words themselves were not threatening, her tone dripped with danger.

"I wouldn't worry about that none," Clint said. "My guess, Pearl ain't gonna charge us any coin."

"Damn," Dekker said. "Two of you must have been close if you reckon she'll be willin' to let us stay for free."

"Oh, I never said for free," Clint said. "Been a while, I'll admit, but if I know Pearl, there'll be a price alright. With Pearl, there always is."

"Soundin' better and better by the minute, Clint," Dekker said sarcastically.

"It's the best choice we got," Clint said. "Mostly, you know, considerin' it's the only one. Or has one of you bastards been hidin' an inn inside your trousers and just hadn't let on?"

"Well, I ain't sayin' it's the size of a *building,* mind," Dekker said, "but—"

"Shut up, Dekker," Ella said.

"Yes ma'am," he said instantly.

After a moment, they all looked toward the wanderer, as always leaving the final decision to him. Trusting in him to make the right one. He considered, then finally nodded. "Clint's right—it isn't exactly as if we're spoiled for choice, and the sooner we can get off the street the better. We've been lucky so far, but a man can't count on luck anymore than he can count on sunshine, or so I was taught. Besides, if Clint says she can be trusted, that's good enough for me."

The Perishables' leader gave a smile at that. "Thanks, Ungr. That...that means quite a bit."

"Oh, don't be too flattered, Clint," Dekker said. "This bastard's just eager to set his foot through that brothel door, that's all."

"He'd better be the only one," Ella warned.

Dekker glanced at Clint. "You sure you don't know a church or somethin' we might stay at?"

"I'm sure," Clint said grinning.

"Well, damn," Dekker said with mock regret. "I s'pose it'll have to be the brothel then."

The big man was grinning, his wife scowling, and the wanderer thought that before someone got murdered, it would be best to get moving on, so he nodded to Clint. "Lead the way."

"Will do."

CHAPTER TWELVE

THE BROTHEL DOOR opened into a hallway the walls of which were draped with velvet cloth, red and orange, sumptuous colors that gave the entryway a warm, inviting feeling.

They followed Clint down to where two men, not quite as large as Dekker but not far from it, stood on either side of a doorway their arms crossed. The two guards—or perhaps bouncers would have been closer to the truth, based on their bulbous noses and cauliflower ears, proof that they'd participated in more than a few fist fights—stood watching them come with expressions that, if they weren't exactly hostile, were also not far from it.

"Welcome to Pearl's," one man said in a growl that sounded like it might as easily have issued from the throat of a bear.

"Thanks," Clint said, starting past him but stopping abruptly as the man stuck out an arm that looked more like a tree trunk than anything belonging to a normal human, barring his path.

"Not so fast," the man said. "Ain't no weapons allowed inside. Better for the girls. Better for you. Understand?"

"I understand," Clint said.

"You can leave 'em there," the man said, nodding his head at several tables lining one side of the hall where a few sheathed daggers and one sword lay. "They'll be waitin' on you when you return."

"We're to take your word on it, are we?" Dekker asked.

"That's right."

Clint glanced at Dekker and the wanderer, then he nodded to the Perishables, and those who had them began removing their swords and crossbows. The wanderer removed his own sword from his back, placing it on the table along with the assorted weapons of the Perishables before they all turned back to the big man.

"I'll have the blade at your back, too," the big man said, jerking his chin at the wanderer and the cursed blade in its scabbard. He started forward, and the wanderer shook his head.

"No."

The word was out of his mouth before he realized it, and he immediately regretted it. "I do not mean any harm, but this blade...it is my burden."

"You don't mean any harm. We're to take your word on it, are we?" he asked, giving a small smile that held no humor.

"That's right," the wanderer said, echoing the man's words to Dekker a moment ago.

"And if my friend and I decided we were going to have that blade, whether you liked it or not?" the first asked, the second only grinning widely as if he could think of nothing he'd enjoy more.

"Then we're all in for a bad day," the wanderer said calmly.

"Look," Clint said, "we don't want any trouble. It's just...that blade, well, it's really important to him see."

"Sentimental value, is it?" the bouncer asked.

"Say that it is," the wanderer said.

The bouncer watched him for several seconds then gave a small shake of his head. "The balls on you. You come here lookin' for trouble, that it?"

"No."

"Could have fooled me."

"The blade is important to me."

"The rules are important to me," the first man countered. "So, if you want to keep your blade, that's fine—fine as a fiddle, my pa'd say. You can keep it. But you can also keep your ass outside. We clear?"

"Very well," the wanderer said, glancing at Clint and Dekker, "I'll wait here, and—"

"*Give up the sword, fucker.*"

The wanderer turned back in time to see the second guard—who up to that point, hadn't spoken—rush toward him, grabbing hold of his shirt.

The wanderer's body reacted before his mind had fully caught up. The man was big, at least a hundred pounds heavier than the wanderer himself, thick with muscle, but as big as he was, his knees, like every other man's, were just cartilage and bone and joints. And his toes—like everybody's toes—did not take kindly to being stomped on, a fact that was proven as the wanderer brought his heel down on the man's foot, and he bellowed in pain, his grip loosening. Before he could react, the wanderer stepped inside his guard, giving a hard—but not *too* hard—kick to the side of the man's leg, and he hissed as his knee buckled, bringing his face down at the perfect moment to catch the wanderer's fist in his temple.

The man let out a breathy groan and collapsed to the ground at the wanderer's feet.

It all happened fast, a few seconds, no more than that, and for a moment silence reigned as everyone took in what had transpired.

The moment of silence, of shocked stillness, stretched then, finally broke.

"Damn," Dekker breathed.

"Son of a bitch," Clint said.

"Wish you hadn't have done that," the still-conscious bouncer said with a note of what sounded like genuine regret as he withdrew a two-foot-long black truncheon from his waist. "Here we were, havin' a nice conversation, and you had to go and get violent."

He took a step forward. Only one step, but it was enough for the wanderer to take his measure, and he knew that this man, at least, would not so be so easily dealt with as his companion. He knelt, slightly, letting his knees bend, and brought his hands up as the man started toward him.

The bouncer managed only two more steps, though, before a voice rang out from somewhere beyond the wanderer's sight.

"Just what in the name of all the Eternals is going on here?"

A woman's voice, ringing with a mixture of authority and outrage, and the wanderer's companions and the bouncer froze at the power, the command in that voice. Even the wanderer found himself tensing at the sound and had to resist the urge to stare at his feet and hunch his head like a turtle seeking shelter in its shell.

A moment of silent stillness once more, one even greater than that which had followed the wanderer knocking the first bouncer unconscious. And into that stunned silence, from somewhere beyond the wanderer's sight, deep in the brothel, strode a woman.

Though in truth the first impression of her the wanderer got was that she was less a woman and more a force of nature, like a tornado or a thunderstorm. She reminded the wanderer of Joan, a fierce independence to her that a man could see at a glance, though in truth she looked nothing like Joan.

Joan had stood tall and never mind that she had been no more than a touch over five-feet high. This woman, though, was six feet at the least, and where Joan's hair had been long and red, like fire flowing down her shoulders, this newcomer's hair, save for a silver streak going through the middle of it, was as black as night and pulled back into a tight ponytail.

She was not beautiful in the largely-accepted sense that the nobles and peasants alike seemed to seek—the diminutive, dainty form. For there was nothing diminutive or dainty about the woman, yet her features were fine and pleasant, though, just then, those features were turned into a scowl as she paused a short distance away from where they all stood, her hands on her hips.

She looked like an annoyed mother preparing to discipline a gaggle of badly-behaved children, and despite a hundred years and more of fighting, despite all his training and mastery of the sword and various other weapons, despite the fact that he was likely a hundred years her senior, in that moment, the wanderer *felt* like a child.

"Just what is the meaning of all this racket?" the woman demanded, glancing around at each of them, and each of them, Perishable and bouncer alike, avoided her gaze.

Even Dekker, who the wanderer had seen face down creatures that most wouldn't believe existed without fear, fidgeted, clearly uncomfortable. When the woman turned in his direction, he managed to avoid looking away but only did so with an obvious effort.

"Well, Shayne?" she said. "Is something happening?" she went on, glancing meaningfully at the truncheon the man still held in a loose grip. "Or is it that you're just happy to see me?"

"Forgive me, ma'am," the big man said, "it was only—"

"Hold that thought, Shayne," the woman said, holding up a hand as she stared at Clint. "Is it really you?" she asked, her voice not sounding imposing or threatening now but confused, perhaps even a little frightened.

Clint met her gaze, some powerful emotion dancing in his eyes. "It's me, Pearl," he said, his voice soft and low.

The woman moved slowly toward him, as if walking through water, seeming almost as if she were being pulled along by some invisible string. She came to stand in front of him, stopping only inches away, and the wanderer noted absently, as she did, that she actually stood a couple of inches taller than the Perishable leader.

"You came back," she said, her voice little more than a whisper.

Clint gave the woman a smile that seemed to the wanderer to be made of glass. "Well, I said I would…didn't I?"

"Yes," she said. "Yes, you did."

They continued to stand that way for several seconds, watching each other. Then, as abruptly as she had appeared, the woman reached up and slapped Clint across the face, the sound of it like a bell ringing in the silence.

The wanderer shared a troubled look with Dekker at that. He didn't know what sort of past Clint shared with the imposing woman, but if she kicked them out, they had nowhere else to go, and without somewhere to hide it was only a matter of time before they were marked by an agent of the enemy.

He was aware of the bouncer still standing with his truncheon gripped in his hand, looking to the woman like a dog waiting for a command from its master. He was aware, also, of two more men, as big as the other, that had followed the woman as she came up and now stood behind her, their thick arms crossed in front of their chests, scowling at the wanderer and those with him.

He glanced at where his sword lay on the table, wondering if he could get it in time if they decided to attack and doubting it. He still had the cursed blade at his back, it was true, but only a complete fool would draw it so close to the enemy. So he waited for what the woman would do, waited for her to give a shout and send the men— and no doubt others that waited beyond his sight in the brothel— on the attack.

Only, the woman gave no shout, and the men did not move forward to attack. Instead, she stared at Clint with an expression that was, indeed angry but more than that, hurt. "You're late," she said. "About five years late."

"I know," he said. "And I'm sorry."

"Will your sorry reverse the last five years? Will it take away five years of hurt?"

"No," he said. "It won't."

"Then you can keep it, for what good is it to me?" she asked. She sighed heavily. "It's good to see you, Clint."

"It's good to see you too, Pearl," the Perishable's leader said. "I've missed you."

The woman seemed to tense at that, as if struck. "Not too much apparently," she said. Clint opened his mouth to speak, and she waved a hand, dismissing it. "Forget it. You had a long time to make your excuses—I will not hear them now. Instead," she went on, her gaze traveling to the wanderer and those with him, "why don't you tell me why you have chosen now of all times to show back up in my life? As if I don't have enough problems already that I'm having to borrow them from my past?"

"What problems?" Clint asked.

"What problems?" she said as if he were a fool. "What, Clint, did you walk here with your eyes closed, that it? Did you stop your nose so you couldn't smell the decay of this dying city, cover your ears so you couldn't hear the cries of the suffering?"

"Listen...Pearl," Clint said, "those problems...what's happening with Celes, I mean...they're why we're here."

"Ah," she said, nodding slowly, her expression hurt again. "I suppose it couldn't be any other reason."

Clint winced at that. "Pearl, that's not what I—"

She waved her hand again. "Forget it. What's done is done. Instead of trying to explain something that you have no explanation for, why don't you tell me why it is that you and your friends here are causing a row inside my entryway? And is that a *child* I see? Damnit all, Clint, I always knew you were a fool, but even I didn't suspect you'd be fool enough to bring a little girl to my place. I mean for the Eternals' sake, have you lost your mind?"

Clint glanced back at the wanderer. "I don't know, you'd have to ask him," he muttered.

"What's that?" Pearl asked, frowning at the wanderer.

"Nothing..." Clint said. "Look, Pearl, is there some place we can talk?"

She glanced between the wanderer and Clint, frowning. Then, after a moment, sighed. "Fine, we can go to my office. As far as your...entourage goes, they can go watch the dancing, but if any of them bothers my girls, Clint, past or not, I'll throw all of you out on your asses and damn your explanations and your charm, understand?"

"I understand."

She sighed again, shaking her head as if she couldn't believe what she was doing. "Fine. This way then before I change my mind. And Shayne, wake that silly bastard up and get him looked at, will you?" she said, nodding to the unconscious man.

"Yes ma'am," the big man replied.

"Alright," she said to Clint, "let's go find a quiet place to talk."

She started away and Dekker glanced at Clint. "Charm is it?" he asked, grinning. "If I didn't know better, Clint, I'd say that lady was trying to decide whether to kiss you or kill you."

Clint only winced, and the big man gave a laugh. "A formidable woman, that one," Dekker said. "One I reckon could give a bear lessons on intimidation."

"Aye, that's Pearl," Clint agreed. "Anyway, we'd best get going—she doesn't much care to be kept waiting."

"From what I heard she's been waiting for five years," Dekker countered. "What could another few minutes hurt her?"

"It's not her I'm worried about," Clint muttered and, with that, he started away, leaving the wanderer and the others to follow.

They stepped through the door into a large common room, and Dekker grunted, displaying a surprise that the wanderer couldn't help but share. Brothels, from his experience, were usually simple enough affairs when it came to decoration and entertainment. After all, the sort of services such places sold weren't the kind that required much advertising.

This brothel, though, was different. The room they stepped into was expansive, four or five times as large as a typical inn's common room. Scattered about the room were half a dozen small stages on which scantily-clad—or, in some cases, not clad at all—women danced while men seated at the surrounding tables hooted and hollered and cheered.

There was even one stage, the wanderer saw, with several women gathered around it, upon which a half-naked man danced.

"Well," one of the Perishables said as he eyed the nearest woman, "you do what you got to do, boss. We'll be here waiting for ya."

"Aye, take your time, sir," another said, grinning. "We'll do our best to keep ourselves occupied."

"I imagine you will," Clint said dryly as the men hurried toward several of the stages to take up seats near the dancing women, not attempting to hide their eagerness.

Meanwhile Pearl walked through the room like a queen meandering down the streets of her capital city. It was an analogy that was maintained by those around her as serving men and women, dancers, and even customers alike nodded and bowed and waved as she passed.

She led them past tables upon which sat lamps draped with warm colors of cloth—reds and oranges, yellows and pinks—that, when combined together, gave the massive room a warm, sumptuous glow. That sumptuousness was also found in the thick, red carpets.

The wanderer could not help but grin as he noticed Dekker walking straight as a board, his eyes locked on Clint's back where the man walked ahead of him as if his life depended on it. Which, if the scowl Ella was shooting in his direction was anything to go by, it likely did.

Pearl led them to the back of the grand room to a door. She opened it, starting through, and her two guards started to follow her.

"No, the two of you can stay here, Rolph," she told one.

The man frowned at the wanderer and those with him. "But, ma'am," he said, "maybe it would be better if—"

"If I hired someone who listened to my orders instead of questioning them?" Pearl finished, arching an eyebrow. "Perhaps you're right."

"F-forgive me, ma'am,' the man said hastily. "We will, of course be here, should you need us."

"Thank you, Rolph," she said, nodding, then glancing at Clint and the others. "Besides, even if they meant me harm, I do not believe this one here could hurt me more than he already has." And with that, she turned and disappeared into the doorway.

Clint turned to give the wanderer and Dekker a sickly smile before following after her.

The door led into a large office. At the room's center sat an oak desk stacked with papers. Pearl made her way around the desk to sit down. There were two chairs on the side closest to the wanderer and the others but no one made a move toward them. They waited in silence for several seconds then until the door thudded shut behind them, and Clint tensed.

Pearl grinned. "I don't remember the Clint I knew being quite so jumpy."

The Perishables' leader winced. "Yes, well...it has been a long five years."

The woman's smile faded at that. "Indeed, it has." She glanced at the wanderer and the others. "Well? Please, lass," she said to Ella, "you and your daughter, help yourselves to a seat," she finished, waving a hand at the two chairs on the other side of the desk.

"Thank you, ma'am," Ella said, moving toward the chairs, seating Sarah in one before sitting down herself.

"Please, just Pearl," the other woman said, smiling at Ella, a far more pleasant, ingratiating expression than anything she'd shown to the others since meeting them.

"I'm Ella."

"A pleasure, Ella," Pearl said, then leaned forward, her eyes going to Sarah. "And what about you, little one?" she asked, her voice as sweet as honey. "What's your name?"

The little girl glanced nervously at her mother, waiting for Ella to nod before turning back to Pearl. "My name's Sarah."

"Sarah," Pearl responded. "My but that's a pretty name, isn't it?"

Sarah smiled. "A pretty name for a pretty girl. That's what my daddy says."

Pearl glanced over at Dekker, favoring him with a smile before turning back to the girl. "Sweet and truthful," she said. She glanced at Clint and although she was still smiling, the wanderer thought he saw danger in her gaze. "Men are so rarely either, let alone both. Tell me, Sarah, have you ever had a chocolate pastry?"

The little girl's eyes went wide at that, her eyebrows practically disappearing into her hairline. "Not in a very, very long time," she said, her voice quivering with excitement.

The woman nodded. "Well, I think I may have some in my sitting room. She paused, nodding her head at a side door. "Just there. I wonder, would you and your mother be interested in having one?"

She glanced at Ella then, and Ella nodded, looking at Dekker who nodded as well. "That would be good, ma'am, thank you."

"Please," the woman said again, "Pearl."

"Very well...Pearl," Ella said. "We thank you for your hospitality."

"Think nothing of it," Pearl said, rising and opening the door to the side room in which the wanderer could see a small divan with a table in front of it, one upon which, indeed, sat a few small chocolate pastries.

She smiled as mother and daughter moved through the doorway, continued to smile as they sat. "If you need anything, please don't hesitate to let me know," she said.

Then the woman turned and the pleasant smile faded from her face as if it had never been as she scowled at Clint while walking back around the desk. "Now that's settled," she said, "why don't you tell me just what it is you're doing here and why I shouldn't have Rolph and his friends throw you and *your* friends out on your collective asses?"

"Pearl...I need your help."

"Help," the woman repeated as if she'd never heard the word before. "Five years of waiting, Clint. Five years without so much as a letter, and now you show up and tell me that you need my help."

"I'm sorry, Pearl," Clint said, "I didn't mean...that is, the Perishables needed—"

"*Damn* you and your *Perishables,*" she snapped. "A bunch of fools that ought to spend their time taking care of their families instead of meddling in the business of the Eternals. Fools like that big bastard, Hank, more like a dog than a man, a mad dog looking for something to bite."

"Hank's dead, Pearl," Clint said. "Him and a lot of others. Dead *because* they were trying to help their families—theirs and everyone else's. After all, the best way to do that is to make the city better."

"Damn the city too," Pearl said with a surprising amount of venom. "But...Hank's dead?"

"Yes. Him and Will. A dozen more," Clint said.

The woman's anger seemed to evaporate in a moment and she sat heavily back in her chair. For the first time since the wanderer had met her, she seemed less like a force of nature and more like a woman and that only. A woman who appeared to be in her mid-to-late forties, a woman whose face was wrinkled with worry lines, a thinness to her gaunt cheeks and face.

"Those poor fools," she said. "What happened?"

"They saw a world, a city that was full of suffering people," Clint said, an angry tone in his voice. "And they decided they wanted to help and so were punished for it."

She shook her head, a frustrated expression on her face. "You still don't get it, do you, Clint? The world doesn't *want* to be helped. Not anymore than a drowning man set on suicide does, and the only thanks someone's likely to get for trying to help him is to drown themselves."

"Doesn't make the effort not worth it."

"*Doesn't it?*" the woman demanded, leaning forward in her chair so abruptly that the wanderer thought she might attack the Perishable's leader. She didn't, but she did stare at him with eyes dancing with fury. "*Doesn't it?*" she repeated. "What about the family of the second man, the one who drowns because he's too much of a fool to realize that the first doesn't want his help? What about the people who love h—" She cut off then, her mouth snapping shut.

Clint looked just about as sad and sorry as any man could. "Listen, Pearl...it wasn't anything to do with you. The city, it needed help and—"

"*Damn the city!*" she shouted then winced, glancing over at the door through which she had led Ella and Sarah. She turned back to Clint and when she spoke further her voice was quieter, though no less angry for all that. "Damn the city, Clint," she said again. Then, in a soft, hurt voice, "What about *me?*"

"I'm...I'm sorry, Pearl," he said. "I...I just did the best I could, what I thought was right."

She sighed heavily then, nodding. "I know you did, you bastard. I know. We're all just doing the best we can." She shook her head.

"Let's leave it, Clint. I'm sorry I was cross but let's leave it. Five years is a long time but, at the same time, it's not so long at all, is it?"

"No. No, it's not."

She nodded. "It is good to see you—I wasn't lying about that."

"It's good to be seen," Clint said.

And just like that, the wanderer thought that it was alright between them. Not great, not perfect, but then human relationships never were.

"So you said some of the Perishables were killed," she said. "Hank and Will. Who else?"

"Too many to list," Clint said grimly. "And we lost more in the Untamed Lands."

"The Untamed Lands?" she said, her eyes going wide.

Clint gave her a humorless smile. "As I said, it's been a busy few months."

"But…by the Eternals, Clint, why would you ever be so foolish as to travel into the Untamed Lands? Damnit even a child knows better."

"Those Eternals of yours didn't exactly leave us with much of a choice," Clint said. "Soldier—or well, not really Soldier but…never mind. Suffice to say that we were chased out of the city. At least, that was, some of us. The lucky ones made it to the Untamed Lands. There were plenty who didn't."

"Lucky ones," Pearl said, shaking her head in wonder. "So that commotion I heard about a few weeks back, that was you all?"

"It was," Clint said.

She frowned at that. "We were told it was a gang fight."

"Wasn't much of a fight at all, truth to tell," Clint said, his voice cracking with anger and sadness. "They butchered them, Pearl. Monsters that you wouldn't believe exist. Cut them down like they were nothing."

"Oh, Clint," she said, her own voice full of compassion. "I'm so sorry."

"Aye," he said, nodding. "So am I."

"Still," she said, frowning. "Are you sure? That it was Soldier? Look, Clint, I know you and the Perishables, you had your gripes with Soldier and the other Eternals but…open murder in the streets? Monsters? Don't you think it all sounds a little…I don't know, like some sort of grim fairy tale?"

"Fairy-tales don't cut men in half without the poor bastards even seeing them coming on account of their invisible," Clint countered. "Fairy-tales don't take sword strikes and arrows without even so much as slowing down."

"Invisible monsters, things that can get hit by swords and arrows and not get hurt? Clint, surely you must know how all this sounds."

"I know exactly what it sounds like," Clint said. "But it's the truth, Pearl. You have my word on it."

She frowned, seeming to consider then shook her head. "I'm sorry, it's all just...too much. The Clint I knew wasn't given to children's horror stories."

"The Clint you knew didn't have those stories try to kill him either," the Perishables' leader said.

The woman leaned back, regarding the wanderer. "And you— you agree with what Clint here's saying?"

"Yes."

She glanced over at Dekker. "What about you, big fella? With your size, surely you ain't scared of the bogeyman."

"He's tellin' you the truth," Dekker said.

She regarded each of them in turn. "So let me get this straight— you would have me believe what, exactly? That Soldier, one of the Eternals, the men and women gods who have looked after the world for generation after generation, is actually evil and is in the business of creating monsters to terrify and torture the people of Celes?"

"If you think that's hard to swallow, you ain't seen nothin' yet," Dekker said.

She frowned. "What's the oak tree saying, Clint?"

Dekker blushed at that, and Clint shook his head. "The Eternals being evil, Pearl...that's just the start of it."

The woman's eyes narrowed, and she seemed to consider for another moment. Then, finally, she shook her head. "No. No, I won't believe it. I *can't* believe it. I mean, damnit Clint, you want me to believe that Soldier is bad? He and all the other Eternals? The same ones who have been looking after us, who have been taking care of us for hundreds of years?"

"Look around, Pearl," Clint said. "I admit I haven't been in Celes in a while, but from what I saw on the way here, things aren't looking all that good. What about you? You feeling taken care of?"

"Things are bad, I'll admit," Pearl said, "but just because we're having a rough patch in the city, that doesn't mean the Eternals are evil."

"You say you never thought the Clint you knew would believe in ghost stories," Clint said. "Well, the Pearl I knew was never afraid of the truth when it was looking her dead in the face. I mean, shit, Pearl, just *look* at the city. Look around you."

"Don't you lecture me, Clint," she snapped. "I haven't just looked! I've *lived* it. While you've been out doing whatever it is you've been doing, I've been *here.* I'm the one that's had to hire extra guards just to keep people from breaking in and looting. I'm the one who's seen the girls that work for me too scared to walk the streets, even with an escort. So scared they've taken to sleeping here instead of daring to go home. I'm the one that's listened to the stories of people being...being *eaten.*" She paused, giving a ragged breath, unshed tears dancing in her eyes. "Don't you *dare* lecture me, Clint."

"Doesn't sound like paradise to me," Dekker said.

The woman turned a sharp look on the big man, but before she could say anything, Clint spoke. "But don't you see, Pearl? That's exactly what I'm saying—what sort of gods are the Eternals, what sort of god is Soldier, if he would let the people of Celes suffer so? I mean, damnit, this isn't some backwater village, this is his capital city. And that's before we talk about all the villages and farms that have been burned at Soldier's command."

The woman's eyebrows drew down into a frown at that, and she pulled her gaze away from Dekker. "They said it was bandits that did for the farms—burned them down."

"And you believe that?" Clint countered. "Look, Pearl, you've dealt with some criminals in your time—"

"More criminals than honest men, that's for sure," she interjected.

"Right. You ever known bandits to burn crops? To kidnap farmers?"

She hesitated then, her frown deepening. "Well...maybe if they were looking for ransom—"

"Ransom on farmers who are lucky if they own much more than the shirt on their backs? Men and women who largely provide for themselves and have almost no need for coin at all? You're right,

Pearl. You have been in Celes and I haven't. But I saw Ingleton—or what was left of it. I saw the stacked ash that used to be homes, smelled the ruins the flames left."

"So let me get this straight, Clint. You show up after five years of silence—five years during which I dreamed of you returning, of what I might say. Of what *you* might say. And now that you're finally here, you want to tell me that Soldier, the man-god who has ruled Celes for decades, is evil?"

"Not anymore."

It was the first words the wanderer had spoken in some time, and Pearl turned to him, raising an eyebrow. "And just what is that supposed to mean?"

"I mean that the creature you know as Soldier was evil, but he is not evil any longer—he's dead."

"Dead," the woman repeated dryly, watching him. "And just how would you know that?"

"Because I'm the one who killed him."

Whatever she'd expected him to say, that wasn't it, and she blinked in obvious surprise. "Let me understand this—you're telling me that *you*, a dusty vagabond who looks one poor decision from homeless—"

"Wrong," the wanderer interrupted.

She paused. "Wrong?" she repeated.

He gave her a small smile. "I am homeless."

"You're telling me that *you* killed *Soldier*. Soldier who, along with Leader, enjoys a reputation for being the greatest warrior ever to live. A man who considered to be more god than man.

Clint winced. "Listen, Pearl, he isn't a vagabond, that's—"

"It's okay, Clint," the wanderer assured the man, then he turned back to Pearl. "To answer your question, I did not kill Soldier."

She nodded. "I thought as mu—"

"The real Soldier died over a hundred years ago. What I killed was no more than a parasite. A doppelganger but one that is capable of, so far as I can tell, near-perfect impersonation."

The woman stared at him for several seconds before turning to the Perishable's leader. "Are you aware that you're traveling with a madman, Clint? Or is this some sort of ill-conceived joke?"

"This is no joke, Pearl," the man assured her, "and Ungr is not mad."

She snorted. "We've a history, Clint—that's the only reason why I didn't turn you and these others out on your heel the moment you showed up at my door. But history only goes so far. I've swallowed a lot of bullshit in my day—you can't make your way in the world as I have without doing so—but even I have my limits. And for you to sit here and claim that this man, this *nobody* who looks like the dozens of bums I see lounging on street corners every day, has not only somehow killed Soldier, but has done so without anyone in the city even knowing...well. That's a bit too much to swallow, even for an old friend."

Clint glanced at the wanderer who gave him a small, single nod, then turned back to the woman. "He isn't a nobody, Pearl. And the reason he can kill an Eternal like Soldier is because he is one himself."

A snort of laughter escaped the woman's throat, and she turned to regard the wanderer. "This man here, this dusty bag of bones— you're telling me that he's an Eternal? Alright, sure, Clint, if you want to play games, I'll play along. Who is he? Dusty? Dirty? Smelly?"

"I am Youngest," the wanderer said, "though I have not been called by that name in some time." *At least by anyone living,* he thought, considering the ghosts in the amulet he wore.

"Youngest," the woman repeated. "You know, if it's a lie you're trying to sell, maybe you ought to pick one of the other Eternals. After all, Youngest is a traitor—that's a story everyone knows."

"A lie everyone knows," the wanderer said, surprised that, despite the fact that he'd been aware of the way the enemy had painted him for a hundred years and more, he still felt anger surge through him at the woman's casual mention of it. "I did not betray my friends—I *would* not have betrayed them."

Pearl frowned. "First you tell me that you killed Soldier, then you tell me that you wouldn't do such a thing. Doesn't make a lot of sense, and I learned a long time ago that the thing about lies is that they rarely make sense. The truth, now, that always makes sense. Usually it makes a lot more sense than folks want."

"Nevertheless, I am who I am. And the creature I killed was not Soldier, for Soldier has been dead more than a hundred years. He and the others...my friends." The wanderer found his hand clenching and unclenching at that, heard a voice whispering in his mind. His voice or the swords, he did not know, and he was not sure that it mattered. And though the voice's whisper was quiet, too low that he might make out the words, he did not need to. The tone was clear enough, the message, too. That voice wished for violence, for blood and death. For revenge. That voice demanded it.

"Ungr?"

He blinked, glancing at Clint, saw the man watching him, along with the others, and realized that he'd lapsed into silence as he listened to that voice. He gave his head a shake. "The Eternals are dead," he told the woman simply, aware of a coldness in his tone. "Those who you have known as the Eternals are the great enemy, the one who killed them more than a hundred years ago and took their place. I alone survived."

"That's lucky," the woman said dryly.

"Not luck," he said. "I only made it away because men and women that were better than me in every way sacrificed themselves so that I might survive. So that I might survive and flee with the enemy's weapon and, in doing, allow the world to survive. At least for a time."

"Hold on a minute," the woman said, "by weapon, do you mean—"

"The blade I carry at my back," he confirmed.

The woman sighed, shaking her head. "By the Eternals but this story keeps getting better and better, doesn't it? Just the gift that keeps on giving. But fine, I'll play along—you're telling me that you ran away with this sword, and if they had it they could what, destroy the   world?"

She said it with a laugh, as if the very notion was ridiculous, but the wanderer only nodded. "Yes."

"Right," she said. "And for the last hundred years they've been chasing you, that it?"

"That's it."

She leaned back in her chair as if exhausted, her gaze traveling between the wanderer and Clint and Dekker, perhaps waiting to see if anyone would laugh.

No one did.

She shook her head. "You know, it occurs to me that if what you're saying is true, the Eternals—or, well, sorry, the evil magic doppelgangers—would be extremely grateful to whoever turned you in."

"Pearl," Clint said, his voice sounding shocked, "you can't be saying that you would—"

"It's okay, Clint," the wanderer said, watching the woman. "To answer your question, yes. Those creatures who replaced the Eternals would no doubt be very pleased should someone come to them with knowledge of my whereabouts. Perhaps they might even thank you before they killed you, but I doubt it. I have enough experience with them to know that they aren't exactly the thanking type."

"You're telling me they'd kill me. For turning *you* in?"

"Yes, and not just you. They would kill you and your family and friends, should you have any. They will do so to make sure that you have not told anyone you know about me—about the truth you have heard here today. But they will not stop there, for the enemy is nothing if not thorough. They will dig into your life, and they will kill the friends of your family, the family of your friends. They will burn this place to the ground, will murder and make disappear any who have any connection to you. When they are finished, there will be not a single jot of evidence left to say that you ever existed at all."

"That sounds like a lot of trouble, if you ask me," she said. She was trying to sound casual but he could hear the fear in her voice, and she was right to be afraid.

"For them it is no trouble, not anymore than it is trouble for a child to play tag with his friends. It is a game for them...the death, the destruction...I do not know much about them, for we did not learn much before that final battle, but this much, at least, I do know. They enjoy it."

Silence fell on the room then, one that was thick as a blanket as each of them was forced to confront, in some small way, the true nature of the enemy they faced. Finally, the woman frowned. "Clint," she said, turning to the man, "you're saying that all this, all that he's saying—you believe it?"

"It's true, Pearl," the man said, his voice sounding regretful.

"What it is is horrifying," she said. "Assuming, of course, that it is, in fact, true."

"Someone once told me that the truth is often pretty terrible," Clint said.

She frowned. "You mean to cut me with my own blade, is that it, Clint?"

"I only mean to ask for your help, Pearl. It's why we came."

"Not to gaze once more upon my wonderful beauty, then?" she asked.

"Call it a bonus," he said, giving her a small smile.

She snorted. "You always were a smooth talker. No doubt it's how you convinced those poor bastards that call themselves Perishables to follow you."

"When a man's drowning, it doesn't take a whole lot of convincing to get him to climb aboard your boat," Clint countered.

"Maybe not," she said. "But then are we sure it's *your* boat the poor bastard should be climbing into?"

Clint glanced at the wanderer who shrugged. "We're not saying it's the best boat—the best choice," the wanderer told the woman. "But it *is* the only one. It's us or the waves."

"So I'm supposed to believe that, what, all the stories about the Youngest Eternal are a lie and that you are him and that, more than that, you're going to save us all?"

"No," he told her. "Only that I will try."

She turned to regard Clint. "Where did you find this one? Escape from a healer's, somewhere, that it?"

"Well," Clint said, "that's a bit of a story."

"Oh, Clint, it's safe to say at this point that I'm an eager audience."

Clint glanced at the wanderer who gave him a nod. "Go on, Clint. Tell her."

And so, for the next half hour or so, Clint did. He told her everything from when the wanderer had first met him, sent there by the young man Scofield with his dying breath, to them being attacked at the nobleman Will's manor. He continued, recounting their desperate flight from the city of Celes, where he and the wanderer and the others were separated. Here, Dekker chimed in from time to time, both of the men outlining what transpired following that flight from Celes until the time where Clint and the Perishables who'd survived the Revenants' assault caught up with the wanderer and the others in the Untamed Lands.

Pearl, to her credit, did not interrupt or mock the men as they told their shocking tale, instead only speaking to ask a question or clarify a point. Finally, in time, the telling was finished and they were caught up to where they now stood in her office.

She stared at them all in wonder for several seconds before finally speaking. "You expect me to believe all of that?"

"It's true," Ella said. She and her daughter had returned sometime during the telling, though the wanderer couldn't be exactly sure when for he had been reliving those harrowing moments along with the rest of them. "So...will you help us, ma'a—sorry...Pearl?"

The tall woman watched her from behind her desk, a thoughtful look on her face, as if she was truly considering Ella's question. However, when she spoke, the wanderer realized that she was contemplating a whole different issue. "You really are quite beautiful," she said.

Ella blushed at that, and Pearl nodded as she glanced at Dekker. "We should all be grateful, I do not doubt, that your girl got her looks from your side of the family."

"Hey now," Dekker said, frowning.

The woman, though, didn't seem to notice that the big man had spoken at all. "I wonder," Pearl went on, "would you ever consider working at my club?"

Ella blushed deeper still, clearing her throat.

"Look here," Dekker said, sitting forward in his chair, "I don't appreciate—"

"Understand that I don't mean as one of the...night girls, not at all. You could dance, perhaps, or even just serve drinks. You see, the men—and women—that come to such a place as mine, they are not always after...*that.* In fact, I would argue that most times that is only a secondary consideration to their primary goal."

"Which is?" Ella asked quietly.

The woman smiled, shrugging, then she glanced at Clint and the smile faded. "Why, they want what everyone wants, of course. To be cared for. Desired. Loved."

"I only love my husband," Ella said.

Pearl shrugged again. "And if not loved, if not desired, then they will settle for someone simply listening to them. A kind face—pretty and kind works best, mind—to smile at their jokes and frown at their hurts. For company, that's all. The pay is good, mind. You will not find better paying work in the city, that I can promise you."

Dekker let out a growl at that, and the woman finally turned to him. "Oh, relax, Fido," she said. "I've got a position for you as well."

Dekker's frown vanished to be replaced by a confused expression that also had more than a tinge of anxiety. The wanderer glanced at Clint to see the man grinning. "I don't...I ain't a girl," Dekker said.

"I picked up on that," Pearl said dryly. "But as I believe I mentioned to your pretty wife here, while the majority of customers that visit my establishment are, indeed, male, there are still some few women who attend—more than you might imagine, in fact. And those women would be eager to pay and pay handsomely to a man of your...size. That is, of course, if the muscles that I see aren't just some clever trick of your clothes or the lighting, perhaps."

Dekker let out another growl at that. "Damn if they are," he said, then frowned as he apparently realized what he was defending. "Look, I ain't just some piece of meat, lady."

"No," Pearl agreed, "you are an abnormally large piece of meat. One that, as I said, many of the women who come here would be eager to pay well to look at. You wouldn't have to do much, understand. Strut a bit, maybe do a dance move or two. A little wiggling—"

"*Wiggling*," Dekker repeated aghast, staring at Clint and the wanderer as if for help.

"Yes, you know," Pearl said, smiling at Ella who was grinning widely, "you know, wiggling. I suspect you would do quite well at it, for I can already see that you are a fine squirmer. Usually the two go hand in hand. Anyway, these women, you would be surprised how well they pay. In fact, in my experience—which is vast, mind—such women pay better and are more...let us say *attentive* than their male counterparts."

"I...that...you—" Dekker said, sputtering, unable to manage anymore than a single word at a time.

The woman shrugged. "Anyway, think on it. After all, what's the point of being that big if you don't put it to use?"

"I...she...you can't..."

"I think what my husband wants to know," Ella said, still grinning, "is whether or not you will allow us to stay."

"We can pay you, Pearl," Clint said.

"Pay me," Pearl repeated.

Clint nodded, glancing at the wanderer. "We...we don't have a lot of coin, I'm afraid, but what we have we'd be happy to pay you."

"Coin," Pearl said, shaking her head. "You really don't get it, do you, Clint?"

The Perishables' leader shot a look at the wanderer before turning back to the woman behind the desk. "I...guess I don't."

She rolled her eyes. "Men. Clint, you could have all the coin in the world, and it'd make no difference. If you came here dragging a dozen wagons full of gold, it would be of no use. Not unless that gold was made out of bread or meat or drinkable water. Nobody cares about gold in Celes anymore—or, at least, not enough to matter. Sure, there are some that are stockpiling it, thinking that when things go back to normal, they'll be rich. But if even half of what you all are telling me is true...well, I'm not all that certain things will ever go back to normal. Shit, I'm not sure if I'd even want them to."

Silence then, one that continued for several seconds, until finally Ella spoke. "So...Pearl. Will you help us?"

The woman smiled, glancing at Clint. "Of course I'll help, lass. Oh, I enjoyed watching Clint squirm, it's true, but the fact is that there was a time I'd have done anything in the world for this man, and now that he's here...well. I realize that time isn't so far gone as I thought. But then, that isn't all."

She turned to regard the wanderer then. "Are you really who Clint believes you are?"

"I am."

"And do you think you're able to do what you've set out to do? To rid the world of these...these creatures?"

The wanderer considered the question for several seconds. Finally, he gave a small shrug. "I don't know," he said honestly. "But I intend to try."

She watched him for several seconds. "I've never known Clint to be a liar," she said, "but it's hard to believe you're over a hundred years old. Why, you look about half my age."

"Clean living," he said.

That got a laugh out of her, but she sobered quickly. "I'll help you all," she repeated, "but not just because Clint's with you. I think I'd help you even if he weren't. Do you want to know why?"

The wanderer thought he knew well enough, but he nodded. "Yes."

"I've seen some terrible things, these last few weeks," she said, and her eyes got a faraway look. "Things I never would have imagined. Seen things happen to people...seen people *do* things that..." She swallowed hard, as if choking back some painful memory, and gave her head a fast shake. "Seen things nobody ever should. Saw people go through things nobody should ever have to go through. If helping you gives me even a chance of fixing that, of fixing what's wrong with Celes, with the world...well, then, I mean to take it. Besides," she went on, "it ain't as if we don't have the room. Time was—and not so long ago—that we'd be packed just about every day of the week. Shit, I was thinking on expanding. Then these last few months happened, and it's all I can do to manage to feed my people. Still, I ought to be thankful—we've at least got food. There are plenty of folk who don't."

"We appreciate it," the wanderer told her, "truly. But..." He glanced at Ella, and she gave a small nod before starting to talk to the young girl quietly, keeping her distracted. "I think we should tell you," the wanderer went on quietly, "that it will be dangerous— helping us, I mean. If the enemy discovers that you aided us he will seek revenge. I have seen the results of such revenge before and they are not pretty. In fact, I am beginning to believe that the current state of Celes and its outlying areas is no more than the enemy's way of getting back at me and Clint and the others for escaping. Else they have some other purpose, and I cannot imagine what that might be."

"You paint a pretty grim picture, Ungr. Is it alright if I call you Ungr?"

"Yes."

"Good, because this is my place, and in my place, I rule, and I bow to no one."

"I've never much cared for bowing—it's terrible on the knees."

She flashed him another smile at that. "So I've heard. I've never tried it myself."

The wanderer nodded. "Some people just aren't born for kneeling."

"I think we're going to get along fine, Ungr. Particularly if your abnormally large friend stops scowling at me."

Dekker grunted. "I don't dance. Or wiggle."

"Still on that, are you?" Pearl asked, glancing at the wanderer with a smile. "Anyway, you and yours are welcome to stay here for as long as you need. And if the big fella here doesn't feel comfortable doing a bit of a wiggle, well, I'm sure I can find some boxes that need moving, maybe some rocks that need crushed. In the meantime, though, do you mind if I ask you to share your plans with me?"

Dekker snorted. "As if we'd just share plans with—"

"With the person who you're asking to risk not just her business and those who work for her, those she's determined to protect, but also her own life in order to help you?" Pearl countered. Dekker was silent at that, and the woman turned to regard the wanderer once more. "I do not think it's unreasonable, given what you are asking of me, what you're asking me to risk, to ask you what your plan is."

"No," the wanderer said, "it isn't, and I would tell you our plan...if we had one."

She blinked. "I'm sorry?"

"Everything that Clint told you is true—we came to Celes in search of what had happened to the people of Ingleton and because of what the people of the city were said to be suffering."

"Sure, right, so Clint said," the woman said. "Only, I was asking for your *plan.* You know, the particulars."

"There are no particulars," the wanderer said simply. "Excepting, perhaps, that I intend to figure out who is behind the suffering of the people of Celes, to figure out why they have caused it and to put an end to it."

"So I'm to believe you're some noble knight out of a storybook, that it?" Pearl asked. "Some hero in shining armor riding on a faithful steed come to risk life and limb to save us poor peasants?"

"I've never been a fan of armor, shining or not, and in my experience noble knights aren't quite as dirty or dusty as the man you see before you. I *do* have a faithful steed, but he is busy taking his ease in a stable right now. As for the rest, well, I don't believe a man has to be noble or just or even decent to try to fix the world he himself and those he cares about lives in. No more than he has to be virtuous to plug a hole in his boat before it sinks. I think, for that, he just has to be slightly less than a complete fool."

"And you are no fool?"

"I like to think I'm not a complete one."

She nodded slowly. "I haven't known many men to admit that they might not know everything. Perhaps you are an Eternal after all." She considered. "Well...tell me, do you have *any* idea of where to start?"

The wanderer glanced at Clint who nodded.

"We're looking for friends of mine, Pearl," he said. "Who lived in Ingleton."

"You mean Murphy and Gerta, don't you?" she asked.

Clint nodded. "I do."

The woman's hard face grew soft as she stared at the Perishable's leader with undisguised compassion. "I heard about what happened at Ingleton...I'm very sorry, Clint. Murphy and Gert...they were good people."

"They *are* good people," Clint snapped. "The best."

Pearl winced, looking far more uncomfortable and nervous in that moment than she had when faced with the fact that the wanderer was an Eternal and the rulers of the kingdom impostors. "Of course, Clint. That's what I meant. Murphy and Gert...they're survivors. You have to be to live out there in the wilderness the way they do. If anyone survived...whatever happened, well, it'd be them."

Clint nodded. "I'm sorry, Pearl," he said. "Really."

"It's nothing," she said, waving it away. "You're worried about your friends—I get it."

"I didn't just mean that," the Perishables' leader said. "I'm sorry...about all of it."

The two stared at each other for a second, Clint's expression earnest and regretful, ashamed. The woman's expression was more difficult to read, and the wanderer thought it even odds that she'd have started to cry or lunge across the desk at Clint. In the end, she did neither, only cleared her throat and jerked her gaze away to look at the wanderer, apparently finding it preferable to confront him—and all that his presence meant for her and her home city— than to address whatever had existed, and seemed to still exist, between her and Clint. "I don't know what became of the people of Ingleton or any of the other areas outside the city. Maybe I should have looked...probably I should have. Only, it's felt like all I can do to care for my own people." She shook her head. "Damnit, Clint, I'm sorry. I should have—"

"It isn't your fault, Pearl," he said. "You ain't got nothin' to be ashamed of. Not a thing."

She nodded slowly, looking grateful. "Well. I can't say as I know where Murphy or Gert are, but I think maybe I know where you might start looking, if you've a mind to."

"We're listening," the wanderer said.

She let her gaze travel between each of them. "It'll be dangerous, but then if even a fraction of what you've told me is true, then I suppose that'll just be another day for you all."

The wanderer would have preferred to deny it, but he didn't think he was really in a position to do so, so he only continued to stand, waiting.

When she saw that none of them were going to back down, she sighed. "There's a place in the poor district called the Sewers. You know it?"

"I'm...not familiar," the wanderer said, surprised, for during his time spent training under Soldier he had been shown and taught about every area of the city of Celes.

"Well, might be you know it by another name," the woman said. "Does Mercy Street sound familiar?"

The wanderer blinked. "Of course," he said. He remembered the place well, just as he remembered the name of every boulevard and avenue in Celes, each of which Soldier had named after virtues to which he believed men and women ought to aspire in the hopes that they would serve as reminders. "Mercy Street, it's where the church used to hand out free food to the homeless and poor, where the healers would volunteer their services some few times a month to see to those who could not afford treatment, all of it paid for by the crown."

Pearl frowned. "Doesn't sound like we're talking about the same place."

"It...at the eastern end of the city," the wanderer said, trying to remember. "There was Honor and then Valor, Truth and Compassion and then, after that, Mercy Street."

Pearl grunted. "Suppose we are talking about the same place after all, though it hasn't been called Mercy Street for months now and that with good reason. What goes on there...it isn't mercy."

"Well?" Dekker asked. "Are you gonna leave us to guess or what?" He sounded more hostile than needed, and the wanderer thought it likely he was still smarting over the woman's last comments toward him.

Pearl gave a small smile at that, a knowing look on her face that made the wanderer think she was well-aware of the effect her words had had on the big man. "Oh, don't you worry none, princess," she told Dekker. "I'm sure these big strong men will take care of you."

Dekker recoiled at that as if she'd slapped him, turning a scandalized look on Ella who was staring forward, making an obvious effort to keep her expression neutral.

"In all actuality," Pearl went on, turning back to the wanderer, apparently unconcerned with the low growl issuing from Dekker's throat, "I would not recommend going to the Sewers. It's dangerous, there."

"I thought we'd been through this already," the wanderer said, giving her a small smile.

"True, true," she said, nodding, "but this...this is different. A man or woman, if she isn't careful, if she doesn't mind herself and her surroundings, might die in any part of Celes just now, might walk out her door and simply never come back. But a person who is brave—or foolish—" here she paused, raising an eyebrow at him, "enough to journey into the Sewers might suffer a far worse fate."

"A fate worse than death?" Clint asked, frowning.

"Sure, ain't you ever been married?" Dekker countered, grinning at his wife who rolled her eyes in response.

"Oh look, he's clever, too," Pearl said in the tone of voice one normally reserved for dogs and small children. The big man's smile immediately vanished, replaced by a scowl. He opened his mouth— no doubt to utter some cutting rejoinder—but never got the chance, as Pearl continued, turning back to the wanderer.

"The Sewers, they call it. Not just because it's filthy and dirty and a man who finds himself there will likely wish he was anywhere else—all true. Instead, they call it that because all the worst of the filth of Celes finds its way there the same way shit flows through a sewer to end up...well. Wherever it ends up. Fact is, I haven't the least idea about where that is, but I *can* tell you this much— wherever all that filth is going, it's a place I have no interest in visiting. The Sewers are a lot like that, you see."

"I see."

"And yet you would go there anyway?"

The wanderer shrugged. "If the sewer canals become clogged then someone has to clean them."

She raised an eyebrow. "Not exactly a job that attracts a lot of candidates, is it?"

"Maybe not, but it's still one that needs doing."

She nodded. "You're determined anyway, I'll give you that. Though, after I tell you what I'm going to tell you, it might be that determination of yours wavers a bit. You see, it's not just the usual suspects a determined man like yourself has to worry about in the Sewers. Not just thieves and murderers, muggers and brutes, although they are all present and accounted for, of course. What you really have to worry about isn't the murderers or the thieves—not the charlatans or the shadows that wait in alleyways hoping to steal a man's coin. Instead, it's the Mongrels. For some of those shadows, you see, have teeth."

"Teeth?" the wanderer asked, but he thought he understood well enough where she was going, understood all too well, in fact.

"Who are the Mongrels?" Clint asked. "Some...street gang?"

"I think 'pack' would be closer to the truth," Pearl said grimly. "They are men and women, sure—or at least what's left of them."

"I...I'm not sure I understand," Dekker said.

"Don't worry, big fella," Pearl said, "I'm sure one of your friends here will be happy to explain it to you."

Dekker frowned. "I mean, why are they called the Mongrels?" he grumbled.

"Seen a lot of mongrels in your time, big fella?" Pearl asked.

"A few, but what does that have to do with—"

"Because I've seen quite a lot," she went on. "I've always had a soft spot for animals, understand. Blame it on the fact I was an only child and my parents always liked to keep a puppy in the house. Either way, I used to take in mongrels when I saw them. Feed them, water them, do what I could to find them decent homes. And there's one thing about mongrels that anyone who's spent any significant time around them knows...they'll eat anything."

"Wait a minute," Dekker said, paling, "do you mean..."

"The Mongrels started as men and women who were starving. Nothing unique about that, of course, particularly right now. Why, I'd say three-quarters of the city's people are starving, likely more."

"You seem to be doing alright," Clint observed.

Pearl shrugged. "People are pretty simple creatures. They want to eat and drink, yes, have shelter from the wind and the rain. But they also want to love, to be loved. And, sometimes, they just want to rut. Some men—shit, some women, come to it—are willing to give up their last chunk of bread if it means they get to spend an hour or two with a beautiful woman or handsome man. Anyway, the nobles are still managing to survive well enough, and they like to rut like pigs in shit. Louder than my girls, they are, and that takes some effort. Of course, my girls are faking it, but then that's what they get paid for."

Dekker snorted. "Poor bastards," he said, grinning at Clint.

Pearl raised an eyebrow, then looked meaningfully at Ella, and the big man frowned, glancing at his wife who was looking straight ahead as if her life depended on it.

"Anyway," Pearl went on, a small smile on her face as Dekker's eyebrows drew down into a frown, "what I mean is the Sewers are a dangerous place. I haven't been there myself—not since the troubles. But there are rumors of what happens there."

"Rumors," the wanderer repeated.

She nodded. "Ritualistic sacrifice, murder, torture...all sorts of stories. But on this much the rumors agree—however it begins, it all ends the same way for the poor victims."

"They're eaten," the wanderer said.

"Yes," she said, and her face grew pale as she nodded. "They're eaten."

"But...I just don't understand," Clint said. "We were here only a few months ago. How could things go so bad so quickly?"

"It might take a long time to build things, Clint," Pearl said, "but in my experience, it doesn't take long at all to tear them down. And you'd be surprised just what a man or woman will do if it means they don't have to watch their wives and husbands, their children starve."

"But...surely you don't mean you would...that you'd..."

"Of course not," she snapped. "Eternals be good, Clint—" She paused, frowning as she glanced at the wanderer at that. "You've been gone five years, but I haven't changed that much, you bastard. I'm just saying that's what's happening. As for how it became so...organized...well. They say there's a man. One they call the Jackal."

"Jackal," Dekker repeated, frowning.

And this time, at least, Pearl didn't have any quip for the big man. Instead, she only nodded, her expression grim. "That's right."

There was really no need to ask why they called him that, not for the wanderer, at least. After all, jackals were well known eaters of the dead. "Who is he? This jackal?"

She shrugged. "No one knows. Shit, the truth is I don't even know if he actually exists. It might be that he's no more than a story, a bogeyman. People, in times of trouble, after all, are always looking for someone to blame."

"To be fair, there pretty much always *is* someone to blame," the wanderer said.

She nodded. "I don't know much about the Mongrels or the Jackal, and I don't want to. What I do know, though, is that the refugees who have been coming into Celes lately have all been sent to the Sewers. I expect that if your friends have come to Celes in the last weeks, you'll find them there. If..." She winced. "Well, if they're anywhere."

She didn't say anymore, but then no more needed to be said. The wanderer glanced at Clint, letting him take the lead, and the Perishables' leader nodded. "Okay. Thank you, Pearl. For everything." He turned to the wanderer. "When do you want to go?"

The wanderer glanced at Dekker and the Perishables' leader, saw their grim expressions and gave a small shrug. "How does now suit?"

"Sounds damn good to me," Clint said, his voice a low growl, clearly considering what he might do to the Jackal or anyone else if they had harmed his friends.

"Are you sure?" Pearl asked. "Look, it's getting late—it'll be dark in another hour, maybe less. Why don't you all spend the night here, get some rest? You can leave tomorrow." There was something almost desperate in her tone as she looked pleadingly at Clint.

The two men turned to regard the wanderer then, leaving it to him, but he could see the desperation in Clint's eyes. If they stayed the night, the Perishables' leader would get no rest, of that he was certain. Instead, he would spend the night in the brothel worrying over his friend. If he spent it there at all, for there was something in his gaze that made the wanderer think that, should they refuse to go with him now, he might well go alone during the night.

"We go now," the wanderer said, noticing the way the woman, Pearl, seemed to shrink just as he noted the way Clint gave an almost-but-not-quite imperceptible sigh of relief.

Clint nodded, starting toward the door. "I'll go get the other Perishables."

"Better if you didn't," the wanderer said, and the man turned and regarded him questioningly. "That many people, traveling together...it could not help but be remarked upon, remarks that might, eventually, reach places we would prefer they not. Besides, to find your friends it may well be that we have to ask questions of some of the people living in the Sewers, people who will vanish at the sight of what they would consider a small army marching through."

"But...but surely you can't mean just...just the three of you will go?" Ella asked, looking at her husband, a mixture of desperation and fear in her gaze.

"Ungr's right, love," Dekker said. "It's the way it's got to be. We'll be fine," he told her reassuringly. "You don't need to worry about us."

"Somebody has to," she said.

"We'll be fine, El," Dekker said again, cupping his wife's cheek in his hand. "We'll be back before you miss us, alright?"

"That isn't possible," she told him. The two shared a look at that, and the wanderer suddenly felt as if he were an intruder.

He glanced at Clint, and the two of them moved toward the door. Dekker gave his wife and daughter a kiss and joined them a moment later.

"I'll walk you out," Pearl said, glancing at Ella and Sarah. "The two of you stay here, if you will—I'll be back in just a moment, and then maybe we'll play a game."

Sarah grinned. "What kind of game?" the little girl asked.

"Hmm..." Pearl said thoughtfully, "why don't you think on it, and we'll play whatever you want, alright? If, of course, that's okay with your mother."

"It's okay with me," Ella said, giving the woman a smile to show that she knew well enough what she was doing and that she appreciated it.

"Good," Pearl said, "now let me help these three find their way to the door—likely they'd get lost otherwise."

Sarah gave a giggle at that, and then the woman turned back to the wanderer, the smile she'd flashed the young girl vanishing as she gave him a grim nod.

The wanderer led the way out of the office, and Pearl paused to close the door, turning to regard the two big men stationed there. "No one comes through until I come back."

"You got it, ma'am," one said.

"Clint, why don't you go on and let your people know that they're welcome to stay. I'll have my assistant get them all quartered. I just want to speak with your friends here a moment."

Clint frowned. "Why do I feel like a child being sent to his room?"

She rolled her eyes. "Go on then."

He was still frowning as he turned and walked away. The wanderer glanced at Dekker, a small smile on his face, but the big man didn't notice, for his own gaze was still on the door, behind which were his wife and daughter.

"No harm will come to them unless it comes to me first," Pearl said. "You have my word."

Dekker pulled his gaze away from the door with an obvious effort and looked at the woman, nodding. "Thanks."

"Don't mention it," she said. "Anyway, maybe you can do me a favor in return. Clint and I...well, I'll admit that we have a bit of a past. Just as I'll admit that, when I saw him, I was tempted to kill him myself. But..."

"We'll look after him," the wanderer said.

She nodded, a grateful expression on his face as she turned to regard Clint who had walked off and was now speaking with some of the Perishables. "Understand," she said, "I...I hate Clint. But..."

"But you love 'em too," Dekker said. "We get it—you can't hate nothin' more'n if you love it. That's a fact my wife'd no doubt attest to."

"I thought wrong of you, before," she said. "I thought you were a big fool."

"And now?" Dekker asked.

"Well," she said, smiling. "You are big." Her smile faded then, her expression growing serious. "I will do everything in my power to keep your family safe—you have my word. But please, be careful. I was not exaggerating before—the Sewers are not a kind place."

"Sorted."

They all turned to see that Clint had walked up, apparently finished with his brief conversation with the Perishables. The Perishable's leader turned to Pearl. "If anything happens, if anyone should try to bother you or your people, like if they come looking for us, you can count on them to protect you."

She frowned. "You've known me for a long time, Clint. Have you ever known me to be the type of woman that needs protecting?"

He winced. "No," he said, "no I haven't. But then...well. This time's different."

"That's true enough," she admitted. "Fine—I'll tell you what. If I end up needing saving and my own men can't manage it, I suppose I'll allow yours the honor."

"No doubt they'll feel privileged to do so," he said, giving her a small smile.

"No doubt," she said, smiling back, then she met his eyes. "Be careful, Clint."

"You too," he said.

The two stared at each other for several seconds, and Dekker grunted. "Shit, Clint, why don't you just kiss her already, get it over with so we can get on with business?"

The Perishable's leader's face colored a deep red at that, and it was the woman's turn to sputter, which only made Dekker grin all the wider, clearly enjoying making her uncomfortable for a change.

"Good luck," she said again, then turned and retreated back toward her office.

The three men watched her go, and Clint shook his head. "I'm sorry, Dekker, for the—"

"You're a fool, Clint," the big man said.

The Perishable's leader blinked. "I know she can be a bit...abrasive, but I assure you she didn't mean anything by the things she said."

Dekker looked over at him as if he was a complete idiot. "What, you think I'm offended by what she said, that it?"

Clint glanced at the wanderer who shrugged, then turned back to the big man. "The...thought had crossed my mind."

Dekker sighed. "No, Clint. What I meant was, you're a fool for not marrying her when you had the chance—a chance you still have, by the way. And you'd be an even bigger fool if, when all this is sorted, you don't take it."

Clint blinked, an expression on his face that said he was clearly as surprised as the wanderer. "I...that is...maybe some time in the future, when all of this is cooled down and..."

"There's always going to be something, Clint," Dekker interrupted, his voice not unkind. "It might rain tomorrow, it might not. There's just no way of knowing, and even if we did know it would be well beyond our control to change it." He glanced at the wanderer. "At least most of our control. Anyway, the point is, you can't control what's going to come. But what you can do is make sure that whatever tomorrow brings, sun or storm, you spend it with the people you love. Just think on it, alright?"

"I will," Clint said, nodding. "Thanks. Oh, and Dekker?"

"Yeah?"

"Pearl was right about you," Clint said, then a smile spread its slow way across his face. "You are big."

The wanderer laughed at that, and Dekker gave a sour grunt. "Come on then, you bastards—I think I'd rather face cannibals than sit here jawing with the likes of you any longer."

"Let's hope it doesn't come to that," the wanderer said, and then they turned and started toward the brothel door. The bouncer who the wanderer had knocked unconscious was nowhere in sight, but the two stationed there filled his role well enough, scowling at them as they retrieved their weapons and stepped out into the city.

CHAPTER THIRTEEN

THE WANDERER REMEMBERED the city of Celes as a thriving example of civilization, a beacon of light in an often dark world. Certainly he had thought it so when he had first visited it over a hundred years ago to train with Soldier. He had loved the city, and its shining white marble walls had come to represent to him, as they did for so many others, hope. Hope that mankind was capable of greatness, that he himself *aspired* to greatness, that he could learn to repress the darkest urges within himself and become something...fine. Something noble.

And in walking its streets, the wanderer had felt, long ago, as if he had not only been witnessing that hope, but that he had somehow been a part of it. The city had inspired him to be better, to grow, so that he might, in his small way, be a part of that beacon shining in the darkness. It had given him comfort.

It did not do so now. The white marble walls still stood, it was true, and from a distance, at least, they looked as fine as they ever had. And a man, not knowing what had transpired within the city walls—what was *still* transpiring—might have been forgiven for thinking that the city was as it had always been. But it was not.

It had become something twisted, something ugly, its shining walls no more than the face paint an undertaker might put on a corpse to give the illusion of life. But when a man drew closer, he could not help but see the paint for what it was—a disguise, nothing more. A trick. A ruse.

So it was with Celes, but the city's decay was far worse than that of the corpse. After all, years passed, and men and women died. It was natural. But what had happened to the city, what was *still* happening, was as far from natural as anything could be.

They passed shops with their windows and doors boarded up, and most of these had paint of various colors spattered about them. Some of it was random splatters, no more, but from time to time a word could be made out, always a curse. And on rare occasions the unknown artists had not been satisfied with a single expletive but had chosen instead to write out some of the foulest things—and acts—that the wanderer had ever heard.

"Damn," Dekker breathed, stopping to gaze at one such scrawl, this one written not in blood as some had been but a far browner, far fouler substance.

"What...what does this mean?" Clint said, his voice sounding panicked and confused, the voice of a man who has just discovered just how thin the veneer of civilization really is.

The wanderer frowned, staring at the disgusting scrawl. "Nothing good," he said. It was a sign and not a good one. This he knew, for he had seen such things before. It had been a long time ago, back before the enemy had come or, at least, before they had known of them, and it had been in a village of a few hundred, not a city of tens of thousands, yet he remembered it well, could not have forgotten it even if he'd wanted to.

It had been an assignment from Healer when he had been under her tutelage. There'd been a village in her domain, one she hadn't heard from for several months, and the tax collector who'd gone had never returned. She had feared bandits or some marauding band, and so, scared for the villagers' safety, had sent him.

He had been accompanied by two dozen soldiers, all well-trained, but in the end it had been unnecessary. For when they arrived at the village—Whispering Glen, a name he would not soon forget for it, like what they had discovered, was etched into his memory—there was no one left to fight.

There was only death, only destruction and decay of the sort he now gazed upon. Buildings that had been broken into, scrawled expletives on the walls of the homes and tradesmen's shops. And the bodies, of course. Those he remembered most of all, for they had been in a terrible state. Even at a passing glance—at first, he had been able to do no more than that—he had noted that they had not fallen in battle, the victims of sword thrusts and arrow piercings. No, they had been torn about, ravaged as if by some attacking beasts. Only, when he had managed to gather up the courage to inspect the bodies further, he discovered that it had not been a bear or pack of wolves that had accounted for the villagers. Indeed, their broken nails and blood-stained mouths made what had happened all too apparent, even if he had found it nearly impossible to believe.

The villagers had not been attacked by animal or bandits. They had done it to themselves. In only a few months and for reasons he had never understood, the village had become twisted and corrupted and, in the end, destroyed itself. He had recounted what he'd found to Healer and even as he'd spoken, tears glided their way down her face for then, as always, she had been profoundly touched by the suffering of others, almost as if she experienced it for herself, capable of an empathy he'd never seen before or since. He suspected then—and now—that that empathy was largely the reason she'd become a healer in the first place, in an effort to stop the suffering of others and, in that way, assuage her own anguish.

When he had finished his recounting, she had not spoken for some time, and he had been unable to keep from asking her why, why it had happened, why the villagers had destroyed themselves. It had been a silly thing to ask, an impossible question, like a child asking his father why things died. Yet it had been a question that, in that moment, he had *needed* to ask.

It was a sickness, she had told him. A sickness not of the body, like fever or chills. Not even of the mind, like that sickness which made people forget. No, it was a sickness of the heart, of the soul, and the hardest, she'd said, to heal.

A few months. That's all it had taken. A few months since the last tax collector had come, a few months during which the village of Whispering Glen had gone from a peaceful hamlet to a mass grave. That was all it had taken for the trappings of society to be ripped free, for the façade of civilization to crumble into ash.

He would not have believed it was possible had he not seen it for himself, had he not witnessed that crumbling, had he not sifted through that ash. Yet it had happened. And now, in Celes, a city of tens of thousands, it was happening again.

"Ungr?" Dekker asked. "Everything alright?" He winced. "Sorry. Stupid question."

"Come on," the wanderer said, glancing at the big man, then letting his gaze travel to Clint. "Let's go find your friends."

***

They journeyed farther down Mercy Street, each step harder than the last as they were confronted with one grim sight after another. Another defaced building, another looted shop, cobbles stained with what could only be blood. They saw much, but what they did not see, what were conspicuously absent in a city as crowded as Celes, were people.

At least, obvious ones. The wanderer was aware of shadowed figures tracking their progress from the mouths of some of the sidestreets they passed, was aware, also, of the eyes peering at them through the slats of some of the boarded up windows of the shops and homes they walked by.

"How are we going to find them?" Clint asked. "Murphy and Gert and all the rest of Ingleton, I mean?" he went on, looking around at the dark buildings on either side of the street, without so much as a light to illuminate them. "They could be anywhere."

The wanderer shook his head slowly, thinking. "I need a minute."

Clint and Dekker shared a glance at that. "Sure, why not?" the big man asked. "It ain't like we've got nothin' on just now."

"Right," Clint said. "You know, except walking around in streets apparently full of cannibals in a city that seems to be destroying itself, hunted by creatures out of nightmare and trying to locate Murphy and Gerta."

Dekker gave a single-shouldered shrug. "Suppose there is that. But hey, you take your time—wouldn't want those little aggravations to bother you."

The wanderer gave a small smile. "I won't be long."

"Good," Dekker said, glancing around them at the shadowed street, the dark buildings that seemed to crouch and watch them. "Because, for what it's worth, Ungr, I don't think we have all that long."

The wanderer stepped away then, not far, but far enough that he could concentrate, could think. He knew that Dekker was right—

they did not have much time. Neither did the Perishables and Ella and Sarah where they waited with Pearl. Even if the brothel owner was genuine and kind—and he believed she was—there were still plenty of other dangers to consider. After all, each step they'd taken since walking through the gates had been a step in enemy territory. It was not a question of if the enemy would discover their presence…only when. When that happened, the enemy would send everything he had at them, and when *that* happened…well. The Perishables were brave, Ella and Sarah and Dekker too, but they would stand no chance against such a force.

The wanderer would do anything to keep that from happening. *Anything.*

The word rang in his mind, and he found his fingers toying with the locket hung about his neck. There had been a time, not so very long ago, when he had trusted the ghosts implicitly, had valued their opinions and thoughts far above his own. But since speaking with the Wizard of the South—Earl, and that name for a wizard still brought a small smile to his face, even now—he realized that he had rarely consulted them or asked for their advice.

He'd given himself excuses, of course, that he'd been too busy, that he was being hunted, chased, and he had to focus on staying alive. But then, that had always been true, and he had always found time in the past. No, the truth was that he had lost faith in the ghosts, the truth was that his conversations with the wizard had made him begin to think of them more as just men and women instead of gods, men and women with shortcomings, men and women who made mistakes.

And yet, while that might even be correct, it was also correct that, flawed or not, their wisdom and counsel had saved his life—and thereby the life of every man, woman, and child walking the planet—dozens, hundreds of times over the years as he'd fled from the enemy.

And so, considering what was at stake, not just Clint's friends, not even just his own friends, but the entire city of Celes and its people, the wanderer put aside his doubts and questions.

He opened the locket.

A deluge of voices as always, all of the ghosts speaking at once as if trying to make up for the prolonged silence all in a moment.

Then, finally, he came to a stop in an alleyway. "Are you finished?" he asked.

Sure we're finished, Tactician snapped. *Just as soon as you come to your senses and leave this cursed city. Do you have any idea what will happen if the enemy realizes you're here?*

"Some," the wanderer said. "And I'm not leaving."

Then you're a fool, Tactician said, not sounding his usual mixture of sarcastic and angry but sounding, more than anything, tired. Resigned.

Listen, Ungr, Leader said, *we know what you're trying to do. It's noble. What the people of this city, what they're going through...it's unacceptable. But—*

"But you would have me accept it," the wanderer said. "You would have me leave."

Yes, Leader said. *For the fate of the world and all its people, not just those of Celes, I would have you leave.*

"I will not," the wanderer said simply. "But I would like your help."

With what, I wonder? Tactician asked. *The fastest way to die? Because it seems to me, Youngest, that you are on the right track. And how not? After all, it's a goal you've been driving at for some time now, it seems.*

The wanderer decided to ignore that for now. After all, the argument had been going on for months now since he'd deviated from their wishes—in large part it had been going on since the moment he'd fled with the enemy blade—and it was not likely to be resolved soon.

We will talk later, Youngest, when there is time, for there is much we must discuss. For now, though, tell us what it is you wish of us.

"I would find Clint's friends, if I could," he began, "but I don't—"

"Sure, risk the world for a man and woman you've never met," Tactician snapped. "It makes perfect sense."

"But I don't know where to begin," the wanderer said, ignoring the ghost.

Perhaps...perhaps the government of the city might—Scholar began.

What government? Tactician snapped. *Celes is in chaos, can't you see that, you addled old fool?*

See here, Scholar began, *I won't—*

Somebody ought to be able to see anyway, Tactician countered.

"Enough," the wanderer said. "I do not have time for your bickering. Thank you for the suggestion, Scholar, but Tactician is right. From what I've seen of the guards, if there is a governing body, it is as corrupt as it has been since the enemy took over."

Then how do you mean to find them? Healer asked. *I suppose you could ask around, but—*

Go asking door to door, is that what you mean? Alchemist asked. *Surely you've got to know a better way than that.*

"I don't," the wanderer admitted. "It's why I asked."

The ghosts started to bicker again, but they cut off in another moment when Assassin spoke. The ghost did not speak much, so when she did speak people—and even ghosts—listened.

But you do know, Youngest. If a man searches for a rabbit in the tall grass, he will not find it. For the rabbit is small and the grass is high. So then, if a hunter seeks the easiest way of finding the rabbit...

"Then he should seek out the lion who will call it his meal," the wanderer finished, remembering a time, very long ago, when she had first taught him the lesson.

Yes.

"You mean the man Pearl spoke of, the Jackal."

Lions and wolves, jackals and coyotes, they are all the same.

The wanderer nodded, closing the locket. He turned and walked the dozen or so feet back to where Clint and Deker waited.

"Well?" Dekker asked, raising an eyebrow. "Have any great epiphanies?"

"One," the wanderer said. "I know what we have to do." He let his gaze travel first from one man, then to the second. "You won't like it."

"Ain't that a shame," the big man said dryly. "What with today shapin' up to be such a fine time. Well, go on, let's hear it."

"Who better to ask about the whereabouts of a rabbit," the wanderer said, repeating what Assassin had told him long ago, "than the lion?"

"How about the poor rabbit's wife?" Dekker said. "Shit I know mine always knows where I am."

Clint gave a soft laugh at that then sobered. "The thing about lions though, Ungr, is that...well, they bite."

"Yes," the wanderer said, scanning the area around them. "Yes, they do. If they think they can."

The big man frowned. "What does that mean?"

"We do not face lions," the wanderer told him. "We face a jackal. We face scavengers. And scavengers do not rouse themselves unless they spot what they believe to be easy meat."

"Easy meat," the big man repeated, his frown deepening. "And just to make sure I'm understanding you here—we're the meat?"

"That's right."

Dekker sighed, glancing at Clint. "Alright, Ungr. Let's hear it. What are you thinking? But I'll just say at the outset that, if it's all the same to you, given a choice, I prefer to lead a non-chewed-on life."

"Well, we all got our dreams, don't we?" Clint asked dryly. "Go on, Ungr."

"Simple," the wanderer said. "Those who mark us from the shadows will not come out, not with the three of us. Just as the vultures will not pick at the meat of a creature they fear."

"So...?" Dekker asked. "What are you suggesting?"

"I'm suggesting that we make ourselves look weak so that we will attract some of those waiting in the shadows. And when they show up, we will ask them about the whereabouts of this Jackal Pearl told us about. And then—"

"We'll ask the Jackal about where we could find Murphy and Gert," Clint said.

"That's right," the wanderer said.

"So...you mean to set a trap, then," Clint said.

"Yes."

"A trap, sure," Dekker said. "But for who?" The wanderer and Clint turned to look at him, and the big man shrugged. "Just sayin', I knew a fella once was havin' problems with foxes gettin' at his chickens durin' the night, so he set a trap, a real nasty one too. One meant to close on the furry little bastard's leg and not let go. You see, this fella got into his cups one night, thought he heard somethin' and stumbled out to check on his chickens. In the end, it weren't the fox that found that trap but him. He never did walk right after that."

"What are you saying?" the wanderer asked.

Dekker grunted. "I think you know well enough. Sometimes a fella sets a trap for himself, and he don't even realize it. Or," he went on, glancing at each of them meaningfully, "sometimes it ain't a fella but several—maybe even three."

"Not three," the wanderer said.

The big man's eyebrows drew down into a frown. "I think I know what you're thinkin', and I'm thinkin' I don't much care for it."

"Maybe try thinking a little less," the wanderer said, giving the man a small smile, one he did not return. "Look," the wanderer said, "we all know what's at stake, what we came to do. And the sooner we do it the better. I'm not saying it's not dangerous—all I'm saying is that, sometimes, a man has to risk a little danger to avoid a lot of it."

"Like sharpenin' your sword can be dangerous, if you ain't careful, but then you'll need it when the bandits show up," Dekker said without inflection.

"Exactly," the wanderer said.

The big man grunted. "Got a story about a fella sharpening his sword, too, if you've a mind to hear it."

"Maybe another time," the wanderer said. "For now, I've got to get ready."

"Ready," Dekker repeated. "You mean you need to make yourself into bait."

"That's right."

"Might be you'll want to start by getting rid of those two swords of yours. It'd be a shame to have something to defend yourself with when the vultures come snooping around lookin' for somethin' to munch on, wouldn't it?"

The wanderer could hear the sarcasm in the man's tone, but he chose to ignore it. Instead, he reached behind his back and withdrew the two swords in their sheaths. He handed his own over to the big man who took it, still frowning, but with the cursed blade he hesitated.

"We'll take care of it," Clint said.

The wanderer winced, nodding. *You shouldn't have to*, he thought. And then, following that, *No one should.* But in the end he handed it over.

"Just hold on a minute," Dekker said, and the two men glanced at him. "If we're going to be makin' one of us bait, I'd just as soon as it be me. After all, if what you're sayin' is true and its meat that'll bring the bastards out, well then I've got what—a hundred pounds on you? If its meat they want, then I'll give 'em meat."

"Sure, enough to choke on," Clint said, a small smile on his face.

Dekker frowned. "What's that supposed to mean?"

Clint glanced at the wanderer then back to the big man. "Look, Dek, I've known you a long time, alright? So I know that there's a lot more to you than shoulders so wide you got to walk sideways through doors and hands big enough to crush boulders in 'em. Thing is, there's other folks—folks who haven't had the, let's call it *pleasure,* of your company—who would be a bit…well, they'd be put off, wouldn't they?"

"Put off?" Dekker demanded. He jerked a thumb in the wanderer's direction. "He's a damned Eternal, ain't he? Fella that kills giant snakes and monsters for fun. And you're sayin' that won't bother these would-be feasters?"

"Oh, it'd bother them," Clint said. "If they knew it. Thing is…they don't."

Dekker frowned. "Fine, you bastards," he said. He scowled at the wanderer. "But just so you know, I'd be a damn sight better to chew on then you. Why, you look like you taste like dried-out meat left out in the sun. Nothin' but skin and bones."

"I'll take your word on it," the wanderer said. And then they were preparing. They took a moment to make him appear like just another dusty, desperate refugee. And since that was, to a very large extent, exactly what he was, it did not take long.

Soon, they were ready, and the wanderer gave them a nod. "Remember, stay far enough back that they don't see you—they'll be watching."

"Sure, far enough back not to be seen but close enough that you don't get *too* chewed on," Dekker grumbled, obviously still sore about the fact that it was the wanderer being used as bait and not him.

"Look, Dekker," the wanderer said, "maybe you're a bit more…intimidating than I am at first glance, but, if it helps, you could feed dozens."

"And you couldn't," Dekker said, nodding.

"Look at me," the wanderer said. "I'm just skin and bones. Remember?"

The big man nodded, still looking grumpy but a bit less so. "Fine. Just...be careful, alright? And give a shout if you need us. If anybody's going to kick your skinny ass, I'd just as soon it be me."

The wanderer gave them a small smile then turned and stepped into the darkness alone, looking for those who called it home.

It did not take long.

***

He walked alone.

He had done it before, of course. Sometimes, it seemed as if his life had been little else but traveling through the shadows in search of the light.

He wondered why, then, that this time seemed different, wondered why he felt more alone than he could ever remember feeling, why he felt as if he were the only man in a world full of nothing but shadows.

A moment later, he realized why. For the last century he had not actually been alone, not really. Through all that he had suffered, all the dangers that he had faced, Veikr had been there. A more loyal companion, a better friend than anyone could ask for, a fact not diminished because he was incapable of speech but, likely, enhanced by it.

Loyal and steadfast, that was Veikr. Loyal and steadfast and *there*. Always. At least...almost always. The wanderer glanced to his side, to the place Veikr always occupied but not now. Now it was him, and he was alone in truth.

He continued on into the shadow.

He couldn't say what alerted him—a slight sound, nearly imperceptible, perhaps, or a smell. Perhaps it was neither of these, perhaps it was simply instinct, ingrained over many years. In any case, the wanderer was suddenly aware that he was no longer alone.

He half-turned to look behind him, not surprised to find that figures were filtering out of the alleyway he'd just passed. What *did* surprise him, however, was the number of them. Six in all. They were men but they did not move like men. Their shoulders were hunched, their knees slightly bent, and there was a sort of shifting lope to their movements, a walk that made them seem far more like half a dozen wolves than men, and the similarity did not end there.

As they moved closer, seeming almost to walk as one, they stepped into a part of the street illuminated by the moon, and the wanderer saw that they wore what were little better than filthy rags, and their mouths were stained red, the way a wolf's muzzle might be stained after a kill. He would have liked to think that the stain was from berries, perhaps, or wine, but he knew better. The men were not drunk. Or at least if they were, it was not on wine but madness.

So strange was their appearance, so inhuman, that the wanderer found himself reaching for the sword at his back by habit and never mind that he knew full well he had left it with Dekker and Clint, a fact he regretted very much in that moment.

"May I help you?" he asked.

One stepped forward, the largest of the six, the alpha. The wanderer thought that he might speak but he did not. Instead, he bared his teeth—his fangs, the wanderer thought—in what might have been a grin, and started forward in a shifting, hunched lope.

The wanderer did not much care for facing these men that seemed more like beasts but he reminded himself that this was why he had come, that this had been the plan. Which likely meant that it had been a shit plan, but it was too late to question it now, so he stood and waited as the six approached.

"I've come looking for Jackal," he said.

The front man paused at that, his smile spreading wider still. "And you found us," he said.

"Ah," the wanderer said. "So you do speak. I wondered."

"That isn't all we do," the man said, making it a point to display his blood-stained teeth yet again, as if it was possible the wanderer had somehow missed them the first time.

"No," the wanderer said, "No, I don't suppose it is. Before we get started...know that it doesn't have to be this way. You have fallen deep into the shadows, but you can come back to the light. A man, so long as he still breathes, cannot fall so far that he cannot return."

The men did not respond to that, at least not with words. Instead, they let their actions talk for them, fanning out in the street the way wolves might surround their prey to bring it down.

The wanderer watched them. Men with tangled, knotted hair and filthy clothes, looking as if they hadn't taken a bath in a lifetime. Men who had given way to their bestial sides and thought themselves stronger for it. But it was not their wildness that made men strong. It was their capacity to grow, their discipline. "Last chance," he told the men. "Tell me where Jackal is, and you can go on your way."

The lead man, the alpha, moved so that he stood no more than ten feet from the wanderer, letting out a growl. The wanderer nodded. "I thought as much," he said as he drew the knife he kept at his waist and bent his knees slightly, getting into a fighting stance. "But I had to try."

They roared a yell that sounded far more like the howling of wolves or baying of hounds as they chased their prey, and then they all rushed forward. The first man to reach him—not the alpha, the wanderer couldn't help noticing—either didn't see the knife or took no heed of it. Regardless, it was a mistake, one that cost him his life.

The man lunged at him, his teeth bared, his eyes wide and wild and growing wider still as the wanderer stepped to the side, avoiding his grasping hands, and buried his blade in the man's stomach. The wanderer's attacker folded over the blow which made it all the easier for him to rip his knife free and bring the elbow of his other arm down on the back of his attacker's neck. Dead or unconscious—the wanderer didn't much care which—the man collapsed to the ground.

No sooner had the wanderer straightened than two more were on him. The closest growled as he swiped his hand at the wanderer, his long, dirty fingernails cutting through the air. The wanderer leaned back, the man's fingers swiping no more than an inch or two in front of his face, then he gave the man's shin a hard kick. His attacker howled in pain, leaning forward by instinct to clutch his smarting leg. As he did, the wanderer grabbed hold of the man's chin in one hand and the back of his head with the other and gave a savage jerk. There was a *crack,* and the dead man collapsed to the ground.

The wanderer tried to spin but only managed to get about halfway before the third man bowled into his side, knocking him from his feet.

He grunted as he struck the cobbled street. He tried to rise, making it to his back, but the man was on top of him, his hands wrapping around the wanderer's throat, his eyes bulging with madness, red, frothy spittle leaking from his mouth.

The wanderer tried to pry the man's wrists away, but he had no leverage, and the man's madness had given him strength.

As shadows crept into the corner of the wanderer's vision, the man atop him bared his teeth in a grin, anticipating his victory—and likely his next meal.

That made the wanderer angry, and some part of him rose up in answer.

Kill, that part said, and the wanderer did as he was told. His cast his gaze about him and saw that his knife had fallen on the cobbles beside him when he'd been tackled. He let go of one of the man's wrists, and the pressure on his throat increased immediately, black spots growing in his vision. His fingers scrabbled against the hard stone of the street, and he hissed as they found the sharp end of the blade, cutting into his flesh. He sought the handle, found it, and then buried his knife in the man's stomach.

The grip on his throat loosened immediately as the man gasped in shocked pain. The wanderer gasped too, the air burning in his lungs, but that did not keep him from ripping the blade out and burying it in the man again. Then again, and again, his enemy's warm blood sluicing over his hand and arm, his chest. He might have kept at it for an hour, so lost was he in his fury, but then something struck the side of his face, hard, and he was knocked onto his side, the man atop him, already dead, spilling off.

The wanderer's mouth filled with the coppery taste of blood, and he started to his feet. He'd made it to his knees when a grimy bare foot struck him in the chest. The wanderer took the blow—largely because he had no choice—but turned his fall into a roll that took him over his shoulder and to his feet just in time to see his latest attacker charging him.

The wanderer ducked, his leg lashing out, and the man's roar turned into a cry of surprise as his feet went out from under him, and he crashed into the cobbles face-first with a *crack.* The wanderer rose, vaguely aware that there was a growl issuing from his own throat as the anger took full hold of him, and he regarded the man lying on the ground with a dark satisfaction as the man rolled over, displaying several broken, bloody teeth.

The wanderer glanced at his knife, then back at the man and started forward. Part of him, some small, distant part tried to warn him that there were others, that the man before him was not the only one, but he found that he didn't care. All he cared about was the man on the ground, his enemy. The man let out mewling sounds of fear and pain, all the fight gone from him now, and he turned and started to crawl away.

The wanderer followed.

The man had only made it a few feet when the wanderer slammed his blade into his back. The man screamed, clawing at his back, trying to grab the blade, but he could not reach it.

"I warned you," the wanderer growled, "you should have told me what I wanted."

"P-please," the man said. "I'll t-tell you, j-j—"

"It's too late for that now." He ripped the blade free and was just about to bury it in the man's back again when someone grabbed him roughly from behind.

Before he could react, there was a sweaty, hairy arm wrapped around his throat, and his knife slipped free of his fingers as he was jerked backward.

"Guess I ought to thank you for doin' for some of those bastards," a voice who the wanderer recognized as belonging to the leader hissed in his ear, and the wanderer felt his stomach turn at the rancid, fetid smell of the man's breath. *"After all, that's a few less mouths to feed."*

The man's arm tightened around his throat. The wanderer hissed and struggled, finally managing to work his fingers underneath the man's arm. Try as he might, though, he couldn't break his attacker's grasp, so the wanderer did the only thing he could do—he bit deeply into the man's arm.

The cannibal apparently didn't enjoy being on the other end of things. He screamed, jerking his arm away, and the wanderer turned on him, launching into an attack while he was distracted.

Or, at least, he meant to. He'd only just managed the turn when something struck him on the side of the head, and then he was the one distracted. Mostly because, the next thing he knew, he was lying on the ground, staring up at the dark sky, an agonized thumping in his head, his vision cloudy.

A moment later a form appeared above him. The world was spinning around the wanderer from the blow he'd taken, but blurry vision and spinning world or not, he could not help but notice the sharp, short length of steel held in one of the figure's hands.

"*Hey!*" someone shouted from beyond the wanderer's sight. The man standing over him raised his head just in time to be struck with something. The wanderer couldn't tell what exactly it was, so quickly did it happen, only that it was large and wooden. He doubted if the man had an opportunity to identify it either before it—whatever *it* was—crashed into him, sending him hurtling backward.

It seemed, then, that he was saved from imminent death, at least for the moment, but he was well-aware that the leader of the group was still active—though with a good-sized chunk out of his arm. So the wanderer tried his best to ignore the dizziness and sickening nausea roiling through him from the pain in his head and get to his feet.

Suffice to say that it wasn't his finest performance—one of his worst, in fact, and that with no small competition. After all, it wasn't the first time he'd been struck in the head. He'd only made it so far as to one knee when he heard a familiar voice.

"Need a hand?"

The worst of the wanderer's double-vision had begun to settle, and he looked up to see Dekker standing over him. "I thought they taught you Eternals how to fight."

The wanderer frowned. "You're late," he said, taking the big man's hand.

"Yeah, you know," Dekker said, lifting him effortlessly to his feet. "Got caught up sight-seeing."

"Sight-seeing," the wanderer repeated, clearing his throat and fighting back the urge to throw up as a fresh wave of pain pounded through his head.

"Well," Dekker said, "it turns out jackals run in packs." The wanderer was about to ask the man what he meant by that, but then he noted the fresh blood stains on Dekker's shirt, noted also that the knuckles of the big man's right hand were skinned and raw.

He grunted. "How many were there?" he asked.

The big man shrugged. "Three is all, not so many as you have here. They came up on us from behind."

The wanderer nodded, a fact he immediately regretted as a fresh sickening throb of pain lanced through him, and he would have fallen had Dekker not reached out and caught him.

"Woah there," Dekker said. "You alright?"

"I've been better," the wanderer admitted.

Dekker grunted. "Looks like somethin' got a hold of you alright," he said, glancing at the side of the wanderer's face. He cast his gaze about the area around them then took a couple of steps, knelt, and picked up what the wanderer saw was a loose cobble, one that must have come from the street. What he noticed most about it, though, was that it was stained with blood, and it didn't take much effort to figure out where that blood had come from.

"Damn," Dekker said. "You're lucky."

"I feel it."

The big man snorted. "Good to see you haven't lost your sense of humor. All I meant was it's a good thing the gods blessed you with that rock-hard head of yours. A lesser man's skull would have been crushed like a grape."

The wanderer winced. "I'm feeling a little crushed right now." Something caught his eye beyond Dekker, and he leaned to look past the big man's shoulder, frowning as he stared at a large pile of wood from which protruded two boots. He blinked. Perhaps it was from the blow he'd taken or just how incongruous what he saw was, but it took him several seconds to decide what it was he was seeing. In the end, it was the large, wooden-spoked wheel that confirmed his suspicion.

"Speaking of crushed," he said slowly. "Did...did you throw a wagon at someone?"

The big man shifted from foot to foot, looking uncomfortable and more than a little embarrassed. "Don't be ridiculous," he said.

"Good, because—"

"Only part of a wagon."

"Part of it."

The big man nodded. "Wreck somebody left in the street. One of the wheels was missing."

The wanderer stared at the big man for several seconds, not sure of his own thoughts, not sure what a man might, should, or even *could* say to another who he'd just witnessed hurl a wagon the way most people might hurl a ball. He found himself annoyed, somehow, though he couldn't explain exactly why. He sighed. "Where's Clint?" he asked.

"*Here,*" a voice called, and they both turned as the Perishables' leader came jogging up, breathing heavily.

"No luck?" Dekker asked.

"Bastard got away...at least, most of him." Clint glanced at the wanderer. "Seemed like there was a chunk out of his arm. Speakin' of, Ungr, you, uh...you got a little something...on your face."

"Suppose we ought to commend you," Dekker said slowly. "You know, on tryin' out the customs of the places you visit. Only...cannibalism might be one you ought to take a miss on, Ungr."

The wanderer sighed and was about to answer—likely with some choice curse words—when there was a groan from nearby, and he and the others turned to regard the man he'd stabbed in the back.

Dekker glanced at him. "I was always told a man ought to finish what he started."

"I meant to," the wanderer said, "only, I was busy being choked at the time."

"Anyway, this is good for us," Clint said. "We can ask him about Murphy and Gert and all the rest."

"I ain't sure what all this is, Clint," Dekker said, glancing around at the dead men, his gaze settling on the one that was even now trying to crawl away, leaving a bloody trail across the cobbles, "but I'm sure of this much—ain't none of it good. Not for anybody. But let's go ask the poor bastard some questions."

The three of them walked toward the man who raised his eyes as they came to stand in front of him, a desperate look on his face. And he *was* a man now, not the creature he had seemed when confronting the wanderer with his five companions. His fear had made him human once more, for there was no creature beneath the sun who felt fear the way men did. "P-p-please," he said, "please don't kill me."

The wanderer let his gaze travel to the man's back, to the bloody hole in it. The blood was black, and that was a bad sign. A definitive sign. "You're dead already," he told the cannibal. "Your body just hasn't realized that fact yet, but it will. Soon." And then, because the wanderer felt shame at the way he had enjoyed stabbing the man, shame at how he'd wanted to torture him before when the sword's influence had been on him, "I'm sorry."

The man let out a little moan at that, and Clint spoke next. "Maybe you are dyin', but we all are. You can do some good before you go—that's all any of us can hope for. There's a man and woman, Murphy and Gerta by name, from Ingleton. We're looking for them."

"I-I don't know who that is," the man sobbed. "Please, I'm begging you, help me—"

"I told you, we cannot help you," the wanderer said. "No one can."

"W-water," the man said. "C-can I have some water, please? B-Billy has some, just there..." He nodded his head at one of the dead men and the wanderer saw a flask hanging from the man's belt.

"Of cour—" Clint said, cutting off as the wanderer put a hand on him, stopping him from moving toward the body.

"In a minute," the wanderer said, "if you tell us what we want to know."

"P-please," the man begged, "I told you, I don't know who those people are."

"And I believe you," the wanderer said. "Maybe you don't, maybe you have no idea where we might go about finding them. But maybe you know how we might find someone who does. Like the Jackal."

The man swallowed hard at that. "T-the Jackal? I don't—"

"I wouldn't waste time, if I were you," the wanderer said. "You don't have much."

"P-please," the man rasped. "Just a little water."

"Ungr," Clint said, "maybe I should—"

"Not yet," the wanderer said. "Not until we figure out what we need to know." He looked back at the man.

"O-okay," the dying man said, his voice shaking. "H-h-he s-stays at Th-The Stumbling Sailor. It's a t-tavern."

"Where is it?"

"That's alright," Dekker said, grimly. "I know it."

Clint and the wanderer looked at him, and the big man shrugged. "From a long time ago," he said. "Before I met El."

The wanderer nodded. Dekker had told him, more than once, that he had been a criminal once, a bruiser who'd worked for a crime lord in the city. All that had changed once he'd met his wife which meant that if he knew of the place from before then it was because of his shady past. Not surprising, perhaps, that a man like the Jackal would choose to stay at such a place.

The wanderer nodded, starting toward where the dying man had indicated the flask of water. "Ungr—" Clint began.

"It's alright, Clint," the wanderer said. "I'm not so injured that I can't walk."

"No, what he's saying, Ungr," Dekker said, "is that...there isn't any point."

The wanderer frowned, turning back to the big man and preparing to ask what he meant. But then, suddenly, realization struck, and he turned to regard the man he'd stabbed. He noted the way the man lay, his head down against the cobbles, his body looking like a discarded doll. Slack and lifeless, without breath.

"He's dead, Ungr," Clint said, his voice soft. "He died."

The wanderer stared at the dead man, a storm of emotions waging within him. And chief among those emotions was guilt, shame. The anger, for the moment, at least, was gone. What remained was self-recrimination, self-hatred. The flask slipped from his fingers to fall to the cobbles, but he barely noticed. In that moment he was not aware of it anymore than he was aware of the two men, his friends, standing nearby. For him, the world had become nothing but the dead man lying there.

Nothing but the dead man.

Nothing but the dead.

The man had wanted water, that was all. Just a sip of water before death claimed him. "I don't...I can't..." he said, but he did not know how he meant to finish that sentence. He could not find the words.

Dekker put a hand on his shoulder. "Come on, Ungr. Let's go check out this tavern, alright? Find this Jackal bastard and figure out where Clint's friends are."

"Okay," the wanderer said, his eyes still on the dead man.

"Here, Ungr."

He pulled his gaze away with an effort to glance at the Perishable's leader and saw that the man held his two sheathed swords out to him.

The wanderer took his own, slinging it over his back into its customary spot. He reached for the cursed blade next but hesitated, remembering the anger he'd felt. Anger that had made him want to torture the dead man, anger that had made him hold back from granting his simple request for water.

"Maybe...maybe it's best that you carry it," he told the Perishable's leader. "I...I do not know that I trust myself with it anymore."

"What are you on about?" Dekker asked.

The wanderer found himself staring at the blade as if it were a terrible threat, like a snake waiting to strike. And indeed he thought that was close to the truth, or at least in so far as it differed from the truth it was because the sword represented a far greater danger than any snake could ever hope to. A snake, after all, the worst of them, could only kill a man. The sword...he thought that the sword, the weapon of the enemy, could do far worse. He thought that it could rob a man of the person he was, make him into someone, some*thing* else.

"The enemy's weapon...I have drawn it," the wanderer said. "It...it works at me. Makes me...angry. I...I don't trust myself with it any longer."

"Huh," Dekker said. "Well. That's stupid."

The wanderer frowned at him. "What?"

The big man shrugged. "I mean, come on, Ungr. This weapon, you said if the enemy gets their hands on it, it'd be bad, right?"

"Catastrophic," the wanderer said, unsure of where the man meant to go with this. "The blade contains immense power. Coupled with the enemy's own strength, it would be enough to destroy everyone...everything."

"Right. And considerin' that me and my family are part of that everyone, then I'd just as soon avoid that," Dekker said. "And out of the three of us, who would be the most likely to be able to keep them from it, if they had a mind to take it?"

"You don't understand, Dekker," the wanderer said, glancing at the dead man. "He...he just wanted some water and—"

"And the people that bastard ate just wanted to go on not being eaten," Dekker countered. "You didn't attack him, Ungr—he attacked you. He chose it, not you."

"But the sword..."

"Is just a sword," Dekker said. "A tool, like any other."

"But it's dangerous."

Dekker snorted. "Of course it's dangerous. So's any blade in the hands of someone don't know how to use it. So's a hammer, for that matter, but it's damned hard to build a house without one."

"This isn't a hammer."

"No, no it ain't. But let me ask you this—would you have made it this far without it?"

The wanderer frowned. "What—"

"Like back when you fought those Revenants at Will's place, or when you escaped those giant armored spiders?"

"No, but—"

"So there you have it. It was a tool you used and, because of that, you're still here. Because of that, because of *it,* we're *all* still here. As for the rest, for being scared of it, that's alright, too. A man ought to be scared of any weapon before he's learned the use of it."

"And I suppose you know how I'm supposed to learn the use of it?" the wanderer asked.

"That's an easy one," the big man said. "The same way a man learns the use of anything, the same way a man figures out how to make his wife want to strangle 'em. Practice."

The wanderer frowned, considering his words, thinking of what the ghosts would say. They would caution him against it, would call him a fool for even considering ever drawing the blade again. This he knew, for they had made their thoughts on it clear enough over the years. But then, they were all dead, slain at the hands of the enemy, and the wanderer thought that, if someone meant to learn how to swim, the last person they ought to take lessons from was a drowned man.

He took the sword. It felt good in his grip as if it belonged there, and that scared him.

"You said you know the tavern, the one he spoke of?"

"I do," Dekker said. "Though if the Sailor is anything like I remember it, I'll warn you that it's a pretty long way from some noble's ballroom."

"Good thing I didn't wear my fine suit," the wanderer said.

Dekker grunted. "That one bastard—the one you took a chunk out of—reckon he'll let them know we're coming?"

"Yes."

"Might be they'll set a trap for us then."

"Might be they will."

Dekker glanced at Clint then back to the wanderer. "So what's the plan?"

The wanderer shrugged. "They're waiting on us—it'd be a shame to disappoint them."

"Be a shame to get eaten, too."

"Don't worry," the wanderer said, giving the man a small, humorless smile, "I'm sure there'll be some wagons or trees, maybe a few buildings nearby you can throw around if anyone gets out of line."

"You're a bastard, you know that?"

"Well, sure," the wanderer said, "as you said—I've had practice. Now, come on. Let's go find Clint's friends."

CHAPTER FOURTEEN

IT TOOK THEM another hour to make their way to the tavern the man had told them about. An hour of walking through what felt like some world of the damned where, around every corner, waited another horrific scene, another degradation.

So it was that, despite what they meant to do, despite the many dangers they would face when confronting the Jackal, the wanderer was relieved when Dekker finally held out an arm larger than some trees he'd seen, stopping them. "That's the Sailor across the road there," the big man said quietly.

They stood in at the mouth of a dark alleyway, hidden in the shadows which was just as well as, when the wanderer turned to regard the building Dekker had indicated, he saw two big men, their arms folded across their chests, scowling out at the night as if it had personally offended them.

"Reckon they take kindly to visitors?" Clint asked.

"Only one way to find out," the wanderer said.

"I hate it when he says shit like that," Dekker told Clint.

The Perishable's leader nodded. "What's the plan?" he asked the wanderer.

"Wait here," the wanderer said.

"Wait?" Dekker said. "I don't much care when he says shit like that either," he told Clint. "Musta got hit harder than I realized back there," he went on, frowning at the wanderer. "There's two of 'em, in case you didn't notice. Big fellas, both, and that's before we consider how many are inside that'll come out when they hear them yell."

"Best they don't yell then," the wanderer said, starting away.

"And how do you mean to keep 'em from doing that?" Dekker asked. "Ask them nicely?"

The wanderer paused, turning to give the man a small smile. "Something like that. Will you stay?"

Dekker glanced at Clint. "And avoid having a chat with a couple of fellas that like to eat people? I reckon we'll get over our disappointment. Just don't go getting your fool self turned into dinner, eh?"

"I'll try not to," the wanderer promised. Then, he nodded at them and started back down the alley.

"Uh, Ungr?" Dekker asked.

The wanderer glanced back to the two men, looking at him strangely. "The uh...the Sailor's over there," the big man said, jerking his thumb at the building across the street.

"I know," the wanderer said.

"You...you sure you're feeling alright after takin' that hit?" Clint asked.

"I'm fine."

The two men shared a troubled look, but Dekker nodded. "Alright then," he said, "just...don't be too long."

"Wouldn't dream of it," the wanderer said, then he started once more into the darkness.

***

He was alone again, and that was alright, was as it should be. For one, alone, might slip through the shadows unnoticed. And if he were to have any chance of getting into the tavern without being confronted by what might conceivably be a small army of cannibals, he must remain unnoticed.

The wanderer moved down the alleyway and turned, taking a circuitous route as Assassin had taught him, one that would eventually lead him to the side of the tavern. As he walked, he found himself thinking of the Eternal's lessons.

The work of an assassin, she had taught him, was far different than that of a soldier.

A soldier had a goal and moved toward it, taking the most direct route possible, not bothering to pick the lock of a door when he could tear it down. Bumbling oafs, she had called them, though she had shown respect for their discipline. Assassins were different. For the most difficult task of being a successful killer, the Eternal had said, was not the killing, not one's talent with knives or bows. Instead it was patience, discernment, observation.

He traveled far enough away from the tavern that he would not be seen crossing the street then worked his way down alleyways to draw closer to one of its sides. When he was at the sidestreet closest to The Stumbling Sailor, he crept toward the opening and peered around the corner.

The two guards stood as they had, staring out at the night not just as if they were ready for a fight but as if they wanted it.

Not that they would have been likely to have gotten into a scrap on any normal night. After all, what sort of fools—or fool, as the case may be—sought entrance into a tavern filled with known cannibals, of all things?

Only the most foolish, he thought.

He took his time, considering the distance between him and the two men. Twenty feet, a bit more. Too much to cover at a sprint before they'd be alerted to his presence. Which meant that a subtler approach was required.

Not the heavy trod of a soldier, but the stealthy, whispering walk of the assassin. The wanderer frowned. He had been taught by the very best assassin in the world, of course, taught in the ways of moving silently, of slowing even the beating of his own heart, of gliding through the darkness like a shadow among shadows. The darkness, Assassin had taught him, was one's greatest ally. For through it anything might move, any*one.*

It was as if a whole other world existed beyond that of the light, beyond the shops and cities, the taverns and brothels. A world of silhouettes and mysteries, and only those who understood how to travel within it could find entrance.

He had been shown the path to that world, how to venture into it, but that had been a very long time ago. A hundred years and more, and he was not sure if he remembered the way.

Some people believe it is a talent one never loses, Assassin said into his mind, nearly causing him to let out a cry of surprise that would have doomed him, for he had not realized, in his distraction, that he'd fingered the locket open.

"Some people?" he whispered, doing his best to get control of his suddenly panicked breathing.

Fools, the Eternal said.

Not exactly helpful, but then Assassin had never been particularly concerned with being helpful—it was, after all, largely antithetical to her chosen profession.

You must not be seen, Assassin said. *You must not be heard. So do not be seen. Do not be heard.*

The wanderer winced. "How?"

Be silent, the Eternal said as if it was the most obvious thing in the world, *be invisible.*

"I'm...finding it difficult to be that."

The shadow does not find it difficult to be a shadow, does not try to be a shadow at all. Not anymore than a swan tries to be a swan. It simply is. Or it is not. Perhaps the swan is no swan at all but a chicken. In which case it will likely be dinner.

Not the most encouraging of words, perhaps, but the wanderer knew he was wasting time. He took a deep breath, closing his eyes and doing his best to gather the darkness, the stillness about himself like a cloak, a mental exercise Assassin had taught him.

And if he did, in the end, don that cloak, then it was a frayed, pitiful thing, but he was not capable of making any better, so he took a deep breath, opening his eyes. Then, shooting another glance at the men to make sure they did not look in his direction, he stepped into the street.

He moved slowly, carefully, on the balls of his feet as Assassin had taught him, yet for all his efforts, he felt like a bull charging around a ballroom, like a once-sharp sword that had lost its edge and so was of little use to anyone.

Still, there was no help for it, so he moved forward slowly, not trying to walk but to glide and despite his fears, despite his own insecurities, the men did not glance in his direction as he approached.

Twenty feet shrank to fifteen, and still they did not look. Fifteen to ten, ten to five, and still he remained unnoticed. His swords were strapped to his back, but he did not draw them, for they would not do for this kind of work.

He drew his knife.

He crept forward until he was behind the closest man, and still he had not turned.

He started to reach the knife forward, preparing to stab it into the man's heart, an action that would quickly end his life before he could scream. But he hesitated.

He thought that the man should die, that he *needed* to die for them to gain entry. After all, he was a bouncer for a tavern full of cannibals. Almost certainly the man was a cannibal himself. And yet...the wanderer didn't *know* that. In fact, he knew nothing about the man. Perhaps he sought only to feed his family, to do any work to keep them from starving in a city that seemed damned.

Perhaps the wanderer only felt like he needed to kill him and his companion because of the influence of the cursed blade. There was no way to be sure. So, frowning, he chose a separate course. Instead of stabbing into the man's heart, as he'd planned, the wanderer brought his knife up and struck the man in the temple, hard.

He let out a small grunt, no more than that, but in the quiet stillness of the night it was enough to alert the second bouncer who turned, opening his mouth.

Perhaps he was preparing to ask his companion—who was currently collapsing to the ground—what was happening. Or perhaps he was preparing to yell in alarm. Either way, the wanderer couldn't take the chance, so before the man could utter a single syllable he lashed out, striking the man in the throat with a ridge-handed blow. Not hard enough to collapse it but hard enough that he let out a strangled, choking sound, stumbling away in shock and pain, his hands lashing out wildly.

The man's wild swing struck the wanderer's arm, knocking the knife free, but he didn't hesitate. He lunged forward, sliding underneath the man's guard and getting around behind him, wrapping his arm around the man's neck, grabbing his own elbow in a choke. The man was big, strong, and he tried to use that strength to dislodge the wanderer who was forced to jump up and wrap his legs around the man's midsection, linking his ankles as he continued to choke him.

In desperation the bouncer slammed himself backward. The wanderer winced at the sound—and, more specifically, at the pain—as he struck the tavern wall once, then again. He did not strike it a third time, though, for the bouncer's lack of air began to tell. He stumbled forward, collapsing to his knees. The wanderer remained as he was, continuing to choke him until, in another few seconds, the man collapsed face first onto the ground, unconscious.

The wanderer rose, breathing hard from the brief but intense struggle, and turned to the tavern door, waiting to see if there were any shouts of alarm from inside or if anyone came rushing out of it, eager for his blood.

He was still waiting when a voice spoke.

"Damn."

The wanderer spun, going for the sword at his back until he realized in another moment that the voice he'd heard belonged not to some unseen attacker responding, but instead to Dekker, for the big man was walking up, Clint beside him.

"Huh," Dekker said, glancing at the two unconscious men. "I gotta be honest, Ungr, I figured you meant to kill them."

"I did."

"Mercy, eh?" Dekker said, nodding slowly. "Well, can't say as I have a lot of it for people that eat people, and I don't think they're likely to thank you for it, but...I get it. So what now?"

"Now we go find your friends," he said to Clint.

"Wait...you just mean to walk in there?" Dekker asked.

"I suppose we could skip," the wanderer said, "but I expect that might draw some unwanted attention."

The big man frowned. "But...but won't they attack us?"

"Probably they will assume that anyone the bouncers let in is okay to be there."

"Uh-huh," Dekker said. "Who knows, maybe they'll even invite us for dinner."

"Let's hope not," Clint said squeamishly.

"And what of these two?" Dekker asked, glancing at the two unconscious men. "I mean, they're going to wake up sooner or later."

"Best we hurry then," the wanderer said.

Dekker scowled, making it clear that he didn't like the plan, and that was alright, for the wanderer didn't much care for it either. Still, since it was the best plan they had—largely by virtue of being the only one—he gave the two men a nod, turned, and stepped into the tavern.

He wasn't sure what he'd been expecting—tables where men hunched over the corpses of the dead, their mouths stained with blood as they tore into the flesh of another like demons, perhaps. Certainly, that was his fear.

But what he found upon entering the tavern was, at least at first glance, a normal common room that might be found in hundreds of cities across the world. Wooden tables were scattered about the area and a haze hung in the air, filling the room with the smell of smoke. Men and some few women, about two dozen in all, sat around the room talking. A bartender stood behind the bar, a thin man, but not starving, polishing a glass with a rag. He saw the wanderer glancing in his direction and gave him a wink.

"Huh," Dekker said.

"Huh," the wanderer agreed. The tavern looked like any other tavern in any other city. In fact, a man stepping inside might be forgiven for thinking that there was nothing wrong with Celes at all, that the city was doing as well as it had always done under Soldier's rule.

But the wanderer had been taught to notice things—it was one of those lessons all the Eternals had taken time out to teach him, particularly Assassin. For, according to her, an assassin's life and death depended, more than anything, on his or her ability to observe, to catch things that others missed and to react accordingly.

And so he noted that, while the tavern common room might, on the surface, at least, appear like any other, there were differences, too.

The most obvious of which was the door at the back of the room, one at which stood two men of a size with the unconscious ones in the street. These two, though, were very conscious and alert, frowning out at nothing in particular. The wanderer wondered if bouncers practiced that look, how much time they spent scowling at their reflections to perfect that expression, that stance. Both of which communicated their point as clearly as if they'd spoken it aloud—don't mess with us, unless you want to suffer for it.

But while that might have been the most obvious difference separating the common room from any other, it was not the one that bothered the wanderer the most. First of all, there was a smell—the cloying smell of cooked meat. Then there were the stains he noted here and there on the tables and floor. Crimson stains that had seeped into the wood. They might have been from wine, but he didn't think so. He'd been in plenty of taverns and some of those had been the rougher kind, the kind where a night hardly passed where a fight didn't break out, where someone didn't end up stabbed or bleeding. He'd seen such stains there too.

He'd talked to a tavernkeep about it once, after such a scuffle which he'd helped to bring in order. A leg had been broken off a chair during the row, but the man hadn't cared much about that—instead, it had been the fresh blood stains that had bothered him most. For he'd said that while he might fix the chair leg himself or, if it were too badly damaged, he might pay a carpenter a few copper to do the job, the blood would remain. For blood, he said, never came out, not fully. It seeped into the wood, became part of it, and no amount of scrubbing or washing ever got it out.

There were plenty of such stains on the floor of the tavern, on the tables, too. But even that wasn't the thing that bothered the wanderer most. It was the way the men and women of the room looked at him and the others. They weren't friendly, those looks, but neither were they the unwelcoming scowls one might expect from the recalcitrant, often insular regulars of a tavern who always seemed to feel as if any newcomer was an intruder.

The wanderer had gotten such looks as that, many times, when coming in off the road, his cloak and boots dusty from hours spent on the trail, looking only to get something to drink to wet his parched throat. He'd gotten them many times, and so he knew them well. The looks the tavern's patrons shot in his and the others' direction were different. Not overtly hostile but instead a sort of sizing up, the way a man might size up a cow he was looking at buying at market.

"Anybody else feel like a piece of meat?" Dekker asked quietly, echoing the wanderer's thoughts.

"Come on," the wanderer said, starting toward the bar. The other two followed him to the counter where they sat at three empty stools.

"Three ales, please," the wanderer told the barkeep. He didn't have any plan on drinking, of course, but if a man wanted to blend in then he didn't go to a bar and not order anything.

The barkeep gave him a nod, moving toward the other side of the counter where the tap was. "Don't reckon it's all that hard to figure where this Jackal is," Dekker said quietly, glancing at the door at the back of the room, the one at which stood two thickly-muscled bouncers.

"No, no it doesn't," the wanderer agreed.

"Might as well be a mile away for all the good knowing it will do us," Clint said, frowning. "It ain't as if we can make a move toward it—shit, for all we know, the moment we did this whole room of folk'd up and attack us. I want to find Murph and Gert, but I don't much like the idea of becoming dinner for a bunch of psychotic cannibals in the process."

"What these fine folks?" Dekker asked in a whisper. "For shame, Clint," he said, the sarcasm thick in his voice. "Anyway, what can we do?"

The three of them were silent as they considered that. "Maybe...maybe we could sneak in?" Clint asked, his own doubt of the idea clear in his voice.

"What, like wait for those bastards to go to sleep?" Dekker said, tilting his head at the two men flanking the door. "Or maybe convince them to let us through?" He shook his head. "Not likely. I've been in that position before—door watchin'. Just about the most boring thing you can imagine. Gets to where you *hope* someone tries to force their way past just so you'll have something to do."

Clint nodded, clearly having expected as much. His eyes traveled around the room, and the wanderer followed his gaze to a small stage at its center. A stage that had no doubt been placed there so that entertainers—musicians, jugglers, and all the rest—might perform for the tavern's patrons. Not that the wanderer thought they were likely to see such a performance any time soon, not if the layer of dust coating the platform was anything to go by.

"A shame Sheriff Fred isn't here," Clint mused. "He said he was a juggler, didn't he?"

"That would have proven a fine distraction," the wanderer agreed.

"So...how are we going to get in?" Clint asked.

"I...I don't know," the wanderer admitted. He was still considering it when Dekker let out a sour grunt.

"Might be I've got an idea," the big man said, his voice little more than a low, rumbling whisper.

The wanderer and Clint shared a look. "Well?" Clint said. "Don't keep us in suspense, Dek. I'd just as soon not hang out in a—" He paused, glancing around to make sure no one was close then leaned forward, speaking in a whisper. "*In a tavern full of cannibals, anymore than I have to.* In fact, I'd say it's just about the worst thing I can imagine."

"Wouldn't be so sure of that," the big man said quietly, avoiding both their eyes. He sighed, rising. "If I keep the rest of these bastards distracted, you reckon you two can deal with the ones at the door without causin' all that much of a stir?"

The wanderer and Clint shared another look. "I believe so, yes," the wanderer said.

Clint gave a soft, nervous laugh. "What is it, Dekker, you plannin' on givin' these folks a show or what?"

"Something like that," the big man said grimly. "Let's just hope they don't think dinner's included." He rose then, shifting his massive shoulders and popping his neck, tilting it one way, then the other. Then he took a slow, deep breath, looking to the wanderer like nothing so much as a man preparing to march into battle.

"Be ready," Dekker told them.

"For what?" Clint asked, his tone of voice making it clear that he was just as confused as the wanderer.

The big man closed his eyes, taking another deep breath. "I'm going to sing," he said, the words issuing from his throat with the same solemn gravity that a man might say that he was walking to his own death.

Then, before either of them could say anything else, Dekker turned and started toward the stage.

A few of the taverns' patrons marked Dekker as he moved among them, shooting him appraising glances that, if not overtly hostile, were far from friendly. As he took the stage more turned to regard him, some few nudging and whispering to those seated nearby.

The wanderer would have judged that about a third of the tavern's few dozen patrons were paying attention to the big man by the time he was standing at the stage, clearing his throat and looking just about as uncomfortable and miserable as a man could look.

Then he began to sing.

The wanderer had heard a lot of singers over the years. Troubadours and traveling bards, men and women who sang in dirty, forgotten hamlets and famous vocalists who spent their time performing in the courts of nobles who counted themselves lucky for the honor of hosting such talent. He had heard master musicians at their trade, men and women who had dedicated their lives to their performances. Yet he had never heard anything quite like the big man's voice.

He'd heard people—mostly the bards themselves—describe the voices of others or mostly themselves, saying things like smooth as silk or sweet as honey, deep as a well. The wanderer wouldn't have used any of those to describe Dekker's voice, at least not separately. Instead, it was somehow a mixture of all of them, a powerful voice, smooth and rasping at once, one that did not sound trained like the voice of a court musician or singer, and was not diminished but instead enhanced by that.

And in only moments Dekker did not have the attention of a few people, nor of a third of those in the tavern, but every single living, breathing person within it, all of them watching the man as he sang, his deep, baritone voice filling the room.

"Son of a bitch," Clint breathed beside the wanderer. "Bastard never told me he could sing."

The wanderer meant to respond, but he only found himself nodding distractedly, caught up in the ballad the big man sang. He was so caught up, in fact, that as he sat there, watching the performance, he all but forgot what they had come for, why the big man was singing in the first place.

At least that was until a minute or two later when Dekker glanced at where the wanderer and Clint sat, raising his eyebrows as if to ask what they were waiting for.

"Come on," the wanderer said.

The Perishables' leader nodded, and the two of them slowly began making their way across the common room, taking their time, moving carefully so as not to draw the attention of its patrons. Not that they needed to bother with much subtlety, for everyone in the room appeared to be enraptured by Dekker's performance.

Soon they were at the back of the room, less than a dozen feet between the two guards who didn't even notice them. They, like the rest of the tavern room, were engrossed by Dekker's performance. The wanderer glanced at the big man who shot them a quick look and then, suddenly and seamlessly, as if he had planned it perfectly, the slow, melodic ballad transformed by some trick into a fast-paced, tavern song. One with simple—and bawdy—words that allowed the tavern patrons, after a single verse and chorus, to join in with singing and clapping, which they did with alacrity.

Even the guards left off their grim, happy-to-kill-you stares and began to clap along, grins spreading on their faces.

The wanderer nodded at Clint, motioning for him to wait there, then began to walk toward the guards. He didn't need to worry about them hearing him, for the whole room was filled with the thunderous sound of clamping and feet stomping and, of course, Dekker's voice.

He suspected he might have yelled his plans as he approached them and still it would have made no difference. He didn't, though, nor did he waste time. Instead, as he moved up to the two men he grabbed a hard glass tankard from a nearby table, its owner too engrossed by Dekker's singing to take any note. The first bouncer didn't take note of it either. At least, that was, until the wanderer struck him in the back of the head with it.

The second managed a half-turn but no more than that before the glass struck him, too. The two collapsed to the ground, and the wanderer stood staring at the ale glass. He'd half-expected it to break on the first man's head, had been sure it would break on the second. He glanced back at Clint, motioning the man forward, and the Perishables' leader started toward him, blinking.

"If I ever piss you off, Ungr," the man said as he came to stand beside him at the door, "let's talk it out. Alright?"

The wanderer gave him a sidelong glance. "I've been told I'm not all that much for small talk."

"Well," Clint said, clearing his throat as he stepped carefully over the sprawled form of one of the unconscious men. "You got a way of gettin' your point across anyway. Besides, I s'pose we all have our talents." He glanced at the door. "Reckon we ought to knock?"

"I think we left politeness behind a while ago."

The Perishable's leader nodded. "Probably right."

The wanderer tried the door and was unsurprised to find it locked.

"Too bad Dek's busy," Clint said. "The big bastard could probably look at the damned thing, and it'd fall over out of fear of bein' contrary."

"Probably so," the wanderer agreed.

Still, while he might not have possessed Dekker's strength—he was pretty sure there were gorillas who couldn't make that claim—the wanderer had been taught the arts of stealth and subterfuge by the greatest master the world had ever seen.

He knew how to stalk his prey, how to study them, learn their habits and use their habits to exploit their weaknesses. He knew how to disappear into the shadows—or, at least, come as close as any man could. He knew dozens of poisons, each with different effects and purposes...and he *also* knew how to pick a lock.

He retrieved his knife from his waist. There were tools made specifically for the purpose, ones far better suited to the task than the short, thin blade he held, ones that would do the job completely silently, but he thought the knife would do well enough. He slid the blade into the space between the door and its frame near the handle, working it around until he felt the clasp that held the door shut. Then, slowly, he worked at it, wiggling the blade underneath it. When he was satisfied that it was as good as it would get, he gave the knife a jerk and, at the same time that he loosened the clasp, he slammed his shoulder into the door, which flew open.

The wanderer held his blade up, ready to react if someone rushed him but no one did. The door led onto an office that looked, at first glance, no more out of place than the common room had. A large desk sat at the room's back with what appeared to be a ledger, one that likely documented the finances of the tavern, along with some fresh parchment and a few books.

Yet, something about the desk, about the entire entry room, felt strange, to the wanderer, off somehow. It didn't feel...real. Instead, he got the impression that he wasn't looking at something completely normal but something that had been carefully crafted to *appear* normal and safe. An illusion similar to the one some animals created, pretending to be dead so that their prey would approach only to pounce on them when it was too late to escape.

The room—the entire tavern, in truth—felt like that. All the way down to the bookcase to the left of the desk. But that wasn't all. There was something else bothering the wanderer, something he couldn't put his finger on.

"This isn't right."

"I'll say," Clint said, his voice grim. "You don't...you don't think that fella told us wrong, do you?"

"In my experience dying men rarely lie."

"Got a lot of experience with that, have you?"

"Too much," the wanderer said honestly. "People generally lie either to save their own lives or to make them better, somehow."

"Or to make someone else's worse, maybe."

"Which makes a certain type of person's life better. Or, at least, they think it does. Dying men though have no hope of living, let alone making their lives better."

"Then what?" Clint asked. "Seems a little much to think that this Jackal just happened to step out right before we came."

"Yes, it does," the wanderer said, his gaze traveling around the room, trying to figure out what it was about it that bothered him so much, what had set his nerves on edge. Aside, of course, from the feeling that it was all staged for his—or anyone else's—benefit.

"Well, no one's here," Clint said, "that much is obvious. It ain't exactly as if the room's big enough we might not see 'em."

The wanderer frowned at that. "You're right," he said slowly. "It's a small room."

"Yeah, some are," Clint said. "Surprised you didn't know that. Anyway—"

"Wait," the wanderer said, holding up a hand. It was close, the thing that was bothering him. Close but trying to slip away from his mind again before he could get a good hold of it.

"Ungr, we really don't have time to—"

"Wait," he repeated, still looking around the room. "Please."

To his credit, Clint did, standing in silence as the wanderer let his gaze travel around the room. "It's a small room," the wanderer said, thinking. Something about the words. There was something there. Something that didn't quite fit. Then he was no longer grasping for it but had it in truth. Realization struck, and he turned to Clint. "The room—it's what doesn't fit."

Clint blinked. "Well, I ain't no carpenter, Ungr, but I might have to disagree with you on that one. On account of, you know, it's here. Fittin' and all."

"No, don't you see? It's too small, Clint. The room's too small."

"I'll admit, it aint biggest office I've seen, but it's big enough."

"No," the wanderer said, shaking his head. "No, it isn't. This building—it's bigger on the outside."

The Perishables' leader frowned. "I'm not following you."

"Try to," the wanderer said, moving toward the back of the wall, a wall that, he knew, ought to have been at least fifteen or twenty feet farther away.

"Wait," Clint said, "are you sayin' you think someone, what, built a hidden wall? Why would they..." He trailed off as the wanderer turned to glance at him then cleared his throat. "Right. I'll help you look."

The Perishable's leader moved toward the wall on the opposite side of the desk from the wanderer. Meanwhile, the wanderer stepped toward the bookshelf, letting his gaze trail along it, searching for any tell-tale sign of a hidden hinge or clasp. He didn't see anything at first and so began pulling the books out one at a time until he came to one that did not seem to want to move, as if it had been glued in.

He frowned. *Or,* he thought, *as if it isn't a book at all.* Or, if it was, he decided when another tug still didn't budge it, then it was a book that was not meant to be read.

"Got somethin'?" Clint asked from beside him.

"I don't know yet," the wanderer said quietly. He traced his fingers along the book, then instead of trying to pull at the spine, he grabbed the top of it—the way a man might grab a lever—and pulled it down.

He was rewarded a moment later as the "book" moved, and there was a shifting, creaking sound as the bookshelf—and the wall behind it—pivoted outward like a door.

"Damn," Clint said.

The wanderer nodded, staring into the opening, ready to draw his blade at the first sign of someone charging toward him out of the dimly lit room. When no one did, he glanced at the side of the bookshelf and wall, noting the hinge that had been hidden moments ago. He could not help but be impressed by the work and found himself wondering how much such a thing would have cost. After all, there could only be a handful of artisans in the city that could do it so well. But then he remembered where he was—a tavern that was reportedly full of cannibals—and decided he'd rather not think about what the craftsman's payment might have been.

He glanced at Clint then he drew his blade, moving through the door. He stepped into a small antechamber, and at once the smell which had first struck him when entering the tavern seemed to increase dramatically. The odor of rotting meat and blood. He heard Clint gasping behind him.

The wanderer couldn't blame him, for the smell was far from the worst of it. There were tables on either side of the room, their surfaces covered in blood-stains of varying ages and here, at least, no effort had been made to disguise or clean them. And worse than the blood were the metal implements scattered along their surface. Knives and prying tools, others he recognized as tools used for flaying, peeling away the flesh of an animal when it was butchered.

And judging by the blood and bits of hair and flesh coating their surfaces, all of the implements had been used and used often. And, in several cases...used recently. He did not need to wonder upon what they might have been used and the wanderer felt something very primal rebel in him as he looked at them, felt that alien anger that he attributed to the cursed blade rise up in him, demanding...not justice. No, for that anger cared nothing for justice, only revenge.

Only a reckoning.

He heard Clint gagging behind him, getting sick. The wanderer did not feel sick, though. He felt only rage.

There was a door at the end of the small room, and he thought he could hear the muffled sounds of whimpering or moaning from beyond it. "Come on," he told the Perishables' leader then, without looking back, he started toward the door.

As he approached the door, the whimpering was easier to make out, a rasping desperate voice, begging for help.

The wanderer did not waste time picking the lock this time. He braced himself, then shouldered into the door. The door cracked as it broke off the hinges, swinging open. The smell of blood and death and rancid meat crashed into him, so powerful that he felt as if he was rocked backward by it.

A body—or, at least what was left of it—lay sprawled on a table at the center of the room. At the opposite end was a cage, and in the cage the wanderer got a vague sense of several bloody bodies, no more than that, before someone spoke. *"Son of a bi—"*

The man—who had been standing at the side of the room—charged at him, brandishing a butcher's knife that was less a weapon than it was a tool for preparing meat. The blade in the wanderer's hand *was* a weapon, though, and with the smell filling his nostrils, the knowledge of what had been going on here filling his mind, he did not hesitate to use it.

He lashed out with his blade, the sharpened steel, driven by his rage, cutting through the man's wrist. The wanderer's attacker screamed as the butcher's knife he'd held—along with the hand that had held it—was flung away.

The man reeled away, stumbling and turning as if to run. The wanderer grabbed hold of his shoulder from behind and rammed his blade into the man's back. He ripped the blade free and planted a foot in the man's back, sending him hurtling forward so that he crashed face-first into the ground and did not move.

The wanderer, satisfied that the man was dead or well on his way, certainly far enough gone to cause them no more of an issue, turned back to Clint and the rest of the room.

"Eternals save us," the Perishables' leader breathed, staring at the cage at the back of the room which appeared contain three or four dead bodies, though it was hard to tell for all the blood and the way they were all laid atop each other.

We tried, the wanderer thought in response to the Clint's words, but he did not say them. In fact, neither of them spoke for a few seconds, for there were some horrors, some tragedies that made words seem empty and hollow, a vain attempt at self-soothing that was destined to fail. This, the wanderer decided, as he looked at the cage and the bodies lying within it, was one of those moments. His gaze traveled to the table at the room's center. A table that had been fashioned with iron manacles at both ends, manacles that, even now, held bits of flesh and skin and human hair.

"P-please," a hoarse voice said in a low whisper. *"Please help me."*

The wanderer and Clint turned to look at the man with the missing hand. But it was not him, for the voice had not come from that part of the room. It had come from the cage.

"Eternals be good, please....oh, please."

The wanderer and Clint both hurried forward to the cage. Whatever else they had done, the Jackal and his cannibal-followers had clearly not skimped when it came to the construction of the cage in which they planned to hold their victims. It was fashioned from iron, with a lock as solid and convincing as any a man might expect to see in a king's dungeon.

"A key," Clint said, his voice hoarse and breathless. "There's got to be a key."

The wanderer cast his gaze about and spotted it on the table. He was a bit surprised by that, for he would have thought that the Jackal—if the man lying on the ground missing a hand was indeed the Jackal—would have kept it on his person. Still, he didn't waste time wondering. He hurried to the table, retrieved it and moved back to the cage, unlocking it.

The bodies inside the cage were coated with blood, slimy with it, so sprawled together that it was difficult to figure out where one wretched soul ended and another began. As he looked for the man who'd spoken, the wanderer noted chunks missing out of pieces of the thighs and arms of the men inside, noted, too, the raw places around their wrists and ankles where they had clearly struggled—in vain—against the manacles he'd spotted on the table.

Finally he caught sight of a blue eye staring out at him from that mess, saw it blink. "Help me," he said, and then they heaved the bodies aside.

Clint hissed in shock as soon as they were able to get a good look at the man. *"Murphy?"* he said. "Is that you?"

"C-C-Clint?" the man said in shock as they pulled him to his feet and began leading him out of the cage. *"Wha...what are you doing here?"*

"Looking for you," Clint said, his voice thick with emotion, sounding close to tears. "What...what happened? Where's...where's Gert, Murphy?" he asked, his fear clear in his voice.

The shirtless, blood-soaked man, was shaking his head. *"Sh...she's alright,"* he said. *"She's...safe. Told me...told me not to go out, lookin' for work, but we were hungry, and..."* He trailed off then, beginning to sob, and Clint pulled him into a hug, looking over his shoulder at the wanderer, his expression a mixture of fury and unbelievable sadness.

"That's alright, Murph," Clint said. "That's alright. You're safe now." The Perishable's leader pulled away after another moment, his hands on either of the man's arms, looking him over. "Where are you hurt?" he asked, but before the other man could answer, Clint gave a hiss as he took in a wound on the man's upper arm where it looked as if someone had cut a strip of flesh free and then a deeper one on his thigh. Clint hurried to rip off strips of his shirt, bandaging the wounds as best he could.

He was just finishing when there was a guttural croak from the other end of the room. The wanderer and the others turned to look in the direction of the man whose hand he'd cut off to see that the man had managed to turn himself onto his back and was staring at the ceiling, not quite dead but dying.

The wanderer started toward him, kneeling before him. "Are there others, Jackal?" he said. "Others suffering in this way? Where are they?"

"*Not...*" The man gave his head a ragged shake. "*Wrong...Jackal—*" He never got to finish whatever he'd been about to say for suddenly the man, Murphy, was there, moving with a speed the wanderer wouldn't have credited to most men, particularly when those men were injured.

He held a knife in both hands, and he brought it down, hard, into the man's heart. The man let out a gasp of shock and then he was dead.

Murphy let go of the knife with his trembling hands and gazed up at the wanderer. "*Y-you wouldn't believe what he did...to us,*" he said.

The wanderer had wanted to ask the man questions before he died, but he nodded, glancing at Clint. "We need to leave. Now."

Clint nodded, reaching out his hand to Murphy and pulling him to his feet.

"How long have you been here?" he asked the man.

"I...I'm not sure," Murphy said.

"And the others? In the cage?" the wanderer asked, trying to understand, for there was something strange about it all, something he couldn't put his finger on. "Why did they kill them?"

"I...I don't understand," Murphy said.

"You *know* why they killed them, Ungr," Clint said. "We all know why."

The wanderer frowned, nodding. He still thought it strange, for the men he'd seen had not been dead for very long. He had never raised livestock before, but some of the men in his village when he'd been a child had, and he knew that if a man wanted meat he didn't slaughter all his cows at once, lest the meat go bad. He wanted to ask about that, about a lot of other things, too, but he decided to let it go for now. After all, if a man wanted to tarry there were better places to do so than in a tavern full of cannibals, and he imagined there were few places where the people would be less likely to behave logically. "Can you walk?" the wanderer asked the man.

"I...I think so."

"Alright. Keep him close," he told Clint. "And follow me. We don't stop for anything."

The Perishables' leader draped one of his friend's arms over his shoulder and gave a grim nod.

Then they were moving, back through the antechamber with the tables and their bloody instruments to the door leading into the tavern's common room. The wanderer paused here, glancing back at the two men to make sure they were ready. He considered sheathing his sword but decided against it. While it might attract attention, he thought that he'd rather have it out in case they got more attention than they wanted.

He opened the door and stepped into the common room.

The two unconscious men lay as they had, still decidedly unconscious, and no shouts or yells of alarm greeted him and the others as they stepped out, for everyone in the common room's eyes were instead locked on the small stage upon which Dekker continued to perform. The big man sang a loud, bawdy tune, and whatever reluctance he'd shown when ascending to the dais was nowhere in evidence now. He was grinning widely, singing and clapping along, the crowd following.

The big man's gaze traveled to the wanderer and the others, only for a moment, and while he couldn't be sure the man had noticed them, the wanderer thought he had. "Come on," he told the others.

"What about Dekker?" Clint asked.

The wanderer considered that then shook his head. "He'll meet us at the front, I'm sure."

"But what if they don't let him?"

The wanderer raised an eyebrow at the other man. "Have you seen what happens to things—or people—that get in Dekker's way?"

Clint nodded. "Right. You lead."

"Stay low as best you can," the wanderer said.

Then they were moving again. He did his best to lead them behind the circle of people who were all standing now, engaged in Dekker's performance, but one man stood a little farther back than the others, not leaving enough room for the wanderer and his companions to squeeze through.

"Hey," the man growled as the wanderer pushed his way past. He glanced at them, his gaze moving to the wanderer and the sword he carried, then beyond him to Clint and the blood-soaked Murphy, and he cleared his throat. "S-sorry," he said, moving out of their way.

The wanderer frowned at that, for he would have expected the man to have had more of a reaction, but he decided he could think it over later. For now, he didn't dare waste time questioning their luck that the man hadn't alerted the others in the common room.

And, in another few minutes, they were standing at the door. The wanderer turned back to the stage, waited until he caught the big man's eye then gave a nod, motioning his head to the door.

The big man returned the nod without so much as a pause in his performance, and the wanderer led the two men out of the door.

The guards were still sprawled out as they had been when he and the others had gone inside, so still that they might have been dead. Not that he would lose sleep over it, not after seeing what they and the Jackal had been about.

There was an uproar from inside the tavern, and the wanderer tensed, thinking that now, finally, someone had raised an alarm and that, any moment, the tavern's patrons would come charging out at them, eager to reclaim their prize, Murphy, and add some few others, like the wanderer and Clint, to their menu.

Indeed, the door swung open a moment later, and it wasn't a pissed-off cannibal standing in the doorway but instead Dekker himself.

"Done?" the big man asked.

"Done," the wanderer agreed.

"This him?" the big man asked, turning to scowl at Murphy. "This that Jackal bastard?"

Murphy gave a soft laugh that sounded almost nervous—no surprise, that, for anyone who wasn't nervous at such a scowl from the big man could only be insane or unconscious.

But before he could say anything, Clint spoke in a hurried voice, as if afraid that Dekker would pummel Murphy—one of the big man's favorite ways of dealing with problems. "This is Murphy, Dek," he said. "We found him in a cage in the back room. Him and some others. They were..." He cleared his throat, unable to finish.

Dekker seemed to understand well enough though, for he frowned. "Right. So what now?"

"Now we get out of here," the wanderer said. "Unless, of course, you want to do an encore."

"Kiss my ass," the big man said.

"If ass kissing is what you want, I'd judge you could get it," the wanderer said. "Why, if you go back in there, I imagine your fans would form a line for the privilege."

"You're a real bastard, Ungr, you know that?"

"So I've been told," he said. "Now, come on—let's get out of here."

"You ain't got to tell me twice," Dekker said. "Back to Pearl's?"

"That'd be best," the wanderer said. "If—"

"Please," Murphy said. "Please, Clint," he went on, his expression as pleading and desperate as his voice, "we have to get Gert. She...she'll be wondering where I've gone, and I've got to make sure she's okay."

Clint glanced at the wanderer who gave a nod. "Of course, Murph," he said. "We'll find Gert. Where is she?"

"N-n-not far," he said. "Th-there's an o-old abandoned church we t-took shelter in. I-it's safe enough. I only w-was caught because I left it looking for food."

"Show us," Clint said.

The man nodded, a grateful expression on his face. "It's...this way," he said, pulling his arm away from Clint's shoulders and starting down the street, Clint following after.

Despite the wound in his leg that Clint had bandaged Murphy moved well enough, leading them through first one side street, then another. Murphy had said that she was close, in an abandoned church. The wanderer knew every inch of Celes—for he had been taught the layout of the city in depth—and so he was surprised when the man led them toward the northeastern part of the city where, at least so far as the wanderer knew, no churches stood.

They walked for more than half an hour, a winding course that was inevitably taking them toward the edge of the city. That was unusual, too, for the wanderer would have thought that refugees, such as Murphy and Gerta arriving at the city, would have taken shelter closer to where they'd entered—the southern gate—instead of all the way across the city.

And why come to the northeastern part at all? After all, that part of Celes was the least populated—home only to the warehouses and storehouses used by merchants and traders and if his memory served him correctly, possessing not a single church.

"Are you sure you are going the correct way?" the wanderer asked.

Murphy glanced back at him, and perhaps by some trick of the light there was a clever, cunningness in his gaze that the wanderer did not care for. "Of course I'm sure," the man said, sounding considerably less in pain than he had half an hour before. "Gert's just this way—no more than a few minutes away."

"You said that a few minutes ago," Dekker said, glancing at the wanderer curiously.

"What are the two of you on about?" Clint asked, sounding defensive. "If Murphy says she's here, she's here. Go on, Murph," he said, shooting the two of them a scowl. "Let's go get Gert."

"Of course," Dekker said, "we didn't mean nothin', Clint."

Murphy nodded, giving the wanderer what seemed like an appraising look before turning and starting down the street once more. The wanderer hesitated, though. "Where did you say you took shelter again?"

The man turned back, regarding him. "An old church."

"Right," the wanderer said. "I only ask because there aren't any churches in this part of the city, unless they're new—certainly none that one might consider old."

The man watched him for a second, then shrugged, giving an apologetic smile. "Well, maybe it wasn't a church. What with all that happened to Ingleton, all that happened since we got here, maybe I was wrong. You can see whatever it is for yourself in just a few minutes. It's just this way." He started away again, pausing at the metallic whisper of the wanderer's sword as it left his scabbard.

"Ungr," Clint demanded. "What are you doing? Murphy's a friend."

"Maybe he was once," the wanderer said, still watching the man's back, for he had not turned around. "But he is no longer. Step away from him, Clint."

"What are you talking about?" Clint said, his voice angry. "Damnit, man, we just found him in a damn cage! They, they tore pieces of him off, damnit!"

"Someone did," the wanderer agreed, "and I believe we found what we were meant to find." He turned away from the Perishables' leader, back to the man standing in the street, his back still to him. "Didn't we?"

"This is ridiculous. Tell him, Murphy, it—"

"What gave it away?" the man asked, tilting his head to glance back over his shoulder at the wanderer. There was no sign of the pain or fear in the man's voice now. He sounded calm, even amused.

"Your wrists and ankles for one. They are not scarred from the manacles as the others were."

The man gave a slow nod, still not turning. "I didn't think of that."

"Then, of course, there are the bandages," the wanderer said.

The man glanced down. "What about them?"

"There is no blood on them," the wanderer said. "Perhaps you knew it once but you have forgotten—a normal man bleeds from such wounds. But what of the man back at the inn? The one you stabbed? It was all just play-acting?"

"Not to him," Murphy said, flashing his teeth. "Anyway, he was going to give me away. There wasn't much of a choice."

"You don't seem all that tore up about it."

The man shrugged. "Everything that lives dies." He smiled, an expression without humor. "It's funny, I was afraid the trap was too convoluted. Thought maybe it was too hidden, hidden so well that nobody'd step into it. But then they kept talkin' about how clever you were. Turns out they were right. I'll have to tell 'em, the next time they come 'round. Not that it'll matter much to you—you'll be long dead by then."

"I...I don't understand," Clint said, his voice sounding confused and afraid. "What...what's going on, Murph?"

But the Perishables' leader might as well not have spoken for the other man paid him no attention at all. "You should not have come to Celes," he told the wanderer. "You will die here."

The wanderer considered that, wondered, in that moment, who he was talking to. Murphy, Clint's friend—or one of the enemy. "Every man has to die somewhere," he said.

"Funny words from a member of a group who fashions themselves the 'Eternals,'" the man countered.

"I do not call myself such."

"What is all this?" Clint demanded. "Murphy, what are you talking about? What about Gert?"

This time, Murphy *did* take note of the Perishable's leader, turning on him with an expression of abrupt, insane rage. *"Gert's dead, Clint,"* he screamed. *"She's dead because of you! Because of him!"* he finished, jabbing a finger at the wanderer.

"What?" Clint asked. "But how—"

"They came in the night," Murphy said quietly. "Shadows in the darkness. Some, the lucky ones, were killed. The rest of us...the rest of us they took back here, to the city. They experimented on us. Did things...things you could not imagine. Things I could never have imagined. I don't...I can't remember much...screams in the darkness. Blood. And pain, that most of all."

"Murphy..." Clint said, his voice little more than a whisper. "What happened to Gert?"

"She didn't survive it," Murphy said. "None of them did...except me."

"You're wrong," the wanderer said softly.

The man finally fully turned, regarding him. "Oh?"

"You did not survive what they did to you," the wanderer said. "No one did." His gaze traveled to Clint who was looking scared and confused and hurt all at once. "He is not your friend, not anymore."

"Perhaps you're right," the creature said. "Certainly I have experienced certain...changes. But then what is life without change, right?" he asked, a cold, humorless smile spreading on his face. "What is life without pain?"

"Murphy...I don't...I don't know what's going on here," Clint said. "But...I'm so sorry...about Gert."

"Don't you speak her name," the other man growled. "Don't you *dare,* Clint. My Gert is dead—don't you understand? *Dead!* And now you and your friends will also die."

"But...but don't you get it, Murphy?" the Perishables' leader asked. "This, here, is the man who is trying to fix everything, to fix what's gone wrong with Celes, to make sure that no one else gets...experimented on."

"I know full well who he is," the man said, his voice dripping with venom. "Just as I knew the moment you set foot in the Sewers. Just as the ones I work for knew when you came to Celes. I knew you were coming. That's why I decided to set a trap."

"But...why would you do that?" Clint asked. "I mean, Murph, we came here to save you, to save Gerta."

"And you're too late," the man said. "For both of us. For *all* of us. Do you know *why* they...did what they did, Clint? Why they came to Ingleton in the first place? Because of you and this new friend of yours," he finished, finishing the last in a snarl. "I don't remember much, but I remember that. They could not punish you, could not find you, and so they went to those you knew, to your friends, and they asked us where you were. Asked us hard. And when we didn't tell them where you were—I would have, understand, had I but known—then they decided that while they might not punish you, they could punish us in your stead. And so they did." He flashed his teeth in a humorless smile. "You have no idea how much they punished us, how much they punished Gert. I do not hold them responsible for that, Clint. I hold *you* responsible," he growled in a voice that barely sounded human at all, and that, the wanderer thought, was as it should be. "After all," Murphy continued, "it is not the fox's fault for going into the henhouse—he acts only according to his nature. Instead, it is the fault of the man who left the gate open. You left the gate open, Clint," he said. He brought his hands up into what appeared to be an apologetic shrug. "And now the feathers must fly."

"How far ahead do they wait?" the wanderer asked.

The creature turned to him, and in that movement he saw evidence of its inhumanness. Whatever had been done to Clint's friend had stripped much of his humanity away. What remained was only a memory of it. "Not far," it told the wanderer.

"How long before they come to find us?"

It bared its teeth. "Not long."

"Best we get this over with then."

"Murphy," Clint said, sounding desperate, "look, please, don't do this. We're...we're friends."

"You are the reason Gert is dead, Clint," Murphy said. "I live in shadows, in the darkness, and it is you who cast me into it. You will die. Your new friends will die."

"That won't bring your wife back," Dekker said.

"No," the creature said, regarding him with cold, lifeless eyes. "But I will have company in the shadows."

"Murphy, we can help you," Clint said. "Whatever they did, whatever—"

"You cannot help me, Clint," the man said. "You cannot help yourselves. You are all dead men, and dead men are of no help to anyone save the worms."

"Leave it, Clint," the wanderer said. "He will not be dissuaded—I have seen the products of their experiments before, have seen those like him."

"No," Murphy said, and this time there was humor in his wide smile. "Not like me."

And then, with a roar, the man charged toward Clint. He was fast. Not as fast as an Unseen, maybe, but far faster than a normal man, fast enough that he would be on Clint before the man had time to react in his defense. Thankfully, the wanderer was also faster than a normal man, a product of the rituals he'd gone through to become an Eternal.

He dashed to Clint, shouldering him aside just in time to knock him out of the way of the man's charge but not, unfortunately, with enough time to get out of the way himself.

The wanderer had been hit before, plenty of times.

He'd been hit hard.

But he'd never been hit like this.

The man couldn't have weighed anymore than a hundred and sixty pounds soaking wet, yet he hit the wanderer like a runaway carriage. Numbness shot through his arm, and the next thing he knew the wanderer was flying through the air, tumbling end over end like a castaway ragdoll. Only ragdolls did not feel the amount of pain and shock he felt when he finally struck the side of a building hard enough that he heard the wood *crack.*

"Son of a bitch!"

Groaning in pain, his left arm completely numb, the wanderer braced his weight on his right hand and worked his way to his feet. He looked up in time to see Dekker charging at the man. *"Dekker, don't—"* he began, but it was already too late.

The big man let out a roar that would have been at home on some ancient battlefield, then charged. The creature who had once been Murphy flashed a toothy smile at him, and the wanderer tensed in dreaded expectation. But he needn't have worried, for Dekker lifted Murphy easily off the ground, not bothering to slow his charge but instead rushing headlong into the wall of the nearest building, slamming his burden into it.

Murphy's head rocked on his neck, and there was a loud *crack* to match the one that the wanderer had heard—and felt—when he'd struck the wall of the building he currently propped against.

And yet, the toothy grin remained on the man's face even as Dekker slammed him against the wall, then again, growling as he did, each blow one that might have crippled a normal man.

And yet, the toothy grin remained.

It remained even as Dekker let out another roar, hurling his opponent through the air where he sailed across the street and into the boarded-up window of what might have been a tailor's shop. Whoever had boarded the window had done a fair job at it, no doubt figuring their possessions safe enough from all but the most determined of looters, the most vicious of blows. In most circumstances, they would have likely been right, but then there was no accounting for strength of the kind Dekker possessed.

Murphy flew into the boards, and then flew *through* them. Wood splintered and cracked, and the man-turned-missile disappeared from view somewhere in the shadows of the shop.

The wanderer, his arm still numb, limped down the street. When he arrived Dekker stood with his hands on his hips, scowling in the direction of the tailor's shop while Clint blinked in shocked surprise. The wanderer couldn't blame him. Each of them had seen the big man's strength on more than one occasion, but it simply wasn't the type of thing a man got used to.

He came to stand beside them, and Dekker paused in his scowling to look over at him. "Alright?"

The wanderer glanced at the broken window and gave a shrug. "Could be worse, I suppose."

Dekker grunted, looking over to the Perishables' leader. "Got to be honest, Clint—your friend's a pain in the ass."

"You won't hear any argument out of me," Clint said.

Dekker didn't notice, though. He was busy staring at the hole in the building across the street, not scowling now but frowning. "You see that?"

The wanderer followed his gaze to the tailor's shop where he could make out what might have been movement in the shadows. "I see it."

"Huh," Dekker said. "Ain't that a thing?"

"What's that?" Clint said, also staring at the tailor's shop.

"It's just...well. You know. When I crush things—or folks—they normally stay crushed."

"First time for everything I suppose," the wanderer said as they watched the man, Murphy, climb out of the rubble.

"Still want to make peace with your friend there, Clint?" Dekker asked.

Murphy finished extricating himself from the broken debris, stepping into the street. His clothes were tattered—or even more tattered than they had been—but that was far from the worst of it. His left arm was bent at an unnatural angle, as was one of his ankles, his foot facing ninety degrees to the side of where it should have.

But as Murphy raised his head the wanderer saw that neither the man's arm nor his leg were the greatest signs of Dekker's attention. Instead it was the wooden splinter—though at over a foot long the wanderer wasn't sure it qualified as a splinter anymore—protruding from the man's eye and out the back of his head.

"No," the Perishables' leader said as the creature pulled the shard of wood out of its eye and tossed it aside as if it were no more than an inconvenience. "No, I'd say we're past making peace. Whatever that thing is, it ain't Murphy."

"You'll come to regret coming to Celes," the creature shouted, and even as it spoke the puckered wound in its eye mended itself as if by magic.

"Fella," Dekker called back, *"I'm already there."*

The creature flashed its toothy smile again even as its broken ankle and broken arm twisted and jerked themselves back into their proper places.

"Just how do you reckon he managed that?" Clint asked.

"Painfully, I'd imagine," the wanderer said.

Dekker grunted sourly.

"What, Dek, still upset that the fella didn't remain crushed?"

"Just rude is all," Dekker agreed. He turned to the wanderer. "How tough you reckon this fella is?"

The wanderer shrugged. "One way to find out."

The big man sighed. "I was afraid you'd say that." He raised an eyebrow. "Well, go on then. You been on this quest—we just started. Only right that we let you lead the way."

"Thanks," the wanderer said, and then he started toward where the creature stood in the street. "I have not seen your kind before," he said. "You are the second new creation of the enemy's I have seen recently. It seems they have not been idle."

The creature that had once been the man, Murphy, bared its teeth once more. "Well, you know what they say—necessity is the mother of invention and all. You've made yourself a bit of a thorn in their side, Eternal. One they'd give quite a bit to have removed."

"And what will they give you?" the wanderer asked.

The smile faded then, and the creature's eyes danced with madness. "Revenge," it said. "There is nothing else I want. Now, enough talk. It is time for you to die."

"Don't mind if we fight back, do ya?" Dekker asked.

The creature didn't bother responding, at least not with words. Instead, it charged forward. In another moment the creature was on him. It brandished no weapon, but then considering the strength it had displayed when striking him, the wanderer knew that it had no need of one, thought that the fists it swung at him, should they land, would be more than enough to finish it.

The wanderer bobbed and weaved and dodged, managing a few counterattacks under the creature's barrage. Not that they seemed to do any good, for no sooner had his blade passed through the creature's flesh then that flesh began to knit itself back together.

The assault continued until the wanderer found that his constant retreat under the creature's strikes had brought him so that his back was against a building. He was forced to spin to the side then and wood cracked and groaned as the creature's fist struck it with the force of a blacksmith's hammer swung by a master of his trade. Again and again the creature's fist punched holes into the wood as the wanderer continued to spin to the side, narrowly avoiding the blows.

Finally the creature growled in frustration, lashing out in an effort to grab the wanderer. The wanderer lunged to the side, but the creature managed to get hold of his shirt. Enough that it gave a pull, jerking him toward it so that its other hand could grab hold of his upper arm and the next thing the wanderer knew, he was sailing through the air again.

This time, he managed to gain control of his flight so that when he struck the ground, he landed in a roll, coming to a crouch and facing the creature. His sword, though, had flown from his grip when he'd been thrown, and it now lay at the creature's feet.

The creature stared at the blade then bent and calmly retrieved it, rising to regard the wanderer. "I used to have a fine sword myself," it said, glancing at Clint. "Noticed you carrying it at your side there, as if it's yours." It shook its head slowly. "Not enough to take my wife, my *life* from me. You'd have my blade as well. But that's alright," it said, baring its teeth. "I have no need of such things, not anymore. What, with what I am, what I can do...well, there doesn't seem to be much point, does there?"

"I don't suppose there is," the wanderer panted, rubbing at his shoulder where he'd struck the ground.

The creature grinned again then, grabbing his sword in both hands and then, without any apparent effort at all, nonchalantly snapped the length of metal in half.

The wanderer stared at the blade in shock, the sword that he'd had for so very many years, the weapon that had protected him and those he cared about countless times. He was surprised by the sharp pain of anger and loss that he felt as the creature casually tossed the broken pieces to the ground.

"Now then," it said, flashing him a grin, "shall we continue?"

The wanderer, for the moment, at least, was lost for words, which was just as well as the creature didn't wait for him to respond before rushing forward.

He sidestepped the first fist that flew in his direction, ducking under the second. Then he countered, pivoting and burying his fist in the creature's stomach. Murphy, for his part, didn't seem affected in the slightest by the blow, and the wanderer growled, striking him again, then again, pivoting and turning, planting an uppercut underneath the creature's chin that rocked its head backward and made its teeth snap together.

The creature stumbled away, then brought its head back down, flashing a smile that displayed a missing tooth as proof of the wanderer's attack. "Not bad," the creature said. "Now it's my turn."

It started forward again, and the wanderer did his best to hide his exhaustion and pain, knowing that he didn't have much left. His left arm was still tingling and numb, and his shoulder ached, not to mention the fact that his breath felt like fire in his lungs.

But before the creature reached him, there was a bellow and the wanderer and creature alike turned to see Dekker charging at it. The creature might have stepped out of the way of the big man's attack—after all, the wanderer had seen its speed and knew it capable of it—but instead it only continued to smile, accepting the blow as the big man tackled it around its midsection. Dekker, carrying the creature, charged into the wall of a nearby building with an impact that made the entire structure shake as if it might come apart.

Yet the creature did not seem terribly put out. Instead, it grabbed Dekker's arms, peeling them away, then planted a foot in the big man's stomach. The air exploded from Dekker's chest in a *woosh,* and he was flung backward toward the wanderer who only just managed to catch him and keep him from falling.

Dekker glanced over at Clint who was standing there holding his sword and watching the creature with wide eyes. *"Your...turn,"* the big man gasped.

Clint started forward then paused, letting out a gasp of his own. The wanderer wasn't sure what had caused the man to do so at first, but then when he looked he saw that the creature, Murphy's, hair—which had, moments ago, been midnight black—now possessed a dull, gray streak. That wasn't all, though. Murphy's face was considerably more wrinkled than it had been, and his eyes were sunken in a face that was nearly cadaverous. As if somehow becoming aware of this fact, the creature brought its fingers up, running them along its face.

"The enemy's gifts always have a price," the wanderer said quietly, trying—and largely failing, he suspected—to keep the pain out of his voice.

Murphy blinked, his expression a mixture of confusion and fear, but in another moment that was gone, replaced by anger. *"Then I'll pay it gladly,"* he screamed.

Then he was charging again.

Clint met him first, stepping forward and swinging his sword in a competent, two-handed downward stroke. The creature didn't even bother trying to dodge, just caught the blade in one hand and with a savage growl jerked it free of the Perishable's leader's grip.

Then it jerked Clint up by his shirt, lifting him easily off the ground with one hand. *"You killed Gert,"* the creature growled. *"Now it's your turn to die."*

Before the creature could do whatever it intended, though, the wanderer reached into his belt, withdrawing the blade he kept there, then he pivoted and threw in one smooth, practiced motion. The blade embedded itself in the creature's throat—not that it seemed to do much good. It reached up with its free hand, ripping the blade free. "Do you really think you can—" it began, but it didn't get the chance to finish before Dekker was on it, bringing a meaty fist into the side of its face.

Again, and again, and again the big man struck, until on the fourth punch, the creature caught his fist, stopping the blow in mid-air. Then it pulled its gaze up to the big man, revealing a face that's features were so broken and misshapen as to barely be recognizable as belonging to a man at all. But even as the wanderer watched the creature's nose and lips and eyes began to heal, going back to their proper places.

Then, the creature squeezed, and the wanderer heard something *crack*. Dekker screamed, stumbling away, his good hand clutching at the other where several fingers, the wanderer saw, had been broken.

"Now then," the creature said, turning back to Clint who still hung in the air, kicking at it and fighting its grip but to no avail. "Where were we?"

The Perishable's leader's answer came in the form of a boot to the creature's only-just reformed face, smashing its nose and lips.

Murphy growled in anger, grabbing the offending foot and spinning, hurling Clint through the air where he struck a nearby building.

"*Damnit,*" the wanderer hissed. He could not beat the creature, not unarmed, and if he didn't do something and soon his friends would die.

He became suddenly very aware of the cursed blade sheathed at his back. He did not want to draw it, found that he was afraid to, but he was more afraid, he decided, of what would happen if he did not. Dekker had told him it was only a tool—one that he might use to his purpose. Of course, the blade had its own purpose, this the wanderer knew for he had heard its voice often enough, seeking murder, seeking death.

And at that moment, at least, their purposes aligned.

The wanderer drew the cursed blade.

Power flooded through him, a tidal wave of it, one that he felt swept up in, but more than that, he felt as if he were being pulled apart.

Kill, a voice thundered in his mind, roaring like some terrible, all-consuming storm.

That maelstrom tried to tear him apart, but the wanderer stood in the midst of it, refusing to be moved.

Kill, the voice boomed again.

"Okay," the wanderer said.

His pain was forgotten, in that moment. It wasn't that it no longer existed—it simply did not matter. There was no place for it, just as there was no place for his fears or his worries. There was only the rage, the *need.*

He charged. Perhaps the creature had some inkling of understanding, for its eyes went wide as he came upon it, the blade flashing out again and again, and its smile vanished under his assault.

Its flesh still healed from each blow, but each time the wanderer noted that it healed a little slower than the last, and then a little slower still. As he pressed the attack, as he forced the creature back under the assault, he noted other changes in it, too. Noted the way its face took on a skeletal, drained, look, one that grew worse with every strike.

This continued until finally the creature's movements began to slow, the wounds and its use of strength robbing it of its vitality, its life. And then, the wanderer plunged his sword into its chest, through it and into the wall behind it where it stuck, pinning the creature against the wall.

Murphy stared down at the sword in his chest then raised his head to regard the wanderer and Clint and Dekker who had limped up to stand beside him, the big man cradling his wounded hand against his chest.

"I'm sorry, Murph," Clint said.

The man bared his teeth in a bloody grin. "Not...yet," he said. "But you...will be. Did you think...I...was alone? That I...alone...knew you were here...in the city?" He laughed then, a laugh that turned into a rasping, gasping cough. "*They* know. They know, don't you see? They know you're here. Knew as soon as...you set foot. In the city. You and that...big horse of yours...They know...and they're comin'. Be here...soon. Shame about that horse of yours, though...there's some men of mine that have done for him by now...lot of good eatin' on a horse. Not that you'll have much time to mourn...they're comin'."

"And I'll be waiting," the wanderer growled. He ripped his sword free and before the creature could say anything more, he lashed out, lopping its decaying head from its shoulders. Then he turned to Clint and Dekker. "Are you—"

"Go on, get your horse," the big man said. "We'll be alright."

The wanderer nodded to the two men.

Then he was running into the darkness, the cursed blade still in his grip, an anger rising in him to match it as he charged into the shadows.

And now, dear reader, we have reached the end of *City of Steel and Shadow.*

The next book in The Last Eternal is coming soon. In the meantime while you wait, I've got some other books you might want to give a shot.

Want another story of an anti-hero in a grimdark setting where a jaded sellsword is forced into a fight he doesn't want between forces he doesn't understand?
Get started on the bestselling seven book series, The Seven Virtues.

Interested in a story where the gods choose their champions in a war with the darkness that will determine the fate of the world itself?
Descend into The Nightfall Wars, a complete six book, epic fantasy series.

Or how about something a little lighter? Do you like laughs with your sword slinging and magical mayhem? All the world's heroes are dead and so it is up to the antiheroes to save the day. An overweight swordsman, a mage who thinks magic is for sissies, an assassin who gets sick at the sight of the blood, and a man who can speak to animals...maybe.
The world needed heroes—it got them instead.
Start your journey with The Antiheroes!

If you'd like to reach out and chat, you can email me at JacobPeppersAuthor@gmail.com or visit my website at JacobPeppersAuthor.com.
You can also give me a shout on Facebook or on Twitter. I'm looking forward to hearing from you!

Turn the page for a limited time free offer!

Sign up for my VIP New Releases mailing list and get a free copy of *The Silent Blade: A Seven Virtues novella* as well as receive exclusive promotions and other bonuses!
Get your copy now at JacobPeppersAuthor.com!

NOTE FROM THE AUTHOR

And so, my friend, we have reached the end of *City of Steel and Shadow*. I hope you enjoyed journeying once more with the wanderer, with Dekker and Ella, and little Sarah.

We have found new enemies, it is true, but then so, too, have we found new allies. Pearl, a proud, resourceful woman, as clever as she is intimidating. Merle, a man who stands when others flee, and that is good. There will be much courage needed in the days to come, for it takes a brave man to stand against the shadows.

And then there is Jessup, once a great man fallen far into the darkness. But no matter how far a man falls, he might always rise again, just so long as there is breath in his lungs and will in his heart. Jessup has lost that will, but he might yet find it again.

And he will need it—they all will. For dark days lie ahead.

The wanderer has fled for a hundred years and more, but he flees no longer. He has chosen, instead, to stand. To fight.

And so, as always when a man chooses to stand and fight, there will be blood.

The wanderer races through the streets of a city fallen to murder and cannibalism to save his friend, Veikr, with nothing but a washed-up drunken duelist standing between his friend and the rising shadows.

The wanderer is fast—far faster than any normal man.

We can only hope he will be fast enough.

I'd like to take this opportunity to thank all of those who have been instrumental in the creation of this book or, in the case of my wife, the continued survival of its author.

Thank you, first, to my friends and family. Thank you to my wife, Andrea—I live a blessed life, it's true, far better than I deserve, and I count you and the children first among those blessings. Thank you to Gabriel, Norah and Declan, too. You don't help much with the book—being attacked by pretend dinosaurs or shin-kicked with princess shoes isn't conducive to writing. But you help with life, and that's a lot more important.

Thank you to my beta readers. As always, your comments and thoughts have proven invaluable and, as always, I stand in awe of your kindness to dedicate your time and energy to wading through what can sometimes be a particularly thick murk of plot holes and story tangles.

Thank you, lastly, to you, dear reader, my friend. Can I call you friend? After all, we have traveled far together, in this world and in others, and I would presume as much. For such travels bring close companions, do they not? We have traveled far, but we have far to go yet. It is my sincere hope that you stick around, and whatever end comes, that we face it together.

Happy Reading,

Jacob Peppers

ABOUT THE AUTHOR

Jacob Peppers lives in Georgia with his wife, his son, Gabriel, daughter, Norah, and newborn son, Declan, as well as their three dogs. He is an avid reader and writer and when he's not exploring the worlds of others, he's creating his own. His short fiction has been published in various markets, and his short story, "The Lies of Autumn," was a finalist for the 2013 Eric Hoffer Award for Short Prose. He is the author of the bestselling epic fantasy series *The Seven Virtues* and *The Nightfall Wars.*